INTERNATIONAL ACCLAIM FOR

Adele Parks

—who delivers "cleverness to spare"* and sharp, savvy portrayals of relationships, sex, and marriage in her sensational bestselling novels!

Game Over

"Parks' style is down to earth and very, very funny."

—*OK*

Larger Than Life

"Entertaining and sophisticated."

—*Marie Claire*

"Parks has scored another surefire hit with *Larger Than Life*. . . . Expect to see it peeking out of handbags near you soon."

—*Heat*

"An engaging read."

—*Independent*

Playing Away

"Compulsively addictive!"

—*Elle*

"An affecting first novel . . . a cheeky first-person narrative. . . . A balanced exploration of the rules of marriage."

—*Kirkus Reviews*

"*Playing Away* is a very edgy book. It's also wickedly funny and very sexy."

—*Publishers Weekly**

ALSO BY ADELE PARKS

Larger Than Life

Playing Away

GAME OVER

A Novel

Adele Parks

downtown press

New York London Toronto Sydney

DOWNTOWN PRESS
1230 Avenue of the Americas
New York, NY 10020

First published in Great Britain in 2001 by Penguin Books Ltd

ISBN: 0-7434-5761-7

First Downtown Press trade paperback edition March 2004

10 9 8 7 6 5 4 3 2 1

DOWNTOWN PRESS and colophon are
trademarks of Simon & Schuster, Inc.

Manufactured in the United States of America

Designed by Jaime Putorti

For information regarding special discounts for bulk purchases,
please contact Simon & Schuster Special Sales at 1-800-456-6798
or business@simonandschuster.com

Game Over and *Playing Away* are unlikely tributes to Colin Douglas, Mary Peacock, Dick Parks, Mryra Wilkinson and Emma Blythe, with love.

GAME OVER

CHAPTER ONE

"WHAT AN INAUSPICIOUS START to married life," Josh comments.

"Is there such a thing as an auspicious start?" I ask. He grins at me and Issie scowls. *She* likes weddings. The rain is falling so hard it's bouncing off the pavements and up my skirt. I'm bloody cold and wish the bride would stop hugging her mother and simply get in the car. I look closer. Maybe she isn't so much hugging as clinging. Maybe the seriousness of what she's done has hit her and she's having second thoughts. Issie shakes the remnants of confetti from the blue box but misses the bride and groom. The confetti settles on the grubby road. The filthy street is a stark contrast to the finery of their clothes, the car, the flowers, the smiles that radiate.

"Josh, what's the proper name for a squashed cube?" I ask, pointing to the little blue box of confetti. "They should redesign this packaging," I add.

"No!" Issie looks horrified, as if I'd suggested exposing my bikini line to the vicar. "Weddings are about tradition."

"Even if tradition means tacky and predictable?" Two big sins in my book.

"By definition," she defends. Then she leaps forward to jostle for a front position to catch the bouquet. She nervously hops from one foot to the other, her sleek, blonde, shoulder-length hair brushing her right shoulder, then her left, then her right again. Issie is a fidget. I am a still person. She continually rubs her hands together, taps her feet, jerks her knee. She once read that this constant nervous activity uses thirty calories an hour, more than a Mars bar a day, pounds in a year, a whole dress size in a lifetime. Her constant unfocused activity strikes me as a fairly accurate metaphor for how she lives her life.

I don't try to catch the flowers. I don't try for two reasons. One, Issie will lynch me if I catch them. She's spent the entire reception spiking the drinks of single women, in the hope that this will diminish their co-ordination. And two, it's bollocks.

No really, the whole marriage thing is bollocks. I mean I'm as happy as the next one to have an excuse to wear a hat and drink champagne. Generally, wedding receptions are a laugh, a big, fun party. But that's as far as it goes for me. Beyond that, it's bollocks. I'm not a man. And I'm not a lesbian. I'm not even a man hater— Josh is one of my best friends and he's a man. I'm a single, successful, attractive, thirty-three-year-old, heterosexual. I just don't want to get married. Ever.

Clear?

Issie doesn't catch the flowers and she looks as though the disappointment will break her.

"A drink, Cas? Issie?" asks Josh, in an effort to cheer her up. He doesn't wait for a response but turns back to the hotel and heads directly for the bar. He knows that we'll willingly join him for a drink Martini-style: any time, any place, anywhere. We elbow through the elegant crowds. This morning they sat demurely in church pews but they have now abandoned any semblance of civilization. The exit of the bride, the groom and the oldies leaves the rest of the guests free to indulge in what brought us to the wedding in the first place. The opportunity for some hedonistic, no strings attached, unashamed sex.

I selected my target in the church, before the "I dos." I relocate him. He's tall, dark and handsome. Admittedly, he doesn't look that bright. Rather too in love with himself to allow room for anyone else. Perfect. Deep and meaningful is an overrated phenomenon. Shallow and meaningless but well endowed gets such a hard press.

It's important to pick out a target early on in the proceedings and it's important to let him know he's it. I smile. Directly at him. If at this point he looks around and tries to locate the recipient of my smile, I'll instantly go off him. I like my men to be arrogant enough to know that I'm flirting with them.

He passes the test by grinning back at me. Only turning to catch his reflection in the mirror that hangs behind the bar. He grins again. This time at himself. The difference in appreciation is fractional. I don't mind. Vanity is a safety net. I flick my hair and turn away. Job done.

Issie and Josh are still fighting their way to the bar. I call them back.

"What? I was nearly at the front," Issie complains.

"Don't worry, drinks are on their way," I assure.

"Oh." She relaxes into the chintz chair. Josh lights a fag, trusting me. We are all familiar with my routine. Josh and Issie know all about me.

Josh is like a brother to me. We met aged seven over our suburban fences. It is this meeting that makes me believe in fate. We met when our families' stars were crossing. His in the ascendant. Mine spiraling downwards.

That summer we shared Rubik's cubes, cream soda and an uneasy sense of impending change. Our childish sixth sense told us that we were both powerless in the face of adult whim. The five-bedroom detached, in Esher, Surrey, that my mother and I had thought was a dream home turned out to be a temporary residence. That summer my father announced that he was in love with another woman and couldn't live without her. My mother showed rare wit and emotional honesty by asking whether he'd prefer cremation or burial. My father moved out immediately following his announcement. I was to see him three more times in my life. A week later when he came to collect his records and he brought me a Lundby doll's house (presumably to replace the real home he was destroying). A month later when he took me to the zoo (I cried the entire afternoon, saying that the animals behind the bars upset me. In fact, they didn't, but I was determined that both my father and I would have a terrible afternoon—after all, my mother and I were having plenty of them). And the following Christmas (when I refused to open his present or sit on his knee). After that, he just sent Christmas and birthday cards, which petered out before I was ten. Josh's seventh summer wasn't great either: he was told that he was to be wrenched from his comfortable local primary school and prepped at the hallowed ground of Stowe. Thinking about it, perhaps it wasn't so much a sixth sense. The prep-school prospectuses and the endless rows were a giveaway. Although very nearly entirely submerged in our own terror, we settled into an uneasy mutual sympathy that passed as companionship. Sulkily learning to rollerskate and eating raw gooseberries has an enormous bonding effect. I still think he got the best deal. At that time we had lived in identical homes, distinguishable only by the color of the Formica on the kitchen units. I was never to live in anything so spacious again. He, in anything so compact. As a child I identified the difference. His father kept quiet about his affairs.

I suspect that our childish friendship, although intense in a sharing gobsmacker type of way, would have petered out except that we met again, aged twelve, at a county tennis tournament. Josh recognized that knowing a girl, any girl, would improve his standing at Stowe. I was attracted by his rounded vowels, and even at that early age had recognized that competition was healthy, a challenge that the boys at Westford Comprehensive rose to. It turned out that we still liked each other. We liked each other so much that Josh insisted on disappointing his teachers and parents by joining me at Manchester University. They'd had their sights set on an establishment that was a little older and altogether less red-brick. I was determined to go to Manchester; for the trendy bands, the radical students union, the men in turned-up Levis and DMs, but mostly for the outstanding media studies course.

Josh is tall, six foot two, blond. If I look at it objectively, I have to admit he is the most attractive man I know that I haven't slept with. Whenever I introduce him to my girl friends and colleagues, they unilaterally swoon, they go on and on about how fanciable he is. He is what's described as "handsome" or "dashing." Invariably, because they lack imagination, they assume we are an item. I explain that I like him far too much to complicate things by having sex with him.

In fact, I love him. He is one of the three people I love in the world. I love my mother in a no-nonsense, non-demonstrative kind of way. And I love Issie.

Issie and I met at Uni. In her first term she read biology, then chemistry and finally chemical engineering. It wasn't so much that she'd finally found her vocation, it's just that her tutor wouldn't hear of another change of direction. Issie is frighteningly intelligent and alarmingly optimistic. It's an unusual combination, which largely leaves her dissatisfied. She's a little taller than most women are (five foot nine) and a little thinner (U.K. size ten), achieved through the constant fidgeting rather than gym visits. Therefore she's slim but untoned. She bewails her wobbly upper arms and potbelly but hasn't, in the fifteen years I've known her, ever seriously considered stomach crunches or lifting weights (unless you count carrying heavy shopping bags). She's a natural blonde: eyelashes and brows prove it. Therefore she doesn't tan but has a sprinkling of freckles on her (wide) nose and (slim) shoulders. She has the sexiest mouth in the Western world. It's broad and red. Women describe her as stunning. Men are diametrically opposed; they either fail to notice her at all, her paleness rendering her invisible, or they want to be her knight in shining armor and put her on a pedestal. I don't think either of these responses suits her. Issie's fierce intellect and brutal honesty ought to be dignified with something more than indifference or insulation. But then there's a lot of things that ought to happen and won't. I don't hold much hope for Issie finding a man that is worthy of her. Especially since her optimism has overpowered her intelligence and she has spent her adult life in a stalwart but senseless crusade to discover hidden depths in the men she dates. I've explained on countless occasions that there isn't a pot of gold at the end of the rainbow.

It's really Josh who is responsible for Issie's and my friendship. He spotted her at Freshers' Week and developed an intense crush on her. He begged me to befriend her. I did. By the time I discovered how much I liked her and how ethereal and fragile she was, Josh had slept with half of the students in Withington and Fallowfields. I decided that she was far too special to allow him to have his wicked and transient way with her. I discouraged both parties, in what I admit to be a Machiavellian manner. I pointed out his shortcomings to her and other women's attractions to him. It was a successful ploy.

I still think I made the right decision.

If they'd wanted each other so much, they'd have found a way to make it happen.

We settled into a healthy flirty relationship where we often confused who fancied whom. Instead of any of us sharing each other's beds, in the second and third years, we shared a student house. Just the three of us, loath to let anyone else into our inner sanctum. This was sensible, as arguments over who bought the last loo roll and put an empty milk carton back in the fridge put a full stop to any romantic notion any one of us harbored.

We were typical students. We avoided lectures, joined clubs and societies—rugby (Josh), Literary Soc. (Issie), wine appreciation (me); we drank copious amounts in the Uni. bar, relied on last minute cramming for exams and shagged relentlessly. We were atypical in that none of us fell victim to the statistic that says one third of all graduates meet their long-term partner at university. We were all hopeless at anything long-term. Issie fell in love with every man she shagged. It was a warped attempt at respectability. She shagged until the men she was shagging got fed up of her reading metaphysical poetry as foreplay. Josh fell in love with every woman he screwed, at least until he'd eaten breakfast and sometimes for days on end. He was forever breaking hearts. I never fell in love and often got bored before the first post-coital cigarette.

This youthful pattern set us on the path we would follow throughout our twenties and, likely as not, until we draw our pensions. This thought doesn't bother Josh or me. The law chambers which he so successfully wafts around offer enough intelligent and willing women for him to fall in and out of love *ad infinitum*. The same can be said of my job in the media. The abundance of loose-moraled young men is a necessary criterion for any job offer I accept. I have no illusions about commitment, which makes me a deeply attractive proposition to men who have no intention to commit—99.99 percent of them. So I use and abuse. It's easier all around. Actually, I don't do too much abuse. To abuse someone they have to be emotionally involved and in my experience men are happy to forgo this nicety if good head is on offer. So when I leave their beds failing to leave my telephone number on the empty fag packet or when I shoo them out of my flat with the empty promise that I'll call, no one really minds that much.

Issie is a lab technician at a huge pharmaceutical company. Her white coat is quite fetching but I know Issie is still looking for something more than a quick game of doctors and nurses. I'm always telling her it will be a fruitless search and she wants to count herself lucky that we have each other to love.

• • •

"Can I offer you a drink?" I never say yes to this question without first checking out the origin, however busy the bar is. I look up and see Mr. Tall, Dark and Handsome. On cue. He is presumptuously holding a bottle of Bollie and a fistful of glasses. I like presumption, extravagance and the recognition that my friends will want a drink too. He has sparkling green eyes and the floppy-haired look that was all the rage when I was nineteen. I resist telling him that since *Brideshead Revisited,* no man (other than Hugh Grant) has ever successfully pulled off this look. I resist because besides the height, eyes and cheekbones, I like his suit.

"Fine." I grin.

He does the usual stuff: he asks me my name, and I tell him it's Cas and he says, "Oh, what's Cas short for?" And I explain it's short for Jocasta and I grin and add, "I was named after my father's mother, very Oedipal." And sometimes they get this reference and sometimes they don't but it doesn't matter because either way they grin maniacally. Because usually by this time the men I talk to are well and truly in lust with me. They may not be interested in references to Greek plays but they are extremely interested in the possibility of steamy foreplay. They are checking out my full, pert tits or my long, brown, muscular legs, depending on whether they are breast or leg men. And, if their tastes are more sophisticated and long, black, glossy hair, or clear skin, or slim hips, or blue eyes, or straight white teeth turn them on, I can offer all these things too.

Believe me, I know I'm blessed.

I wear my hair long, because it drives men wild. They look at me and see a sexy bitch or a nineteenth-century heroine, whichever is their bag. Strictly speaking, I think my personality would suit a razor-sharp, chin-length bob, but I work in television and "give them what they want" is my war cry.

I ask his name and try to commit it to memory. I ask what he does, and he does something or other. It doesn't matter. His prospects only matter to women who want a future. I notice he has very large feet and this is exciting. In my experience (wide and varied) the old adage is true. I constantly touch him. Little light touches on his arm and shoulder. I even pick off an imaginary piece of lint from his breast pocket. It always amazes me that men fall for this clichéd crap but they always do. I run my tongue around my lips, my teeth and the olive in his Martini. He is not vulnerable. He knows this routine. He's played it himself on countless occasions. He's a little bit taken back that it's being played to him but my audacity excites. He tries to regain control of at least the conversation and asks what I do for a living. I tell him that I'm a TV producer for the new terrestrial channel, TV6, and this, if we were in any doubt, clinches it.

My glamorous job has huge pulling power. My job *is* glamorous, especially in comparison to most people's jobs. It is an affectation of those who work in TV to continually deny that the job is fun or alluring. It's a way of neutralizing our guilt at the hideously high salaries we earn. It is undoubtedly more glamorous to sell TV airtime than baked beans at a leading supermarket. It is unquestionably more exciting to spot Des O'Connor in the lifts than Dave Jones from accounts. However, TV is also bloody hard work. I've been in the business for twelve years now. I started as a gofer on *Wake Up Britain* straight after Uni. The pay was a pittance but I was thrilled. I had a job in *television*. I spent most of my time in a state of perpetual fear. I had no responsibility so the level of misdemeanour that I could aspire to was putting sugar in someone's coffee when they'd distinctly asked for saccharin. My most constant dread was that my clothes, hair, figure, accent, jokes were unacceptable. I spent all my money on the right clothes (black) and the right hairstyles (long, short, very short, long again, black, blonde, red, black again), happily reinventing myself until I could be myself. It was vital to me to do well. Not just well but best. No job was too small for me to accept it cheerfully. No ambition was too large for me to hold it greedily.

I worked obscene hours, even working once on Christmas Day, which wasn't really a hardship. Holidays bore me. It was worth it. I leaped ahead of my peers and by the time I was twenty-three I was chief researcher. I rushed through the ranks of associate producer and producer, and I reached the dizzy heights of executive producer the week before my thirtieth birthday. It's who I am. It's what I am.

"That must be fascinating," Mr. Tall, Dark, Handsome with Green Eyes comments.

"It is. As we are now living in the digital age and there are hundreds of extra channels all fighting for the consumer mind share, it's extremely tough." I don't bother to tell him that besides the terrestrial channels, BBC 1 and 2, ITV, Channels 4 and 5 and TV6, there are 200 digital satellite channels, 500 digital cable channels and 70 digital terrestrial channels on offer, not to mention interactive television, the Internet and home shopping. Yet viewing time per capita has declined. The more we have to watch, the less often we tune in. So the challenge hasn't let up; I'm constantly being asked to introduce more demanding or aggressive promotions, programs or plans. I don't bother to mention it because even Josh, my most devoted listener, glazes over when I give too much detail. I know I can be boring about my work but it means so much to me. I try to think of an entertaining star story. In the corridors of power I often bump into someone famous, especially those who are famous for being famous—they make themselves very available. I like them the least and admire them the most. It's much harder than being famous for being talented. I know a story about has-been soap stars won't interest.

"I eat my sandwiches in the same canteen as Davina McCall." That gets him.

I wake up to birds screeching and a swarm of bees hovering threateningly above me. I fully expect to open my eyes and see a fan whirling from the ceiling. It takes me some seconds to understand that my pounding head is not because I'm on set in *Apocalypse Now and Again* but that the audibility of feathered friends is due to the fact that the windows of the country-house hotel bedroom are wide open. The night before it had been a good idea. I'd insisted on it. Naturally, as I am paying £170 a night (not on expenses), I wanted my money's worth. Shortbread biscuits, mini bottles of shampoo, shower cap and fresh air.

The swarm of bees turns out to be a lone ranger. This is a relief. I survey the room. The debris suggests I had a really good time last night. I move my head a fraction; the hangover confirms it.

I concentrate on focusing: empty champagne bottle, empty mini bar, horizontal wardrobe and handsome stranger in my bed.

A result.

His name eludes me. This is not a disaster but it is an irritation. It seems rude, even by my standards, to ask a man to leave without addressing him on a first-name basis. Big boy, although an adequate term of endearment last night, seems faintly ridiculous in the harsh light of day. I'm saved from immediately confronting this dilemma as the phone rings.

Tring, trinnnnnng, tring, trinnnnnng. The tone is definitely getting more insistent. I feel around for the handset.

"Cas?"

"Issie." I pull myself on to my elbow. "You OK?"

"No."

I try to concentrate on her story. It starts good—scored with one of the ushers. But it gets muddled through her tears. Seemingly she had a passion session last night. Peppered with orgasms, blowjobs and him murmuring, "You are amazing." This morning she'd woken up to him trying to sneak out of her room. She'd asked for his number. He gave her one but it was made up. It was one digit too many.

"He called me Zoë," she wails. It's true Zoë isn't generally the accepted shortening of Isabelle, however familiar the parties involved. "How could he forget my name?"

"I don't know, honey. I really don't. What's your room number?" I want to stroke her hair, hunt a tissue from my handbag, blow her nose and pour a substantial G&T. I want to make her better. I hurriedly climb out of bed. Momentarily noting the slight strain in my groin. I turn and have a last wistful look at big boy. I wouldn't have minded a bit of early morning naughtiness. But it is out of the question. Issie needs me. I don't even have time to wash off the sperm and smell of rubber.

"Hey big—" I stop myself. "Hey." I shake him gently. He opens his eyes and tries to pull me back into bed.

"What's the rush?" he asks with a lazy grin. I maneuver away from all his hands, pull a jumper on and throw his shirt at him.

"My friend called. I'm going around to her room."

"I'll wait for you," he offers.

"No, that would be"—I play with the idea of saying tedious and opt for the more polite approach—"too kind but unnecessary. She's very upset; I might be gone all morning. All day."

"Should I leave you my card?"

"Yes, great. Do that." I kiss him on his forehead and feel a bit like his mother. How young this guy looks in the daylight. Of course I have no intention of calling him, but I'd like to have his name. I keep immaculate mental records in these matters.

Issie opens the door; she's wrapped in a sheet.

"Oh Issie." I hug her. Fighting down the swell of irritation that washes over me when I see her tear-stained face. I'm annoyed at him for doing it to her. I'm annoyed at her for doing this to herself. "Have you called Josh?"

"He's incognito."

"Oh, makes sense. I saw him slope off with that woman in the huge navy hat."

"Which one?" asks Issie. "There were a dozen navy hats."

"The Emu one."

"Oh." She grins, despite herself, and I think, not for the first time, that Issie is too nice to be treated like this.

I put on the mini kettle and throw the biscuits to her. She needs the sugar. She catches them with one hand and this simple gesture makes my heart swell with pride. It is so unfair. There is no way Issie would ever have managed to do something so cool in front of a guy she fancied. Women are always so much nicer, more composed and funnier when blokes aren't around. Why can't we be our best selves in front of them?

"Did you have full sex?" I ask, trying to establish the level of disappointment.

"Yes." She sounds guilty.

"Don't sweat it, forget it. I'm not your mum." But I know she's wracked with shame and an overwhelming sense of self-loathing. She's explained it often enough. I try to cheer her up. "I also had full sex and I'm not expecting to see him again either."

"But you don't care. You have no feelings." Fair point. I shrug. I'm as hard as nails on the outside. Scratch the surface and I'm as hard as nails on the inside. Impenetrable. Well, emotionally impenetrable, not the other. Not frigid. Technically, I guess, for want of a more user-friendly term, I'm a slapper. I start to run her a bath. I'm overly generous with the bubble bath. Bubbles are so frivolous. They never fail to cheer me up.

"Was it good sex?" I shout above the running tap.

"Not particularly—we hardly know each other."

So why is she so upset? I walk back into the bedroom and start to drag her toward the bathroom.

"What did I do wrong?" she wails. I've heard this question so often that I have a stockpile of answers. *"You* did nothing wrong." "Men are simply incapable of more." Etc., etc. None of it helps. She still regularly has her heart stomped upon.

Whilst she's in the bath I order room service. We require serious comfort food so I order a big, greasy fried breakfast (powerful medicine for hangovers and broken hopes), a pile of pastries and huge steaming mugs of hot chocolate. I quickly shower while Issie flicks through the Sunday papers. We eat breakfast lying on the massive bed, wrapped in luxurious, white toweling dressing gowns. I couldn't be happier. To me this is a perfect Sunday morning. I know Issie would be happier if I were a man.

"But why does it matter?" I ask, genuinely confused. "You had your servicing and you don't have to put up with the inane conversation this morning. Best of both worlds."

Issie sighs. "What if the conversation wasn't inane but stimulating?"

"It's a bit unlikely, isn't it?"

She sighs again, very deeply this time. I know I am trying her patience.

"No, it's not unlikely. Men are people, Cas, and they are capable of relationships."

It's not that I think men are any more awful or dishonest than women where such matters are concerned. That's such an archaic view. But as soon as sex comes into the equation, integrity, candor and decency invariably make a swift exit. Someone is bound to get hurt. I simply prefer it if it's not me. Or Issie. Or Josh.

I catch sight of my reflection in the dressing-table mirror. I can see what other people see, a five-foot-seven, size eight woman, with huge blue eyes and long dark hair. Sexy, cool, flawless. But it *still* surprises me that they can't see what I can. The seven-year-old chubby tyke, left behind by her father. Not only was I not pretty enough to make my father stay, I actually suspected it was my fault he'd left. Had I been naughty? Was it something to do with digging up his vegetable plot with Josh? By the time I realized this wasn't the case at all, and it was actually more to do with Miss Hudley—his buxom, blonde and willing secretary—it was too late. I'd spent a decade blaming myself. Rationale and reason were too tardy. The psychology isn't difficult to figure out. Intense feelings of betrayal, blah, blah, blah. I have a complex about men not loving me enough to stay and about their general ability to be faithful. My defense is a life awash with cynicism, constraint and calculation. And it's an extremely effective preclusion to pain. I hurt before I can be harmed. I dump before I'm damaged. I never get involved.

"The mistake everyone makes is thinking sex and love are at all compatible. Why? No one imagines they are in love because they feel hungry or tired or cold. Why imagine you are if you feel randy?"

"Oh, you are too clever for me." Issie evades my argument. She doesn't think I'm clever, she thinks I'm cruel, but she's too polite to say so.

I had planned to spend Sunday afternoon with my mother, and Issie decides to join me, as she can't face a Sunday afternoon on her own. I'm pleased she's joining me but frustrated that she thinks there is such a thing as "on your own" when you live in a city with seven million inhabitants, dozens of museums, scores of galleries, hundreds of shops, and millions of bars and restaurants.

When we arrive at my mother's, she is sitting in the garden reading a romantic novel. I pointedly put down the bag of improving books that I have brought for her. She thanks me, but I doubt she'll swap the stolen glances and passionate embraces to learn more about the trials of the Irish during the potato famine. My mother is delighted to have both Issie and me to fuss over and immediately scuttles to the kitchen to put on the kettle.

Mum lives in a small, immaculate house in Cockfosters. The house is cramped full of furniture that she rescued from her marriage. My mother brought everything from our five bedroom detached home and put it into her two-bedroom terraced house.

The result is overpowering. It is impossible to walk through a room without banging your hip on a sideboard or stubbing your toe on a chair. In some rooms furniture is literally piled up on top of other bits of furniture. Chair on table, poof on chair. There are two beds in each bedroom, although no one ever stays. I wish she'd throw it all out. I wish she'd start again at Heal's. The house is stuck in a time warp and so is Mum. When she married my father everyone commented that there was an amazing resemblance between her and Mary Quant. It was a very successful look at the time. She's never been able to leave it behind. Over thirty-five years later she still wears her hair in a thick dark bob. She applies a home dye kit every three weeks. She wears her skirts too short and a ton of eyeliner. I find her look mildly embarrassing. Not simply because she's unfashionable and being a trend leader is important to me, but because of what her look signifies. It is a very public statement that she has not been able to move on since my father left her. She's never said so, but I know that she's preserving herself in this way. She hopes that one day Father will come home and the last twenty-six years will be magically erased. A modern-day Miss Haversham.

My mother is a tall, strong-looking woman. The height comes from her thighs, which are slightly longer than average. She's kept her figure. The only concession to her age is that her tummy is gently rounding, comfortably protruding but certainly not huge. Her back is broad and her shoulders wide. Her body tells of capability. Her face is thin and she has high cheekbones. Her nose is narrow and straight, giving the impression that life's discomforts slip from her without disturbing her. But her chin is pointy and juts out to catch all pain and atrocity. She has watery blue eyes that punctuate the solidness of her face. And because her eyes are the window to all her delight and disgust she often hides them behind dark glasses. Even in the winter. I've inherited this from my mother. Whilst I don't actually wear dark glasses I do see the world as a slightly shady place.

"Did you get my message on Tuesday?" Mum asks. I don't say yes and that it made my day. I say yes but I've been too busy to call back. She nods.

"How was the wedding?" She knows all about my social life and what I do with myself on a daily basis. It's a tactic to avoid living a life of her own.

"Fluffy," I reply.

"Beautiful." Issie smiles.

"What a shame about the rain, especially as today is so beautiful. Isn't that always the way?"

"They must have expected rain or at least thought there was a fair probability. It is August, it is England." I don't know why I do this. Behave badly. But I always do. My mother always brings out the worse in me. The moment I am in her presence I am incapable of being polite, let alone charming. I become petulant, sulky, churlish and unreasonable. My mother authorizes this appallingly childish behavior by silently indulging me. The harder she tries to please, the meaner I become. I always leave her house ashamed of myself.

"Ignore her," says Issie.

"Oh, I do," giggles my mum.

"You know how she hates weddings."

I pretend to have an overwhelming interest in the yellow patches of grass on the lawn. My mother cuts me a piece of chocolate fudge cake. It was my favorite as a child. I consider telling her I'm dieting but it's a lie. I'd only be doing it to be pathetic.

"Did Josh enjoy the wedding?"

"Seemed to," I mutter. I know where this conversation is leading. It's leading where every conversation my mother ever has about Josh leads. She mistakenly labors under the apprehension that Josh and I would make a "lovely couple." She insists on deliberately misconstruing his innocent acts of friendship as overtures. Her inference would irritate me, but I comfort myself with the thought that my mother knows absolutely nothing about the male psyche.

"Didn't he want to come for tea too?"

"He was otherwise engaged." I haven't the heart to elaborate—she looks crushed as it is. Rallying herself, my mother turns to Issie.

"Issie, are you courting at the moment?" asks Mum as she passes Issie a slice of cake. Issie and I avoid catching each other's eye because although we are thirty-three years old we still think the word "courting" is hysterical. Hearing it said out loud is enough to send us into peals of helpless giggles.

"No." Issie manages the single syllable by cramming a load of fudge cake into her mouth.

"Oh. What a shame. Are you working too hard? You're not neglecting your social life are you? Don't forget there's more to life than work." My mum and I agree on one thing. If Issie wants a man it should be possible.

"It's not work. It's just that all the men I meet are bastards." Mum blushes at Issie's expletive. I'm amused and watch the exchange with interest. My mum and I run through this routine every week. It amazes me that while her marriage made her so unhappy, she still thinks it's the answer to everyone else's dreams.

"I met someone last night." I catch Issie's eye—we both know she is giving my mother false hope. "But I took his number down incorrectly, one digit too many." She's just bending the truth to protect the feelings of an older lady. Anyone would do it. My mother and Issie then spend an hour looking at the telephone number working out which is likely to be the wrong digit. This is one of the most pointless exercises I've ever witnessed. I spray the roses, which have a spot of greenfly.

CHAPTER

Two

HE IS APPALLINGLY UGLY. And while most people are embarrassed by their physical drawbacks, Nigel Bale, my boss, is blissfully unaware that he looks like Hissing Sid. His mannerisms are, by some way, less attractive. He is very tall and should be skinny, but he has wide, middle-aged woman's hips and a pot belly. The pot belly is a testament to the numerous occasions he's cornered some poor, defenseless junior in the pub and drunk them under the table or, more accurately, into bed. He has large feet and fat fingers. He's balding. The hair he does have is greasy, serving to glue his dandruff to his exposed scalp. And yet he is inconceivably arrogant, confident and vain. So much so that he will not recognize himself from this description. He considers himself to be the most intelligent of the male species and although he doesn't come across crushing competition on a day-to-day basis at TV6, he is mistaken. He firmly believes he is irresistible to the opposite sex. Sadly, to many he is.

It's his bank balance. It is huge. Massive.

And he is powerful. Extremely so.

Two compelling aphrodisiacs. I am ashamed to be female when I see Hissing Sid surrounded by an entourage of young vixens, willing to lie back and think of the Bank of England. It disgusts me that these women, always attractive and often intelligent, are too lazy to think of anything more creative than sleeping with the boss to ensure a promotion.

I can sense his presence, and this isn't entirely to do with his body odor and bad breath. A deathly hush has fallen. Hissing Sid is oozing his way across the open-plan office toward me. I brace myself for his visit by starting to breathe through my mouth.

I force myself to look up. Nigel is leaning over my desk. He has no perception of personal body space and does not seem to understand that I don't want to be close to him. Could his mother? I think of dead fish in a fishmonger's window.

"A word, if you please," he sprays. He mistakenly believes that the fake Dickensian language is distinguished. Flapping my arms, encouraging the air between us to circulate as quickly as possible, I follow him back to his office. As Controller of Entertainment and Comedy (a position he secured by uniquely blending bullying, bullshitting and—much as it pains me to admit it—a genuine business acumen) Bale has three offices. The executive office on the sixth floor, which is bigger than my flat, heaves with mahogany and teak, deep shag-pile carpets (literally), and numerous pictures of Bale with celebs. It doesn't work for me—I still don't think he is interesting, I still think he is offensive. This office is straight out of a set from *Dynasty*. This man is blissfully unaware that New Romantics are passé and even their retro revival has been and gone. His second office is a *pied à terre* in Chelsea. I shudder to think what kinds of contracts are negotiated there. I've never visited. The third office is the one on our floor, which he is currently leading me to. Again, huge—this time very modern and open. Not so that we are encouraged to drop in on him (no one wants to) but so that he can terrify us through constant surveillance.

Although visiting Bale's office is unpleasant, at least I am one of the few heterosexual women in TV6 who is safe from his advances. He obviously asked me to sleep with him when we first met, but I refused. He quickly became distracted by a far prettier but less fastidious PA. By the time she received her P45 (following her justified but failed attempt to bring a sexual harassment case to court)

I'd proved that I was actually quite good at my job. Lascivious Bale is, but stupid he is not. He realized that actively pursuing me as a lay was unlikely to be successful and would certainly limit my productivity. More concerned with the bottom line than any bottom, he's since left me more or less alone. He occasionally takes the odd pot shot, when he's had one or two dozen too many. He leers at me or sprays his spittle in my direction, but a friendly hint that Mandy in Comedy finds him really attractive is usually enough to distract him.

Bale nods toward the leather chair that is strategically positioned to be four inches lower than his. It's a ham-fisted attempt at intimidation. I sigh; this man is a parody. I sit down and wait.

He waits too.

Silently.

Then he grins. It's the cruelest smile I've ever seen and it totally fails to ignite his eyes. I wonder if he is going to sack me. I feel a bead of sweat run down my back. It's cold. If he calls me Jocasta this is serious.

"Jocasta, I want an idea." He bangs his fist on the desk. I force myself not to jump. I know we are at war. But then, I always am. His gesture is unnecessary but I understand his motivation. He knows, as well as I do, that every eye on the floor is turned toward us. He likes to appear passionate; it's very new millennium.

"We're in trouble, Cas." Because he calls me Cas, I realize that *we* may be in trouble but *I* am not. He needs me. I allow myself to relax enough to take in what he is saying. He flings the channel's weekend viewing figures over the desk. I don't pick them up to examine them. I don't have to. I checked them this morning at 7:30 A.M. They are terrible.

Not content with being one of the youngest executive producers at ITV and managing some of the strongest shows for a main commercial channel, two years ago I decided I needed new challenges. I took a leap of faith and joined a consortium led by a group of guys with enough venture capital and balls to bid for the franchise of a new channel. Our team won the bid for TV6 by insisting that instead of being yet another publisher broadcaster, filling airtime with programs shipped in from the U.S., we would produce new programs. I had visions of producing challenging, dynamic, informative and startling programs. I threw away my six-figure salary, company Porsche, obscene expense account, private healthcare, pension and gym membership, and moved to TV6. To be clear, this was not an act of altruism. My end goal was not to educate and entertain the great British public. I just thought that this novel approach would generate huge viewing figures, that the channel would be an unprecedented success and that I'd get more material reward than I've ever had before. The added benefit, the incalculable advantage, would be that I would have control. A smaller pond to swim in perhaps, but I'd certainly be a much bigger fish. A shark.

I'd honestly believed that the public wanted new programming. New thoughts, new ideas. It pains me to admit that this was a misjudgement on my part. It's unusual that I miscalculate human nature and it's unprecedented that my miscalculation is roseate. It appears that the general public is very happy with repeats of *Diff'rent Strokes* and *Fame*. Channels that, three years ago, looked as though they'd never sail are beginning to race in the white waters. It could be that I am on the *Titanic*.

"The competition are whipping our ass. Have you seen their Internet policy? They're not fucking around." He throws a competitive annual report in my direction. I've read it. "And they are capturing the youth market." He throws another annual report my way. Again, I've seen it. "Youth is the name of the game. We should go after that."

"What and be a 'me too?' " I comment scathingly. I notice that the slats in the blinds in Bale's office are damaged. I briefly wonder who he's fucked up against them. Bale ignores my put-down.

"Let's employ some designers with trendy jeans. We could get the girl on reception to serve our clients vodka and Red Bull." He looks at me hopefully. My eye falls on his desk. He has a mug with a dozen identical, yellow, sharp pencils. All this in the digital age. Oblivious, he carries on. "They could listen to trance music and send their friends text messages. They could wear blades to work."

"And that would help with the schedule, would it?"

"It would bring fresh ideas."

"Bale, we are too old. Even the lads and ladettes we know are aspiring to 'me-time' and their own pads. We can't do anything for the teen market."

"Well what, then?" he asks petulantly. I bet he'd already chosen the bunny outfit for the receptionist.

"I don't know. Late twenties and early thirties are always rich pickings." I know I'm clasping at straws. "We should think of a schedule that targets them."

"Yeah, they all have more money than sense, no direction and lots of time. How about sport?"

"I've never believed in encouraging sports fanaticism, and besides, the next thing you know they are actually playing, which involves turning off their TV sets. We don't want them out playing sport. We want them slouched in front of the box. Besides, ASkyA are there."

"Yes, while I think about it, write a complaint letter. ASkyA are running sports updates throughout their ad breaks on sports programs. They'll be charging advertisers a premium for that. Where there's advertising there is money for program development," he warns.

"You could argue that it distracts the viewer from the advert. Maybe it's worth less money."

"Yeah, send a spoiler letter to the advertisers," he instructs.

"Get your secretary to do it," I counter.

We glare at one another. Both livid and arrogant.

And scared.

"I want an idea," he yells again. "A single idea, but a big one. A humongous one. A bloody big-dick-swinging one. An astonishing, unique, bang-those-bastards-and-their-new-shows-in-to-the-ground-idea." He changes tack. He leans toward me and starts to whisper menacingly, "The tabloids and the men's mags have a host of new wannabe babes who present meaningless shows and are prepared to pose topless for publicity." I'm about to condemn this, when he adds, "You're going to have to come up with something really good to top that." He wipes his mouth with the back of his hand. The idea of topless wannabes has made him salivate. "Got it?"

"Something arresting." I'm trying to sound cool but I keep my hands by my sides so he doesn't see them quiver. I hope my mastery of understatement irritates him.

"A ginormous, fucking, ratings-rocketting idea. Now go away and have it." He dismisses me.

I get back to my desk and give in to the shaking. I light a cigarette and swallow back a cold double espresso. Artificial stimulants are a way of life. For all Bale is as ugly as a slapped arse, he is good at his job. I do, grudgingly, admire him. He has a point. I've been trying to ignore our flagging ratings, positively denying the competition's success. But the weekend runs are indisputable: TV6 is in big trouble.

Our office is in north London. A peculiar idiosyncrasy in the microclimates means that it rains more than average here. Or so it's seems to me. It's late August. It has certainly been summer in every other part of London. I have seen pavement cafés exploding throughout Soho; crowds of office workers have exploited every coffee and lunch break by pouring into the streets in the West End. Girls in skimpy sundresses and strappy sandals have been spotted as far as Hammersmith. But in Islington it's bleak. To be specific, in TV6 it's bleak.

"Everything OK?" asks Fi. Fi is my assistant and has been for eighteen months. I employed her because she reminds me of myself. She is committed, ambitious and dedicated. She's cold comfort in times of a crisis.

"Fine." I turn to my PC and hope she'll get the hint. I like to work things out for myself.

"Is there anything I can help with?"

"No," I reply automatically. Although I employed Fi, I don't trust her 100 percent. It isn't that Fi has done anything to lose my trust. In fact, when she first joined TV6, she worked very hard to be a "chum," but eventually she realized I don't do "chum." And I don't trust. These are policies.

"If it's Bale, maybe I can have a word," she offers. I sigh, depressed by the implication. Am I supposed to think she's being helpful? I look up at her and she is twirling her fine blonde hair around her finger, tapping her foot and smiling to herself. The implication is that she has a special relationship with Bale. Has she? Has she slept with him? Oh, awful thought. I look closer and she defiantly returns my gaze. Her ice-blue eyes, sparkling out above her high, chiseled cheekbones, lock on mine for a fraction of a second. Then she starts to walk away. She is striking. Her mother is Norwegian and she has inherited her Scan. confidence and good looks. She's one of those women who can make a beady bag and a friendship bangle look cool rather than childish. She is five foot ten; she has no hips, no thighs, no stomach. She is the ideal woman, as far as women are concerned. Generally Bale likes his women a little curvy, but then that is a generalization. It's possible they've had sex. However, I don't want to ask her. What's the point? She wouldn't have to tell me the truth. If she has slept with him she will have no influence over him, whatever she thinks to the contrary. But it is possible that he's still trying to seduce her, and if this is the case I can't afford to alienate her. She could be useful.

"Hey, Fi. Yeah, you can help. Organize a meeting between our team after lunch. We need a brainstorm." I smile. We both know the smile is business. She grins back and I'm relieved. She probably hasn't slept with him yet. I normally know about such things long before the participants do. I consider warning her but decide not to. She'll either think I am jealous or too old to know better. Advice, by its very nature, is there to be ignored.

Our office is a huge glass building that seems to rise endlessly upwards. It's turned inside out like the Pompidou Center. There is an odd mix of ritz and tat. Diet Coke and watery hot drinks from vending machines are consumed around Conran aluminum tables. There are plants oxygenating the room but I suspect the nod toward green and leafy is a losing battle. Since television studios are some of the few places left in London where people can still smoke, most feel it is obligatory. A dense smoky haze fills our days. People don't move around much, they stay at their desks. This suggests that there is substantial amount of genuine industry but not much communication. Calling a meeting indicates the seriousness of my issue. Through the glass partition I see my team congregate. It's like watching a bunch of anxious relatives waiting by a sick bed. The analogy is frighteningly close to the reality. I'm pleasantly surprised to see that they possibly realize as much; everyone appears slightly nervous and sweaty. They are trying hard to look as though they are not trying at all. Their names are Thomas and Mark (the creative team), Jacquelyn (production secretary), Diana (marketing manager), Graham (sponsorship and advertising manager), Deborah (PR officer), Richard (broadcast strategy and scheduling manager) and Fi. Because we work in TV they are known as Tom, Jaki, Di, Gray, Debs, Ricky and Fi. There was nothing we could do with Mark.

The team look to one another to discover a suitable expression to draw their faces into. They are trying to decide whether to look wracked with professional concern, coolly indifferent or bright and optimistic. The problem with my industry is that a very large part of it is populated by those who refuse to leave their student years behind them. They dress like students. Everyone is ill-looking thin. Dressing down is an art form. The merest hint of trying, an iota of personal pride, will be condemned. Everyone looks as though they do too many drugs, and smoke and drink too much. It's fair. Besides looking like students, the attitudes are similar, too. It is only students who could have arrived at the concepts of "essay crisis" or "no milk in the fridge crisis." These are not crises. Crises are earthquakes, famines and tidal waves. My team understands that the cancellation of the Christmas karaoke act is a crisis but have no concept that twelve weeks of plummeting ratings is a crisis. If they do get the concept and panic about it for fifteen minutes or so, they can't hold the concept. It's usual that mid-brainstorm or meeting, someone suggests that we need to go to the pub for a "break from the intensity." On our return the original subject of the meeting is forgotten and the debate has moved on to whether salt and Linneker are a better flavor crisp than cheese and onion.

I don't feel like this. There is nothing more important than my job.

I never enter a meeting room without first thinking through exactly what I want to say, how I want to say it and what effect I want to have. Fi being keen and ambitious, while slightly threatening and nauseous, is useful. She'll really want to crack this. I've slept with both Mark and Tom, although neither of them knows about the other. (FYI, Mark is better-looking, Tom is better in bed. He tries harder.) It should be easy to keep their attention. Especially as by happy chance I am wearing an unnecessarily tight T-shirt and bootleg jeans that cling in all the right places. I haven't slept with Gray so the outfit will be doubly effective. Debs and Di like to keep in with me as I occasionally give them tips on hair conditioners or the latest "must have" fashion statement. Ricky's gay so he does the same for me.

"Afternoon," I breeze.

"Afternoon," they mumble sulkily. For a nanosecond I think they are going to add "miss," but they don't.

"What's this?" I ask, pointing skeptically toward a cardboard box in the center of the table. It's overflowing with balloons, Christmas decorations, crayons, sticky-backed plastic, old magazines, a toy trumpet, several Comic Relief noses and a cappuccino.

"Oh, that's my coffee," says Di, reaching into the box and rescuing her drink. She takes a huge slurp, oblivious to my disdain.

"Yes, that's clear. What is the rest of it?" I fear Debs has been let down by her childminder again and had to bring her five-year-old son into work. I hope not—Bale just isn't in the mood.

"It's the creativity box," pipes up Fi, enthusiasm oozing from every pore. I look at her, waiting for a more meaningful explanation. She tries, "It's to help stimulate more creative thoughts." Even if I hadn't read Fi's CV I would know by this comment that she had an idyllic childhood, went to the best public schools for young ladies and had a father who adored her. How else could she be this happy with life? I think I'll piss on her parade.

"Remind me, Fi, which industry do we work in?"

"TV." She looks cautiously around the room, unsure where this questioning is going.

"And wouldn't you agree that TV is generally considered a creative industry?"

"Well, yes, but—"

"We're not bloody management consultants, we don't need sticky-backed plastic to prove we are capable of ideas." I don't raise my voice. I don't have to. She sheepishly drags the box off the table and tries to hide it behind the more conventional ideas aid, the flip chart. The others disloyally look away, distancing themselves from her. That doesn't impress me either.

"OK. You have read the brief. We have to come up with a hero show, something that will draw in the viewers and the advertisers; interest of the press would be a bonus. Mr. Bale has articulated the problem here, rather succinctly, I'm sure you'll agree." I read, "We need a 'bang-those-bastards-and-their-new-shows-in-to-the-ground-idea.' " The team treat themselves to a nervous giggle. I'm tough, but Bale is a tosser and our common loathing of him unites us again. I roll up my sleeves and sit on the side of the table, smiling and allowing the good humor to penetrate. "So what's the competition doing?"

"ITV are concentrating on their main stable of shows, successful soaps, quiz games that make people rich and buying in blockbuster films that earned a fortune in the box office. Here's their schedule for the next four months. The docusoap features heavily too," says Ricky. He's done his homework efficiently. Unfortunately the news is depressing. The room falls silent again; the good mood has evaporated.

"What about Channel 4's scheduling this year?" asks Fi hopefully.

"Just as strong," adds Ricky, embarrassed to be twisting the knife. "They have everything. Arts, music, drama, comedy, entertainment, lifestyle, leisure, documentaries, film premieres and something called '4 later.' "

"What's that—porn?" asks Mark.

"I don't expect they even need porn," answers Tom.

I read the descriptor. "It's porn," I assure. No one knows whether we should be glad that C4 have resorted to this or depressed because it will be a crowd pleaser. I clap my hands. "OK, to business. No idea is a daft idea, any thoughts, please?" I pick up the marker and stand with my pen poised in front of the flip chart.

Silence.

"Come on," I encourage. "Don't let those schedules intimidate you. I really think you can overestimate a period drama with high production values, big stars and great plots. I think they are too highbrow. Let's catch another niche market."

Fi gets it. "Drama is too expensive for TV6. Entertainment is cheap."

"Exactly," I bolster. "With entertainment the main outgoing is people's pride and common sense."

"What about a game show?" offers Tom. The look on his face suggests that he thinks he's just invented electricity.

"Good," I assure. He'll be the first to go, when the P45s are being dished up. "Now try and think of what *type* of game show." I consider whether, if the worst comes to the worst, I could retrain as a primary school teacher. I have all the core skills.

We bandy a few game show ideas around but they've all been done before. Often on bigger budgets than we have available. We talk it around and around.

"We could diversify. We could buy a publishing house or a football team," suggests Gray. He's thinking of the free tickets that he could blag for his friends.

"That's a stupid idea," comments Di.

"Gary, the commercial director, likes it."

"I think it is a great idea," says Di.

"Can we keep to the point, please," I instruct. It's getting hot and late. I call out for more coffee and Coke. The rest of London's workforces teem out of their offices and escape into pubs for a long cool lager. This isn't an option for my team.

"How about a 'fly on the wall' program?" asks Jaki. "They are cheap and popular."

"Absolutely. On which subject?"

"The police force?" offers Mark. "We could expose their ruthless tactics and racist tendencies."

"They do a pretty good job of that themselves, without TV," points out Jaki.

"The fire brigade?" offers Ricky. I know he's simply getting hot and sweaty over the idea of them swinging down their pole. He's a sucker for uniforms.

"Been done."

His disappointment is criminal.

"Banker-wankers?"

"Same as the police force, really."

"The gas board?"

"Done."

"Electricity?"

"And water. Nothing left to be said on the utilities scams."

"Nor builders or mechanics."

"It's all been done before," sighs Mark. "It's all too undemanding and formulaic."

"We are talking about an escapist medium," I remind him. "No one wants demanding. Demanding is how we describe our kids, red bills and the lover we no longer want to have sex with."

We fall silent again. I look at the trash that's lying on the table. Numerous empty cans of diet Coke, overflowing ashtrays, curling sandwiches. This mountain of debris and my Patek Philippe watch tell me it's time to call it a day.

"OK, go home. Go and see your partners and kids." I flop back into my chair and put my head on the desk. The cool surface is a relief. "But don't stop thinking about this. The idea may come to you on the tube or in the bath or while you're making love."

"You're sick," grins Jaki. She seems to think that part of her job description as production secretary is to tell me how it is.

"Look, Jaki, football is not a matter of life and death, it's more important than that. And TV? TV is more important than football."

She laughs and closes the door behind her.

But I'm not joking.

CHAPTER
Three

I LIVE ON MY OWN, in a spacious pseudo-loft apartment in a trendy part of East London. I say pseudo because it's not in the loft, it's on the second floor. But I do have exposed brickwork and genuine iron girders that keep the roof from falling in. My space is the antithesis to both the abandoned family home in Esher and my mother's two-up-two-down in Cockfosters. It's modern and light and empty. I only allow things into my flat if they are both useful and beautiful. Except for the men who visit, which would be asking too much. My two favorite possessions are my charcoal-gray B&B Italia couch that seats umpteen and my B&O TV, which is the size of a screen at a small local cinema. I love my flat and Issie hates it, for the same reason: it's clinical and impersonal. Issie keeps trying to introduce chintz by buying me floral bathmats and tea cosies for Christmas. I return the favor by buying her aluminum, slim-line pasta jars, which she can't open.

Josh and Issie both have keys to my flat, as I do to their homes. We are Londoners so we don't literally drop in on one another. But sometimes we make arrangements to go around to each other's pads for supper, as it's nice to occasionally come home to the smell of cooking and the clink of someone pouring you a G&T. Tonight I'm delighted we've made this plan. I need their company. I push open my door and am hit by delicious cooking smells.

"You're late," shouts Josh from the kitchen. He's responsible for the delicious smells. I drop my bags and PC and head straight for the kitchen.

"What's cooking?" I inquire, lifting lids and spooning small amounts of heaven into my mouth.

"Out," he snaps, playfully swiping at my hands and trying to replace the lids. "You have to wait." But he can't resist showing off. "It's *pepperoni con acciughe capperi.*"

"Chargrilled peppers with anchovy and capers," translates Issie, as she hands me a glass of Australian Chardonnay. "Mountadam, Eden Valley 1996," she assures, knowing it's important to me.

"And *maiale arrosto con aceto balsamico,*" interrupts Josh.

I turn helplessly to Issie. She fills in, "Roast pork with balsamic vinegar."

"Fantastic." Funny, I'm never irritated by Josh's pretension of insisting on calling every dish he cooks by its Italian name. "Have I got time to shower off my shit day?"

"Yes, if you are quick."

Sometimes we chatter nonstop throughout supper and sometimes we watch TV, entertaining ourselves by hurling abuse or a book at the commentary, but tonight we eat in comfortable silence. Or at least I think it is comfortable until Issie asks, "What's up, Cas? You're really quiet tonight." She's given me authority over the remote control. Normally I love this but tonight, as a diversionary tactic the remote control is a failure.

I realize I'm grateful to be asked and I slip into child mode, hoping that surrogate Mum and Dad can sort things out for me. There's only Issie and Josh, in the entire world, who I let see me when I feel vulnerable or down.

"It's work," I whine.

"Naturally. We never expect you to say it's man trouble," comments Josh. I don't have man trouble—that's the advantage of seeing them as sex objects rather than soul mates.

"The channel's viewing figures are down for the twelfth week in a row. It's serious. Bale's talking redundancies. Problem is we haven't got a hero show. We haven't even got a strong soap."

"What about *Teddington Crescent?*" Issie is as intimate with my programming schedule as I am.

"The lives and loves of the inhabitants of Milton Keynes don't have what it takes to knock Corrie or Brookie off their spots. We haven't got a principal game show, or a lead chat show host. Poor ratings—that's viewership," I translate, but it's unnecessary as they are both educated in my media speak, "affects the advertisers we can draw. Without advertising money we can't invest in cool shows. It's a vicious circle." I pause. They don't interrupt but allow me to find the words. "The worst of it is that Bale has made it into my problem." I check to see if they are as pissed off as I am. They both make an admirable job of looking horrified. Satisfied, I continue. "Despite his obscene pay check he has renounced all responsibility and said I have to come up with a winning idea. He's—"

"So rotten. He's repellent, revolting, ridiculous," jokes Josh.

"A plethora of R words." Issie grins and tries to get me to cheer up.

I scowl. "He's a shit." I'm not going to allow them to brighten me out of my despair. "I'm scared."

Everyone is silent. They know my job is my world. Josh sits down next to me and puts his arm around me.

"I'm fucking scared," I say with unusual honesty.

"I don't see the problem. You'll come up with the idea," he comforts. Normally I love his confidence in me but I shrug, because right now, I don't think his confidence is founded. My head is aching. Everything's fuzzy.

"Maybe." I know that it is my problem and neither of them can really offer a solution, so I change the subject. "Did I get any post?"

"It's on the mantelpiece."

Two bills, council tax and water—marvelous. Three pieces of junk mail, all for pizza delivery services. I spy another heavy white envelope.

"Hell, another wedding," I sigh. "It's nearly September, for Christ's sake. Haven't these people any decency? Plaguing me throughout my autumn months as well as the summer." I'm only half kidding, but it's great to see Issie look het up.

"Who is it this time?" she asks.

"Jane Fischer is marrying Marcus Phillips," I read. "Have we met him?"

"Yup," confirms Josh. "He was at Lesley and James's wedding last week. He was an usher. The blonde one, with the red waist-coat. Jane wasn't there—some prior commitment, probably another wedding."

Issie and I freeze.

"Bastard," we assert in unison.

I pass Issie the invite so she can see the betrayal for herself. Issie fingers the white card, caressing the embossing, and sighs. It's not turning out to be a good day for either of us.

"That explains the reluctance to give a real telephone number."

"Will either of you marry me?" asks Josh, realizing that Issie's had a disappointment but not knowing the exact nature.

"No," I say.

"Yes," says Issie, "but only for the dress."

We all laugh. We've run through this routine zillions of times. When we graduated Josh promised to marry whichever one of us wasn't married by the time we were twenty-five. Twenty-five came and went. None of us had managed to find a life partner but we were forced to admit that, at that precise moment in time, we didn't fancy each other. We decided not to go ahead but put the deal back to when we hit thirty, assuming that we'd be so desperate by then we'd all be less fastidious. Thirtieth parties came and went, but Josh said he couldn't chose between us and as bigamy is an offense, punishable in the highest courts in the land, we all agreed to think about it again in the year 2005. However, Josh does regularly ask us to marry him, just so we feel good about ourselves. He often tries to coincide it with our menstrual cycles, which with the passing of time he has reluctantly become intimate with.

"Can you believe that Marcus guy slept with me just days before he sent out invites to his wedding?"

"Yes," I reply.

She scowls and mutters, "Well, of course you only expect the worst from people," she grumbles. "Can *you* believe it?" Issie turns to Josh. It's an annoying habit of hers to think that there is a male and a female point of view on these things. She often dismisses my point of view and turns to Josh, "because he's a man and he knows how men think." Invariably Josh agrees with me.

"It's commonplace. The last fling and all that," says Josh, and although I know that what he is saying upsets Issie I feel vindicated. "I make a conscious effort to lookup ex-girlfriends just before they get married, on the grounds that I might exploit the last fling thing," he adds.

"Do you?" cries Issie, horrified.

"Do you?" I say, and once again my respect for him is renewed. Josh tries to settle his face in an expression that will please both of us, a subtle mix between contrition and pride. He gives up and ends up just grinning at me.

"Tell me," I beg. Josh is a wonderful friend and I love him for very many reasons and one of them is that he's unscrupulous and we can share tactics.

"It never fails. It's the combination of the near-legalized indiscretion. Women figure that once they've slept with you, they might as well sleep with you again." I raise my eyebrows. Personally I'm not too fond of repeat performances—they give the wrong message. Josh catches my glance and understands my skepticism.

"I'm generalizing," he explains. "Normal women. Everyone wants a final fling but a safe final fling. The ex is that. It's worked for me on several occasions. One last night of unbridled passion but without the complications that Marcus risked by starting up a new liaison." Issie scowls. Josh shrugs apologetically. But what can he do? He's spent years apologizing to Issie for his half of the human race, but really it's not his fault. Now he simply shrugs off her disappointments.

"That's it! That's it! Genius," I congratulate. "You are a genius," I cry and hug Josh. Josh happily accepts my hugs but he hasn't got a clue why I'm so excited. "That's the idea for the fucking amazing ratings-rocketing program. A *Blind Date* meets *The Truman Show*."

"What?" asks Josh. Issie simply stares; she rarely expects to follow my devious mind.

"A fly-on-the-wall plus. We get couples, the week before their wedding, to come on to the show and tell us all about why they are getting married." I rush to explain but my tongue can't keep up with my gray matter and I doubt I'm making sense. "Loads of sucker stuff about how they knew from the moment they saw each other and how there could never be anyone else for them. Then we find out which one of them is gagging for a bit of extra-curricular—"

"But—" Issie tries to interrupt me.

"There will be one," I assure forcefully. "Then we maneuver a meeting between that party and an ex. Then we let nature take its course."

"Will it work?"

"Of course it will work. There is nothing more seductive than an ex."

Issie eyes me skeptically.

"Except perhaps Gucci," I concede. I'm thrilled. "It has everything! Voyeurism, trivialization of sex, manipulation."

"It's a terrible idea," shouts Issie.

I'm genuinely bewildered. "It's brilliant."

"It's the principle I object to," she adds.

"I don't deal in principles—they are no longer legal tender."

"More is the pity."

I start to imagine the marketing and PR. "He's put on a pound or two, maybe lost a bit of hair, but otherwise he's unchanged. He was the love of your life when you were twenty-one and ten years have gone by. Yet, he has that same boyish grin, he still calls you by your nickname and he remembers that you bought your hair gel in goldfish bowls at Superdrug. How can you resist?" I'm warming to my theme.

"Flirting with nostalgia is perilous," warns Issie.

"That's its selling point," I confirm.

"You could wreck lives. Be responsible for canceled weddings," she squeals.

"We'd pay for the wedding if it fell through."

Josh looks at me as though I've just crawled out from under the rim of the loo. This surprises me.

"What?" I demand, hotly. "I'm saving taxes. Your hard-earned taxes." I think this will get him. Josh is in the 40 percent bracket. He has private healthcare and went to public school, so my very reasonable argument that taxes aren't just for the building and reconstruction of our roads but for the building and reconstruction of our healthcare and future has never washed with him. Now I'm grateful.

"If these people married, they would sooner or later divorce, dragging their five children through the courts. The children would be emotionally scarred and, no doubt, perpetuate the scenario by re-enacting their parents' failed marriages. The total legal aid costs could run into hundreds of thousands."

"Christ, Cas, you deserve a medal," bites Josh sarcastically.

I choose to ignore the sarcasm. "I knew you'd see it my way."

• • •

I can hardly sleep with excitement. I fine-tune the details. I consider that perhaps it is too much to expect every couple, weeks away from marriage, to have cracks in their relationships, but I could advertise. I reason that no one is going to come forward and volunteer that they are feeling restless or randy. People lack such emotional honesty or self-awareness. I know—I've operated in the so-called adult world for sixteen sexually active years and I've yet to find anyone who is prepared to call a spade a shovel. But perhaps there is another way. Perhaps I could attack it from the other side. I've seen countless examples of paranoia, jealousy, insecurity and mistrust. Now *that* is an angle! Maybe I could advertize for people who doubt their partners and want to test them before they make that final commitment. Then all TV6 will have to do is maneuver a situation where the mistrusted party comes into contact with the threatening ex and then . . . And then! I hug myself. Obviously it depends on the mistrusted partner never having a clue that they are being tested. Total secrecy. But that shouldn't be too hard to achieve. In my experience secrecy between couples is pretty commonplace. I know this is big. I can see it now. The reaction of the duped, the hypocrisy of the rogue partners. All on live TV. It is pure brilliance! It's so cruel. It's so honest. I can smell my success and it makes me feel sexy.

I switch on my bedside light and feel under my bed in an attempt to unearth my electronic diary. I hesitate, problem with repeat performances is that they invariably lead to unnecessary complications. The guy involved thinking I really care, him thinking he does, or his wife finding out and thinking both of us do. Yet, needs must. I really can't be bothered to get dressed and drag myself to my club to pick up something fresh. The diary beeps at me. Steven Arnold? No, I think he just got married. That would be awful timing. Keith Bevon? No, psycho, stalker tendencies. Phil Bryant? Didn't he emigrate? George Crompton, or perhaps his brother Jack? Oh no, too late in the day for the complex sibling thing to "Why did you ring me rather than my brother?" "Is mine bigger than his?" Lord, it's enough to bring on a headache. Miles Dodd? Good idea, not too clingy, not too involved—with me or anyone else. Prepared to hold back until I come. Yes, Miles will do nicely. Disappointingly his line is engaged. Well, at least it's just his line. Joe Dorward. It takes me a moment to place him. Oh yes, the researcher on that pop quiz show on Channel 4. I met him at a workshop several months ago. I hadn't found him sexy at first— good-looking, yes, but not clever enough to really turn me on. I figured I could run verbal rings around him, which is rarely attractive. However, after three or four glasses of champagne I was less fastidious. It had panned out quite well. As Josh says, it's not *verbal* stimulation you want in bed. I call his number. He picks up.

"Hey, Joe," I murmur.

I wake up and Joe is already up. I can hear him in the kitchen, whistling and fixing breakfast. He brings up a coffee and tells me that he's been to the 7-Eleven to buy croissants, that they'll be ready soon. I tell him I don't eat breakfast and struggle to sit up.

"Water?"

He rushes to the bathroom and returns with a glass of water. I'm so dehydrated that I ignore the fact that this glass of water has undoubtedly passed through five other bodies before me. Joe climbs back into bed and starts nibbling my shoulder. In the cold light of day I realize that first impressions are always right. He is dumb. Admittedly, he is extremely handsome and, I suppose, sexy, in an obvious sort of way. But how come I hadn't noticed those puppy-dog eyes shining with devotion? That overloud laugh that erupts every time I say anything, even unfunny things like my name and that nodding bloody head that agrees with *everything* I say. It's nauseous. He still smells good and, thinking about it objectively, he is a shag. But he's so certainly besotted. I try to think of the things that could put him off me. Perhaps if I showed him my cellulite or my untrimmed bikini line he'd leave the flat, (unlikely). Maybe if I insist on watching Oprah, or pick the pubes from between my teeth with my toenails. I can't think of any antisocial behavior that is antisocial enough to discourage him. I realize that the only way to get him to lose interest is to pretend to be in love with him. I doubt I have the energy. His large legs, erotic last night, look overwhelming today. I push him away, get out of bed, locate his trousers and throw them at him.

"Get dressed. I've a big day today."

"Bale, I have the answer." I charge into his office, shooing his secretary away with a single, withering glance. I decline the seat and the cigar he offers. He really is a twat. However, he is my twat boss and I want to impress him.

"I have the Idea."

"I'm all ears," he sneers. Actually, he does have jug ears but he's all teeth, not all ears. I resist the jibe and start to tell him about my idea. Although I've stormed into his office at 10:50 A.M. to give the impression of an employee who knows her worth and won't be bullied, I have actually been in the office since 8:15 A.M. rehearsing this meeting. I have perfected a pitch that guarantees punch but appears spontaneous, that is irresistible and, most of all, assured. Besides the presentation of the pitch, I have paid immaculate attention to the detail of the presentation of the person. I'm wearing a Dries Van Noten white cotton slip dress with heavy boots on bare legs. The look I've achieved is naive charm, but the boots hint at something a whole lot tougher. I'm showing enough cleavage to secure his attention.

"OK," I take a deep breath. "The brief was to have a high-profile program that will attract viewers, advertising budgets and the press." Bale nods cautiously. "You want notoriety on a shoestring," I add for clarity.

"I never said notoriety."

"But you agree we need to be noticed." He nods. The nod is fractional. I know this is because if there is ever a debate with the executive committee regarding this program, Bale will deny he gave consent. Sod him. I tell him my idea.

"It's a bit unlikely, isn't it?" says Bale cautiously.

"Why do you say that?"

"Well, the premise you're working from is that we need couples who are just about to skip toward the altar but are paranoid enough to think that their dearest is not 100 percent kosher and he fancies a bit of pork with his ex-totty."

The analogy is repulsive. Offensive to a number of religions, vegetarians and women, but yes, basically Nigel has it. I try to encourage him.

"Look, I've done my research. There are 6.6 marriages per 1,000 population in the U.K. Which is roughly 11,000 per week. It's one of the highest marriage rates in the world, twenty-ninth highest, actually. But we also have one of the highest divorce rates too—"

"Well, you can't divorce unless you marry," says fucking Einstein. I smile icily.

"The divorce rate is one in three marriages. Ninth highest in the world."

"And your point is?"

"Do you know how in many cases the ex is cited in court? Thirty-seven percent. There are countless rekindlings of old flames and remarriages to ex-partners each year. The ex is so compelling, I give you Liz Taylor and Richard Burton, Fergie and Prince Andrew, Melanie Griffiths and Don Johnson." Bale's beginning to be interested. He knows a good idea when he sees one.

"Isn't that Melanie one with that Banderas one now?"

I sweep his objections away by ignoring them. "Bale, we can't fail."

"Would there really be people who would do this?"

I can't believe Bale is questioning whether there are enough exhibitionist/paranoid/jealous types in the world.

"We are looking at a pilot series of six episodes. Two couples per episode. We only need twelve couples. We have the entire British population to choose from."

Bale nods. "People are so hideous."

He should know. I fake cordiality. "It makes good television. Think back to 1974, Paul Rogers' documentary *The Family*. You know what I'm talking about?" The show has superstar status in the history of TV. Everyone knows of it. It was the first fly-on-the-wall.

"Oh, the one where Rogers sat, for months, with a camera in the front room of some family from the commuter belt? The marriage broke down as a consequence."

"Yes. I don't think it was simply to do with Mr. Wilkins's dislike of audio equipment. It was because Mrs. Wilkins admitted on national TV that her husband was not the father of her last child."

"That's right." Bale is leering and chuckling at the same time. "Dirty bitch."

"But ask yourself why Bale. Why would she divulge such a thing to the entire world? Maybe it *was* simply stress, but she invited that stress in to her home. Why would she do that? Maybe she wanted to make the confession? Maybe she wanted to blow apart her sanitized semi? Or was it to guarantee that she didn't pass from this world to the next without her Andy Warhol requisite fifteen minutes of fame?"

"Or maybe she wanted to teach him a lesson?" adds Bale. "Hurt him? Or beg his forgiveness in a forum too public to allow him to reject her?"

"Exactly. We don't know. There are myriad reasons that motivate people. Think of the radio wedding a few years back. People are prepared to trot down the aisle, with absolute strangers, to get their Warhol fifteen minutes of fame. Although in the Birmingham couples case, it wasn't so much fifteen minutes as seven and a half months, 185 minutes of TV air time, 207 minutes of radio airtime and 58 column inches in the press."

Bale taps his pen on the desk. He's getting excited. I go for closure.

"There are countless fly-on-the-wall programs about marriage: the run-up to the proposal, the wedding, the first year. I've heard that Channel 4 are developing a documentary on consummation." I'm making this up, but I want Bale's budget. I am immoral most of the time and amoral where business is concerned. I'm proposing a twist to a proven formula. The contributors are to be in the studio when the actions of all parties are exposed. The live audience is key. It's overpowering. The thing about ex's is that they never go away. Even those to whom you haven't given a second thought in over a decade, who you've never seen since you parted, are important. There is always a nagging curiosity about what happened to the one that got away, or the one you threw away."

Bale, a true businessman, sees the potential. "You think it will work." He states this as a fact rather than as a question.

"Yes," I enthuse. "I admit that it is dependent upon the credulity, stupidity and vanity of the British population." I take a deep breathe. "It can't fail."

"But if it gets as big as you say it will, how will we keep attracting people on to the show?"

"We'll film enough shows for a series before we go live. We'll have watertight release forms so that the guests can't retract their permission. Bale, I'll work out the detail. Don't you worry." I'm desperate, so I gently pat his arm.

Bale nods. "OK, Cas. Go to finance and work out a budget."

I want to punch the air. He senses it. "Hey, don't get carried away. I'm not a millionaire."

That's another one of Bale's relentless lies. But I don't care. I've got a program and it's a winner!

CHAPTER
Four

JOSH, HI, IT'S ME. Guess what? Bale went for it! The infidelity with an ex show."

"And I'm supposed to think that's a good thing."

"Oh, come on, Josh." It's not like him to be down on me. "I'm back on top."

"Which is where you most like to be," Josh laughs, despite himself.

"Both literally and metaphorically," I add cheekily.

"Are you flirting with me, Cas?" Josh asks, but not seriously.

"I'd be flirting if it was anyone but you," I assure him.

"Cold comfort."

"We're going to call it *Sex with an Ex.* What do you think?"

"I'm trying not to think about it."

I sigh, disappointed by his lack of enthusiasm. "Look, I've got to ring off—there's so much to do. I just wanted to tell you my good news. After all, you more or less gave me the idea,"

"Oh, horrible thought. Bye now."

I put the phone down and do my best to push Josh's reserved response to the back of my mind. Instead I focus on the fact that Bale's is as grateful as I could hope. He has offered to pay me a bonus related to the ratings we secure. I'm likely to make a killing. My success has duly subdued Fi and I have decided to be magnanimous. I don't trust her, but practically speaking she is my assistant and I need her to be closely involved in this project—there is so much to do.

We start with the advert.

Are you about to get married? Do you trust your affianced 100 percent? Is there an ex in his or her past who could still affect your future? Please write in complete confidentiality to P.O. Box . . .

Such a simple call to action.

"Will it work?" asks Fi.

"If I know anything about human nature, this will work."

"Where should we place the ad?"

"Initially in the sad, loser magazines, *Gas* and *Gos*." I throw a couple of mags over to her. I respect Fi enough not to expect her to be familiar with them. She picks up the mags and begins to flick through them.

"My God, these are obscene. Don't these people have any self-respect?"

I don't look up from my budget sheets. "No."

She starts to read the contents page. " 'I Had Sex with 100 Men in Three Years,' 'I had a Threesome with my Mate and his Girlfriend,' 'The Crotchless Knickers are by the Booby Drops—Working in a Sex Shop,' 'We're Sex-perts—Women Who Really Rate Themselves in Bed!' "

"It's ideal," I interrupt. "The readers are willing to bare their souls and their bodies for a measly fiver and a couple of column inches on the letters page. These people are looking for platforms. They're a gift. However, Fi, I don't want to be another Jerry Springer. I don't simply want the oddballs of this world. We are going to have to think of an extremely clever incentive to attract normal people."

Fi groans. "But it will be easier to get horrid people on the show. They have no self-awareness and also they've had fewer opportunities."

I glare at her. Easy (unless relating to my sexual morals) is not a word I like in my vocabulary. I know that the success of the show will lie in whether I can make the average viewer feel uncomfortable. There are zillions of fly-on-the-wall and chat show programs where the guests are modern-day ghouls. Normally the viewer sits back, cushy on their chintz. They comment that the characters on talk shows are priceless, pure escapism. Chat shows do a public service: people watch and thank God that their own lives are better than these are. I want *Sex with an Ex* to be a different sort of show. I want cosy couples to stiffen in each other's company. I want them to struggle for conversation in the ad break. I want them to move apart a fraction and doubt each other. This show is their lives, whatever class, age, race or religion they are.

"So who do you want to attract?"

"Joe and Joanne public. The people we trust. Policemen, nurses, librarians, teachers, the guys at Carphone Warehouse." Fi eyes me skeptically.

Eventually we agree to place the ad on the TV6 web page and the internal electronic noticeboard, to send a researcher to gyms and clubs to do some on-the-spot recruiting, and to place a telephone line after our *Don't Try this Alone* program. It does quite well on the early evening slot.

Any reservations Fi had regarding the number of volunteers we'd find are soon swept away. Within days of placing the adverts we are inundated with responses; they arrive by the sackful. The world, it appears, is full of those who are about to pledge love until death do them part but actually fear a much more secular separation. It was as I'd expected. They are the most depressing reads ever.

My girlfriend, Chrissie, is the sweetest, kindest, most loving woman I have ever known. I'm honored that she accepted my proposal and agreed to be my wife. We are due to marry in four weeks' time. We are having a big do, no expense spared. After all, you only do it once. We plan to have a large family and one day live by the sea. I love her and she loves me. She says so all the time.

Do you think she'd ever be unfaithful?

I only ask because my best mate reckons he saw her in a pub with an ex-boyfriend of hers. I'm sure it was innocent but when I asked her about it, she said he must have made a mistake . . .

I get married in seven weeks' time. I love my fiancé so much and I'm sure that he loves me, pretty sure. But not absolutely certain. There was a girl he went to college with. She ditched him for an American rower. My best friend got very drunk at a dinner party last night and said some really mean things. She said that I caught him on the rebound, that he's out of my league. I wonder—if he had the choice, would he choose me?

. . . I found letters, you see. Why would she keep his letters?

. . . When you marry you give up your past. You have to. I'm ready for it. But is he? He's always been a bit of a one for the ladies. Nothing serious. He's just a flirt. He can't help himself. He doesn't mean any harm by it. It doesn't bother me. Too much. It's just that my mum says that men like him never change. It's not that there is an individual ex that I'm threatened by. To be frank there are dozens . . .

There are a number of psychotics. People who said they'd rather see their partner dead than unfaithful. I believe them and pass their letters on to the police.

We employ a team to trawl through the responses, but Fi and I can't resist an occasional morbid dip into them. Although the letters are in many ways individual there is a commonality. There is a mustard ripeness of those desperate to confirm their own supremacy in their partner's affections.

"Do you think they'll all look hideous?"

"Why do you suppose that, Fi?"

"Well, to be so desperate, so insecure?"

I throw over to her a picture of one of the letter writers. The woman in question is thirty-two, slim, blonde, elegant. She has enclosed a CV detailing that she has a first from Cambridge and a Ph.D. from Harvard. Fi looks amazed. To shake her further, I pass a photo of the fiancé. He is smart and mediocre. Fi looks bewildered.

"He is so ordinary."

"Yup, to you. But to her he is a god."

"I don't get it." She shakes her head wearily.

"Nor do I, babe. Maybe it's London." I don't believe this, but I think it might be a comfort. "Anyway, get her on the show."

The team is gathering around the mountain of letters, which appear to have a magnetic force. I take advantage of their presence, "OK, status. Have you seen the lawyers, Jaki?"

"Yes. We have to be extremely careful, but the terms aren't impossible. For those who know they are being filmed and are part of the set-up we can use any footage we like, as long as the punter is informed that the tape is running. 'Informing' them can be as simple as posting a notice saying cameras are in operation, and to be super-safe, we must get the guests to sign this." She waves a weighty document, about the thickness of the *Yellow Pages*. "The fine print will bore the proverbials of most guests and they'll sign. You can use CCTV footage as long as the local council agrees. I'm working on clearance. Those cameras are everywhere—shops, garages, on street lamps in dark alleys"—I like the fact that she's been thinking laterally—"libraries, public car parks, hotel foyers."

"I can't imagine these bodies will agree, though, will they?" asks Fi.

"As I say, I'm working on clearance but as long as all the correct legal documents are in place no one seems too squeamish about blowing the whistle. Restaurants and hotels see it as free publicity. However, taping the dupe is much more difficult. If someone doesn't know they are being taped it's illegal to show footage of them, unless they are committing a criminal act and it's to help the course of justice."

"Oh," I sigh. This isn't good news. The whole premise of the show depends on catching these guys and gals red-handed, so to speak.

Jaki continues. "The only way around it is to conceal their identity. Do it all through implication. So, for example, show stills of the dupe and current fiancé/fiancée, which the fiancé/fiancée will have released. Then show stills of the 'tempting party' and then when filming the actual seduction scene we'll have to be creative with those black banners that obscure identity or body parts. It will be clear whether the dupe has fallen or not, without having to actually say so."

I think about it. As the film will be shown for the first time in front of a live audience and all the parties, it will be impossible for the dupe to deny if he/she is the person committing infidelity. And even if they do, the guaranteed ensuing row will still make great TV. I can't loose. "Sounds manageable. Anything else?"

"In addition, you can't show any actual lewd acts, even after the watershed. We must bleep out the C word, at a minimum, and other expletives if you want to avoid controversy."

"Which I don't."

Jaki shrugs. "It's your call. In summary Mr. and Ms. J. Bloggs have very few legal rights over their privacy."

"Fantastic. Document everything. Remember the golden rule."

Jaki nods. "Yes, I have it tattooed on my cranium, 'Thou shalt cover thy arse.' "

"Precisely. OK, Ricky, what did the scheduler say?"

"Oh, you know, the usual bollocks that their responsibility is to heighten the built-in tension between random luck and rules in a game structure—between the predictable and inconceivable, the controllable and the frenzy, which creates enjoyment, blah blah. Need I go on?"

"No. What slot do we have?"

"They offered us seven thirty on Saturday night, going out against Cilia."

"That's stupid. *Blind Date* has been running for sixteen years. It still pulls in over seven million viewers. I'd never think of running a head-to-head." I pause. "Well, at least not until toward the end of the series. What else did they offer? It's hardly as though we are flush with brilliant programs."

"Monday at ten."

"Take it. Gray, how are the sponsorship and advertising deals coming along?"

"Good. The advertising is all in place. The TV trailers are set up and we've optioned press and poster adverts—the exact placement will be confirmed a few weeks before the first show. As for sponsorship, we have a lead. A teenage retail store is interested in sponsoring the show. It would be a cash-and-barter deal. You know the type of thing: the guest would be obliged to wear their gear etc. The creatives have come up with some suggested break-bumper ideas."

Gray cautiously puts the ideas on the table. It's an unsubtle play on the words "top shaft." The creative team annoy me on a number of counts. They are incapable of accepting a creative brief without whining that they are overworked, which is unlikely to be the case in a channel struggling to come up with programs; they take long lunches; they switch off their mobiles; they never accept advice, use dictionaries or attend meetings. They proudly admit to reading the *Sport* and comment on the size of the tits of their female colleagues. And finally, worst of all, their ideas are puerile. Gray reads my face.

"You think they're puerile, don't you?"

"Yes," I confirm. "It won't work. The Independent Television Commission won't touch it. And even if we could get it through, it says the wrong things about the show. Get Mark and Tom to come up with some more up-market directions."

I push open the pub door and am hit by the familiar and comforting smell of beer-soaked carpets, cigarette smoke and salt and vinegar crisps. It's mid-September and although the sun is weakly trying to battle with the autumnal winds I'm glad Josh has decided to sit inside rather than in the beer garden. I spot him immediately. He is sitting in the corner reading *Private Eye,* oblivious to the adoring looks he is attracting from the small gaggles of women office workers. I weave my way toward him and kiss him on the cheek. He puts down his reading matter and, grinning, points to the vodka and orange which is waiting for me.

"Cheers." We clink glasses. "How did you know it was a vodka day?" I normally drink gin and tonic except when I'm under extreme pressure at work, when I drink vodka and orange. I like to think the orange cordial will somehow compensate for the fact that I haven't eaten a proper meal for days.

"Well, since you started this *Sex with an Ex* project, neither Issie nor I have heard from you. I figured if you hadn't had time to call us in ten days you wouldn't have had time to eat either."

"Sorry," I mumble. Josh shrugs. I don't have to say much more. I'm still reeling from the ticking off he gave me this morning when he finally got through to me at work. He'd made it quite clear that he was sick of talking to my answering machine. I'd insisted that given a choice, of course, I'd prefer to be drinking with him and

Issie, but developing a new show monopolizes my time, whether I like it or not. Josh swept aside my objections and bullied me into coming out for a drink with him. To be honest I was grateful to concede. "Where's Issie tonight?"

"Yoga. She said she might join us later. So in the meantime you'll just have to put up with me boring you with stories about court."

"Bore away." I grin, because Josh is anything but boring. He is a good storyteller. He practices criminal law and is always full of amusing anecdotes about his day-to-day dealings with the dregs of society. We chat about his work and his flat (he wants my advice on bathroom tiles and I agree to go shopping with him next Saturday); he tells me about his latest flirtation, which he doesn't appear to be that enthusiastic about—although he assures me that she has stunning legs. The chat is comfortable and relaxed. I listen intently and while I'm bursting to talk about *Sex with an Ex* I resist. Josh knows me well enough to know I am practicing extreme self-restraint and so finally allows me center stage.

"And what about you? How's *Sex with an Ex* panning out?"

This is what I've been waiting for. I know that I can discuss all aspects of the show with Josh without the reserve I have to employ when talking to anyone else. In the office it is of paramount importance that I appear confident and assured at all times. I can't express any doubts or misgivings even about small things, like the color of the set design. With Josh, on the other hand, I can bounce from extreme confidence to misgivings and back again in one easy move, without him thinking any the less of me. I sigh.

"I don't want this show to be tacky, but I am working against the odds. When we don't have good ideas we have to employ amazingly expensive actors and construct lavish set deigns—it's an attempt to distract the viewer." I explain. "*Sex with an Ex* is a good idea so we are investing sweet FA in the production. I've seen the set—it shivers dangerously whenever anyone sneezes or shouts loudly. If only Bale would dig a little deeper into those pockets of his. I know they are not limitless, but they are fathoms deep."

"Is Bale being tight?"

"He did, at least, agree to a warm-up act—you know, someone to keep the audience amused during the commercial break."

"Well, that's something."

"Yes, the epitome of generosity. He suggested we pick up some act from Covent Garden and pay them thirty quid," I bite sarcastically.

"Who are you getting as the presenter?"

"Well, I wanted Zoë Ball, Yasmin Le Bon or Nigella Lawson, but Bale instructed me to go and get 'some new totty' straight out of drama school. That way he won't have to pay her more than a few grand for the series."

Josh laughs. "Typical Bale."

"Absolutely. Even so, I'm optimistic. After interviewing forever we found the perfect presenter. She is busty, with short spiky hair and personality. She wears cropped tops and baggy trousers. She's young." I don't add that I see this as an advantage because she's too young to feel particular about the tragedy bus she is, if not driving, certainly stamping tickets on.

"Have you worked out the detail of the show's structure?"

"Yup. We advertised and were inundated with responses from the paranoid and jealous. We interview these individuals on tape. We draft in the threatening ex and interview them too. The motivation of the ex is usually revenge or desperation (if they were dumped), curiosity or vanity (if they were the dumpee). We then follow all parties (including the unsuspecting dupe) for a week, intercutting the preparations for the wedding and the possible betrayal. The key to the show is that we bring all the guests back and play the footage live. The unsuspecting dupe thinks they are going to be on *Who Wants to be a Billionaire* or something similar, right up until the moment they are on stage. It will be on stage that the letterwriter gets to either faint with relief or discover if their worst fears have been founded." I stop and check Josh's reaction. He's very pale and sweaty-looking; perhaps he's been drinking too much. "You do think it will work?"

"Yes, sadly I think you are on to a winner."

Pleased, I stand up to get the drinks. Issie calls Josh's mobile to say that she's not going to join us because she doesn't fancy being in a pub after meditating. We stay until last orders and I have a great time.

As I climb into a cab, Josh wishes me luck with the show and makes me renew my promise to help him shop for bathroom tiles. I nod, blow him a kiss and fall back on to the leather seat. My slightly inebriated state brings with it a sense of well-being and all is right with the world. I really should make more of an effort to see more of my friends.

I find the interviews with the selected couples obscene and fascinating at once, and have insisted on conducting as many of them as possible myself.

"So, Jenny, you wrote to us in response to the article you saw in *Gas*. Let's run through the details of the letter, so you can confirm them for me and I can get them straight in my head." I laugh in a jolly oh-silly-me-I-find-it-so-hard-to-retain-information way. I find it gets them onside. "Do you mind?"

Jenny shakes her head. The movement is exaggerated. She is trying to appear confident and assured. However, she is chainsmoking full strength Benson & Hedges, lighting another before the first stops smoldering—not the actions of a confident woman. Jenny is skinny but not the fashionably anorexic skinny that is prevalent in the studio. She's skinny because she can't afford to smoke and eat. We all have choices. According to my notes Jenny is twenty-three. She looks forty-five but then I suspect she was born looking forty-five. I suppose the advantage is she'll still look forty-five when she's sixty-five. Her face is pinched and reminds me of a balloon the day after the party, all shriveled and twisted into a knot. She's had a lifetime of poor school results, no chances and no splendor, which is why she's here.

"Jenny, you must be very excited by the chance to be on TV?"

"Too right, yeah."

"And it's been explained to you exactly how the show works?" This is code speak for "You know the humiliation you are about to undergo?"

"Yeah."

"You wrote to me because you think there is a possibility that your fiancé, Brian Parkinson, is being unfaithful. Or at least he would be, given the chance." I tilt my head and quietly cluck.

"Yeah."

"And you mention in your letter that you have your suspicions as to who the object of affection is."

"Too right, yeah. My best friend, Karen."

"Karen Thompson," I read from my notes. She nods again and swaps stub for fresh fag. "Can you give me a brief history."

"Brian was going with Karen when I met him."

"And that was when?"

"I was seventeen."

The story is bleak. Brian has yo-yoed between Karen and Jenny for the past six years. It's hard to understand what drives the change of allegiance. I think it is something to do with which of the two women is employed at the time and can supply money for his fags and booze. The only cheering thought for humanity is that the women have not allowed Brian's indecision to come between them. More often than not, all three of them go to their local together. I'm not delicate but I wonder how any of them live, not knowing whom Brian will want to go home with on any given night.

"She'd be better getting it on with Roy, Brian's brother. After all, she's my bridesmaid and Roy's the best man. It's traditional, ain't it?" She slaps my thigh and laughs. But the laugh is tinny and nervous. She stops suddenly and leans close into me. I know from Issie and a number of my other friends that she is about to indulge in a confession. In a more religious age she would be offering up prayers to Mary the virgin mother, saint of desperate cases.

"I really wouldn't like to lose him, darlin.' I love him. But if I'm going to lose him, it'd better be before the wedding."

I back away, disentangling myself from the woman's cigarette fumes and her earnest stare.

My interview with Karen is almost identical, except Karen is as fat as Jenny is skinny. Her arms wobble when she raises a glass of beer to her mouth. Her life has been one of steaming hot chips wrapped in newspaper and pastry cakes with custard. She's wearing a flowered tent. I pull Fi to one side.

"Fi, has she had her clothing allowance?" I ask, horrified. There are some shows that encourage their guests to wear bright outfits, so that they look like fat sugared almonds. This isn't supposed to be one of those.

"Ya, but we couldn't find anything in Harvey Nics to fit her," Fi whispers back.

"Well, what about a high-street store?"

"We couldn't find a researcher who was prepared to go and find out."

I sigh and resign myself to the tent. I wonder how the colors will work against the backdrop of the set.

Karen, the "other woman," explains that she thinks she has as much right to Brian as Jenny has.

"After all, I was with him first." But people aren't like pieces of furniture or clothes; "I saw him first" isn't exactly a reason to lay claim to someone. I remind Karen that Brian must love Jenny, or else he wouldn't have proposed. Karen corrects me and points out that it was Jenny who proposed and in fact she bought her own ring too. She admits that she is still sleeping with Brian. She shakes her tits at the camera: "He likes something to get hold of." I leave the room.

"That is so depressing," comments Fi.

"What is?" I ask.

"The way both of those women want the same man and by this time next week one of them will have been rejected. Don't you think that's awful?"

"I think that's the point of the show. Now, here's the rest of the schedule. I want you to take a cameraman and stay with Jenny. Get lots of shots of her trying her wedding dress on, interviews with her mum, something to depict their financial struggle to put on the best wedding reception they can afford and a shot of her on her own, preferably in a church."

"So you are expecting Brian to choose Karen, then?" asks Fi.

"Not so much actively choose, more like his dick will jump out of his trousers through habit. Now, I need the logistics crew to work out where the camera should be for the grand seduction. Karen is planning to seduce him over a pint and some pork scratchings in their local."

"Very glamorous," says Fi wryly.

"She's not a glamorous girl. And he's not a glamorous boy. It should be on their usual turf—we don't want to arouse suspicions. Besides which our budget is a pittance. Now go to it."

Next I interview Tim Barrett. I think that Tim has a good career ahead of him as a criminal. Not because he appears particularly vicious, immoral or crooked but because he would be impossible to identify in a line-up. He is neither extraordinarily skinny nor obscenely fat. He is, in fact, of average build, average height, average looks and average intelligence. His hair is mid-brown; his eyes are a brown/gray/green color. I forget which. After close investigation I discover that the only thing that distinguishes him at all is his fanatical, obsessive jealousy in relation to his fiancée, Linda.

He runs through his suspicions regarding three of her exes. I don't think his suspicions are founded. But that's irrelevant. As he tells the stories he fidgets on his chair, moving from one buttock to the other. His hands appear to have developed an independent personality. *They* are animated. He picks up his coffee cup, puts it down again, he picks up a pen, pencil, ashtray, clipboard, biscuit. Everything, other than the biscuit, is put into his mouth. After he has spent fifteen minutes boring me with his paranoia and insecurity I think that this girl deserves a fling. If we do manage to cause a rift between them we will be providing a public service. I instruct a private detective to track down some of her exes immediately.

My next interview is with a petite brunette, Chloe. Chloe is an advertising executive in a small advertising agency in Bristol. She is more like the type of guest that I crave for the show. She is certainly attractive, with shoulder-length, curly hair, a winning smile and a neat, sharp body, which she is obviously and justifiably proud of. She's aged twenty-five. She's bright, funny.

And insecure.

I imagine that generally she hides it quite well. I imagine that her acquaintances and colleagues describe her as confident. But behind her back her friends discuss her ugly neediness. After chatting to her for four and a half minutes it is obvious to anyone who has ever read any popular psychology books (and I've read them all) that she is a woman who loves too much. She believes she is half a person unless she has a boyfriend. The men she meets believe she is an entire person, until they become her boyfriends. On sensing her dependency, their cocks go limp and they leave her. However, as I listen to her chat, it seems to me that her fiancé, Rod, breaks the mould. He actually likes her dependency; it makes him feel valued. But her historical, consistent failure has eroded her trust and faith in the concept of fidelity. Instead of being grateful to have found Rod and keeping her head down, Chloe is hitting the self-destruct button by testing him.

On national TV.

As the interview comes to a close and I have all the details I need regarding Rod's exes, I ask Chloe why she feels compelled to verify his fidelity on TV. She must know that she is risking personal humiliation and universal disdain.

She shrugs and with a bravado which we both know to be fake replies, "I think if you are going to be a failure, you should try to be as conspicuous as you can about it. Who wants to be a run-of-the-mill failure?"

I love this wisdom. You've got to hand it to the British public. There's an Aristotle in every one of them.

"The queue for the live audience is massive—it stretches the entire length of the car park," laughs Fi excitedly. This is a good sign. The PR vehicle must have done its job.

"What do they look like?" I ask. The correct live audience is essential. There are lots of things that the majority of us will do in our homes that we wouldn't do in public. Things like: cheer at other people's insecurities, rejection and fear, encourage savagery and disloyalty, positively celebrate humiliation and distress. I need people who are either honest or stupid enough to have these reactions on live TV.

"Generally poor and unhealthy-looking. But they appear oblivious to their aesthetic drawbacks—they're oozing excitement," says Fi.

This is exactly what I want to hear. An anonymous voice cries, "Spot checking, ladies and gents." Nobody has a clue what that means, if anything at all, but it has the desired effect and the audience squirm with nervous expectancy. I don't blame them. It is exhilarating. We put on a bit of a show to get them in the mood. The runner's bleep pings incessantly; she ignores the increasingly desperate calls. The director (long-haired and self-important by necessity), production manager (a grumpy git—it's a professional qualification) and the stage manager (careworn and exhausted) huddle in a corner debating furiously about some technical point or other. The production executive is running around the set as though her life depends upon it. A plethora of cameramen—dressed entirely in black, baggy combat trousers and Ted Baker shirts, Cats or DKNY trainers—are standing around, trying to look casually indifferent, as though their lives *and* souls depend upon it. The set, although flimsy, is attractive. The backdrop is a close-up picture of dozens of fat red hearts. At first glance the impression is romantic; a dip in the lights and the effect is satanic, open-heart surgery on stage. There are the compulsory comfy couches in the middle of the stage, ensuring everyone gets the best view of the gallows.

"Where did he come from?" I am referring to the warm-up act. He is a fat, northern comedian who has blatantly been on the circuit longer than Schumacher. He looks like a pantomime dame and his requests for the audience to "Go wild, go crazy" illicit nothing more than a few embarrassed titters. Fi shrugs, "He does well with the *Kin's Kismet* audience."

I listen to him telling a few mucky jokes. He is the only one laughing.

"What were you thinking of? I've told you I want an up-market show. Which bit of the word up-market is it that you don't understand?" I snap. Somewhere I can hear someone say, "Thirty seconds to live."

"You told me to deal with the detail," she defends.

I'm not in the mood for debating. "I want him off the show by next week, Fi." The voice in my earpiece says, "Twenty seconds." I tune back in to the fat man.

"It's a live show tonight, so if you are sitting next to somebody you shouldn't be, move." The audience finally begins to smirk. "Ten seconds."

"Did you see anyone move, Fi?" I ask. I'm always thinking

about potentially adulterous relationships. "Eight, seven, six." There is a swell of expectancy.

"Now a big hand for Katie Hunt, this evening's presenter." The audience starts to clap their hands raw for the remote chance that there may be a nanosecond mug shot on TV. The fat man tries to get Katie to twirl like a modern-day Anthea. This is proof, if we needed it, that he has had his day. Katie wouldn't twirl if Robbie Williams asked her to. Katie casts him a withering look. I'm relieved—at least she understands what type of show I'm making here.

"Three, two, one—we are on air." The roving camera sweeps magnificently across the audience and set. The camera reminds me of an internal. It must do the same for Fi, as I notice she writes "smear" on her hand with a felt tip. The emergence of the cameras acts as an aphrodisiac on the audience. Everyone visibly brightens; they grow a couple of inches, smile a bit wider.

"Hello, and welcome to the very first *Sex with an Ex.*" The stage manager initiates more applause; the audience catch on quickly and begin to cheer. Katie smiles back at the camera, appreciating their appreciation.

"You smell the same."

"Smell? What do I smell of?" He is mildly irritated. Scrupulously clean at all times, he has made a particular effort tonight.

"My youth." She smiles.

She leans closer to inhale him again. She notices he is quivering. She notices she is. He turns a fraction and he is staring into her eyes, straight past the pupils, and directly hitting her mind and soul. She is sixteen again. Which makes him eighteen. She has been propelled back to the doorstep of her parental home. The season is irrelevant; she feels warm and safe. It's late at night, very late, because although they abide by the curfew and get her home by 10:45 P.M., they are literal: she is home but not in her home. It's past midnight and they are still sitting on the step. They can't go in because her mother is waiting up in her nylon dressing gown. Her mum will want to know what the film was like, and she'll make a cup of coffee and stay up and drink it with them. They don't want to talk to anyone else. They never do.

Did. 'Did' is the correct verb because she's not sixteen, she's twenty-six and she's not on the step of her mum and dad's house in Croydon. She's actually just bumped into Declan outside Pronuptia bridal shop.

"Big box," he comments, grinning, and he's just the same. The grin is just the same; it lights up her stomach and a bit lower.

"Er, yes." She hesitates. The natural thing to say next is, "It's my wedding dress," but Abbie doesn't say the natural thing. She says, "Wow, it's been a long time."

"Yes. Ten years." He pauses for a moment and then adds, "Four months, two weeks and about eight days,"

Delighted and shocked, Abbie blushes and glances both ways up the street. She's not sure what or who she's looking for. But she's relieved not to see anyone she knows. "I don't believe you've been counting."

"Fair cop. I haven't. I just made up the stuff about months and weeks." They both laugh because it always was easy for him to make her laugh.

"Fancy a drink?" he adds casually. And why shouldn't she? It's just a drink. She hasn't anything else planned except a night in with a face pack. Lawrence is out tonight—rugby practice.

They make their way to a nearby wine bar that he knows. She is impressed with the way he takes charge and really he couldn't have chosen better. As she pushes open the door, she is overwhelmed by the smell of fags and booze, by the litter of noise and dark suits. Money and irresponsibility, the most potent aphrodisiacs. The wine bar is packed. Smart bods forcing their way to the bar, into each other's psyches and beds. The suits are Armani and the bed linen will be Egyptian cotton. It's Abbie's kind of bar, full of deeply attractive and arrogant media types, all of whom have disposable incomes matched only by their disposable lifestyles. She hasn't been to a bar like this for *ages. It was in a bar like this that she met Lawrence. But once they'd been together for a few months such dens of sin were superfluous. It was easier to sin on the settee in his flat.*

The music pumps through Abbie and Declan's brains and rushes to her knickers and his cock. Music just does that. No one is dancing, it's a bar not a club and although Abbie is tempted to sculpt out a space on the designer scuffed wooden floor, she's far too shy to do so. Besides which she's still carrying her huge box with her bridal dress and six-foot veil. Where would she put it? What is she thinking of? Bringing her dress in to a smoky bar? She notes that she's tapping her foot. In fact, her leg is jerking almost uncontrollably. She wants to dance. She needs to whoosh and swirl. Suddenly she understands stripping. Music does equate to sex. It thumps and jars and consumes and fills and ulti-mately relieves. Abbie prefers to make love to music, rather than in silence. It helps create the mood. Whichever mood she wants. Fast and frantic or slow and seductive. Abbie shakes her head. What is she thinking of? Sex, that's what. Why is she thinking of sex? She's not out with her fiancé; she's with Declan. She should not be thinking of sex.

"Drink?" she yells. She orders him a Becks and herself two gin and tonics. She downs one at the bar and then returns to her seat with the other. She doesn't normally try to calm her nerves with drink. Then again she's not normally nervous with men. She's been with Lawrence for three years so she can't remember the last time she felt flirtatious or sexy. But she is nervous with Declan.

And flirty.

And sexy.

"So you don't drink Bacardi and Coke any more?" He smiles.

"No." She smiles back. "And I assumed you'd moved on from Woodpecker cider. Cheers."

They clink glasses. They fall silent, as they have so much to say. She wants to ask him why he never wrote once he went to university. Why didn't he reply to any of her letters? She remembers the endless waiting for the postman, the fruitless, pointless hoping. The answer is he met a girl from Nottingham in Freshers' Week. For the first two terms it seemed like love. He reads her mind and says, "I never was much of a letterwriter."

He wants to ask her who she lost her virginity to and was it good. The answer is that, furious and bored with waiting for his letters and calls, she eventually climbed into bed with his cousin within hours of blowing out the candles on her seventeenth birthday cake. Yes, it was good, very good.

She reads his mind and assures him, "Pretty average, really. Like everyone's first time."

They both start to laugh at the cosmic connection that seems undamaged by the years of neglect. They had always found talk easy. Indulging in endless outpouring of thoughts, views, dreams and emotions. Now they exchange suppositions, opinions, histories and sentiments. They don't notice the difference. It is still there, the familiar but indefinable sense of possibility. He'd always filled her with such a pure sense of adventure. She loves Lawrence dearly, but he doesn't create that sense of future possibilities; he brings with him a sense of future stability. She thought it was impossible to feel sixteen unless you were sixteen, but now she is within inches of Declan, it's back, that overwhelming sense of YESness. Her mood is buoyant as she drinks those first few G&Ts. Quickly they pass a respectable G&T hour, so they swap to red wine.

"Aren't you hot?" he yells over the crowd.

"Hot?" she asks with feigned nonchalance.

"You are still wearing your gloves."

Slowly she peals them off, revealing her engagement ring.

"When?" he asks.

"Two weeks," she answers. The answer does not create the same rush she experienced this morning when she checked her countdown calendar.

"He's a lucky man," says Declan, but he won't look at Abbie. "We should be celebrating. I'll buy us some champagne."

Occasionally when she wanders around Heal's furniture department or sits at a dinner party with Lawrence, Abbie finds herself idly wondering whether, if she'd met Declan later in life, would he have been "the One"? Occasionally Abbie has wondered what sleeping with Declan would be like. The front step of her parents' house didn't offer the correct opportunity. As she watches him at the bar she believes that it can't hurt to find out.

As Abbie pushes back the hotel sheets and climbs on top of Declan she is sixteen again. As she leaves the hotel room, three hours later, under the cover of darkness she feels her twenty-six years and to be frank she rather likes it. Declan was a lovely part of her past and that's where he should be. She's walking with a swagger. It's the swagger of a confident young woman who knows she's marrying the right man.

When Lawrence watches the tape he misinterprets the John Wayne stance and is disgusted.

For a moment the studio is silent. Awash with betrayal, regret and fear. Lawrence is staring at Abbie. His jaw is hanging open, which is unbecoming. He looks like the dumb animal Abbie has reduced him to. It's complex. I admit that. I signal frantically for camera two to move in tightly. Close up, close up. I want to see every muscle twitch, every emotion exposed. Abbie is shaking so violently that I think she may spontaneously combust. I suspect she wishes she could. She resolutely stares at the floor. Too humiliated and ashamed to think beyond how she can get out of the studio, she doesn't even attempt to catch Lawrence's eye. She's forgotten that Declan ever existed. Declan is trying to look unconcerned. He is sitting back in his chair, with his long legs casually crossed, and he's tapping his toe. His brave performance is exposed as the act it is when camera three picks up the fact that he is tearing at his own skin, digging his nails so deeply that his quicks are brilliant white. Boy, are they regretting it now. They are a mass of sweaty palms, quivering lips and knotted intestines. Their faces ask what they've done.

I wish I'd never written the letter.

I'm sorry. I'm sorry.

Fuck.

Lawrence breaks the silence. "Why did you do it?" he upbraids.

"Why didn't you trust me?" accuses Abbie.

"Fuck," says Declan.

That's the cue for the audience. They become animals. They boo and hiss and spit and claw. They are collectively relieved that, in this instance, it is someone else who has been fucked over. Unscathed, they fly into an uncontrollable frenzy. The savages hurl abuse and insults. I think that if they'd had rotting fruit to hand they'd have used it. They despise Lawrence for being cuckolded. They loathe Abbie for being a slut. And they forgive Declan because he has got a cute grin and he's a bit of a lad. The synthesized music pipes cheerfully through the studio. Oblivious to the fact that Abbie is sobbing hysterically and has to be carried off the stage. Her legs buckle. It's a sad pathetic sight. I hope camera two got a close-up.

"Good job, Cas."

"Thank you."

"Way to go, Cas."

"Thanks."

"High five, Cas."

"Yes, very high." I efficiently accept the congratulations and charge through the corridors with the air of someone who has a mission. Thing is, I have. My heart is pounding; the blood is rushing through my being. The show only finished minutes ago but already I know it is a huge success. Massive. The audience won't leave and we have had to call in security. Lawrence punched Declan. Live on stage! I'm delighted. It couldn't have gone better if

I'd scripted it. Then Jenny, Brian and Karen—what a horror show! Brian wasn't sure if it was the worst or best day of his life. The audience loved his unashamed cockiness.

I walk into my office, which is awash with flowers and champagne. Good news sure does travel quickly. I had expected to be doused in congratulations and good wishes. After all, nearly everyone at TV6 is scared of me and therefore try hard to ingratiate themselves. But I never calculated a result as big as this. I'm delirious, but I know that it is essential that I appear unmoved.

"Where should I put these flowers?" asks Fi.

"Anywhere." I casually read the cards. There's one from Josh and Issie. It reads, "You are an unscrupulous, overly ambitious, single-minded exploiter. Well done. Love, your best friends."

I grin. There is another from Bale. It reads, "Big things get bigger very quickly."

"You are *so* profound," I mutter.

"I'll crack open this bubbly, shall I?" asks Fi. She's holding a bottle of vintage Veuve Clicquot.

"If you like. As long as you understand that this isn't a celebration."

Her smile vanishes. "Isn't it?" She is genuinely dumbfounded.

"No, it isn't. We need to see the overnight runs and also the log call book before we can really celebrate. In fact, I think I'll go and sit in the log room now to talk to the duty manager."

"But I've booked Bibendum. The team's looking forward to it. They've worked so hard over the last eight weeks."

It's true we've all worked regular fourteen-hour days.

"On whose budget?"

She's crushed. She's silent. I relent. "OK, you guys go along and I'll catch you up. If the news is good, I'll pay. If it's not, I'll pay."

Sometimes I'm nice like this but it's just to confuse them.

I make my way through the rabbit warren of corridors, leaving the sound of popping champagne corks behind me. I stumble past piles of A4 paper and mountains of clip files (the paperless office is a figment of management consultants' imagination). I note dozens of plastic crates that haven't been unpacked in the twenty-four months that we've been here. I wonder if someone knows something that I don't. As I approach the normally silent log room, where all complaints and compliments are handled, I am struck by a general buzz of activity.

I wake up with aching back and neck, a furry mouth and a fuzzy brain. Not enough sleep. It's a huge effort, but I force concentration. I establish the following facts: I'm not in a bed, my own or a stranger's; I'm not hung over, but there is a glob of saliva on my desk where my head has been. I consider that this is one of the reasons I'm careful about intimacy. Imagine if I had woken up with the man of my dreams, if such a thing existed, and there had been a string of saliva on the pillow. It would certainly put him off. Far too human. However, such speculation is irrelevant, as my pillow last night was a box file, my bed companion a portable computer. I try to think it through. I'm here because—

The phone rings. I reach for it and automatically chant, "Cas Perry, TV6. Good . . ." —I hesitate and check my watch. It's 7:15 A.M.—"morning," I confirm, confident that it is morning, but I'm less sure why anyone would be calling me at this hour.

"Thank God," says Josh.

"Oh, hi," I mutter, reaching for my fag packet. I light up and inhale. The nicotine hits me behind the eyeballs. That's better.

"We were so worried. Where the hell have you been?"

"Hey, don't come on all marital with me," I laugh. "I've been here all night. Did you see the program?"

"Yeah."

"Wasn't it brilliant?" The tar and bad stuff have helped. I now know why I slept at my desk. "We were taking calls all night. I took the last one at 4:45 A.M. The lines were jammed. TV6 has never seen anything like it!"

"Lots of complaints, then?" asks Josh sympathetically.

"Complaints, sure," I say dismissively, "but compliments too and applications to go on the show." I check the latest figures in the log book. "Two hundred and forty-seven calls!" I do some quick mental arithmetic. "One hundred and thirty complaints! Can you believe it? I only have to get fifteen before I am obliged to take the program to the ITC for reappraisal."

"So that's good news?" Josh asks hesitantly. He simply doesn't get it. "All those complaints are good news?"

"It's caused a national outcry. It's huge. It's fantastic. It's—look I can't chat. I need to call PR—we'll have to put out a press release. I wonder if any of the papers have picked anything up yet."

"It's a shame you didn't make it to Issie's last night. We had ricotta and basil risotto, as planned." Josh slices through my euphoria. I suddenly remember that I had promised to go straight to Issie's after the show. In fact, I'd begged them to meet up. I'd insisted that Issie miss her pottery class and that Josh skip his rugby practice. I'd worried that the show would be a disaster. We'd all known that if that was the case Issie and Josh would be the only people I'd be able to face.

"Oh, shit. Josh, I'm sorry. Fuck, I'm really sorry. I'll make it up to you. Both of you. I just got caught up here on the telephone lines. Shit. I'm sorry." This is genuine. I feel awful. There have been occasions when Issie and Josh have let me down, always due to circumstances they couldn't control. I've sat endlessly staring at the clock wondering where they were. Why they didn't call? My irritation that their supper is ruined has turned to fear as I imagine they've been abducted or murdered or involved in a road accident. Worse, that they are dating someone unsuitable. I know that standing each other up is a bishop sin.

"I should have called," I add meekly.

"Yes, you should have. We were worried." Josh can't stay angry with me for long. "The risotto was ruined. I've had to soak the dish but the stubborn bits of cheese won't come off."

I know I'm off the hook. "Try Fairy Liquid extra concentrated king-strength," I laugh. "Look, I've got to go. I'll call you tonight."

"You'd better."

I can see my reflection in my computer screen. By rights I should be looking rough. Last night I secured just a few hours' sleep. Over the past eight weeks I've been averaging six hours a night at best, even at weekends. I haven't had a night out in all that time. I've existed largely on sandwiches from the staff canteen and double espressos from the Italian deli around the corner. I can't remember when I last saw natural daylight or a vitamin. Either boxed or first-generation.

And yet I look *fantastic*.

Well, there is no point in my being falsely modest. I look keen and lithe and sharp and I'm glowing. I know I look like a woman who's just fallen in love. And the reason for this, the little beauty secret, tip for the top, is that the show is a *success*. I rattle around in my desk drawer looking for a toothbrush and all the other necessary toiletries. I open my stationery cupboard. I keep a full wardrobe at work for all events. A few basics: trousers from Jigsaw, T-shirts from Gap, white cotton knickers from M&S. Plus a couple of Nicole Fahri trouser suits and shirts from Pink, in case I'm unexpectedly called into a big meeting. Some Agent Provacateur underwear and a number of garments that vary in their size and transparency but are reassuringly, constantly black. These are for when I get lucky. None of this is appropriate for today. I see what's lurking behind the plastic file dividers. Eventually I select Miu Miu trousers, a slash-neck Cristina Ortiz wool jumper and Bally boots. I find a pair of clean knickers and a tiny lacy bra in my filing cabinet. I know today is my day and it's important to look the part. I go for a brisk workout and then shower in the office gym. By 8:45 A.M. I'm back at my desk.

Fi is in too. It looks like my budget was thrashed at Bibendum.

"You look crap," I tell her, as I generously offer a can of Red Bull.

"Thank you. You look as fresh as a daisy."

I graciously accept the compliment. After all, I do. "Was it worth it?" I ask.

She grins, "Yeah, I had a fantastic time. Or at least I think I did." She holds her head steady for a moment trying, no doubt, to chase a faint memory. She gives up.

"Well, that's the main thing," I assure.

"We went on to the Leopard Lounge. I didn't go home—I've come straight in."

I'm impressed by her dedication. I try to ignore the brewery smells she's exhaling and fill her in on the excitement of the night in the log room.

"Sounds a gas." She stifles a yawn. "I'm glad it went so well." She starts to tell me some funny tale about Di getting off with Gray, and Ricky trying to pull a transvestite. I'm glad they've had a good time. But I'm not interested. I know I'll lose most of today. The team's productivity will be severely depleted because of the necessary administration of Alka Seltzer and intravenously dripped black coffee. They'll spend hours discussing the pros and cons of the various hair-of-the-dog cures. Choices being Bloody Mary, a pint of Guinness, fried eggs with gin. Most importantly they will all be extremely ashamed of themselves and so tomorrow I'll get commitment overdrive.

My phone rings again.

"Cas Perry, TV6. Good morning."

"Jocasta?"

"Mum."

"How are you, dear?"

"Brilliant. Mum, did you ring about the show?" I'm thrilled.

"Show?"

"My show. You did watch it, didn't you?" I'm devastated. I can't believe that my mother has forgotten about the show. Even when things were really hairy and busy around here, in the penultimate couple of weeks before the show went live, I'd religiously visited my mum on Sundays. I had been there in body, although, I admit, not always in spirit. I'd had to spend a lot of time on my mobile. But when I wasn't on my mobile I had taken time to tell her all about the show. Now my mother is acting as though she's never heard of it.

"Oh yes. Erm, *Best with an Ex.*" She demurely avoids the S word. Actually, I'm quite impressed with her title. I should have consulted her before the show went out. *Best with an Ex* is so much more subtle than *Sex with an Ex.* I wonder if there is any chance of a name change at this stage. My train of thought is interrupted as Mum mithers on.

"I did watch the first ten minutes but then Bob, from over the road, popped over to fix that drawer that's been sticking. You know, the third one down in the kitchen."

Bob, one of a small number of names that my mother floats past me on a regular basis. "Mrs. Cooper said that there's a buy two and get one free offer on shampoo at Boots at the moment"; "It's Albert and Dorothy's fortieth wedding anniversary on Saturday—they are having a supper"; "Dr. Dean was asking after you." It's tedious keeping up with the comings and goings of these tiresome people.

"I couldn't have the television running while he was in the house," comments my mother.

I'm disappointed, so move quickly to get her off the line. A non-offensive exit demands a certain amount of self-sacrifice. I agree to go shopping with her on Saturday. I regret the offer almost the moment the words are out of my mouth. It will be a disaster: it always is. For a start she will want to find a bargain in the Army and Navy store, while I will want to spend obscene amounts in Bond Street. If we do go to Bond Street, her face will settle into one of the expressions I can only assume she most favors, shocked or cross. Shocked at the prices and cross at life. I can't bear her sudden outbursts in small boutiques. "That's how much? There's nothing to it! Look at the hemming. I could run you one up on the sewing machine." Which is odd, as she has never sewn in her life. Worse than her audible disgust will be her silent condemnations of my frivolity, the incessant tutting at the cashpoint as I hand over one of my magic pieces of plastic. Therefore we usually shop at the Army and Navy store, where I destroy her pleasure by continually pointing out 'nice' things and adding for clarity, "Nice for you, Mum." Revenge is always hers as she buys whichever monstrosity I've picked out and gives it to me for Christmas or my birthday. All this accepted, we regularly put ourselves through this purgatory on earth. What else can I do? She's my mum. I wonder if I can get Issie or Josh to meet us for lunch.

By the time I put the phone down most of the team have arrived. Except for Tom and Mark. Their status as creatives excludes them from having to appear at work at all if they are hung over. The scene is as I'd predicted: I am in an office with the walking dead. They are pale and unshaven, and they smell of booze, sweat and sex. There is a certain amount of squabbling, the excuse being that the vending machine is all out of non-dairy creamer, the real reason being the bad heads. However, the atmosphere is immediately dissolved when Ricky bursts into the office.

"Have you seen the rating?" he screams.

Shit, the ratings. I must have been affected by the booze fumes to allow the rating figures to slip my mind. The number of calls we have received that have been duly logged suggests we have a stonking success on our hands. However I can't count my poultry just yet. Ratings are the accurate measure of exactly how many people watched the show. This is the acid test.

Ricky is breathless. I know it is good news.

"Well?"

He grins. Enjoying his moment.

I humor him and extend my grin a fraction wider. "Well?" He hesitates again. This time I consider firing him. A girl can only be so patient.

"1.4 million viewers tuned in at 10.00 P.M." There is a whoop. The team throw off their hangover to cheer and shout and clap and generally behave like delinquents on E, which is not so far from the fact. I stay calm.

"Well done to marketing." I smile across to Di and Debs. I know that the number of viewers we draw in as the initial credits roll is 95 percent down to the marketing. Keeping the viewers for longer than five minutes is down to the quality of the program. I am at the mercy of the remote control. It's so undignified.

"And what were the numbers after the center break?" I ask.

"1.6 million!"

Now I scream.

Really loudly.

CHAPTER
Five

"CAN YOU BELIEVE IT?" I ask Fi for the fourteenth time "The ratings went up. That means people actually called their friends and told them to tune in!"

"Or something good finished on the other side," adds Fi.

I scowl. "I've thought of that and checked the schedules. It wasn't the case. Not unless you count a documentary on the hibernation habits of bugs on hedgehogs as good TV."

"Fair point."

"*Can you believe it?* A follow-up interview with Declan in the *Sun.* I've got to hand it to him: he's a natural the way he worked the tabloids. And now they are begging us for the names of the people in the next shows. We'll have to work really hard to keep the can on the interviews we've already got. The trick is going to be in continually surprising the mark." The "mark" is the official name for the person we are tempting. We also call them Grouchos, stooge and victims. "Can you believe it's such a success?" I complete my circular diatribe.

"Not really." Fi grins. I glare and she corrects herself. "Well, obviously it is a brilliant idea. We all knew that it would be a fantastic show. But the public isn't always as perceptive as we'd like to imagine. There's always a risk."

I'm mollified by her obvious flattery. "Very true. Exactly my point. Want another drink?" I survey the debris in front of us. It's roughly half past seven. I'm not certain. The hands on my watch have shrunk and they are randomly bending. We've been in this pub since four thirty. Celebrating. We have drunk my week's calorie allowance and smoked an entire tobacco field. I'm beginning to see Fi's more sympathetic side. In fact, I'll definitely be buying her a Christmas pressie.

"I shouldn't, but OK then. A gin and tonic. Go easy on the tonic. Best make it slim-line," says Fi as she reaches for the bowl of cashew nuts. She offers them to me but I decline.

"I'm allergic."

This isn't true. I'm very thin and very fit. Whenever anyone asks me how I manage this I smile and say it's genetic and effortless. This is, of course, bollocks, but I know that if there is anything more annoying than a thin woman, it's a thin woman who professes that she never diets. There's no such thing as effortlessly thin. It comes as a direct result of one or more of the following: dedication to a relentless fitness regime, being a slave to the calorie counter, drugs or an unreliable bastard of a boyfriend. I work out at the gym five times a week—minimum. I'm also an expert kick boxer, although I don't enter competitions; it's just for fun. I own a Z3 series BMW but cycle to work, six miles there and back every day. I club once a week and I never touch any saturated fat. In addition I indulge in every detox program known to womankind. I can regularly be found swathed in seaweed or mud at Champney's or the Sanctuary.

I place the double G& (slim-line) Ts on the wooden table. Fi is chewing an ice cube thoughtfully.

"Is there anything you haven't tried?"

I think she has telepathically understood that I'm concentrating on detox programs. But before I tell her that I've never done colonic irrigation—I just can't stand the idea of a hosepipe up my bum—she puts me on the right track.

"I mean with men?"

This is easier to answer.

"I never do three in a bed."

"Oh?"

"Yes, I think everyone's entitled to some exclusive devotion, even if it's between twenty minutes and a few hours." Not much of a moral, I admit, but one I'm faithful to.

"Is there an ex in your past, then, Cas?"

"No," I say without hesitating.

"Then again you're not on the cusp of marriage."

"Nor am I ever likely to be."

"Then how did you know the show was going to be such a success? How did you know both Brian Parkinson and Abbie would fall? And, for that matter, all the other couples that we've already recorded?"

"I didn't *know*, absolutely *know*, but I thought the odds were with me."

"You are so cynical."

We have fast become confidants. This is entirely due to the copious amounts of alcohol we've consumed; still, I am quite unable to resist the illusion of companionable intimacy. Whilst I talk about work Fi is more keen to discuss her dearth of men in relation to my plethora. On one hand it is odd; after all, she is an extreme beauty. She's also got that exotic twist of a Scandinavian parentage. If I were male I wouldn't be able to stop myself. The matter is cleared up when she admits to me that secretly all she desires is a large family and a log cabin. Men can smell women who want commitment further away than they can smell those who wear Poison perfume. The odor is just as overpowering and off-putting.

Fi is looking through *Tatler's* "Little Black Book." She throws it aside and picks up *London Guide to Restaurants*. She isn't looking for somewhere to eat but she's looking at the photos of the chefs. She fancies the idea of bagging a creative, temperamental kitchen diva. I'm skeptical.

"I'd stick to the methods which are proven," I advise.

"Like what?" asks Fi grumpily.

"Supermarkets or the company telephone directory. I don't know. I never have any trouble meeting men."

"Yeah, you'd get lucky in a convent." She throws the guide to one side. "But it's such a waste. You are never even grateful."

I stare at her. Surely that is the point.

"Why are you so eternally unimpressed?" she asks. It is the drink that has given her the confidence to ask this. "Your first!" She's fallen on some inspiration. "Tell me about that."

She's looking for insight. I don't normally indulge. But a bottle of Merlot has magically appeared from nowhere and we'll have to talk about something as we drink it. Fi's stories have dried up pretty quickly. I feel obliged to entertain.

"My first." I cast my mind back through the numerous tangled sheets and emotions I've shagged my way through. "Maybe if he'd been faithful I could have believed in fidelity, even after my father's rather poor attempt as a role model."

"He wasn't, then?"

"What do you think?"

"The odds are definitely against it," admits Fi. She pours some wine into my glass. "What was he like?"

"Beautiful," I admit. "I mean, I was just like the next seventeen-year-old. OK, my parents had gone pear-shaped, but you know I was *seventeen*. I was hopeful, I hadn't been sitting at the dining-room table sticking a fork into my hand to see how much pain I could sustain, like some psycho." I sigh. "He was twenty-six. He was beautiful and shallow. And married, as it happened."

"No." Fi is shocked. I grin wryly. I remember being shocked. Now disreputable behavior never shocks me, it doesn't even disappoint me—I see it as an inevitability.

"Yeah. Slipped his mind to tell me. Until his wife turned up on my mother's doorstep. To quote the great Holly Golightly, *"Quel Rat."*

Fi sits silently, trying to take it in. It's true it's not the conventional first lover story. That's meant to take place in the back of your parents' Volvo or at someone else's house while you are babysitting. It's meant to take place with some acne-ridden youth who is equally inexperienced and as smitten as you are.

"Which made me a paramor at seventeen years old," I joke. But really it was no laughing matter at the time.

"Inadvertently," says Fi, loyally.

"Still." I inhale deeply.

"Still," she admits, taking a large swig.

I'd cried for months and when I stopped crying I started hating. It took several more months for the hate to cool and when it did I was left in a pool of icy resentment. "So I figured I should try and turn it to my advantage. No more shocks. No more surprises. I decided to have a very low expectancy threshold on what should be gained from a relationship. I don't think unconditional love is a possibility, never mind a probability, which guarantees no disappointment."

Fi is concentrating on what I've just said as she taps out the tune on the jukebox with her fag pack.

"Sounds a bit extreme. Couldn't you have just dated someone your own age and sort of"—she pauses—"I don't know, muddled along like the rest of us?"

I raise an eyebrow and she shrugs, perhaps realizing how unappealing the alternative is.

"I did date someone my own age next. He was a fop. Lovable, I guess." I think about it, perhaps for the first time. "Yes, certainly. But his willingness to please, at first a novelty, quickly became tiresome. Why don't we value those who most deserve to be valued?" I turn to Fi, but she's concentrating on drawing a loveheart on the table with drips of wine. "Answers on a postcard please. Before I knew it I'd sort of fallen into a series of one-night stands, mostly with married men or commitment phobes and, on one occasion, a homosexual."

This gets her attention. "How did you know? Did he make you dress up and do funny things with strap-ons?"

"No, Fi, he had an opinion on my wallpaper." I run through my sexual misadventures in my head and it could be the alcohol but this reminiscing is making me decidedly morose. I rouse myself into my more acceptable, tough, public persona. "Just take it from me it's easier to enjoy the moment and not expect anything more because really there isn't anything more. I heartily recommend the married man." I swallow and then refill both our glasses.

"Doesn't it bother you that someone else is getting the best bit?"

"The best bit?" I'm genuinely challenged to understand what Fi means.

"The companionship, the stability, the history, the future."

"The dirty washing, the belching, the rows, the incessant football results."

"But it doesn't make sense. You suffered first-hand because your father had a mistress. Why would you want to inflict the same pain on someone else?"

To be fair this is a pretty good question. Especially considering the units we've consumed on an empty stomach. It is a question I'd asked myself, once upon a time. The first time I fell for a married man it was purely accidental. I didn't really expect it to happen again. I did hate the very idea of "the other woman." Women who are compliant in this perpetuation of misery repelled me. After all, if there hadn't been a Miss Hudley, there wouldn't have been a deserting father and a deserted mother.

A deserted daughter.

The problem is, of course, you can take out Miss Hudley but a Miss Budley or a Miss Woodly would replace her. The choice is clear to me: become a Miss Hudley because the alternative role is worse—become the deserted wife. My mother's face, worn and weary with clinging to her pride while loosing her husband, her home, her name and her identity, burns into my consciousness. Fear flung me into relationships with men committed to someone else. It was safer. I should have been struck by lightning when I broke the taboo the first time. I sometimes wish I had been. With alarming ease I've broken every rule and never been punished—in fact, I've often been rewarded. It seemed that what I was doing was sanctioned. Whilst I collected compliments and Cartier, tenaciously avoiding commitment or Kleenex, my friends who hoped for the Happily Ever After were discovering that the road to fairyland was long and winding. And often heartbreaking.

Somehow I've developed secret signals that repel available men or men with a penchant for commitment yet simultaneously attract married men or any of the others who don't want anything more than sex. Or maybe it's just that the numbers are in my favor. I don't say any of this to Fi. I turn back to her question and simplify.

"I'm not threatening. I don't want to be someone's girlfriend, or, horror of horrors, wife. Therefore I'm not a risk. I never demand. I never call at inconvenient times; I never criticize his wife-slash-girlfriend. And in return he has no right to ask me where I'm going or when I'll be back. He has no ability to make me fall in love with him."

Fi stares at me. It may be that she is impressed. It may be that she is horrified. It may be that she is pissed.

"Christ, how depressing," she moans.

"Tell me I'm wrong," I challenge.

We are both silent for a long time. Eventually Fi suggests, "Another bottle?"

I return from the bar with a bottle and, because we both need cheering up, a couple of bankers.

"Fi, let me introduce Ivor Jones and Mike Clark. They're bankers." Fi starts to giggle. "That's with a 'b'," I hiss through clenched teeth. I've seen Ivor and Mike in this pub before. Over the last couple of months we have nodded to each other and occasionally I've accepted a drink from Ivor. They've been watching us all evening. Then I started to watch them watching us. When it got to the point of them watching us watching them watching us I knew it was time to say hi. They are well and identically dressed. Dark Boss suits, striped shirts, probably off-the-peg rather than Savile Row, saffron Hermes ties. They probably don't even know they are saffron—they probably describe them as yellow. Ivor distinguishes himself by having a killer Welsh accent that largely renders him incomprehensible but is very sexy. I don't mind incomprehensible. Most importantly Ivor is wearing a wedding ring and so I leave Mike to Fi.

Ivor's attractions are not what one would describe as classical. His face reminds me of a soundly slapped bottom. He is pale with a sprinkling of freckles and a small snub nose. On the other hand he is tall (six-foot-two-ish), ridiculously intelligent and appallingly arrogant. Besides which he is begging for it. It would be rude not to sleep with him. His hungry, alert eyes boar into me as he showers us with awful sexist jokes. As he hands around bottles of Becks he asks, "How many men does it take to open a beer?" Without waiting for a reply he tells us, "None. It should be opened by the time she brings it." Mike and Ivor laugh heartily. I do too, even though I've heard the joke before. Fi scowls. Ivor is doing an emotional borderpoint check patrol. Just checking the amount of commitment I'll require. If I take his blatantly offensive jokes seriously he knows he's on dangerous territory. If I don't nettle but counter with a few sheep-shagging jokes, he knows he's in the clear. Ivor catches Fi's scowl.

"Oh, no offense. There's nothing worse than a male chauvinist pig, is there? Well, except a woman who won't do what she's told." Again he laughs. Fi is obviously unimpressed. I'm refreshed to find a man who is honest enough to tell it as he sees it. However, for Mike's sake I hope Mike tries a more conventional chatting-up approach with Fi. If I could, I'd advise chocolates and compliments.

Ivor is bored with trying to control the group dynamics and his interest now lies in drawing me into a more intimate conversation. He takes advantage of Fi going to the loo and Mike going to the fag machine to invade my body space. He's sitting on my right and he edges closer. I have nowhere to move, even if I wanted to. He puts his left arm along the back of the scruffy tartan settee. It reminds me of being in the pictures, aged thirteen.

"So how old are you, Cas?"

"Thirty-three." I never hesitate here. I'm proud to be thirty-three. I think it has much more kudos than, say, twenty-six or eighteen. I certainly feel better than I did then. It's only women who have a biological Timex who have a problem with saying their post-thirty ages out loud. Pointless really—it's not as though denial will turn the hands back. Anyway, I know I don't look thirty-three. As if to prove a point and somewhat predictably, Ivor raises his eyebrows. He doesn't bother with the cheap compliment that I don't look my age. He knows I'll have been told this often enough. Instead he keeps the conversation on track.

"So when are you going to settle down and make an honest man of your boyfriend?"

"Honesty is not my thing. I don't have a boyfriend and I don't want to be a wife." I smile efficiently. So Ivor's scored a hat trick, discovering the three most important facts in one conversational turn. He taps my leg with his right hand.

"You're a wicked woman, Cas."

This isn't strictly true. But for immediate purposes it will do as a character ensemble.

"So what do you want?"

I could tell him that I want world peace. I want Issie to find the man of her dreams. I want Josh to stop having wet dreams. I want my mother to redecorate and I want massive ratings on the next episode of *Sex with an Ex*.

"That's for me to know and you to find out," I whisper as I move closer, allowing my breast to rub against his arm. I realize I'm not conforming to the traditional role of coy female. But playing hard to get is only useful if you want to keep the man in question, which I never do. I approve of the invention of paper knickers, cups, napkins, knives and forks. I adore the disposable. I smile broadly. He gulps his designer beer. Amnesia has hit. The words "for better, for worse" etc. are temporarily erased from Ivor's mind.

"You know, just before you joined us Fi and I were discussing the fact that I make an adorable mistress." My voice is devoid of emotion and I could have just commented on the autumnal weather. The contrast between the piping hot statement and the arctic delivery causes Ivor's cock to stiffen. It's just too much fun to resist. I look from his cock to his eyes, back to his cock. His gaze follows mine. He blushes and crosses his legs. But to be honest, he hasn't a chance. "You see, I enjoy it. All of it. Dressing up, having food eaten off me. I never worry that the chocolate ice-cream will stain the sheets."

"Meet me outside in ten minutes," he says, leaving before he's finished his beer. I wonder how he's going to hold his erection for ten minutes, as he looks fit to explode. "I need to call my wife. It's just—" I stop him saying any more. I don't need his excuses.

"Save it for her."

He shows willing, in fact too much willing. His enthusiasm briefly battles with his ludicrously macho self-image. The enthusiasm wins. Ivor manages to restrain himself in the short cab ride that takes us to a hotel, and while he checks in. If "restrain" can be used to describe a man who is intermittently swilling out my ear with his tongue. However, somewhat disappointingly for us both, he shoots his load in the hotel lift. I have very little to do with the act. Besides being there. It's a depressing thought, but I have to face it. He could have downloaded some images from the Pamela Anderson website. His premature ejaculation has sobered both of us. I'm left frustrated. Hardly the culmination to the evening celebrating my ratings that I was expecting. I stare at Ivor, who can barely face me. The lift stops.

"I haven't spoken to my wife for eighteen months." Inwardly I sigh. If I'd realized this I wouldn't have touched Ivor with a barge pole. I look at him. He's grinning. "I don't like to interrupt her."

Another one of his jokes. We are both relieved and indulge in juvenile sniggers. His humor, for what it is, has saved the day. It's not that I think this man particularly irresistible but I do admire an ability to laugh in the face of adversity. Although I no longer want carnal knowledge of him I am aware that he has just shed out £185 for a hotel room. The least I can do is help him attack the mini bar. By the time he unlocks the hotel bedroom door it's pretty clear that neither of us wants sex. We do both, however, need a bit of a confidence boost. I've never had the Pamela Anderson thought before but now I can't shake it.

"I've never done this before," he offers as an explanation, justification and apology all at once.

"You don't—" I plan to say, "You don't say," but I catch a glimpse of Ivor sitting on the edge of the bed. His head is in his hands. It could be the alcohol, but I think he is genuinely upset. I change tack. "You don't have to apologize. There's a first time for everyone."

"It's just that recently my wife and I haven't been getting along too well."

"Married long?" I ask as I light a cigarette.

"Four years."

Ah, the seven-year itch. Everything is fast-track in London. I inhale deeply.

"We're moving house and trying for a baby. Things are tense."

"Oh." I'm engrossed in the mini bar. The hasty offload I can forgive, but if it's marriage guidance he's after I'd prefer it if he got a counselor. I pour myself a brandy and try to change the subject. "Know any more jokes?" It appears that the sexist and irreverent jokes have dried up. He's insisting on showing me that he's a decent bloke. He's wasting his time; it's an oxymoron and it's late. He fishes in his wallet and pulls out a picture of his wife.

"This is Julie." I hate this name and face business. I light another cigarette and realize that I haven't smoked my first one yet. Irritated I stub it out.

"Very nice," I comment, after taking a cursory glance at the picture. Julie looks like a pleasant enough woman, curvaceous, jolly, uncomplicated. She looks like a wife.

"I do love her," pleads Ivor.

I take pity. Which is unusual. Am I due? It could be that. When I'm hormonal I'm moved by *Heartbeat*.

"Look, it's OK." I sit next to him on the bed and stroke his head as if he is a Labrador. I am practiced at letting them off the hook. Admittedly it's usually post coital rather than pre. Normally I use the gentle let-down as an efficient way to get them to vacate my bedroom. "Nothing happened," I insist. I consider sharing my Pammie theory but I'm not feeling *that* charitable. I wonder if he'd have resisted me if I was an ex of his. I doubt it. It's the uncharted waters that are scaring him. "It was the combination—availability and alcohol. My availability and your alcohol. It gets them every time." I try to grin. "Now go home to your wife."

He readily accepts my suggestion and scrambles to his feet. He pushes his arm into the sleeve of his jacket, which, I note, he hadn't let go of. His readiness to leave me momentarily stings, so just before the bedroom door slams closed I yell, "And don't get mixed up in capers you can't handle."

It's useful advice.

CHAPTER
Six

I COULDN'T HAVE WISHED for a better outcome. Declan enjoyed his fifteen minutes of fame so much that he ached for more. He has a talent for the kiss-and-tell. Which arguably isn't a nice characteristic, but it is commonplace. And commercially admirable. Within a week of the first show he has appeared in most tabloids, giving sordid details of various aspects of his and Abbie's relationship, immediate and distant past. Some of it is undoubtedly true. He has been interviewed on local radio and TV stations, he has an agent and rumor has it that he is reading a couple of screenplays. There's no truth to this rumor. I know. My PR team initiated it.

Lawrence has asked his boss for an overseas posting but this has not shaken off the rat pack. It simply means he has become the Pied Piper for the European paparazzi as they maniacally search for him.

Abbie has gone underground. However, her actual presence isn't such a loss, as a number of her friends, family and associates are available to make comment. The woman who sold her the wedding dress offered extraordinary insight, as did the vicar who should have married them, three or four of Abbie's other ex-boyfriends and perhaps, most questionably, her hairdresser.

"Fi, can you believe her hairdresser betrayed her?" I ask, aghast.

Jenny, Brian and Karen have gone one step further. They've happily handed over letters they've written each other, posed for photographs with their families and finally invited *OK* to cover their wedding, although we are still unsure whose wedding it will be.

We have created a real live soap opera. By week two we have secured ratings of 1.8 million. By week three there've been two articles in the serious press discussing the nature and motivation of betrayal. The ratings tip 2 million.

"What's making you grin so much?" I ask Jaki, looking up from the letters commenting on the show. "Have you been promoted and they've failed to tell me?"

Jaki laughs. "No, but they should." I admire her; she never misses a trick. "No, it's something else. I was at a dinner party on Saturday night."

"Oh yeah, what did you eat?"

She perches on my desk and Fi stops working on her laptop. There is nothing we like better than a good conversation about food. Conversations about food have an advantage over actually eating. You can take an avid interest without jeopardizing your waistline. Conversations about food are better than conversations about sex, which are often mildly pervy or frustrating. I'm not sure how to rank conversations about food and actually having sex. It's close.

Jaki details her menu comprehensively, taking an inordinate amount of time to describe the chocolate soufflé. We hungrily hang on her descriptions of double cream and blackberry sauce. When she's told us that the mints were Benedict, I drag her back to her original point.

"So what's nearly as exciting as a promotion?"

"Well, after dinner we usually play games. So that the boys can get competitive legitimately."

"And the girls whip their arses openly," adds Fi enthusiastically.

"Exactly. Sometimes we play Outburst or Trivial Pursuit but more often than not we prefer the more revealing Truth or

Dare. This week someone, not me, suggested playing *Sex with an Ex.*"

"Nooooo," Fi and I chorus. We both immediately understand the importance of being absorbed into real-life popular culture. And so damn quickly!

"It was brilliant. Everyone had to name *the* ex in their past. You were right, Cas: there is always one who can send a thrill through the groin or heart. Then they had to say whether they would risk an uncomplicated, no-strings-attached, one-for-old-times'-sake bonk."

"But wasn't it all couples at that dinner party?" I protest. We are a small team; the stuff we don't know about each other's private lives isn't worth knowing. Believe me.

"Yup. Ellie and James, Daisy and Simon, Nige and Ali and Toby and me. That was the attraction. A public outing."

"So what happened?" asks Fi, excitedly playing with a staple gun. I take it from her before she causes serious bodily harm.

"Well, to start with everyone lied through their teeth. Those who I reckoned would do it became extremely demure. Those who wouldn't tried to pretend they had an experimental streak—which they blatantly don't have. But as the alcohol flowed the truth began to emerge."

"And?" Fi and I chorus. We both know the result we want.

"Huge rows. Ali walked out, Ellie burst into tears, Daisy and Simon's party was ruined."

"Wheeeey heeeeey," Squeals Fi. "Our first row."

"But think," adds Jaki, "if we were having this row in Clapham, how many similar rows must be taking place both north and south of the river, up and down the country! It's become a matter of national debate."

"Jaki, go to marketing tell them to slap a copyright on the board game, if they haven't already. They should be talking to game manufacturers before anyone else does. I wonder if we could get it out before Christmas?"

"That's only four weeks away," Jaki protests. I silence her with a glance. She rushes off. Her dark Afro hair and pert bum sway jauntily.

"Did you notice, Fi, Jaki never said how her evening panned out with Toby?"

By the end of November, on week four, the ratings rip through the 4.5 million viewers mark, and Bale insists I start interviewing again for a second series. The initial pilot series was scheduled to run six episodes. I have enough material to go to ten.

"Ten," yells Bale. "You are far too conservative. Interview enough couples for twenty shows." I try to object and explain that the show will only work while we can surprise the stooges—that's why we filmed so many shows in advance.

Bale glowers away my objections. "Cas, have you seen last night's ratings?" I shrug. I hope my shrug implies that I am far too busy having a fabulous social life, juggling several other projects at work and actively contributing to society by doing charity work to have checked the ratings. The reality is I checked them this morning, before I went to the gym. I have worked out my ratings—related bonus and mentally spent it half a dozen times.

"Have you any idea how big this is? It's more ratings than this channel has ever had on a single show. It's the same number as ITV get for"—he names one or two really big shows that ITV have as staples on their schedule. "It's more ratings than"—he names one of our competitors—"have ever had." He's not telling me anything new. I know this. "I've had offers from other channels to buy us out."

I startle. I didn't know this.

He reassures me, "Of course I'm not going to take them. Our lawyers are selling the idea to networks in the States, Australia and Asia. Murdoch wants to meet me!"

"I'm very pleased for you," I reply coolly as I help myself to tissues from his desk and wipe his heinous spittle off my face. "Yeah, it's good. I think we were helped by Melvin Bragg and Sue Lawley both condemning the show."

"It's good. You're good." Bale smiles. He's genuinely pleased with me. And why not? I've just saved his channel. More, I've probably made his career. I smile back and hand Bale the latest draft of my terms and conditions. It's not at all eighties in its scale. I'm not looking for a Boxster convertible or a six-figure salary. Although I'm confident that the bonuses will take me there. Bale picks up the paper and holds it at a distance. He eyes me suspiciously. He doesn't need to be afraid. The most demanding perk I've requested is that my mum gets to meet Tom Jones when we do *Audience with Tom Jones* show on Christmas Eve. I've also suggested that Issie's younger brother gets a temporary placement as a cameraman during his university vacation and that Josh can have half a dozen tickets for the Cup Final. Bale doesn't know this and naturally assumes the worst. He feels compelled to be nasty.

"Yes, you are good. It is relatively easy to reach the dizzy heights of your chosen profession if you're not hampered by morals and squeamish sentimentality."

"You'd know best, Bale," I reply and leave his office. I'll give him some privacy to review the T&Cs.

Kirsty had thought long and hard about this after the private detective contacted her. At first it'd seemed ridiculous. She thought some of her mates were winding her up. But then she began to understand. A new show. Something to do with confidence in fidelity. To be specific Eva Brooks had contacted the T.V. station to say that she had some doubts about her fiancé Martin McMahon. Did any of those names mean anything to Kirsty? They did. They meant the taste of metal and bile in her mouth.

The private detective was not wearing a long raincoat and a beret. In fact, she looked rather more like one of those women who stop you in shopping centers and ask if you'll spare a few minutes for market research. The private detective, Sue, liked her tea strong with two sugars.

Kirsty considered the proposition for two days solid. She was unable to keep her mind on her job and kept irritating the doctors by giving them the wrong patient notes. They nagged and grumbled at her. Ironically it was their irritation that coerced her into accepting the role, rather than a wish to wreak revenge on Martin. Well, why shouldn't she be on TV? It had to be more glamorous than her job here as a receptionist, in the dowdy little practice, in her small town. The same small town she'd been born and bred in, and if she wasn't careful would be buried in too. Sue promised that Kirsty would get a complimentary haircut and makeover, an allowance for her outfit for the show and some publicity photos afterwards. Sue thought Kirsty had a great chance as a model but she warned time was of the essence.

Kirsty didn't care for Martin at all any more. She was surprised to hear that Eva thought of her as a threat. He'd chosen Eva over her before, hadn't he? Oh shit he had. What made Kirsty think he'd choose her over Eva this time? Her knees nearly buckle under her. The humiliation was painful last time—the stinging, scorching disappointment as he explained that Kirsty was a really fun girl but not absolutely marrying material. Whereas Eva, with her posh university qualifications and green Wellingtons, was. Kirsty had tried to comfort herself with the thought that their kids would look like horses. But the thought didn't really keep her warm at night. Still, it was a long time ago and she was far too sensible not to move on. In the last ten months she'd only thought of Martin occasionally, like when her sister had a baby, her birthday or when one of the patients did something hilarious at work. But that was natural—that wasn't hankering. Christ, what if he rejected her again? Still, the channel didn't want her to get him to propose, just to have some fun. To compromise himself. She figures it will be easy.

Kirsty waits for Martin outside the high-street bank where he is assistant manager. She doesn't often come into London and she remembers why. It's busy and cold.

"Martin." She steps through the throng. He is with a couple of colleagues. They are all dressed identically, even the women.

"Kirsty, my goodness. What are you doing here? God, it's nice to see you."

And Kirsty knows him well enough to know that he is being genuine. She sighs, relieved, not just because the channel will get what they want but because something, somewhere very deep inside her melts. He cares. Not enough. Not consistently. But he does care. Maitin nods his colleagues away, assuring them he'll catch them up in the pub.

"Erm, I came up to meet a friend for lunch. I heard you got engaged so I thought I'd pop by and drop off a congratulations card." She holds out the card and beams, "Congratulations."

"Thanks." He reaches for the card and their fingers bump.

"I'm really pleased for you." Kirsty stretches her amazing smile a fraction wider.

"Yeah, thanks." Martin seems quite embarrassed and quickly thrusts the card into his suit pocket without reading it. "Do you fancy a drink?"

He's not wasting any time.

"Should we catch up with your friends?" offers Kirsty.

"No. I know the bar they are going to; it's really loud. We won't be able to hear ourselves think, let alone talk. Let's go somewhere quieter."

"I know just the place," says Kirsty.

It surprises Martin that Kirsty knows a local pub, which turns out to be absolutely perfect, because she doesn't come up to town that much. Then Martin sighs to himself. Maybe she does come into town now. He doesn't know much about her life. He always felt it pointless to keep in touch with old flames, especially ones who obviously have such different ambitions and expectations in life. Besides which, Eva wouldn't hear of it.

He only expected to have a quick one, but this is their third round.

It is good to be out with a bird who drinks pints again. Instead of the obligatory gin and tonic. Nice that she gets a round in, too, and isn't above going to the bar herself. Christ, Kirsty has fantastic tits. He'd forgotten how magnificent they are. She's still very chatty, too. She still makes little sense. She keeps wittering on about cameras. There again he's not being that rational either. Psychologists rate getting married as equally stressful as bereavement; people do odd things under stress. For example, right now all he wants to do is snog the lips off Kirsty.

With every day a new triumph emerges. The *Evening Standard* runs a story on the weddings that have been canceled by couples who have appeared on the show and the financial implications for the industries involved. The *Express* picks up the story and runs a story on how many weddings, up and down the country, have been canceled since the show began.

"A 120 percent increase on the exact same period last year!" cries Debbie. We are ecstatic. The *Express* hasn't said that *Sex with an Ex* is responsible, but the implication is there. If the show is responsible we are creating a national reaction. It's big. It's bigger than the "Free Deirdre Campaign" that ITV ran in reaction to a *Coronation Street* storyline.

The *Mail* spots the same potential story as we do. They track down a couple who have called off their wedding recently to ask them why. People quite unconnected with the show, people who've never appeared, had no desire to appear and would probably be horrified with the idea of appearing, admit that frank discussions on the sex appeal of an ex-lover have led to a discovery of fundamental disagreements, which can't be ignored.

Debs is reading from the morning paper. "This is it. This is the quote we need to use for our latest press release." She is literally jumping up and down.

"What does it say?" I ask.

"I am regretful," says the would-be-groom. "I believe our parting of the ways was a direct result of staying in to watch TV on Monday." Debs stops reading and asks, "Why do people use such ridiculous and pompous vocabulary when talking to the press? I'm sure he doesn't normally say such stupid things as 'parting of the ways'."

"Very astute, Debs. What else did he say?" I ask, trying to keep her on track.

"I wish we'd gone to the pub as we'd originally planned. But you see we were saving up. I wish I'd never heard of the show *Sex with an Ex.*" Debs puts the paper down with a satisfied flourish.

"Ah well, he sounds like a prick. By the way, Kirsty is doing well. I saw her in *B Magazine* the other day and I understand she has a contract with some modeling agency."

All this points to the fact that the show only has a shelf life of one or two episodes. It is becoming almost impossible to lure people on to the show, as the entire nation appears to be on infidelity alert. The plan is to use the kudos from this show to launch other programs. My phone rings, interrupting Debs's newspaper review.

"Hi, stranger."

"Hi, Issie." I wait for her justified complaints. I never ring her, or Josh. I'm totally absorbed in my work. Have I visited my mum recently? It's a relief that she skips it.

"Fancy a night out?"

"Well, yes, but it's just that I'm still interviewing. Bale's keen to commission another series."

"Then what? Another and another?"

"He seems to think so. I'm skeptical. I mean how gullible does he think the general public is?"

"Well, you may as well have a night out. You can't continue working at this rate *ad infinitum.*"

"What have you got in mind?" I ask.

"A drink? Grab some pasta? Somewhere where we can talk and catch up. I feel I haven't seen you for weeks."

I wonder if this is code for "I've been ditched."

"OK, let's try Papa Bianchi's," I suggest. "The food's fine, not exactly Michelin star, but it's cheap and cheerful and most importantly the waiters understand the importance of having a laugh and getting lashed." I don't mention that it is also in spitting distance of the studio and I'll be able to return to work after we've dined, but when I give her the address she'll guess.

"OK, hold the line until I get a pen."

I can hear the music from Issie's radio drift through the telephone line. I hear her scrabble around for a pen. I know where she's looking. She'll be starting in the telephone table drawer—futile. She'll progress to the kitchen drawers, the jamjar on the windowsill and then behind the cushions on the settee. She'll find a number of pens but none of them will work, the pencils will be blunt. For a scientist Issie is extremely disorganized. She's back on the line.

"Couldn't find a pen. An odd earring that I've been looking for, a telephone number and a recipe but no pen."

"Try your handbag."

"Good idea." She leaves the line again and this time the hunt is successful.

Issie takes down the details of where and when we are going to meet and I put down the phone. I'm pleased to have averted the inevitable disaster of her arriving late because she's lost or going to the wrong place and not arriving at all. My life is made up of a series of these small services which make other people's lives more comfortable. If only people realized.

I turn back to Fi and the problem of an increasingly moral nation. I know this squeamishness is hypocrisy and I don't expect it to be sustained, but it is an irritation.

"You know what, Fi?"

"What?"

"This new morality that the British public have so inexplicably developed"—I'm scornful—"may work to our advantage."

"How come?"

"Well, as I predicted, they've fallen. One after another. We really are living in a faithless society. Fidelity, or the lack of it, knows no boundaries. Indiscriminately it rages and rocks the lives of anyone who dares to trust."

"But it is brilliant television," adds Fi, not getting my drift.

"But somewhat depressing," I assert.

"Well, yes, it is," she confirms. "In fact, we had a letter from a silkworm farm in Ireland today."

"Really?" This trivia momentarily distracts me.

"Yes. Apparently last year, this farm—I forget its name—won the Queen's Award for industry and some other shield thing for their exports. Apparently this year demand has dipped percepti-bly."

"Honestly." I'm delighted. Fi doesn't catch my drift.

"I know, it is a huge responsibility, isn't it?"

"Responsibility bollocks, it's a huge story." Sometimes Fi lets me down. "Anyway, what was I talking about? Oh yeah. Whilst interviewing next week I want you to actively look for those you think have a chance of resisting."

"I thought you said people like that didn't exist," protests Fi.

"Prove me wrong." She looks nervous. I try to be helpful. Tick the underconfident who don't believe they are attractive to one individual, let alone two. Or pick those who are too driven by public recognition to risk public humiliation."

"What, like budding politicians?"

"Yes, or Freemasons."

"You are a sensation! You are a fucking marvel."

"Thank you, Nigel."

"Where did you find them?"

"Believe me, it took some doing."

"Your timing is immaculate. We've had six shows and just

when there was a danger of infidelity becoming a foregone conclusion, you find a couple who resist."

I smile at him. I'm trying not to look excited but to be honest I'm delighted too. We found a couple who although probably tempted were not stirred, so to speak. These people amazed me. They resisted not simply because the ex turned out to be a Clash bore or knew all the lyrics to every Duran Duran song, not just because they were worried about the chiffon and lace industry, not just because they feared being caught. But because they believed in it. Fidelity.

Loving.

Cherishing. They wanted to be exclusive lovers. Forever.

"Suckers," I comment.

"Still, it's brilliant television," adds Fi.

This it is. It brings the house down. This is what people want to believe in. It tantalizes. I've made it a possibility again, the Happily Ever After. We plan to do a massive follow-up show. By paying for the most OTT wedding. We are investigating the possibility of getting Westminster Abbey. It's short notice but providing there are no obscure foreign royalty or minor members of the aristocracy booked in I think we'll pull it off. I'm going to give the public what they want.

"Next week we can go back to the cheats."

It's late and it's 24 December. I look up from my desk and note that there is no one else left in the office except the cleaner. I note that he is wearing a Santa hat and a red nose. The red nose is real. I close down my PC and decide to lock it away rather than take it home for Christmas. My phone rings.

"Cas Perry, evening."

"Cas, you silly tart. What are you doing in the office on Christmas Eve?"

"Hi, Josh." I sigh, too tired to tell him how pleased I am he's called. "Just finishing off, actually."

"Good. We're in the Goose and Crown. Come and join us."

"Who's there?"

Josh names a number of our friends. I look at my watch. It's 8:40 P.M.—not too late to join them. I can't remember the last time I got pissed with genuine mates.

"I'd love to. I'll be there in twenty minutes."

Suddenly I am awash with Christmas cheer and so give the cleaner a bottle of malt whiskey that some advertiser sent me. He's disproportionately pleased. I received about a dozen similar gifts this Christmas and can't relate to his excitement. I call the lift and experience the unusual sensation of being relieved to leave the building. It is a glass elevator not unlike the one that appears in Willy Wonka's Chocolate Factory; it glides up and down in a graceful, effortless movement. As the lift takes me to the ground floor I mentally checklist the next show. This is the hundredth time I've done this—I know everything is fine but I do it anyway. It's habit. The building is dark, only illuminated by fairy lights. I pass the meeting areas. One has a photocopier in it and is always empty. The other has a Mars bar dispenser and a coffee machine. The latter room is always heaving. It's a good place to catch up on conversations about the male menopause. No one is there now. They've all gone home to start basting turkey or stuffing their wives. I pass a few words with the receptionist, which I do every Christmas. We comment on how quickly it's come around again. This time, however, I mean it. I've been so busy that I've completely missed autumn. Which is a shame because, if I was pushed to comment, I'd say that autumn is my favorite season. I nod to the security guard and then head toward the huge glass rotating doors. I'm already imagining downing my first vodka and orange.

"Jocasta Perry." A voice slices across the tranquility.

I don't have a chance to reply or to establish where it's coming from.

"Do you know what it is like to feel humiliation? Betrayal? Do you understand the pain? I don't suppose you do with breasts like those."

The woman who is shouting at me is in her early thirties. She has presumably been sitting in reception waiting for me but I hadn't noticed her until she'd called out. She has fine, highlighted, shoulder-length hair. It isn't particularly styled. She's a comfortable size twelve or fourteen. I don't think I actively know her and yet she has a vaguely familiar face. She looks a lot like a lot of women. She walks across the foyer and is within a foot of me. She is pointing a plump finger at me: she's so agitated she is actually shaking and as a result the strap of her handbag keeps slipping down her shoulder. Each time it does this she stops for a second and hitches the strap back on to her shoulder. Smart mac. Gucci bag. Where do I know this woman from?

"The people who write the letters—do you know what motivates them? Have you the slightest idea?" I look at the security guard and make it clear that I want him on standby. Whoever this woman is, she is obviously buoyed up by Christmas spirit(s). "I don't suppose you do. You obviously love yourself so much you can't love anyone else enough to be made vulnerable."

As I can't believe I know her, I consider it a near impossibility that she knows me. Even my best friends would be reticent to claim they *know* me. So what right does she have to draw such conclusions? Cast such aspersions?

Still, she's right.

She isn't shouting or threatening, but her powerful anger is obvious. She's controlling the menace, but only to show me she can. I mentally run through my Filofax and index cards. Finally I place her.

"I know you. It's Libby, isn't it?" I hold out a hand for her to shake. Libby was on one of our early shows. She'd suspected her fiancé still had a thing for his ex. She'd been right. I remember Libby because she had had such lovely taste. I remember her showing me her wedding dress and the bridesmaids' dresses; they'd been exquisite. Yes, lovely taste, except for in men, that is.

She nods curtly. "I was scared but I was with him. Now I'm scared and alone."

I touch her arm. She smells of teenage perfume which reminds me of Fairy Liquid. I doubt this is Libby's because of her impeccable taste. I suspect that she went for a quick one after work and with the combination of gin and Christmas songs on the jukebox she has become maudlin. I imagine her mates geeing her on to come and track me down to tackle me. One or two of her really good friends will have tried to stop her. On noting her determination they've done the next best thing—doused her in their perfume.

"He'd have left anyhow," I comfort.

She starts to sob. "Would he? Would he?"

The receptionist gives her a cup of tea and the security guard leads her to the settee. She's telling them how lonely she is. I think she should be evicted from the building, but as it is Christmas I won't report the lax approach of the receptionist or the guard. I head toward the door.

"Merry Christmas, Libby," I shout. I pause, waiting for her to wish me a happy New Year.

She doesn't. Instead she grips my arm and asks, "Have you ever looked in the mirror and been disappointed with your reflection?" I turn to face her and she meets my gaze. "Well, I loathe mine."

CHAPTER
Seven

I'S NEW YEAR'S EVE. I have two things to celebrate this evening. One, Christmas is over. I've watched *The Sound of Music* with my mum and I'm now Julie-Andrews-free for another year. And two, it's not the millennium. That was hell. The horrible expectancy of it all. I started planning my millennium New Year's Eve in February 1997, as I was terrified that I'd choose the wrong option for this once-in-a-lifetime opportunity. I couldn't decide. Cottage in the Cotswolds? Black tie in Vegas? Beach in Mauritius? There was just too much choice and every one of them with its advantages.

It wasn't simply a question of enjoying myself. I presumed that I'd manage to pull that off just about anywhere, but I soon came to realize that wherever I chose said something about me. Did I want to say Vegas or Cotswolds? Did I want glitz or serenity? In the end Josh, Issie and I had a posh dinner at Issie's house. Josh cooked, I provided the champagne. Issie's contribution, besides the venue, was that she managed not to have her heart broken. A first for a New Year's Eve, at least in my memory. We then drunkenly walked up and down the River Thames, getting crushed by the crowds and watching the fireworks and the backs of several million revelers. It was great.

Now, in a blink of an eye, it's New Year's Eve again. With all its hellish accessories. Not only does the thought of the little black dress ruin Christmas indulgence, but this year I'm not spending it with Issie and Josh. Issie is going to her parents' party in Marlow and Josh is in Scotland with the family of his latest girlfriend.

On the up side, I am going to a glitzy industry party and if I'm not going to be with Issie and Josh, this is my second choice. Everyone who is anyone in TV will be at the Gloucester Hotel in Mayfair tonight. I *have* to be there. Especially this year, as I'm riding high. Perhaps the highest I've ever been. My show is the talk of the industry. I also consider that it is actually impossible not to score at these events. And I'm ready for it. Thinking about it I've been going though a bit of a dry patch of late. There was Joe, in late August. And then the botched attempt with Ivor, which doesn't count. I thrust these disconcerting thoughts aside, comforting myself with the fact that the combination of my current success, the fact it is New Year's Eve and the loose morals of those who work in the media industry mean I'm guaranteed great sex tonight. You can smell the testosterone as soon as you walk into the hotel foyer. I bristle. We have tried to disguise it with Calvin Klein perfume and aftershave, bow ties and posh frocks, but lust is tangible. A thick tension is staining the air. And although this may sound lairy, it's not. It's exciting. It's fun. It's fan-fucking-tastic.

Literally.

My targets fall into two categories: victim or sparring partner. I prefer the latter but hey, a time and a place. I see him by the time we sit down to dinner. He's on the next table. He's glittering in the candlelight. He's not wearing a wedding ring. After a few discreet inquiries I discover that he has a long-term girlfriend but she's not here tonight. The very best combination—challenging but not insurmountable. I want this to be a one-night thing and really I can't be arsed to put in weeks of prep. Chances are he'll be going through a rough patch. They always are. He'll tell me that this is because his girlfriend doesn't understand him. Of course the opposite is true.

The dinner passes in a blur of laughter and champagne. Bale is

as pompous as hell, but at least I don't get caught under the mistle-
toe with him, as Di does. Fi, Ricky and I have a huge giggle,
spreading gossip, spiking drinks and strutting our stuff on the
dance floor. I'm having so much fun that I almost forget that I
plan to score. But as the clocks strike midnight and Fi and Ricky
both disappear to snog their chosen boys, I look around for my
target. Of course it's not a coincidence that he is standing just a
few feet away from me. He wasn't oblivious to the smouldering
glances I threw across the melon balls; nor was he averse to returning them.

I don't kiss him on the dance floor because he does have a girlfriend. I can do without the gossip and uproar which would ensue
after such an obvious display of our intentions. Instead I lean very
closely in to him so that my lips are a fraction from his lobe. His
hairs stand up and brush my lips. I move an almost indiscernible
bit closer, letting my tit scrape against his arm. He trembles. My
groin flinches.

"Have you got a room?" He nods. The atmosphere is damp
with lust. "What number?" He tells me immediately. I feel so powerful. "Walk to your room. Don't walk too fast because I need to
leave a respectable interval between you leaving and me following,
but I don't want to lose you." I give his arm a squeeze. We both
understand. He nods a drunken nod, happy to follow my instructions to the letter.

I keep a safe distance and then I catch him up in his corridor.
I'm quite tired so I don't bother with anything too athletic against
the wall, which I could have done to politely fill the embarrassing
gap as he fumbles with the key, desperate to get it in the lock. I'm
not sure if this is drink, nerves or excitement, but it doesn't bode
well. Eventually he opens the door. Unaccountably my mood
changes. I think I'm bored by his inability. I'm no longer looking
forward to this. Still, I'm here. He's on a promise and I think it is
dishonest to pull out at this stage. It wouldn't be polite. I'm many

things but a prick teaser isn't one of them. I make the decision to get it over with as quickly as possible. I really am tired and it would have been wiser to have had an early night.

I shrug away his attempt to offer me something from the mini bar.

"You go ahead."

He pours himself a whiskey. He then tries to light a cigarette but fails and spills the matches on the floor. He's very nervous and I feel almost maternal. Is he too young for this? Am I too old? I take pity and decide to encourage him. Delicate thing, the male ego. I've often thought of those soapy bubbles that you make by blowing a lot of hot air through a little plastic device. Easy to inflate, easy to pop and easy to grow again.

"Hey, tiger." I prize the whiskey tumbler out of his hand and kiss him. Fine. Quite good really. But then, it is just kissing. He lunges for my zip and tugs at it. The dress is Versace and cost me nearly a thousand quid. I play a tactful maneuver where I shimmy out of it doing a little mini striptease. He loves it. And I save my dress. To be fair, he is trying—he just lacks subtlety. He's kneading my breasts as though he's trying to massage a muscle out of spasm. We are lying on the bed and suddenly his fingers are deep inside me. Better. OK one, two is fine. Jesus, I hope he knows fisting is just an expression.

"Would you like me to go down on you?" he asks. That's novel—I've never been called upon to have an opinion before.

"Would you like to?" I ask, grinning.

"Well, I don't mind, if it's really what you want. It's not actually my favorite. But I'm happy to oblige if it will make you come." I guess this is sweet, in a way. But sweet is not sexy. I now seriously wonder if anything he can think of will make me come. Being called a prick teaser seems like an attractive option.

I disengage and go to the bathroom. When I emerge I'm wearing a towelling robe and I've cleaned my teeth. The vibes I'm giving off are Mary Ellen *à la* Walton family rather than Sue Ellen, Ewing family temptress.

"Goodnight." I smile, pecking him on the cheek. I pull the dressing gown tightly around me, turn the light out and deliberately roll away from him. I don't even care that he doesn't seem too disappointed.

I scramble for my mobile, which slices through my dreamless sleep. It's Issie.

"*Happy new year!* Where are you?" Her voice is a unique blend of excitement, frustration, anger and concern.

"In a hotel in"—I scrabble around for the note pad next to the telephone—"Mayfair."

"Who with?"

I look to the empty bed. I feel the sheets next to me. They are still warm. They smell of male sweat. I can hear the shower running.

"His name's Ben." I hear her tut. I know the conclusion she has naturally drawn and I haven't the energy to correct her diagnosis of events. Instead I confirm it. "It was New Year's Eve. It was just physical."

"It's always just physical. That's the problem." She sighs. She doesn't seem impressed. "You are heading for trouble. You are on overdrive. You've been working too hard. When did you last go home?"

"Not sure. What day is it?"

It turns out to be Sunday. I haven't slept or bathed in my flat since Christmas morning and before that a week last Tuesday. I did stay at my mum's on Boxing Day, but besides that I've been using the facilities at the gym and work.

"You need a rest," says Issie. But she's wrong—I thrive on activity. I'm at my creative best when I'm hyper. Ordinary people may need to rest after such intensive work periods but I'm strong. I'm fine.

I think I'm going to cry.

"I'm so tired," I wail. "It was awful. In fact, I can't remember when I last had good sex. I'm so tense. I'm going straight from here to my masseur. My neck is so tight I can barely move."

"You can't go to your masseur, it's New Year's Day. They'll be closed. Look, Josh's called. He's missing us. He's on a flight back down here. I'm going to the airport to pick him up. I'll swing by your flat first. Then we can all go for a walk, clear the hangovers."

Thanks, Issie. What a darling.

It is so bloody cold that the stag that are, allegedly, in Richmond Park are nowhere to be seen.

"They're hibernating," suggests Issie.

Josh wraps an arm around each of us.

"If you think this is cold, you should have been in Scotland. Now *that* was cold."

"How was Scotland?" As I say this I can see my breath on the air. I pull my jacket tighter around me.

"Fine. Alcoholic. Tartan," he comments non-committally.

"Gone off her, then?" The "her" in question is Katherine, Josh's latest girlfriend. Issie and I quite like her. She's been hanging around with Josh for a couple of months now. We had high hopes but I can already tell from the tone of his voice, and the fact that he's back here with us instead of in St. Andrew's with her and her parents, that I ought to start talking about her in the past tense.

"I finished it," Josh confirms. Issie and I slyly exchange glances.

"Nice timing," we chorus.

Josh shrugs apologetically.

"How was your night, Issie?" I ask.

"Really good, actually. Family all well and I met someone really nice at my parents' party."

"Someone really nice and male?" I try to clarify. It sounds unlikely.

Issie grins and nods. The cold wind has whipped up spots of color on her cheeks. I understand why Elizabethan poets used to mither on about their heroines having cheeks like roses. Issie is glowing.

"You look fantastic, Issie. Did you score?"

She grins sheepishly. "I was at my parents.'" Good point, no opportunity. "But I did give him my telephone number."

"Home or work?" asks Josh.

"Both, and my mobile. And my e-mail and my fax," says Issie. This time Josh and I exchange the glances.

"He hasn't called yet, though." Issie suddenly scrambles for her mobile. She checks her message facility and the text messages. Nothing.

"It's far too early for him to call," Josh comforts her. Although neither he nor I think that Issie's chap will call. He'll have detected the fact that while one hand was handing over all her telephone numbers, the other hand was flicking through a copy of *Brides and Setting Up Home*.

"Should I call him?" asks Issie.

"Do you have his number?"

"Yes, his mother gave it to my mother."

I stamp my boots hard on the freezing snow, enjoying the crunchy sound it makes and avoiding confronting the inevitable disaster Issie is driving towards. It sounds to me as though this guy is a social misfit, if his mother has to try to get him dates. I don't share my theory with Issie. Instead I listen to hers on sexual equality.

"I mean, it doesn't matter who rings who, really, does it? I mean we are both adults. We don't have to play games." Neither Josh nor I comment.

We stop and buy a hot chocolate from a caravan, marveling that the guy is open on New Year's Day. The vendor assures us that he'd rather be freezing in his caravan in Richmond Park than "stuck in the house wiv me muvver-in-law and the kids." We all do our best to ignore this condemnation of family life and sip the creamy drinks.

Issie continues. "I'm sure he'd respect me for calling."

She believes the seventies' hype that a man still respects you if you call him, that he'll like you and want a relationship with you. I try to explain that the advice is thirty years out of date. In the seventies, single women would not have accepted the advice of the Land Girls. So why does Issie think that the burn-the-bra brigade have any relevance to how women of the twenty-first century should conduct their romantic and sexual liaisons?

"Call him if you like, Issie. But he'll know that you don't just happen to have two tickets for the opera—no one ever does."

"Should I suggest the Turkish restaurant that's just opened on Romilly Street?"

"If you like, but he knows it's code for 'I like you.' 'I like you' leaves you exposed and will send him running."

"You call men all the time."

"I call because I don't want commitment. They respond because they know that." Issie scowls at me. But doesn't waste her breath arguing. "If you want my advice, wait until he calls you."

Issie gives Josh her phone and makes him promise not to let her ring until January 3, earliest.

"What about your evening?" asks Josh, turning to me.

"Fine," I say, without committing. "Good food. Good company. My Versace dress stole the show. Crap sex."

Josh's charming, confident laugh rings around the park. "Your problem is that you are from Mars and you keep meeting men from Venus."

I grin. "I just wanted some good sex to round the evening off but for all my fascination with other people's sex lives right now, mine is going through a rough patch. I simply can't conjure up the energy. Of course I'm still sleeping with men but it's becoming tedious. For example, this morning I just wanted to slip away. I didn't need a post mortem, but Ben wanted to be all twenty-first century about our encounter. He wanted to discuss what it meant. I told him it meant nothing."

Issie gasps. "Why did you say that?"

"Because it's true," I state simply.

"It is impossible to sleep with a stranger and not risk suffering or inflicting serious emotional carnage. Casual sex is what we enter into, not what we come out of," Issie chides.

I blame Josh for this outburst. He gave Issie the book *Responsibility for Yourself, Reconciliation with Others* for Christmas. Apparently it was intended for me, and the book *Women Who Love Too Much* was meant for Issie. He got the tags mixed up. I thought it was hilarious.

"But I do come out unscathed, without a fractured heart and absolutely free of bitter recriminations," I point out to Issie.

"Do the men you sleep with?" she asks.

"Yes," I say without faltering.

Issie and Josh both draw to a dramatic halt and glare at me.

"Yes," I insist and I try not to think of Ben's hurt look this morning or the pathetic messages Joe keeps leaving on my answering machine or the numerous Christmas cards that I received from men suggesting that we could "do it again sometime." Problem is I can rarely remember doing it the first time. My conquests are a homogenous blur.

"Well, in your case there are two options. Either you are internalizing the damage or you are an animal. I know you are not an animal." Issie is suddenly serious and she lets go of Josh's arm and runs to hug me.

Poor Issie. This constant search for something deep and meaningful in me is exhausting. Why can't she just accept me for what I am? Someone led by hedonism, eroticism and base animal instincts. I say nothing until at last her face settles into sad acceptance. Weary of fighting with me, she grudgingly laughs, "Oh, OK, you *are* horrid."

We all go back to my flat. Josh immediately goes into the kitchen to see what he can rustle up. My fridge is surprisingly well stocked. This is because my mum has a key and must have popped around today. There are fresh vegetables, leftover turkey and a load of mince pies. She's also left a small Christmas cake on the coffee table. Josh starts to chop vegetables and Issie opens some wine while I call my mum to thank her and wish her a happy New Year. By the time I get off the phone, Josh has made a huge pan of thick vegetable soup. We sit with bowls on our laps in front of the TV.

"Didn't your mum want to come around?" asks Josh.

"No. I invited her but she said that she and some neighbor or other are going to put their feet up in front of the TV."

"Bob?" offers Issie.

"Could be," I shrug. Sometimes it seems as though Issie knows more about my mother's life than I do.

It's a big night for me. The wedding episode of *Sex with an Ex* is playing out as an hour special. Half an hour on the wedding, then half an hour on the usual program. The fact that I secured an hour spot on primetime TV on New Year's Day is hugely exciting. For all Issie and Josh have made it quite clear that they don't approve of the program (which I think is hypocritical of Josh, considering his behavior was inspirational to the original concept), they both have to admit that it is compelling. Neither of them has missed a show.

"Why is she wearing a leopard-skin tracksuit?" Issie asks.

"It goes with her hair," notes Josh. "Why do they do it at all?" he adds incredulously.

"Fame," I assert happily. "It's compelling."

"She's awful," says Issie, "she keeps clapping herself. Why does she do that?"

"Too much orange squash as a kid," I offer.

The scene cuts to some moody music, something that builds to a crescendo. The audience, in its entirety, is with Tom. They want him to resist. He doesn't. The cries of protest and defense of the infidel, Tom, bleat from the TV. "It meant nothing—it confirmed the reasons we split up." His girlfriend ignores his wails and punches him. "Whooooo. Whoooo." The audience erupts. Turning at once. Deciding within seconds who they'll support. Who they'll hate. They know they should be supporting people because they seem nice—they ought to prefer the sweetest personality. But invariably they cheer for the bird with the biggest tits or the guy with the cheekiest grin. They whoop and cheer and sing and goad and cry and console and condemn in the space between one commercial break and the next. The overwhelming emotion is fear.

"It's fascinating," comments Issie. "The men justify straying on the grounds that it's not about love and the women that it is."

"I don't find that fascinating. I find it predictable. I'd like a woman to come on the show and say she fancied a shag," I argue.

"It's unlikely though, isn't it? You're the only woman I know who underwent an emotional lobotomy at the age of seven."

"Shush." I'm not embarrassed by what she's saying, but the adverts have finished and we'll miss some of the show with her chatter.

His face is gray and his lips tight. He's sweating from every pore. His eyes are darting left to right. He doesn't know. He can't be sure. Has she slept with her ex or not?

"You know how we could improve the show?" I ask rhetorically.

"Pull it," Josh suggests.

I fling him a filthy look. "No. We should have two signature tunes, depending on the outcome. One for jubilation, the other for . . ."

"Humiliation?" Issie interrupts.

"Mortification?" Josh offers.

"Simply desolation," I say.

I don't shy away from it. I cast my mind back to Christmas Eve and Libby's swollen, weeping face. She thought she was telling me something I didn't know. She wasn't. She looked just as my mother had the day my father left. I know all about desolation. I know the emotion I'm exposing on stage and I'm not frightened of it. *I'm* not the one creating it and I have no reason to feel ill at ease. I know that the couples with unfaithful partners are desolate, horrified, mystified, disappointed. But it won't last. I firmly believe I'm doing them a favor. Better now than after they've signed the form at the registrar's.

We finish the soup and I heat the mince pies and slice the Christmas cake. Issie groans, insists she can't eat another bite and then asks if there's any brandy sauce for the pud. Josh has now put himself in charge of alcohol and is as liberal with the measures as he is with his sperm. We're filthily pissed by 9:15 P.M.

It's brilliant.

"Thanks for the socks," he says, kissing me on the cheek and sitting next to me on the sofa. I grin and put my arms around him.

"You're welcome." I also bought him a number of more desirable pressies: big boy's toys such as a palm pad, a Swiss Army knife and a mobile phone that you can send pictures on. The gift he liked best was the computer headset that gives you access to your favorite website by talking to your computer. He wasn't even perturbed when my mother asked, "But isn't there a button you could push instead?" Buying these presents reaffirmed my belief that even the nicest men are truly incapable of growing up. The socks are a joke. We always buy each other an old-married-couple-gift. We figure that this is as close as each of us will ever get. Josh bought me a perfunctory rolling pin. Not even one of those nice marble ones. He knows I've never had a use for a rolling pin and unless someone comes up with a creative way of utilizing one in the bedroom I'm unlikely ever to. We've offered Issie the chance to join in our game. After all, if Josh bought two women wifey gifts it would be even more realistic. She's steadfastly refused, complaining that it's too depressing a notion. I think she fears she's tempting fate. The irony is she hopes that one day she'll exchange such gifts for real.

"Have you made a New Year's resolution?" asks Issie, squeezing her slim bum between Josh and me and wiggling a bit so that we have to move to accommodate her. I slosh some more brandy into everyone's glass.

"Oh, you know, the usual—lose five pounds in weight, limit my alcohol units to just twice the recommended allowance and cut back to twenty a day. You?"

"I'm going to play it cooler with men."

Josh and I are too drunk to bother to hide our amusement. We both spit out our brandy. Mine is aimed back into my glass; Josh isn't as houseproud and he splatters his all over my cashmere cushions. I'm laughing too much to get cross.

"What?" asks Issie, indignantly. But she knows what.

"Well, at least you are consistent. That's the same resolution you made last year and the five previous to that," I comment.

Josh is kinder. "To be fair, that is the very nature of our resolutions. I mean you always want to eat, smoke and drink less, Issie always wants to love less and I—"

"Always want to screw more," Issie and I chorus.

We all laugh. It's too true for any of us to take offense.

"How about we do it for real this year?" I suggest.

"I do hope to screw more," says Josh seriously. His average is pretty high as it stands—I doubt if he has time for that many more conquests. His behavior is already quintessentially male. I use him as a role model.

"No, I mean this year why don't we resolve to do something different, and really do it?"

"What, like run a marathon?" suggests Issie.

"Yes, if that's what you want to do," I encourage.

"Is it a good place to meet men?" she asks. I sigh.

We drink a whole lot more. In fact, we finish the brandy and start on whiskey. This is on top of the wine that we drank with the soup. I've certainly blown apart my resolutions, but that's all I'm certain of. Everything else is a fog. I hold my hand out in front of me, but it's blurry around the edges. Issie and Josh are both being wildly funny, coming up with more and more ludicrous resolutions that we could pledge, but I can't keep up with their thoughts. My head is smudgy and, try as I might, I can't seem to control the direction of my thoughts. I keep getting vivid flashes of Ben's serious and earnest face as he droned on about his girlfriend and whether she'd forgive him for his near infidelity. I advised him to keep his trap shut. He stared out of the window as though he hadn't heard me and asked how could he forgive himself. I must be really drunk because Ben's face keeps dissolving into Ivor's and Ivor's pleading eyes melt into Joe's. I shake my head. Whisky, the devil's own urine—it always makes me weird.

"Learn a new word every day."

"That's easy."

"And use it."

"Do the three peaks' challenge."

"No way."

Issie's ash misses the ashtray she is aiming for. She doesn't seem to notice but I watch it sprinkle to the floor in slow motion. My eyes see this. My mind sees Ben's matches scatter as he nervously tries to light a fag. I notice I'm surrounded by drooping tinsel and dropping pine leaves.

"Tell the truth for a week, the whole truth and nothing but," suggests Josh. Little white lies are a way of life for him and all philanderers. More natural than breathing.

"No, that's stupid, you'd have no friends."

"More whiskey?" I offer.

"Go on then," they slur and hold out unsteady glasses.

"OK, how about I resolve to get married?"

"What?" Both Issie and I stare at Josh. We're dumbfounded.

"You can't marry, dummy, you've just ditched your girl, remember? And she was great, the best you've introduced us to for a while. You are a commitment phobe, remember?"

"That's not true," argues Josh.

I defend him. "Be fair, Issie, he is committed—very much so—in the beginning. It's sustaining the commitment that he has a problem with."

Josh scowls good-naturedly. It's a fair cop. "I'm very committed to you, Cas. And you too, Issie," he adds. "I've just never been with the right girl."

I'm not sure what he's looking for.

Josh and I are similar in many ways. We've both had numerous sexual encounters. The big difference is Josh does believe in relationships and does expect to settle down one day. He's always telling me so. I don't know why he still expects this with his track record. For eighteen years Josh has followed a pattern. He is always desperately in love or desperately in loath. The difference is only a matter of weeks. He bores easily. But instead of thinking that it's because there is something flawed in the concept of Happily Ever After (which seems obvious to me) Josh insists it's because he hasn't had the opportunity with the right woman yet. He repeatedly and forcefully insists that he *knows* she exists.

"OK maybe promising to get married this year is a bit over the top. The best reception venues will be all booked up anyway. I'll take it in easy stages. I'll find the One and propose."

"Can I be bridesmaid?" asks Issie.

"Yes."

"Can I be best woman?" I'm humoring him.

"Maybe." He swallows back his whiskey and pours yet another.

He swills the amber devil's pee around in the glass and we silently watch him silently watching it.

"You're serious, aren't you?" I ask.

"It's time," he confirms. A cold finger traces its way along my spine. I shiver; it feels a lot like fear. Josh marry? I'd lose him. Or rather I'd lose my position as *numero uno* in his life. I share Josh with Issie but that's different. Issie isn't competition, she's complimentary. I'd miss him.

"You're pissed. You don't mean this. I tell you what, you can retract it in the morning." I smile. I wait for him to smile back and he doesn't, so I move on to Issie. "OK, what's your resolution?"

"I like that one about running a marathon. And you?"

"I'm beginning to feel cheap and bored." She cocks her head to one side, waiting for me to elaborate. I can't. I'm amazed I've said this much. I don't mean it. Or do I? I do.

"I'm giving it up."

"What?"

"Casual sex, shags without thought, impulsive sex, shags with limited thought, acting on drunken whims, sleeping with someone to celebrate a promotion, or the ratings, or a pretty frock in Armani." I pause to be certain that covers all scenarios. It does.

"What will you do?" asks Issie, with the scary honesty that only best friends can employ.

"I don't know," I reply with the same tone. "Celibacy?"

CHAPTER
Eight

"WHAT HAPPENED? Why did you do it, Susie? What made you do this?" Jed is being unusually dignified, under the circumstances. After all, a quarter of the British adult population have just seen his fiancée kiss her ex-lover almost in the vestry of the church, fifteen minutes before their wedding rehearsal, a week before their wedding. The film clearly shows her adjust her skirt as she emerged from behind the tomb stone. Bale's terrified of law suits so we are not explicit but it doesn't take a Mensa IQ to work out that kissing wasn't where the action stopped.

Susie is whiter than the wedding dress that she'd proudly shown the audience just before the ad break. But then that was another lifetime. That was a pre-public outing lifetime. Susie was still playing happy families, Jed was still living in cloud cuckoo land and Andrew was still standing in the wings waiting to expose Susie's infidelity.

"I am so sorry," whispers Susie. Which I think is a good move. Her only chance of winning the audience over is to be immediately and totally contrite. After all, Jed's a good-looking guy and natural instincts are to root for him.

It's an interesting moment, this one: when all three stooges are on the floor and they have to deal publicly with the consequences of a very private affair. Jed had thought he was in control. He hadn't actually believed Andrew was any real competition. He'd imagined that it would be exciting to be on TV, something to tell the grandkids. He'd expected Susie to choose him, despite the fact that all their friends still whispered about Andrew and Susie being a great couple, so much more passionate. I bet he's now wishing he'd simply stuck to the wedding video.

Andrew thought it was his game. He had little to lose as his and Susie's romance ended in a veil of tears and reprimands some years ago (FYI, and it's worth noting, the reason they finished was because Susie found Andrew in bed with another woman). Andrew had happily agreed to tempt her. If he hadn't, it would look as though he was chicken shit, and that foxy detective who'd approached him would think he was only half a man.

"Why did you do it, Susie?" pleads Jed.

"I wish they'd ask more probing questions," comments Jaki. We are both standing in the wings watching the action, live.

"No, this is the crux," I whisper back. "The reasons why the partners fall are massively interesting. The list is endless. Closure, revenge, consolation, opportunism."

Susie has finally found her voice.

"I am sorry, Jed. But I couldn't not. For the last three years since Andrew and I split up I saw him in every square jaw and broad shoulders. Sometimes I'd see him in front of me on the tube escalator and I'd run to catch him up, my feet pounding on the wooden slats, my heart vibrating against my tonsils. And for that heady thumping moment I wouldn't worry how I'd explain it to you. Or why I was forgiving him. I just wanted to heal myself by resting my eyes upon him. I thought then that the throbbing might go away. But it never was him. It was always someone less. Because everyone is less. Even you."

How curious.

The audience knows that Andrew doesn't deserve such devotion, but they are thrilled. Other than Susie's very deep ugly sobs, you can hear a pin drop.

Tears are streaming down Jaki's face. "Aren't you moved, Cas?"

"Yes, I'm delighted there isn't a dry eye in the house. It's great television. What's next?"

She hands me a clipboard. "Interviews for next week's show."

I walk toward the interview room, ushering away a few giggling research girls who are cluttering the doorway. "What's up with them?" I ask Fi.

"Haven't you heard? Your thinking man, he's a Greek god."

"Not very tall, then, and with several heads?" I quip. But my sarcasm is whipped out of me as I open the door and see Darren. I can understand why Marcus is insecure. I met Marcus this morning. He is fine. He is bright enough, more interesting than most, average-looking and extremely wealthy. He obviously adores Claire. Claire realizes this is not a bad deal and I figure she adores him back. However, besides my personal belief that everyone will have an affair given the opportunity, Darren is breathtaking.

He's tall, about six foot two, with long, gypsy hair touching his chin. I don't normally go for long hair. Because, more often than not, it is accessorized with an entirely denim wardrobe and a Meatloaf album collection. But, right now, all I want to do is lose my fingers in his locks. More, I want to lose him in my Conran bâteau wooden bed. He has wide shoulders that taper to slim hips and the cutest bum. He is wearing a pale gray sweater and some old Levis. Just the right amount of effort, without suggesting he is conceited. His eyes are huge, deep brown and framed with the most stunning Bambi lashes. And best of all is his smile. He has the cheekiest smile that provokes his entire face. His eyes, his cheeks, his laugh lines.

He's a babe.

For a moment I am at a complete loss. I don't know what to say, what to do or how to stand. I am absolutely dispossessed of common sense, thirty-three years of precedent, or even a simple grasp at etiquette. I can no more think of the correct words than I could bungy jump from . . . God I can't even think where people bungy jump. My mind is blank. He smiles and I think I can hear music, which is such a cliché that I'm ready to shoot myself. My nipples are getting hard, which I think is a filthy betrayal. Can he tell? I'm literally salivating. Get a fucking grip, I instruct myself.

"Jocasta Perry," I say in a confident, don't-think-I'm-going-to-be-impressed-by-your-stunning-good-looks-I'm-inpenetrable voice. It's entirely fictional.

"Jocasta, how Oedipal." He smiles, taking my hand and shaking it very firmly. I'm amazed not at the firmness of the handshake but at the reference. "Jocasta or Ca—"

"Cas," I confirm. Is this man psychic?

"Darren Smith."

"Yes, I know." I indicate the clipboard, which has all his personal details. Telephone number, address, date of birth. I wonder if we should start including some more intimate questions in the briefing session. Like favorite sexual position, which side of the bed he sleeps on. Mentally I pinch myself. He's just a man. I quickly draw attention to his shortcomings. We both need to be aware of them.

"Daz or Dazza?" I smile icily.

"Darren," he confirms without the slightest hint that he's taken offense. I wonder if he realizes that I am trying to be rude. He doesn't seem stupid. He grins at me. Exposing a row of teeth which the Osmonds would be proud of. How can anyone be this gorgeous?

"Well, Darren, to business." I sit next to him and accidentally bang my knee against his. His touch blisters through my Joseph trousers. I actually flinch. Shaking, I reach for a glass of water.

"You OK?" He moves quickly, reaching the water before I do. Genuinely concerned, he hands me the glass. I'm incapable of telling him I'm OK. The glass slips an inch. He thinks I'm going to drop it and so guides it to my lips, watching me the whole time. His eyes bore right into me. Is he reading my mind? Does he know my knickers are in flames? I take a gulp of the water. And place the glass back on the coffee table. "It is hot in here," he comments and springs up to play with the air conditioning switch. He is so confident. So in control. And I'm . . . ? I'm so lost. Maybe I'm sick. I glance at Fi. She's grinning. This brings me back to my senses with a jolt.

"Something funny, Fi?" I glare at her. She shakes her head and retreats to a corner of the room. I force myself back to my guest notes and back to Darren. Only one of those actions presents a problem. "As you know, Marcus Ailsebury is about to marry your ex-girlfriend, Claire Thomson, on Valentine's Day. Just over two weeks' time. Marcus wrote to us to tell us that he feels"—I correct myself—"fears that Claire may still hold a torch for you." I blush. This script, normally adequate, suddenly appears to be exactly what it is. Bloody awful. I hope Darren doesn't think I'd normally use an expression like "hold a torch." Regardless, I carry on. "Marcus needs to know whether his fears are founded. Now are you familiar with the format of *Sex with an Ex?*" I look up at him.

"*Sex with an Ex?* Sadly, yes." He nods seriously. His hair falls over his left eye. I can't think of anything more attractive. He blows out of the side of his mouth. Except that. The hair almost magically falls back into place.

"Good, well, what we need you to do is—"

"Look, I'm sorry to interrupt, but I don't want to waste any more of your time than I already have." I smile, quite happy to engage in a conversation with him. Answer questions and queries. He can have all evening. I want to hear everything he has to say.

"I'm not going to do this."

Except that.

"I don't want to be on your show."

I stare at him, amazed. Arsehole.

"I feel terrible that I'm letting you down and that I've probably inconvenienced a lot of people, but I had no idea, when your studio invited me here, it was for *Sex with an Ex*." He spits out the title with undisguised contempt.

"Didn't the private detective explain it all to you?"

"No. She just said that Marcus needed some help with the wedding preparations. I thought I was being invited on to a show similar to *Surprise Surprise*."

I consider this. It is possible that our researchers and detective deliberately misled Darren. Or at the very least kept him in the dark. They too must have recognized that Darren would be great for ratings.

"Nothing on this earth would induce me to be on *Sex with an Ex*."

"Why not?" Frankly, I'm stunned. He's saying no. No to the opportunity of being on TV. No to the opportunity of seducing an ex. No to *me*.

"Because you are undermining everything I hold dear. Love, marriage, fidelity, constancy. I can't do it."

I'm amazed. A man who owns up to feeling these things must be gay. But I know he's not. I mentally shake myself. Fuck. Twat. I haven't got time for this. I'm busy. I don't need some half-average-looking bloke, who has too high an opinion of himself, screwing things up for me now. I glare at him. I breathe deeply.

"But Darren, why not? Marcus wants this," I say reasonably.

"Then Marcus is wrong."

"He wants to test her."

"He'd do better to trust her."

"You're joking, right?"

"Deadly serious."

I check my watch. I have to speed this along. I have the other guests to meet still. First interview of the New Year and I run into a hitch immediately. If I were the superstitious kind, I'd think it was an omen. But I'm not.

"Look, Darren, is this a question of money? You see we can't offer our guests hard cash, our lawyers won't let us. But we can make this worth your while in expenses. Clothes, travel, entertainment, etc." I mentally calculate what I can up the budget to. We normally expect an outlay of up to £600 per guest.

"It's nothing to do with money." Darren rests his head in his hands and leans back against the sofa.

"We can go up to eight hundred pounds."

"I just think it's ignoble."

"Fifteen hundred."

He shakes his head fractionally. And casually crosses his legs. They are extremely long. I take a deep breath.

"Two thousand."

He doesn't acknowledge my offer. I make a quick cancellation. This man is extremely intelligent, sensitive, stunningly good-looking. Even I, *fleetingly*, had found him attractive. Until he started arsing around like this. Now I realize he's a wanker. But, generally, people aren't as perceptive as I am. Audiences will like him. Bale will love him. How much?

"Four thousand pounds." I hear Fi gasp. Darren smiles pleasantly, too astute to be insulted. He looks extremely confident. He shakes his head. I lean close to him. My mouth is only inches away from his ear.

"It's my final offer," I whisper. He smiles. I look closer. He's resolute. Damn.

"Big prick," I comment to Fi, as I charge out of the room. I don't even check if the door has banged shut behind me.

"Almost certainly has," she comments.

I glare at her. "I wasn't commenting on his equipment," I snarl. "More his manner."

"I thought he was utterly charming," she confesses, blushing.

I sigh, irritated. "What exactly is charming about fucking up our shooting schedule?" I rage. "Do you think Bale will be charmed?"

"Guess not."

I begin to charge down the corridor toward the other interview rooms. We are on an extremely tight schedule. We've moved *Sex with an Ex* from the Monday slot to Saturday, which has cranked up the pressure by one more near-infeasible notch. We have to complete the interviews tonight. For both liaisons, pre and post advertisements break. We have to choose the location for the temptation scene. Tomorrow we have to arrange all the logistics for all the parties in each liaison. Film on Wednesday and Thursday and then edit on Friday. The entire team regularly work at the weekends. I don't need spanners in works. I don't have time for mistakes, misgivings or misjudgments.

"So who do we have on reserve? Give me the briefing notes," I hold out my hand waiting for the relevant file.

"Err." Fi looks a bit shamefaced. "We haven't one."

I stop abruptly. "What?"

"We did have. But we don't now. Mr. P. Kent marrying a Ms. L. Gripton were in reserve but he called the wedding off. I actually think he was using the show as a way to get rid of her. But he found the courage to do it without us." Fi smiles brightly and I consider murdering her. I don't have time. When did she become stupid?

"How fabulous for him. What a shame for Ms. Gripton and what a bloody disaster for us." I'm not shouting. I'm too angry to shout. "We always have two reserve options. Who are the others?"

"Well, there's a bit of a problem there too," mumbles Fi. "The bride-to-be broke her leg. She's unlikely to try to conduct an illicit liaison when she's in a toe-to-hip cast."

"Such bad luck," I snarl.

"Isn't it? The wedding photos will be ruined."

"I mean ours. Fi, go back to your office and paw over every letter we've received. See if there is anyone who we can reach tonight. Who's on next week's show? Is there a case we can bring forward?

Leave no stone unturned. If you can't find anyone in the letters pile, go on the Internet and set up an emergency telephone line, run it tonight." Fi starts to dash down the corridor. I call after her, "Fi, do you know anyone who's engaged? Check your Filofax. I'll check mine." Fi starts to object. I sweep away her squeamishness. "This is important."

I check my watch. It's 6:30 P.M. I bleep for the *Sex with the Ex* runner. I know it will take some time to locate Trixxie because our policy for employing runners is another one of Bale's economy-driven strategies. Instead of recognizing that the runner on a show is a lynchpin and needs to be astute, willing, energetic and proactive, TV6 employs the defective offspring of our big advertisers. More proof that Bale is a sycophantic stinge. He gets to suck the cock of his most important clients and at the same time is able to pay below the minimum wage, in the knowledge that Daddy will supplement with an allowance. I wait nine and a half minutes for Trixxie to respond to my page. She is undoubtedly doing something really pressing, like smoking hash or fixing her makeup or choosing the correct piece of metal to put in her eyebrow. When she eventually does show, I realize that "respond" is probably too kind a description.

"Like, can I do something?" she asks with a tone that is somewhere between careless and gormless. She is in reality about twenty-two but looks about six, as she is anorexic-thin, wears her hair in bunchies and has a number of bruises on her legs. The bruises are not, however, the result of playground bullying but UBIs—unidentified beer injuries. Unrestrained partying is part of the job. In fact, she thinks it is the job. She's paid a pittance but she's worth less. I tell her to go directly to Darren and delay him.

"Delay him?" she drawls. Redefining the adjective non-comprehending.

"Yes. He wants to leave."

"But he can't, he's filming this week and whatever."

"He doesn't want to film," I explain with what absolutely must be my last ounce of patience.

"That's bad."

I sigh, far too aware that incompetents surround me. Trixxie stumbles on an obstacle. "I can't force him to stay against his will or whatever."

"I know that. You have to persuade him to stay by making it worth his while."

"Sleeping with him?" she asks.

I look at the specimen in front of me. Darren wouldn't. I think on my feet. I need Darren on the show. He'd make a great show and more urgently, because of Fi's incompetence in securing a reserve, he's our only chance at any show. I have to keep this lead, as tenuous as it is, warm until we've explored all other angles.

"No, don't offer to sleep with him. Appeal to his better side. Say that I'm cool with his decision and would like to take him to dinner later, to show there's no hard feelings etc." I'm sure he'll agree to dinner. He's too polite not to.

"That's big of you," says Trixxie, beaming at me. "Really cool. Like you could be pissed off and whatever."

I don't bother explaining that in reality I'd like to dissect Darren into small pieces and feed him to the lions at London Zoo for inconveniencing me so. I don't think Trixxie is up to the deception. In fact, I'm not sure she is up to delivering the message. And there's something else that I don't mention. As irritating as I obviously find Darren, I'm also absolutely fascinated. He said *no* to me. He said no to *me*. Not the type of no which really means "yes" or "maybe." A flat, final no. Try as I might, I can't think of him as the moralistic tosspot loser that he so obviously is.

I interview the two women involved in the other liaison for next week's show. It calms me somewhat. I predict that the guy being tested will fall. I always think that there is a better chance of unfaithfulness if the men are being tested. It's not that women are fundamentally more faithful, it's just that women are more involved in the wedding preparation and are less likely to jeopardize their big day. I check my watch. It's 8:15 P.M. I call Fi and as I feared she's not hopeful about finding a reserve at such short notice. I threaten, cajole and bribe her into working through the night. I tell her to use the overtime quota and call in any reserves from the research department that she thinks is necessary.

"And what are you going to do?" she asks.

"I'm going to take Darren for dinner."

There's a silence. Eventually she comments, "Tough work, but someone's got to do it."

"It really is work," I insist. "I expect he's going to be fabulously dull." I'd like to mean this but my groin obviously disagrees, as my knickers think it's Fireworks Night. "I don't want to spend any more time with him than I have to, but we *do* need a show," I insist. "I'm going to persuade him to see our point of view."

"Well, I could go instead of you," volunteers Fi, with an enthusiasm that has been notably lacking in the past.

"You are not manipulative enough. You'd want to sleep with him."

"So do you."

"But you'd fall for him emotionally. I never do that." She can't argue with this. I continue, "We need to understand where he's coming from. He doesn't want to do the show because he realizes that his actions will have consequences, people will be hurt and humiliated. Irritating as hell. I think all we can do is try to appeal to his disproportionate and displaced sense of decency. I'm going to explain how a program affects more than the people on the show; advertisers will be inconvenienced, audiences will be disappointed and you and I will lose our jobs." I hope it won't come to this but Bale is unpredictable. My head aches. I squeeze my temples.

I'm desperate to see Darren again.

But only because I need a show. I think his moralistic approach is misplaced.

Quite attractive.

Bloody irritating.

"Fi?"

"Yes."

"What should I wear?"

We arrange to meet at the Oxo tower. Trixxie has booked the restaurant rather than the brasserie. Good work. He can't fail to be impressed by the spongy leather tub chairs, the complicated wine list, the blue-white linen tablecloths, the huge, elegant wine goblets which are designed so that even Ten-ton Tessie would feel delicately petite—or maybe that's an exclusively girl thing.

I arrive before him. I survey the restaurant. It is 9:00 P.M. and the restaurant is full of people cheerfully initiating voyages of the heart. By 2:00 A.M. the streets will be littered with the grieving casualties. This is true of every restaurant in London. I am wearing a black roll-neck jumper and on-the-knee black wool skirt. Heavy biker boots that are so chunky my legs look matchstick-thin. I have a hunch that this is more Darren's cup of Typhoo than low-neck lines and high hemlines. This is currently my sexiest outfit, albeit understated sexy. I keep it in the office, if not for this exact occasion, then certainly for something similar. Issue is I'm not sure what the exact nature of this occasion is. I'm clear that I want him in line, on board, part of the family. I do need a show.

But.

Or rather and. And, while I'm not sure *why*, I am sure *that* I want to see him again.

I see him arrive and I'm gratified to notice he's changed clothes too. He's wearing a light gray suit and a wide-collar, open, white shirt. It shows off his olive skin brilliantly. He looks gorgeous. He walks confidently to my table and leans in to kiss me.

Kiss me.

On the cheek.

I nearly knock over the bottle of mineral water that I've ordered, which by anyone's standards would be uncool. His kiss scorches my face. I'm sure I'm branded like an animal. It takes every ounce of courage, sense and control I have to stop myself snogging him on the spot. I feel an overwhelming pull internally. It starts in my thighs and moves upward, enveloping my lungs, intestines and throat. What is wrong with me? I have experienced sexual attraction before. Keen sexual attraction, but this . . . This is something new.

I'm not threatened.

I know I'm cool as long as he's either tediously dull or arrogant.

I already know he's neither.

He sits down and smiles at the waitress. I notice that she nearly keels over on the spot. He orders the wine, giving me a cursory opportunity to offer up a preference, but he has taken control.

"I'm really pleased that you suggested this dinner, Cas. And somewhat surprised. I didn't expect you to take my views so well. Anyway your 'runner' "—he manages to say the term using inverted commas, which is exactly how I describe Trixxie—"your runner informed me that you'd like to take me for dinner. Well, that's daft. I'm very aware that I must have inconvenienced you and I insist this is my treat."

"But I can get this on expenses," I offer weakly. My being weak surprises me. I rarely am. In fact, the last recorded example of my being weak was pre toilet-training. But Darren is breaking all the rules. He's not overwhelmed or intimidated by me, nor is he excessively combative. Every other man I've ever met has fallen into one of these categories.

"I know that but, really, I'd hate to profit from your show in any way and"—he pauses and raises one of his eyebrows—"I'd really like to buy you dinner." He has a soft, velvet voice, so I have to lean close to him to hear him. As I lean close I note that he smells amazing. If I hadn't met him in these circumstances I'd think of fucking him.

No. I wouldn't have to think.

But the thought is irrelevant, as the business I have to concentrate on is not funny business. It's not funny at all. I have four days to get the next show in the can.

I think he's wearing Issey Miyake.

I am extremely aware that the balance of power is definitely not in my favor. I remind myself again: the primary reason for my being here is that I must persuade him to be on the show. And even if he is drop-dead gorgeous, so what?

He's drop-dead gorgeous, that's what.

I stare at the menu, pretending to be interested; a toss-up between wood-roasted squid stuffed with chili, or red mullet in white wine, parsley and garlic sauce. No, not garlic. Really I need to broach the subject of the show.

"Why would you want to buy me dinner?"

He blushes and then drags his eyes to meet mine. "Any man would want to take you for dinner. You're stunning."

Bang.

I am delighted, thrilled to my core. Yes, I've heard it before. Yes, I'll hear it again but really it's never been quite so thrilling. Or terrifying. His up-front approach propels me into a unique position. I'm honest in return.

"Look, Darren. Cards on the table, I'm not here to be social. I'm here to try to persuade you to be on the show. I need you. I'm embarrassed to admit it but I need a show and you're it." I stop and take a deep breath. The bread arrives. He doesn't comment for a while. Instead he chooses his bread. He selects the walnut one. In an effort to ingratiate myself I do the same.

"I'm sorry you didn't want to have dinner with me."

"I didn't say—"

"I'm not going to be on your show."

"Why not?"

"Because I couldn't face myself in the mirror every morning if I did so. Myself or my parents or siblings, friends, nieces, nephew."

No girlfriend. He didn't mention a girlfriend.

"Why not?"

"Because you are peddling the destabilization of family values."

I sigh. I've heard it all before. Somehow the general public has convinced itself that TV is responsible for the disintegration of the family unit. It's a way of avoiding responsibility. It's not fair.

"The family unit is under pressure for myriad reasons. Television is only one," I argue. "There have been countless surveys that have tried to assess the effect television has on modem society but net net, bottom line, psychologists, educationalist and moralists have failed to agree that there has been *any* effect at all. How can you expect little old me to have all the answers?" I'm trying to appear girlish and agreeable.

"You are endorsing the gradual deconstruction of decency. You are encouraging the trivialization of love and sex." He butters his bread ferociously. He has magnificent hands. Very strong-looking. I reach for my wine.

"Darren, no one needed me to do that. There were Blackpool postcards long before TV.".

"So you accept your show is in poor taste, indecent and a contributor to the erosion of public standards?"

The waitress interrupts to take our order.

"Taste is arbitrary, it changes according to fashion. Good taste is revised with every issue of *Vogue*. Decency I understand—a regard for cultural and religious issues, i.e. sending sympathy cards when some old dear pops her Patrick Cox." I fall back on familiar territory, sarcasm. "But standards, are they somewhere between the two? Like giving up your seat to a pregnant woman when traveling by tube, or more emphatically not traveling on public transport at all. And who is the standard setter? The law? The Independent Television Commission? The public? You? Are you the judge and jury in this, Darren?" I'm raising my voice. He's got me riled. The seating is tight; there's no room for hysteria. I lower my voice in an effort to regain control. "I've always avoided racism. I don't patronize people with disabilities. There's no violence, we beep out the bad language and we don't show actual penetration."

"How magnanimous of you."

I'm not sure he means this. I take a deep breath. This conversation is not going in the direction I expected. It's wrong by about 180 degrees, and Issie isn't even navigating. I had planned to be beguiling, flirtatious and coquettish. This is usually a successful ruse. Instead I'm behaving like Attila the Hun's more ferocious big sister. More peculiar still, I actually do want this man to see my point of view. Not simply to get him on the show: suddenly I want him to respect me. Wanting his respect makes it impossible to flirt. How much have I drunk? We both take a break as we sip our wine. It's a '96 Puligny-Montrachet. It's very fine.

"Nice wine, good choice," I comment.

"Thank you." Darren is not going to be side-tracked. He pursues his line of reasoning. "TV has exercised an unanticipated and unprecedented influence. Not since the invention of the wheel has anything been so transforming."

Someone's dropped an Alka Seltzer in my knickers. Although I don't like his argument I am delighted that he sees he importance of TV. So few people do and as I'm passionate about it, I'm thrilled to find someone else who has an opinion, even if it is so condemning. I'm also ecstatic to be debating with him. The sparks, intellectual, emotional and sexual, are all but visible. Darren stares right at me; his divine eyes lock on mine so tightly that I can't, however hard I try, break his gaze.

"You must see how influential TV is, and therefore what a responsibility you hold. Your programs articulate the world we live in. You're saying that deception is OK, infidelity par for the course."

We sit, sulky and silent. Listening to the clink of bottles and cutlery, and the hum of indistinguishable voices. Indistinguishable, that is, except for the table next to mine, where I can definitely hear the nervous pleas of a guy who is being ditched. The waitress brings our food. I sip my soup, carrot and coriander. It's not particularly a favorite of mine but it was top of the menu and I didn't have time to think about my selection. He is chasing skinny bits of courgette around his plate. He doesn't seem much interested in his food either. The silence is thunderous.

"So what else do you do, Cas?"

The sudden change of conversation throws me. Else? Else? Er. I'm too exhausted to think of anything creative, flirty or interesting so I plummet for the truth.

"My friends Issie and Josh, the gym and men. Oh, and my mum—on a Sunday."

Darren laughs. "So nothing conventional like stamp collecting or mud wrestling then?"

I smile. "I've tried mud wrestling."

He laughs again. "Tell me about the men, Cas."

There is another tiny pulse in my groin. Is he flirting with me? Please.

"Men fall into three categories for me. Those I'd sleep with. Those I wouldn't and Josh."

"So who wouldn't you sleep with?"

He is flirting!

Or maybe he's just trying to get a handle.

Why don't I know? I always know men.

"My friends' boyfriends and husbands, ugly or stupid men, and men I've already slept with." He moves his fork fractionally, indicating that he is interested and that I should carry on. 'My friends' boyfriends are safe because, despite the world being awash with infidelity and deceit, I don't do that to my friends." This is true and the nearest I have to a moral code. "Besides which they just aren't appealing."

He raises an eyebrow again. Which is such a cliché and, regrettably, soooooo sexy.

"I'm not saying anyone who would go out with my mates must be unattractive, far from it. It's just that my friends and I tell each other *everything*. By the time I know about their boyfriends picking their toenails, the filthy tricks they get up to loo brushes, the farting in bed then going under the sheets to smell it, they just aren't sexy." He's grinning. I'm being serious. "Intimacy breeds revulsion. The reason for not sleeping with ugly or stupid men is transparent. Men I've slept with have no allure for me. I rarely do repeat performances." I pause.

I wonder if he's noticed that, by definition, he is a man I'd sleep with?

"You seem to have it all worked out." I nod. Which causes his grin to broaden into a smile. Is he being ironic? "Can I ask you something?"

"Ask away and then I'll decide if I'll answer." In my experience, the questions people ask are just as telling as the answers they give.

"Have you been unlucky in love, as they say?" He blushes. "I mean, I only ask because I was wondering why you have such a mercenary attitude toward love."

I choose not to take offense.

"Of course I've been unlucky in love. If you meet a woman who hasn't been unlucky in love, look for the little electronic chip behind her ear." I always use this line. I grin and fork a mound of food into my mouth. I wonder if he's the type of man who finds a voracious appetite on a woman a turn-on?

"So who was he?" Same old question that all men ask. I have an answer rehearsed.

"Er, my first lover," I bluff. I pause with my folk halfway between my mouth and plate.

The implication is that the memory is so painful that momentarily I can't eat. Men like to think women are too sensitive to ever fully recover from a broken heart. It fits in with their view of us as delicate flowers.

"Was it a long-term relationship?"

These incessant questions. I hesitate. "A couple of weeks."

"A couple of weeks." His tone is somewhere between incredibility and hilarity. That's not the script. He's supposed to be touched by the intensity of the affair. "But you said your first lover." He seems confused. "That must have been—"

"A long time ago. Yes. I don't get over things easily. I'm very sensitive."

He stares at me. We've only just met but we both know how untrue this is. Darren's too polite to openly refute my statement.

"But you can't still be getting over an affair that took place over a decade ago and only lasted a few weeks."

Good point. First time it's ever been made, which goes to show that the scores of other men who I've said the same to weren't paying attention.

"What *really* hurt you?"

This is unique and I haven't got a practiced answer to hand. I look at Darren and his face surprises me even more than his original line of questioning. He seems genuinely concerned. I'm genuinely perplexed. I mean, what can I say? "My first lover irritated me but frankly my heart hasn't ever been broken. I'm just a bitch." It seems an unlikely solution. After all, it is the truth. He tilts his head a fraction in my direction. He's astonishingly close. His long hair is falling in front of his eyes and although not quite touching my skin, it is touching the hairs on my forehead. There is acid in my knickers. My throat is dry and my breasts are straining upwards, obviously hoping he'll swoop down and kiss them. Hello, sexual tension. I shake my head.

"Hmmm?" he prompts.

"What?" My mind has undergone a spring clean and I can't remember what he asked me. His eyes are fabulous. Brown. A cluster of really rich browns, like autumn leaves piled up under a tree. Suddenly Darren appears embarrassed.

"Sorry, I shouldn't have asked that. Erm—" He scrambles around for a recovery conversation. "Tell me about Josh."

I'm grateful that he's let me off the hook and garble, "Josh is my only male, platonic friend. I've known him since we were kids. He has too much dirt on me to risk me falling out with him. He could sell to the press when I'm rich and famous."

"Is that your ambition, to be famous?"

"Isn't it everyone's? Frankly I'm confident that Josh wouldn't do that. Despite all odds, tantrums, time and the tenuous nature of platonic love, Josh and I adore each other. We trust each other and would never hurt one another." I pause and consider what I've just said. "Perhaps this is *because* of all the tantrums, time and the tenacious nature of platonic love." I grin at Darren. Suddenly I'm overwhelmed with embarrassment. Why am I saying this? I'm telling him about myself. I'm being truthful and straightforward. What has possessed me? I hate people knowing more about me than I know about them. I *never* do this. I try to hide the sudden intimacy in humor. "Besides which, I have a incriminating photo of him dressed in suspenders and a basque, he claims this was for *A Rocky Horror Show* party but I'm not convinced."

Darren laughs.

The conversation is snappy, intense and truthful. I'm overwhelmed. Darren and I have finished a bottle of wine. We are, in fact, halfway through our second bottle. We drift from topic to topic. My clipboard detailed that he's a tree surgeon, which apparently means that he is based at London University, where he has an office and a lab but he travels to, well, wherever there is a sick tree by the sound of it. This is at once strange—as it is so individual—and at the same time expected. It's extremely fitting; I sort of imagine him working outdoors and with his hands. This connection throws me into confusion, as I have images of rolling around a park with him. I see myself picking leaves out of my hair and twigs from my ruffled clothes. Of course he has no idea what I'm thinking but the way he stares at me suggests that he is privy to my X-rated daydream. I struggle to think of anything suitable to say.

"I've never known a tree surgeon."

He laughs again. I guess that isn't my best line ever. I try another. "Fantastic view of the river from here, isn't there?"

"This is one of my favorite buildings in London, actually," agrees Darren.

"Really." Bullseye.

"Yeah, the view is amazing, as you said, and I like the brickwork."

"You said *one* of your favorite buildings. Which others do you like?" As if I care.

"My favorite, by some way, is the Natural History Museum, I like everything about it. How and why it was conceived. The structure, the brickwork, the lighting, the contents, the concept." How can anyone be this animated by a building full of stuff? Not even stuff you can buy.

"What's your favorite building?" he asks.

"I haven't thought about it before. I don't think anyone's ever asked me." I consider it for a moment. "Bibendum. You know, the restaurant in South Kensington."

"Why?"

I could tell him that I adore the stained-glass windows and the unusual tiling that François Espinasse designed in 1911, but I don't want him to get the impression that I'm anything other than shallow.

"It's kind of a Golden Gate. It heralds the entrance to shop heaven—Joseph, Paul Smith and Conran. Besides which they sell fabulous oysters." I smile coolly and he laughs again.

The evening flies by and I am keenly aware that I haven't really talked about getting him to appear on the show. Which is careless of me—I rarely diversify from my agenda. I drag myself back to the point.

"So why did you and Claire split up?"

Frankly I'm confused. He's clever, handsome and filthily sexy. I only have Marcus's statement, which is an unreliable source. Marcus will have received a sanitized version of events from Claire, which he'll have distorted in his head with neurotic paranoia. If I can get Darren to reveal the reason he and Claire split up, I'll be able to manipulate the facts to justify why he should go on the show.

Besides which I'm interested.

"We were a casualty of cohabitation."

"What do you mean?"

"What's your phrase? Intimacy breeds revulsion. Well, in our case it certainly bred irritation. We liked one another, even loved one another well enough before we moved in together, and then it started. The rot set in."

"What, you started to take each other for granted? Became complacent?"

"Nothing as dramatic. She didn't like the way I kept film in the fridge. I hated the way her beauty product things seemed to be procreating all over the dressing table. She hated Sky Sport."

I gasp, shocked.

"I loathe soaps."

I'm horrified. What that girl must have put up with.

"I like to read in bed. She likes the light out immediately. And then it escalated. She began to hate my friends. I hated her hairs in the bath. She, my laugh. Me, her mother. I'd forgotten all this until I talked to Marcus earlier today. He said she was shopping. I knew that she'd be buying Easter eggs although it's only January. Her organization was always horribly efficient. I hated it. There was no spontaneity. The truth is, we split up because we weren't suited. We're not together because it didn't work and we shouldn't be together. Why else do people ever split up? It's so easy to look back on a past relationship and idealize it."

Thank God. This is the whole premise of my program.

"I've never met anyone as right as Claire was for me but it still doesn't alter the fact that she wasn't 100 percent right."

"90 percent is pretty good."

"She wasn't even that."

"85 percent," I suggest.

"Nearer 65 percent." There is an unaccountable warm glow of delight in my stomach. He's right, 65 percent doesn't sound like the One.

If you believe in the One.

Which I don't.

"So you are really over her?" I'm disproportionately anxious to hear his reply. Which I hate myself for.

"Yes."

"Then what harm can there be in appearing on the show? Can't you just tempt her and leave it at that?"

Darren forces his mouth into a wry grin. Does he think I'm joking?

"You just don't get it, do you, Cas? Your show's a travesty. Besides which I loved her once. Why would I want to hurt her? I doubt she'd be tempted by me—"

"I think she would," I interrupt enthusiastically.

"Thank you." Darren's face relaxes into the widest smile I've seen all evening. Ever, in fact.

Arrogant bugger!

"I didn't mean it as a compliment," I mutter sulkily into my plate. Unperturbed, his smile widens an unfeasible fraction further.

"I'll take it as one anyway."

I scowl but try to appear unflustered by playing with the stem of my wine glass, caressing it as though it were a brand new pashmino. "Well, if you are convinced that Claire wouldn't fall, the program might be good for her and Marcus. We did have one couple, before Christmas, who managed to resist."

"Yes, I read about that. TV6 turned their wedding into a media frenzy," says Darren with obvious disgust. "That must have been marvelous for the ratings. Cas, haven't you been listening to me? It's not about whether she would want me or not. Any association with *Sex with an Ex* is contemptible. A need to 'test' someone you should love exposes the fact that there is a problem with the relationship. I don't want to embarrass Claire or anyone else for that matter. I don't want her to know that her fiancé has this insecurity. I don't want to drag up our past, not even to entertain your—what did you say?—8.9 million viewers." I nod. "I loved her and that fact is still important and private."

He believes all this. I look at him, this six-foot-two specimen of pure sex, sitting in front of me. I don't understand him. He seems to be from another era. One that is perhaps a little more genteel. And trusting.

And pointless.

I try to think about my initial strategy.

"Look, Darren, this show isn't just about entertaining the general public. There are a lot of other serious issues hanging in the balance here."

"Such as?"

"My job, the jobs of about thirty-five other people, advertising revenues."

"I'm sorry." Darren calls the waitress and asks for the bill. It's time to go. I'm disappointed. The restaurant may be empty but I don't want to leave. I try to think of something else that will be damaged if the show doesn't go ahead. There's my ratings-related bonus. I don't think it's wise to mention this. I sigh, resigned. The quiet determined way he explains his views convinces me that he won't change his mind tonight. I suppose it does sort of make sense in a horribly moral way. Never again will I attempt getting a thinking man on the show. I'll stick to Neanderthals.

We leave the restaurant and start to wander back to the tube, past the National Theatre, the Royal Festival Hall, the Hayward Gallery, The Queen Elizabeth Hall. Although it is January my shirt is sticking to my back with sweat. I hope I'm not coming down with flu. Couples are edging up to one another, the foolish myth of intimacy protecting them against the late-night chill that is settling. And it must be chilly because the people who are on their own pull their coats about them. My bag weighs a ton. It's full of my life: notebooks, Dictaphones, research manuals, schedules. The weight of it drags my shoulder down to the right, causing me to lean. I occasionally bump into Darren. Each time I do so I tut so that he, at least, is clear that it's an accidental collision and I don't like it.

My senses are on red alert. I can feel the cold night air not brushing my skin but laying icy hands on my forehead and shoulders. I hear a train rattle across Charing Cross bridge, splitting the night. Sparkly lights outline the bridges and pavements. An adult dot to dot. There is metal on my tongue. I can smell sweat, fresh and stuff that's months old. The fresh twang is mingled with Darren's aftershave. It rinses my nostrils. I tut at the dreamers hanging around the National Film Theatre, lost in nostalgia or stupefied with pointless hope.

"Look at them," I spit. "Incapable of getting off their arses and doing something real."

Darren surprises me by laughing. "Is that all you see?"

"Yes." I look at the jugglers and pseudo-intellectuals. People happier to watch plays about other people's lives than actually live their own. "What else is there?"

"Look again," he insists. He puts both hands on my shoulders and turns me to look at the crowds. "You have to look at everything from as many different angles as possible. In as many ways as possible. Look at it and try to see it differently."

I look again and see scores of people hanging out. Some are drinking coffee sold from the cafés at the theaters. Others are standing around the buskers. Others are debating with one another or chatting animatedly about the performance they have just seen. Others are snogging the face off each other. I shrug.

"Don't you see dozens of people having a good time, improving and enjoying themselves? A mass of humanity buzzing with just being here."

"No."

"Again. Look closer," he insists.

There is one old guy playing a violin. He's ancient; he has a long, white beard. He is playing Vivaldi's "Spring." He skips lightly through the air, barely landing before rising again, his skinny limbs tapering in effortless rhythm. Grudgingly I throw some coins into his battered Panama. He is talented. He moves his head in a slight dip, more dignified than a bow. Darren smiles at me. I smile back.

We cross over the river and reach Embankment tube station. It's heaving. A burly mass of drunks in suits and drunks in rags. Distinguishable simply by their disposable incomes. Darren fights, through the morons and marauders, to the ticket machine. He buys our tickets. Mine for east London, his for south. We're on separate lines and going in separate directions.

"Will you be OK getting home?"

"Fine. I'm a tube veteran." This is a lie. I usually catch a cab but if I say so I'll have to explain why I've just walked half a mile to the tube station. Which I can't explain, not even to myself.

"Well, it's been great to meet you, Cas. A very entertaining evening." Darren stops and turns to face me.

"I bet you've hated every second."

"Not at all." He hesitates, then adds, "The reverse."

I smile broadly, relieved. "Well, goodnight."

"Goodnight." Neither of us moves. Suddenly this feels very date-like. Will he kiss me? Is he going to shake my hand? He leans in and I think he's going to kiss my cheek so I move my head suddenly. In fact, it appears his original target was my lips but my sudden maneuver means that his smacker ends up somewhere between my chin and earring. We jump apart and Darren heads toward the ticket barrier. It's certain. He's going to walk out of my life and back to his trees.

And right now I can't think of anything more soul-destroying.

My reluctance over letting him go *must* be attributable to the amount of wine I've drunk. Isn't it? God, I really fear it's more than that.

"Darren!" My yell slices through the crowds and almost as though he'd been waiting, Darren responds immediately by turning and walking straight back to me. I usher him away from the tube station and crowd back toward the river. I'm buying time as I formulate a plan.

"At the very least I have to be *seen* to have done everything in my power to persuade you to come on the show."

"You have," he assures.

"Not everything."

Darren looks a bit shocked. "Are you going to—"

I read his mind. "No. Not that," I interrupt, understanding at once that he thinks I am going to offer to have sex with him. I'm unaccountably insulted. Darren blushes.

"That's a relief." Then he blushes again. "Not that I wouldn't want to, but the circumstances are—"

I help us both out by interrupting him. Before I've even thought about what I'm going to say, or why I'm saying it, or the consequences of opening my mouth at all, habitual bullshitting kicks in.

"No, my proposition is of a different nature. I'd like to be given the chance to present my side of the story. To do that I'd need to spend some time with you. I'd need to shadow you for a day or so." It's a gamble but I'm a player. He looks at me doubtfully.

"You won't change my mind."

"Maybe not, but at least give me the opportunity to appear to have done my best. It will save my bacon with the guys at TV6."

This isn't true. In fact, what I should do now is return to the studio and help Fi recruit a replacement scenario.

But after spending the evening with him I know that if he were to appear on *Sex with an Ex*, it would be the best show ever. He's delicious-looking, articulate, sexy and moral. If I could publicize his objections and how we overcame them, the entire country would support *Sex with an Ex*. There have been some objections to the show. Few and far between, and in my opinion mostly hypocritical. But those who are squeamish about weddings collapsing like stacked cards would surely throw their lot in with TV6 if someone like Darren has. Who could resist Darren? And although I can't be sure that he will be persuaded I've got to give it my best shot.

I begin to mentally rearrange my schedule and calculate how much Fi will be able to handle on her own if I'm not in the studio. At the same time that I'm making these hurried calculations, trying to predict scenarios, outcomes and consequences, Darren is leisurely weighing up the proposition, which he has taken at face value.

"I was taking the week off work, expecting to be on the show. Now I'm planning on going to see my parents and family." With something near reluctance, he sighs, "You won't change my mind but if it helps you out with your bosses, you can join me for a couple of days."

"Great." I smile. Agreeing before I know whether I mean it. "So where do your parents live?"

"Whitby."

"Where?"

He laughs, "Whitby, you know, in North Yorkshire." No, I don't know. It sounds a long way off. It sounds a different and uncivilized world. But the show must go on. How bad can it be? I nod and try to appear informed without committing myself.

"OK, Cas, I'm happy for you to shadow me, if that's the official term, but I think we'd both have a better time if you started to trust me and enjoy yourself."

I'm not here to enjoy myself and I don't do trust. I bite my tongue and resist pointing out either of these pertinent facts.

"Trust simply leads to disappointment," I state frankly.

"Listen to yourself, Cas. You are not convincing anyone with this super-hard bitch act."

He is very wrong. I've convinced eight primary school teachers, twelve senior school teachers, dozens of fellow students, scores of colleges, numerous girlfriends, exactly fifty-three lovers and my mother. Even Issie, painful as it is for her, admits from time to time, "You can be so callous." What is this obsession with being soft? Isn't it obviously asking for trouble? Asking to end up hurt, abused, alone? I like being impenetrable. I don't want to be discovered.

Darren pauses and stares out at the river. It's twinkling, which surprises me. I always think of the Thames as a rest point for crap and sanitary towels.

"You know what I think?"

"No, bowl me over," I sigh.

"You just want to be discovered. You want someone to make the effort and scratch the surface. You want to be loved. You just want to make it difficult. A modern-day Agamemnon challenges. You are the same as every woman I've ever met."

I didn't realize Darren could be so insulting.

I look at him and he is gorgeous. The streetlights are reflected in the river. The reflection bounces up to illuminate Darren. He looks like an angel. He smiles and he's mucky sexy. He looks like a devil. I've never come across anything so complex and compelling in my entire life. I realize that it's going to be more important than ever, and quite possibly harder than ever, to keep up my super-hard bitch act. And while my mind is resolving that I won't let my guard slip for a second, I hear my disloyal tongue say, "Oh bugger it. Go on then, show me a good time. I don't suppose you'll be able to." I grin my challenge. But even I don't believe me.

CHAPTER

nine

We meet at King's Cross Station. I spot Darren as soon as the cab sets me down. He stands out like a beacon. But then that's not so extraordinary as he's sharing the platform with prostitutes, beggars and commuters. As I approach him he takes my bag from me and briefly kisses me on the cheek. It's comfortable. It's unnerving.

"You look good," he murmurs, smiling appreciatively.

"What, this old thing?" I shrug.

"This old thing" was actually a look achieved after nine hours' searching through Issie's wardrobes and mine. I like the final effect. It's a sort of rock-chic-meets-country-girl ensemble. I think it works, although Issie had doubts. She had questioned whether a six-hundred-quid pony-skin skirt was appropriate for a dash around North Yorkshire. I ignored her advice; after all, she doesn't read the style pages. She also kept going on about how I'd be cold in a short-sleeved jumper. I explained that my upper arms were really toned at the moment and needed full exposure. She sighed and stuffed another cardigan in my bag. I'm grateful now because it is freezing on the platform.

Issie had been a bit irritating all around, while I packed for this tour of duty. She commented, "North Yorkshire sounds very romantic. Isn't that where the Brontës are from?" Is it? I thought it was Lancashire. Didn't all the Brontës die spinsters? I feigned ignorance.

"Besides which, we're going to visit his family. Have you ever known families to be romantic?"

Issie reminded me of the guy she met through her mother, on New Year's Eve. I reminded her that he never called. "So why are you going to Whitby, if you think it's going to be so dour?"

"I explained, Issie, I have to get him to agree to be on the show. It's a matter of professional and personal pride."

"Nothing more than pride?" I've been asking myself exactly the same thing all night.

"I've explained, he'd make a great show. He'd silence our few lingering critics."

"Nothing more than a great show?" asked Issie. She didn't sound as though she believed me. I admit Darren is interesting and funny and ridiculously fanciable. I admit that if Issie were choosing to travel halfway across the globe to visit some guy's family I'd think it was because she'd fallen for him. But the same can't be said of me, can it? I'm only doing this for the good of TV6.

"What else is there?" I asked, slipping my Manolo Blahnik lilac open-toe shoes into my bag. I would have been extremely grateful if Issie could have answered me; however, she just scowled.

"It doesn't sound like you have the faintest chance of getting him to change his mind."

"I don't know, I might have. After all, he agreed to let me shadow him."

"Yes, I wonder why he did that. Does he fancy you? I expect he does."

"More likely wants the opportunity to save my soul."

"Oh lord. His chances are poorer than yours," laughed Issie as she walked me to my waiting cab.

Yes, Issie was extremely irritating all around.

"I've bought your ticket. Come on, the train is in. Platform Three—we have to run," urges Darren.

Despite the fact that we are traveling zillions of miles to (practically) Scotland, the timetable tells me that we will arrive in Darlington in two and a half hours' time. I'm incredulous, but Darren explains it's the electric line. I'm still incredulous. What about the obligatory leaves on the track and the right and wrong types of snow? My heart plummets. Even if by some miracle the train does arrive on time, two and a half hours is going to seem like ten and a half. What will I say to Darren? It was OK chatting in the restaurant last night, but I'd had a shedload to drink. But now, in the cold light of day, I'm beginning to regret volunteering to shadow him. I know my chances of persuading Darren to appear on *Sex with an Ex* are slim. I could be on a wild goose chase! What will I do with myself outside London? How will the studio manage without me? Will Bale buy my reasoning for shadowing Darren? Besides all this, sitting on a train with a moralistic do-gooder is not my idea of fun. Even a devilishly attractive one.

The train journey is awesome.

Besides buying the ticket, Darren also had the foresight to buy up half the magazines and sweets in WH Smith's. I can't remember the last time anyone bought me sweets. Big fancy boxes of chocolates, yes, I get those by the dozen. I just pass them on to my mum. She eats some and gives the other boxes to local geriatrics (cellulite not being a major concern of theirs). But Darren hasn't bought me chocolates in a box. Instead he's bought the sweets of our childhoods, Jelly Babies, Licorice Allsorts, Flying Saucers and Sherbet Dib-dabs. Undoubtedly I'll feel sick by the time the journey is over. Even so, it's a good call. Instead of the slow and stilted conversation I feared, we have an unlimited avenue in discussing childhood. What were your favorite sweets as a kid? (He remembers Spangles, Space Dust and Cream Soda, he agrees that Snickers definitely used to be bigger and anyway they were Marathons.) What was the first book you read? (Neither of us is sure but, satisfyingly, he's clearer on his TV viewing habits; he recalls every episode of *Mr. Ben* and swears his sister looked the image of the girl who sat with the clown when there was nothing on TV.) So what was your favorite TV program? (We agree Mark from *Eastenders* will always be Tucker from *Grange Hill.*) When did you learn to swim? (He learned after seeing the ad with the fairy god-mother. I learned after seeing *Jaws.*) And while I remember all this I completely forget to uphold my icy reserve. Trivia, but this and reading magazines together means that the journey to Darlington flies past.

Reluctantly I acquiesce: he does a great line in small talk.

Grudgingly I have to admit that perhaps we do have some things in common.

But nothing fundamental.

I watch the landscapes change. The parks of the south melt into the woodlands of the Midlands, and in no time at all into the rugged, Gothic hills of the north. Although it's only mid-morning, the sky in North Yorkshire is mauve with damson clouds. Not the cottonwool clouds of textbooks but strong, imposing smudges, more like a painting a child would make with a thick brush. It's breathtakingly beautiful.

But then, once you've seen a scene, it's over with. It's not as though you can wear it.

I call Bale on my mobile to explain what I'm doing. It's a diffi-cult call, as I have to make it from the minuscule British Rail loo, awash with urine and with a dodgy door lock designed to make occupants nervous.

"If we get him on the show I'd put money on the fact that he'll be a pin-up within weeks and he'll have his own chat show within months," I enthuse to Bale.

"That good, hey?"

"That good," I assert.

"And do you think Fi will manage?"

I enthusiastically sing her praises to reassure him (it doesn't—

he's understandably suspicious). He wavers, trying to decide whether any guest can be worth my absence. I sense his indecision, so dramatically turn up the charm. I promise I'll give it two days and travel back overnight on Tuesday in time for Wednesday's filming. In the meantime, I reassure, he can reach me on my mobile.

When we arrive at Darlington station Darren's brother, Richard, is waiting for us. Richard is younger than Darren by three years, but he's beefier (that will be the fish and chips and Yorkshire pudding) and so looks a bit older. Darren's filled me in with details of his family. There is Sarah, who is thirty-seven, married with three kids. Darren who is thirty-three, like me. Richard, thirty, he's engaged to Shelly and finally Linda, who was a bit of a surprise to Mr. and Mrs. Smith. She's seventeen now. Darren is the only one who has moved away from home. I must ask why. Richard and Shelly are buying a house a few streets away from her parents. Sarah and her family live in a nearby village. I commit all these details to memory in an effort to flatter him and ingratiate myself to his family.

The two men slap each other on the back and this action instantly makes them appear boyish, but in the very best sense. Whilst not obviously showing affection by embracing, it's clear that they are delighted to see each other.

"Richard, this is Cas." Darren hesitates and then adds, "A friend." I'm strangely gratified to be described as such and therefore treat Richard to my most winning smile. Naturally he's enchanted and falls over himself to help me with my luggage. I catch Darren's eye; I want to know if he's noticed that I've impressed Richard. I can't be sure; he's laughing to himself.

I am keen to leave behind Darlington station. Not that there is anything particularly wrong with the station—it has everything one expects; small WH Smith, cookie-cut café and smelly loos— but it is a station and I try to avoid public transport whenever possible. However, I'm not thrilled when Richard indicates which is his car.

"The Escort?" I ask, hoping there's been a mistake.

"Yes. The one with the red door," says Richard.

"And the blue body," adds Darren in case the situation demanded any more clarity. I try not to show how disgruntled I am, but quietly climb into the back seat, which I share with furry dice (honestly) and an entire forest-worth of sweet wrappers.

I don't say much in the car journey from Darlington to Whitby. Instead I let Darren and Richard catch up with each other's news. As an only child I'm always fascinated to see siblings' reactions to one another. Richard is obviously delighted that Darren has paid this surprise visit. I can't imagine that my arrival anywhere would be awash with such excitement. Except perhaps for Harvey Nics—my personal shopper is always blissed out when she sees me. When Richard asks Darren how he came to have unplanned holiday, I'm unaccountably relieved that Darren fudges the answer. I'm also mollified when Darren comments vaguely that we "met at an interview." Richard obviously feels bad that I'm not part of the conversation and tries to include me by sharing details of the route.

"We're on the A66, heading east. We could've come across the new road. They both join at A171 to Whitby."

I'm not sure what response is required of me. This fascination with routes, alternative routes and "the road we could have taken" is definitely a boy thing. I nod, not committing, and turn to gaze out of the window.

I'm in a foreign land. Not least because of Richard's accent but also because of the strangeness of the landscape. It's an eclectic mix of the very modern (brand-new and impressive football stadiums, architecturally complex bridges), quaint, old-fashioned poverty (bingo halls and boarded-up shops) and stunning countryside (sheep). I notice that the women standing at the bus stops, in each village, look alike. They are fat and tired—don't they ever work out? Richard's Escort pauses at a red light for a couple of minutes and I look more closely. A woman is waiting at the bus stop; another shouts to her from a fifty-yard distance. The first one makes the bus wait while the other heaves her excessive weight and carrier bags to the stop. The driver of the bus becomes animated and jovial and doesn't seem to be too irritated by the delay. As the woman hoists herself on to the bus all the other travelers shout and wave to her. Am I missing something? Is she famous? I don't recognize her. But she must be because why else would they be so nice to her? The warmth they so obviously feel for one another momentarily sends a freak glow through me.

Which is a bloody miracle, considering that the temperatures I'm enduring are arctic.

As in a wartime era, the men on the streets are either very young or very old. They are malnourished. On the young men, this looks chippy and sexy; on the old men, it looks pathetic. I try to remember some facts from my geography A-level and the news in the eighties. North Yorkshire wasn't a community annihilated by the closing of the mines, was it? No, definitely not. It was a community ravaged by the collapse of the ship-building industry. I wonder where the men of working age are. Have they got on their bikes? Or are they at the Cargo Fleet Social Club doing their best to support the Bass dynasty?

I sigh, bored, losing interest in my own line of thought. A new level of tedium. It must be this place. I light a cigarette. Richard stares at me through the driving mirror. So as not to be rude I wind the window down an inch, which I think is very considerate of me in these sub-zero climes.

"Would you mind not smoking?" asks Richard.

I shift uncomfortably and for a second I'm tempted to say that yes, I would mind very much. I have a thirty-a-day habit to feed. I have a metabolism to send into frenzy. Instead I smile, falsely, and throw the cigarette out of the window. Richard doesn't congratulate me or thank me but simply nods curtly. I'm surprised. I thought he fancied me. The lust men normally experience when meeting me is, if not a license to print money, at least a certificate which exonerates me from obeying the no-smoking signs. What is it with these Smith blokes? Don't they have hormones?

The towns disappear and soon even the villages are spasmodic. The bleak warehouses and graffitied bus stops detailing that, despite the odds, "JEZ LUVS BREND 4EVER," vanish and are replaced by wide open fields of mud, splashed with snow, ice and the odd farmhouse. The sky is still lavender but is now streaked with silver layers of light.

"I can see the sea," shout Richard and Darren at once. Then they both laugh. "It's sort of a family tradition," explains Darren. "Not a very unique one at that. I'm sure you know the sort of thing." I don't, but I follow their gaze anyway.

"It's beautiful," I sigh, despite myself. And I immediately regret saying so. My city platitude hardly captures the breathtaking splendor of the scene and I do try to make it a rule not to say anything unless it is original or cutting, yet I'm at a loss for words that are grandiose enough. I catch sight of Darren's face in the wing mirror. He smiles at me as though he finds my lackluster comment adequate.

"You don't think you'll be too bored, then?" he asks. Does he have a tent at a funfair to practice this mind-reading thing?

"No, I think I'll find enough to amuse me," I answer honestly, with only a smidgen of flirtation.

Richard wiggles uncomfortably.

Whitby is higgledy-piggledy. Built on an undulating coastline, the houses and teashops (closed) look precariously stacked. We steer through narrow streets and climb steep slopes. I'm suddenly in a period drama. Eventually we draw up in front of a row of terraced street houses. I am sure they are going to fall into the sea if anyone coughs too loudly. Darren assures me that the houses are tougher than they look. As they've been in place for over a hundred years. I concede he's probably right; even so I make a mental note not to move too suddenly once inside. From the outside the house looks minute and I wonder how the Smiths managed to bring up four kids in something so small. Isn't property cheaper in the north? I consider passing this comment as a way of making conversation but decide against it. We don't go in the front door but slip up an alley-cum-path, which leads to the back door.

"Alleyways are called ghauts around here," explains Darren, doing his psychic party trick again. I wish he'd stop that, it's freaky.

I realize that the house is in fact deceptively large as it stretches back in a seemingly endless row of rooms. Mrs. Smith and Linda are waiting on the back step to greet us. Mrs. Smith keeps yelling to "Father" that Darren and his friend are here. Father turns out to be Mr. Smith, her husband. He doesn't get up from his chair in the sitting room but waves cheerfully from where he's sitting. This is understandable; he's watching a repeat of *The Waltons*—pretty compelling viewing. Mrs. Smith eyes me mistrustfully. I know from experience that women generally, and mothers specifically, are always wary of me. I also know from experience that if I want to ingratiate myself with Darren I have to make his mother like me. It's amusing that almost always the reverse is true of a man trying to impress a woman. My mother's approval is a grade A turn-off. Mrs. Smith can't drag her eyes from my skirt and mutters something about her "being sure it's all the rage" in London. Linda, by contrast, greets me in a manner with which I am much more accustomed—unadulterated praise and flattery. She loves my hair, likes my bag, adores my skirt and would die for my shoes. Her mother tuts impatiently but I answer all her questions about where I got everything and I let her touch the fabrics. Poor kid, she probably hasn't ever seen anyone dressed in anything other than a shellsuit before. I offer to take a B&B so as not to inconvenience Mrs. Smith but she won't hear of it and in fact appears offended that I've suggested it. She says that Darren can share Richard's room and I can have Darren's old room. Linda enthusiastically offers to take me to it straight away and I agree. I haven't touched up my lipstick since I arrived at Darlington.

Linda is a delight to be with. Adoring me is obviously a point in her favor and she has all the advantages that youth can offer— buoyancy, an uncynical view of the world, hardly any wrinkles and an ability to be oblivious to the humiliation of slavishly following fashion. Besides, she—like Darren—has won the gene lottery jackpot. I much prefer to be surrounded by beautiful people. Linda has thick black curly hair that she wears shoulder-length. She has Darren's to-die-for eyes and Bambi lashes and she's slim. Perhaps her most attractive feature is that she seems to have no idea how beautiful she really is. It's a shame she lives in the armpit of nowhere and won't ever be seen. In London she'd be a hit. She could get a job in media, modeling or working in the city, all of which require more than a pretty brain. Instead she'll be consigned to marrying young, raising a football team of children and counting her stretch marks. Blissfully unaware of her fate, she chatters vivaciously and nonstop as she guides me to Darren's room.

The house, like the county, is a diverse mix of ancient and modern. I spot a warehouseworth of electrical goods: three TVs, two videos, a computer, a number of computer games, radios, hi-fi systems and all white-good mod. cons. Yet the wallpaper and carpets must have been hung and laid before the war (and I'm talking Crimean). I take in endless brass wall hangings and crocheted doilies and make a mental note that next time we are producing a period piece the props department would do well to consider Mrs. Smith as a source. Whilst the fixtures and fittings are old-fashioned and, frankly, ugly, they are immaculate. My mother could run her finger along any skirting board or wardrobe top and fail to find cause for concern.

At first I'd been embarrassed by Mrs. Smith's insistence that I stay in their family home. I don't do family homes. I occasionally stay over at Josh's but his parents' houses (note the plural) are so big that there is never any danger of bumping into a parent on the stairwell. Anyway, you can't justifiably call Josh's places "family homes." His parents are only together in a nominal sense, negating the term family. And the term home. They both take advantage of the size and number of their abodes to avoid each other. If his mother is in the country, you can put money on his father being "up in town"; if his father is in the country, his mother is ensconced in their Spanish villa. Married bliss. Yet despite my reservations about accepting Mrs. Smith's invite I do have an inexplicable, but overwhelming, curiosity with regard to Darren and so I am delighted at the prospect of sleeping in his childhood bed. I casually try to establish if the room I am about to be shown has always been Darren's and Darren's alone. Linda assures me that it has: "This room has seen everything from bed-wetting to"—she hesitates—"well, bedwetting, I suppose." Too much information.

She pushes open the heavy wooden door and we both struggle to get my (extremely large) case into the (extremely small) room. Like a lot of parents, Mrs. Smith has lovingly preserved the shrine of her eldest son's childhood. I feel I've just been handed Darren's diary. The room is a thumbprint. There is a skinny, hard-looking bed pushed up to the wall under the window. It gives the impression that sleeping was a low priority for the youthful Darren. I can't help but wonder if the same still holds true. There's an ancient wardrobe and a small hi-fi/dressing-table unit. It's from MFI and I expect the twelve-year-old Darren demanded it as an act of rebellion against the fifties' bedroom suites. There are posters on the wall that I would expect in the room of any male who had grown up in the seventies and stagnated in the eighties. Original Star Trek, the A

Team and Starsky and Hutch, then Debbie Harry and Pam Ewing. These are the only nods toward a conventional bedroom. The rest is an Aladdin's cave meets Treasure Island meets Batman's cave. There are zillions of books. They line the windowsill and countless shelves, and the overflows are piled in precarious, wavering, waist-high stacks around the walls of the room. There's everything from *Beano Annuals* to a Reader's Digest collection of Charles Dickens's work. His taste is wide but the thing that all the books have in common is that they are well thumbed. Lying on top of the books are a number of models that have obviously been made by a young Darren. I think his mother has arranged them in date order as the ones nearest to the door are childish (although charming in their naïvety)—rockets and submarines, made from loo rolls and corn-flakes boxes. Then Darren must have introduced elastic bands and Dairylea tubs to make helicopters and combine harvesters. The models grow in complexity and size until finally, in the corner opposite the door, there is a massive Meccano model about three foot high and two wide.

"It's a replica of NASA," explains Linda. She must realize that I'm none the wiser because she starts dropping small marbles into buckets, which turn a wheel, which activates a pump, which moti-vates an engine, which launches a rocket etc. It's fascinating and it's more complicated than *Mouse trap*.

"It must have taken him hours to build."

"It did."

"Didn't he have any friends?"

"Hundreds," she grins cheerfully, oblivious to my implied insult. "But he's always been fascinated by ecology and wider than that, the universe, and—"

"The reason we are here." I can hardly keep the smirk out of my voice.

"Absolutely," enthuses Linda. She reminds me of the Americans—they don't do sarcasm either.

She smiles at me expectantly and, unusually, I'm shamed. I'm forced to mutter, "It's very good." Which is honest enough.

The *pièce de resistance* is the ceiling. Darren has painted a night sky. I look closer at the pattern of the stars and realize it's an inaccurate rendition of the Milky Way. Scientific accuracy aside, it's gorgeous. Linda smiles.

"Mam won't paint over it. Darren did it when he was thirteen and Mam loves it."

I can't decide if this interior decorating proves that Darren is the saddest man I've ever met or . . .

The most amazing.

No, definitely a loser.

I look out of the window, which is encased with sparkling net curtains, hanging straighter than Issie.

"Is that his tree house?"

"Yes, it's mine. I built it myself," says Darren. I jump and turn to face him. Linda looks infuriated that he's crashed our girl time. I, on the other hand, can't help but be pleased to see him.

"It's very fine," I say. "Most people settle for one story and forego the plumbing." But I beam, making it clear that I'm impressed. Darren smiles back, and I, for once, am devoid of a sparkling putdown.

We return to the kitchen, which appears to be the epicenter of the Smith household. Mrs. Smith hands me a huge mug of strong, sweet tea. I mean to tell her that I prefer black coffee or Earl Gray but I can't quite find the opportunity. The kitchen is a hive. The radio is tuned into some local station. The DJ has the strangest accent. The washing machine, dryer and dishwasher are all whirling at once. Yet despite this industry there are also great mounds of dirty plates in the sink and clean ones draining on the draining board. There are piles of ironing on at least two chairs. No one is sitting on any of the other chairs, as they are inhabited by fat, lazy, sleeping cats. Intermittently the dog, an aged

Labrador, jumps up from its basket and barks at some sound out-side. It amazes me that he can hear a sound outside. I can barely hear myself think. There isn't a pause in the conversation. In fact, conversation is a generous description. It seems to me that every-one is talking at once, about different things and without regard for anyone else. Yet despite this no one, except me, seems to be struggling to keep abreast and answer the correct people at the appropriate time. Linda and Mrs. Smith regularly try to force food on me, which I try and fail to decline. I quickly realize that it's eas-ier to accept the cakes, biscuits and sandwiches and leave them untouched, on the side of my plate. I do quietly sip my tea, which is surprisingly pleasant. Sarah and her husband and kids explode on to the scene. Sarah unceremoniously drops the baby she is car-rying on to Mrs. Smith's knee and flings her arms around her brother. The two older children, girls who are probably between three and nine years old (it's hard to guess, unless you're into kids), follow suit and climb all over Darren. Sarah's husband quietly melts away and goes to join Mr. Smith watching TV in the front room.

The kitchen, bubbling before, is positively effervescent now. I desperately need a glass of champagne, or at the very least, some soluble aspirin—ASAP. My head is simply throbbing with all this noise. Darren's nieces are demanding "twizzies," and Darren is obliging them. Sarah is demanding a cup of tea and wants to know if her mother's baked this morning. Mrs. Smith assures her she has, which accounts for the delicious smell that's wafting through the house. Mrs. Smith is balancing the baby on one hip and feed-ing it with one hand, while setting up the ironing board with the other hand to iron dry a skirt for Linda. Shelly and Richard arrive. There is more noise and more kissing. Shelly has brought a choco-late cake, which is cut into immediately—with no regard to whether it is a mealtime or not. Richard wants to know if Darren is "up for a kick about" in the back garden. Shelly shows her nieces-to-be samples of material for their bridesmaid dresses. Delighted, they squeal their approval. Sarah is unpacking groceries, recalling some incident to do with her eldest daughter's (turns out to be Charlotte) school teacher, and throughout all of this everyone is interrogating me about who I am and why I'm here.

Mrs. Smith, Sarah and Shelly have jumped to the understandable conclusion that I am Darren's girlfriend. Understandable that is, if you don't know me. I've never been a girlfriend and I have no desire to be one. And if ever I did have the desire to be one, it wouldn't be with someone like Darren. He may be good-looking, sexy, funny and intelligent but he's definitely not my type.

I'm sure he'll make someone a lovely boyfriend.

The kind of someone who wants a lovely boyfriend.

However, it's easier to allow the Smiths to think that I'm a girlfriend than explain that actually I want Darren to seduce his ex for the edification and delight of the now astounding 8.9 million viewers. The Smith women take advantage of Darren and Richard's exit to quell their curiosity.

"So you and our Darren are friends, then?" Sarah hovers over the word "friends" for about ten seconds. I concentrate on choosing a biscuit from the heaving plate proffered by Linda. I barely nod my head.

"Known each other long, have you? It's just that I don't recall him mentioning you," adds Mrs. Smith. I'm glad I'm not into this man—his interfering family would be a nightmare. It's obvious that they don't think anyone is good enough for "their" Darren. I imagine that a number of years hence Mrs. Smith and Sarah will be checking Darren's bride's ability to wash whites whiter than blue white. Awful thought. She'd probably have to sit an exam in pastrymaking before they'd hand him over. Poor Shelly, I imagine that she was subjected to the same hostilities when Richard first brought her home. I look at Shelly, expecting to see the browbeaten shrew of my imaginings. She grins at me cheerfully and confidently kicks a cat off a chair, plonking her own bum in its place.

"Move it, Tabby."

Hmmm.

Charlotte's interrogation lacks subtlety, but then this is forgivable because she's still wearing Winnie the Pooh matching vest and pant sets. She cuts the preamble. "Are you Darren's girlfriend?"

"Er, no, I'm not." I knew the question was brewing, so why am I blushing?

"Oh." Charlotte is unimpressed. The others are simply perplexed. "Have you got a boyfriend?" she continues.

"No." I would never, ever have come here if I'd realized that I was going to be humiliated in this way.

"Poor you," says Charlotte, "I have. His name is Alan Barker and he sings to me." I smile at her encouragingly. She persists, "I'm six and a half. Lucy is four. Ben isn't really a baby. He's nearly two. How old are you?"

"Don't be rude, Charlotte. You should never ask a lady her age," says Sarah. Yet she pauses expectantly, waiting for me to answer.

"Thirty-three," I oblige.

I notice that Shelly, Sarah and Mrs. Smith exchange furtive glances. They think there is something suspect about a single thirty-three-year-old woman. I wish Darren would stop farting around with that football and come and rescue me.

"Do you have a sister?" pursues Charlotte. We haven't lost eye contact since the interrogation began. I wiggle on my seat trying to get a better view of the back of her scalp; I'm looking for a tattoo of 666.

"No."

"A brother, then?" asks Lucy.

"I'm afraid not." Lucy climbs on to my knee, as if to console me. I'm a bit nervous—I don't think I've ever had anything so young on my knee before, not even a kitten or a puppy. How will she balance? It appears that Lucy has got experience in this sort of thing. She expertly cuddles into me and begins to suck her thumb. I can feel her breath on my neck. I look around for approval. No one else seems to think it is at all unusual that I have a child on my lap. But it is. People don't touch me. Not unless they are paid to or it's sexual. An important distinction. I'm touched by my hairdresser, masseur, acupuncturist and personal trainer for hard cash and by men for a more amorphous fee. But this child is sitting on my lap and holding my hand, and doesn't appear to want anything from me at all. How odd.

"So what do you do for a living?" asks Sarah. I am about to offer to fill in a questionnaire but I notice that Darren and Richard have just come back inside. I bite my tongue.

"She works in TV," jumps in Linda. Linda is the only one who is impressed by my career choice.

"What exactly do you do in television, then, dear?" asks Mrs. Smith. I give my dummied-down job description, which I assume will be adequate. No one ever really understands what someone else does for a living.

"I think up ideas for programs."

"Ooohhhh," the kitchen choruses.

"Did you think up *Friends?*" asks Shelly.

"No, it's American."

"Did you think up *Blue Peter?*" asks Charlotte.

"No, before my time."

"Did you think up that game show with the nice Mr. Tyrant? The one that makes people very rich?" asks Mrs. Smith.

"Or *Cold Feet?*" asks Linda hopefully.

"No, not my channel," I add apologetically. Clearly I've failed to impress anyone.

"Oh. Well, what did you think of?" asks Sarah.

Mercifully the doorbell rings and this causes such concern that everyone, other than Darren and Lucy, leaves the kitchen.

"No one ever rings the door bell," he explains. "They all come around the back. It must be a delivery."

I nod as though this outlandish behavior was second nature to me, rather than the extraordinary adventure it is.

"Why didn't you tell them the name of your show?" he asks.

I stare at him sulkily. "I guess I didn't think it was their cup of tea," I mutter.

"Oh, you took a guess that they weren't part of your 8.9 million. Very astute."

I glare at him.

He is so smug. He is so cocksure. He is so sexy.

I think it's the mouth.

CHAPTER

Ten

I AM UNSURE ABOUT HOW I got myself into this predicament. I can't remember the point when I actually agreed to accompany Darren, Charlotte, Lucy and baby Ben to the swimming baths. The noise and confusion that reign in the Smith household is so extreme that it is possible I didn't agree at all but simply was unable to resist their collective force.

I don't do public baths. I do health spas and private gyms. I can feel the foot diseases waiting in the cracks of the tiles and despite the gallons of chlorine that the local council has tipped into the pool, I am sure that I am about to swim in neat child's wee. To add insult, I catch a glimpse of myself in the steamy mirror. It's bad. I didn't bring a costume with me and therefore I've been forced into borrowing Sarah's. Although there is evidence that Sarah has been a very attractive woman in her time, she has had three babies and has let her figure go somewhat. I get the feeling sartorial elegance is not the top of her list of priorities. The bathing suit is high street rather than high fashion. I did explain to Sarah and Shelly that I only ever wear black. They smiled and handed me this monstrosity. I think that initially it was a mass of fluorescent flowers, which thankfully have faded. The cut is all wrong. Damn, why didn't I bring my Calvin Klein costume? It's cut to maximize the length of the leg and minimize the waist. Its padded at the breast, creating a look that is undisputedly flattering. The floral number is baggy at the crotch and hips, plus the straps keep sliding off my shoulders.

As if the possibility that I might fall out of the suit altogether isn't terrifying enough, suddenly I find that I'm alone in the changing rooms with two small people.

The panic rises. Not just because I haven't shaved my legs in over a week, but because Charlotte and Lucy are both looking up at me with expectancy in their eyes. It appears that everyone—Darren, his mum, Sarah, Shelly and these kids—all seem to think I am in charge.

And that I'm capable of it.

Which I am, of course. I mean, I run a show that pulls in millions of viewers per week, for God's sake. I control budgets of hundreds of thousands of pounds, create revenues of millions. I can undress two small children and dress them again in suitable attire.

Surely.

They don't stand still. They slither and slide all over the place. They don't want to wear costumes anyway, much less their armbands, which I abandon altogether. It seems that no sooner have I got the appropriate limb in the appropriate hole than they take it out again. I do manage to get the costumes on but one is inside-out and the other is back-to-front. I realize that above all else, I must remain calm. Like any confrontation it is important not to let the adversary know that you feel menaced or panicked. I can outstare four- and six-year-olds—definitely. If only they would stay still.

"Charlotte, don't run. The floor's slippery. You might hurt yourself." I try to make this sound like advice or a warning. It comes out sounding like I'm threatened or threatening. "Lucy, we didn't bring your pink costume. You have to put this blue one on. Now please, stop crying. Just one more arm. Please." Both the girls are crying (although I suspect Charlotte's are crocodile tears) and I am closer to tears than I've been in twenty-five years, when another mother offers to help.

"They're not yours, are they, pet?"

"No." I'm irritated and relieved all at once. They aren't hers either, are they? But, in a blink of an eye, she has managed to get them both into their costumes, the right way out, and facing the right direction. Why couldn't I? Can it be that there is a mother gene that makes this stuff easier once you are a mum? Not that I ever want to be a mother, not in my wildest dreams. In fact, it's close to my worst nightmare. But I do like to be able to do things properly. I don't like to fail.

I bribe the girls into not telling Uncle Darren that the nice lady had to help with dressing them. I offer them each a pound but Charlotte informs me that the going rate is a new outfit for her Barbie doll and a trip to McDonald's. I would be annoyed but actually I admire her business acumen and I'm sure that she'll go far.

Darren doesn't comment that we've been in the dressing-room for forty-five minutes but waves cheerfully from the baby pool, where he is confidently handling a happy, gurgling Ben.

I lower myself into the pool and try not to think of the wee. I hand him the armbands for the girls. Making it clear that it's his turn.

"Will you hold Ben?" I nod, as I don't want to open my mouth for fear of what will go in it. Darren grins and hands him over. I'm relieved that he doesn't start to cry. I smile winningly at him and hope that my legendary way with men works on someone so young. Darren hoists himself out of the pool.

He is divine.

He must work out. His muscles are taut and developed. He's lean and tanned. I watch the pool water glisten as it clings to his shoulders and legs. I'd glisten too if I was clinging to that Adonis. I'm thrilled to note that his strong chest and legs are hairy but his back is clean. My nipples harden and chafe against the costume. Bloody cheap thing, no lining.

Darren puts the armbands on the girls and lowers them into

the pool with me. He sits on the side, dangling his legs in the water. He drags his feet unselfconsciously through the water, bending and straightening his knees. My knees have turned to Play-Doh. My entire body is on fire. I cannot drag my gaze from him. He is utterly, utterly stunning. From his tanned feet, with neat square nails—rather than the yellow, curled nails that most men choose to sport—to his long, tight, muscular legs, to his neat, flat stomach. Six pack, forget it—this is an entire shelf at the off-license. I want to entangle my fingers in his chest hair. Lose them there and never ever find them again. His shoulders are as rigid as they are broad. They look almost polished. He's staring out at the children and not aware that I'm studying every little droplet of chlorine that's clinging to him. His glossy hair curls rebelliously at the nape of his neck and I'm envious. I want to be that lock of hair; I want to be the drops of chlorine, pool water and pee.

Since he's occupied watching the children splash and bob, I risk taking a look at his swimwear.

WHHHOOOAAA-HHHOOO.

Hello, Big Boy.

"Should I take Ben now?"

"Erm?"

I nearly drop the baby with the embarrassment. Why did he have to choose that moment to start up a conversation? I avoid his eye as I pass the baby to him. I feel like a kid caught with her hand in the biscuit jar. I force myself to look at Darren and he's grinning again. Well, I'm pleased to be so amusing! Irritated and flustered, I sulkily pull myself on to the side of the pool as he climbs in. He tries to make conversation but I won't be mollified. It isn't until I catch him furtively checking out my tits that I start to brighten up. In fact, I feel considerably happier.

When we leave the pool we go to McDonald's. Darren is bla-tantly a bit surprised by my choice of dining venue. I smile and don't offer an explanation. It isn't until Lucy is on to her second chocolate shake and I've taken Charlotte to the loo twice (unaided) that it crosses my mind to check my mobile messages. I can't believe I've forgotten to call Fi or Bale. It's not as though I'm having a good time. I mean, I'm not shopping or clubbing. Normally I check my messages every twenty-five minutes when I'm out of the studio.

I've had six calls.

Hi, Cas. It's Fi. I reviewed the files through the night and have a shortlist of three possible scenarios for next week's show. Should I interview them? If so, you'll need to release more budget. Call me.

Hi, Cas, it's Josh. Issie told me that you are chasing some bloke halfway up the country. What's the angle? Is he a transvestite? Now that would make a good show. Well, call me when you get a mo.

Cas. It's Fi again. Er, I haven't heard back from you so I had to make the decision to go ahead with the interviews. I think I've found a substitute. Hope this is OK. But I didn't really have a choice. What with the timetable being so tight. Can you call me? Er, say hi to Darren for me. Tell him I was the one in baby-blue cashmere. No, scrub that.

Cas, it's Issie. Weeeellllllll? How goes it with Mr. Northern Hunk?

Jocasta, it's your mother. I do hate these things. Can you hear me?

Cas. Bale. Call in.

So nothing urgent. I switch the phone back to the message facility.

By the time we drop the kids back with Sarah, I am exhausted and barely have the energy to turn down the offer of staying for supper. Which under normal circumstances I'd turn down with extreme force.

"Stay—we're having lasagna and Mam and Dad are down the pub, Richard's at Shelly's, Linda's here. There will be no one at home. You'll be rattling around an empty house."

Hearing this, I get another surge of dynamism and almost wrench Darren's arm out of its socket as I pull him from their kitchen and bundle him into the car. Laughing, he turns the ignition.

"Had enough of kids for one day?"

I feel a twinge of guilt. Perhaps he wanted to stay and was too polite to contradict me; after all, he probably doesn't get to see his family much, being based in London. But my arms are aching with playing "one, two, three, swwiiinnnng." I smell of baby puke, my mind is fried with coming up with answers to the perpetual 'why' question (nearly all of which had come from Darren). Most importantly, I haven't reapplied my makeup since leaving the swimming pool.

"To be honest, yes. I'm not used to kids. No nieces or nephews."

"Some of your friends must have children, though," he comments.

I think about it. No, not really. Women in TV rarely nod toward their reproductive capacity and my friends in other lines of work seem to disappear once they have babies. I suppose it's because we keep very different hours.

"No." I smile at Darren and decide to confess, "In fact, until today I don't think I've ever held a child, or dressed one, brushed its hair, taken it to the loo, changed a diaper or fed it."

"Really?"

"Really," I confirm.

I'm slightly shamefaced and don't know how Darren will take this. He obviously values these motherly skills in his women. Indeed all men like to see a woman behave perfectly with kids. Most women like to think they have a natural ability to be patient, entertaining and loving. Not me. I'm not bothered. Well, I was keen to put the shoes on the right feet but that was because I hate to be inadequate at anything. As a kid myself, I didn't like anyone else winning musical chairs. Second place is nowhere. If something is worth doing, it's worth doing well. That's always been my motto. It has nothing to do with impressing Darren. I don't care what he thinks of me. I sneak a look at him to check his reaction to my confession. Richard's car is so tiny that Darren is almost folded double. He's concentrating on the curling roads. He puts on the long beam lights and the windscreen wipers are valiantly trying to clear the pouring rain. I fear it's a losing battle. Without taking his eyes off the road, he mumbles, "You're amazing."

I'm amazing! I'm floating on air. My bum is absolutely refusing to stay in the car seat.

I'm amazing? Oh yeah, and how many times have I heard that before?

I'm amazing! I'm floating on air. My bum is absolutely refusing to stay in the car seat.

I'm amazing. I bet he says that to everyone.

I pretend I haven't heard and close my eyes keen to get some sleep on the short journey back to the Smiths' house.

I wake up and a young Kevin Keegan is smiling down at me. Where am I? I'm in a single bed with itchy nylon sheets and itchy nylon bedspread. They are brown. Different shades of brown. My worst fear—I've screwed someone with bad taste. I hear children laughing in the garden and I look out of the window.

Darren.

And Charlotte and Lucy. It's a gray, bleak day. Gray grass, gray sky. But Darren and the girls are a remarkable contrast, their clothes and laughter, a colorful relief to the horizon. Impetuously I bang on the window and wave furiously. They all look up and wave back. Then I remember I haven't got any makeup on, so I dive back into bed before they can see me properly. There's a knock on the door and, before I answer, Mrs. Smith bustles in. She smiles broadly and I bathe in it. Perhaps she's heard how good I was with the children yesterday and is beginning to approve of me. Not that it matters. I neither want nor need Mrs. Smith's approval.

Much.

She hands me a cup of tea that's so strong the spoon can stand up in it. I take it from her and thank her.

"My, you were tired, weren't you?"

A strange feeling of unease creeps into bed with me; it gets under the sheets and disperses the cosy feeling. Oh bugger, yes, now I remember. Last night I'd been very tired. Too tired to argue my case about the show properly but tired enough to argue petulantly. We were having a laugh. In the absence of wine or gin we decided to raid his parents' cocktail cabinet. A walnut veneer monstrosity, straight from the Ark, justifiably hidden in the "front room." We agreed that tequila was the perfect accompaniment to cheese on toast (desperate measures for desperate times. The other choices were all fluorescent in color and likely to have been radioactive). I had the idea of broaching the subject of the show while the family were out and we had the house to ourselves. I thought that as he was beginning to warm to me he might be open to discussion. He wasn't. The conversation had been brief, powerful and cold.

He turned his back to me and concentrated on grating the cheese. The hairs on the back of his neck were standing to attention. I had an overwhelming desire to blow on them.

"I'm not saying that you should have sex with Claire." God forbid. "Just find out what would happen. Just let fate take its course," I argued to his very wide shoulders.

"But your program isn't about fate or what would happen naturally if everyone was left to their own devices. Your show is designed to distort. To bring out the worst in people." He was watching my reflection in the window against the black night sky.

"The worst in people is the norm."

He tutted dismissively. But he did, at least, turn back to me. Or was he just turning because he needed to put the bread under the grill?

"No, it's not. You just think that the peculiar is normal because it's prevalent in *your* life."

Fucking cheek. What does he know about my life? Well, besides the stuff we'd talked about at the Oxo tower restaurant, on the train and today. But that hardly amounts to revealing insight. He knows little more about me than what my favorite milkshake was when I was a kid. Oh, and admittedly, we had a fairly flirty but extremely coded (due to the presence of minors) conversation about condom flavors this afternoon. But then half the men at TV6 know that I prefer banana-flavor condoms.

None of them know it's chocolate milkshake.

I glared at him and said, "Infidelity is a fact. Disloyalty is a fact."

"OK. Maybe. But it's a horrifying fact and should remain horrifying. By continually showing betrayal as an acceptable form of entertainment you are neutralizing the horror. Are you so damaged that you can't see that?"

I was tired and sick of his sanctimonious attitude. I found I was shouting. I ignored his question and asked my own instead. "You want to shelter who, exactly, from these cultural and moral norms of the West? I'm not suggesting anything that they aren't already endorsing, committing."

We both fell silent as Darren concentrated on retrieving the cheese on toast from under the grill. He set it down in front of me and offered Worcester sauce. I refused it. I poured him tequila;

he'd left it untouched. We ate in silence and then I went to bed, alone, defeated.

Now, I try to find my wristwatch.

"It's three thirty, pet," says Mrs. Smith, cheerfully.

"In the afternoon?" I jump up suddenly. Mrs. Smith clocks my lacy negligée.

"Yes, in the afternoon. By, love, you must have been tired not to notice the cold in that flimsy thing. If you'd said you only had your underwear to sleep in I'd have leant you one of my nighties."

Duly mortified, I crawl back into bed and cover myself from her disapproving gaze. Underwear indeed! I'd especially selected the most conventional and practical nightdress I own, to bring on this trip. I normally sleep naked. If she thinks this is skimpy enough to be underwear, what would she think of my knickers?

"Darren wanted to get you up but I said, 'Let her sleep.' You obviously needed it. He's just taking the kids into town for a ride on the merry-go-round on the seafront. I thought that you might want to get bathed and then we can think about a bite to eat."

I nod politely, although I'm sure my stomach will actively revolt if I try to eat anything more. Yesterday's binge of sweets, chocolate cake, scones, hamburgers and finally cheese on toast was more than I normally eat in a week. It must be the fresh air that's given me such an appetite.

"What time did you say it was?"

"It's nearly twenty to four now."

"What day is it?" I'm not normally so vague, but then I don't normally sleep for seventeen hours. And I don't *ever* sleep in nylon sheets.

"Tuesday."

"Oh shit."

"Excuse me," Mrs. Smith looks horrified but I have no time to placate her.

"Shit. Shit." I scramble in my bag looking for my mobile

phone. "Shit. Fourteen messages." Mrs. Smith tuts and leaves me to my own devices. I think it's safe to assume that any tentative strands of approval she'd been weaving my way are now well and truly snapped. So what? I turn to my messages.

The first is from Issie, reminding me that my New Year's resolution was not to have casual sex. Ha, fat chance. Darren doesn't even seem to want to swap pleasantries, never mind bodily fluids. And anyway, what is she talking about? That's not why I'm here. I'm here to endear myself to Darren so that he can't resist me and finally agrees to be on the show. I thought I'd explained that. All the other messages are work-related.

> Cas. Please give me a call. It's Tuesday morning. What time will you be back? Have you persuaded Darren to be on the show?

Fi sounds nervous and a twinge of guilt bites as I acknowledge that I have left her in the lurch. She's a strong assistant but she hasn't had to make the decisions before. Well, maybe I micromanage too much and it's time that Fi had a bit more responsibility. She's probably doing a good job. I skip a few more messages to listen out for her voice. There are three more from Fi. The first and second are increasingly irate. The third confidently asserts that she's found a replacement for Darren, Claire and Marcus and has made the decision to reschedule the filming. She details how she's going to use the two producers back to back. One in the studio, editing, while the other is at the shoot and then vice versa. This is a good idea as it will help catch up on time. She says she's expecting me back by Wednesday morning and significantly repeats, "As you promised."

Bale is less subtle.

> Cas, where the fuck are you? Getting serviced? Well, fuck that. Call me.

His three messages are all the same. I also have calls from Di, Debs and Ricky. Apparently some bishop or other has written an open letter to *The Times* condemning the show. Which is great news. Di and Debs want to know how to handle the PR. Idiots. Can't they do anything without me? Ricky is lobbying for a schedule change to coincide with Valentine's Day. He's come up against a brick wall. Or, more accurately, a homophobe executive who can block or facilitate such things. Ricky's particular breed of charm will only serve to irritate in this instance. Whereas I could undoubtedly help by just offering to take the guy to lunch. I call Ricky and tell him to set it up for Friday. I call Fi, and it's not until I tell her that I'm not traveling back tonight as originally promised but early tomorrow morning or tomorrow night at latest that I realize I've made this decision.

"But you don't need to stay, Cas. I have a replacement."

"Yeah, but I think Darren is just about to capitulate and I still think he'd make such a good show." This lie is vibrant scarlet but I have no conscience about it.

"He is gorgeous," Fi agrees enthusiastically.

"If you like that kind of thing."

"Are you having a good time?"

"Not really. He's unstable. A delight one minute and a rabid dog the next. I have to schlep around with his tedious family. It's freezing and I'm in the middle of nowhere." It's always been an adage of mine that I don't owe every pertinent inquirer the truth, whole truth and nothing but.

"The things you do for your job."

"Exactly. Listen, Fi. It's probably best if you don't mention to Bale that we have a replacement. He hasn't met Darren and won't understand why I'm so actively pursuing him." Fi titters, so for clarity I add, "For the show."

"Of course." I can hear the smirk in her voice. Cow. "Be careful you don't fall for him."

"Impossible. I could never fancy anyone called Darren. I'm not called Kylie or Sharon."

Fi laughs. "I won't say a word to Bale, but you'll have to get back by first thing Thursday at the absolute latest. We can push the filming back to then but no later. I can't do the filming on my own. We need you."

Of course they do.

After bathing I feel in need of fresh air. Avocado green has never been my color for bathroom suites. I decide to catch up with Darren and the children. Because what else can I do? Play bowls? I walk along the pier and spot them walking down the beach, which is more or less deserted as it's January, it's the north and it's freezing. Anyone with any sense is sitting by their fireside or, less romantically but more realistically, their TV set and radiators. I wave and shout, and surprisingly Lucy and Charlotte start to pelt toward me, their little legs not keeping up with their will to be further ahead than they are. I succumb to the Calvin Klein ad factor and rush to meet them. I stoop down to hug them. I only do this because I'll look good.

"Hi," smiles Darren.

Is last night's spat forgotten? I'm not sure, so I concentrate on the girls. I know he's watching me examine their toffee apples and take due interest in the horrid plastic novelties that they've procured on the seafront.

"You're getting the hang of this kids thing. And Wellingtons too," he comments.

I glare at him. The Wellingtons' are Mr. Smith's. I have just endured the most embarrassing thirty minutes of my life, well beyond anything I have ever encountered to date. Mrs. Smith insisted that my Mulberry wide-leg trousers were "too good to be darting on the beach in" and gave me a pair of her "slacks." She laughed out loud at my Gina Couture mules and set about finding me a pair of Wellington boots. I am a size seven shoe. Which caused much astonishment as the fact was repeated throughout Whitby by Mrs. Smith, who rang all her friends and asked if they had a boot that large. None of them did. It's obvious that they are still binding women's feet in North Yorkshire. I was subjected to the humiliating experience of being the most ugly of Cinderella's sisters as I tried to squeeze my feet into Shelly's size six boots. They didn't go anywhere near. I commented that cheap brands do come up small. Mrs. Smith laughed and gave me Mr. Smith's Wellingtons. They are big and slip up and down as I walk but at least I can get into them. I didn't manage to leave the house without accepting sheepskin mitts, a kagoul, scarf and a duffel coat. The type most people wore at school. I didn't. I refused then. However, no amount of objections could deter Mrs. Smith. She kept insisting that it is bitter in January, and that I wouldn't have known anything like it. The implication is that I'm a softy southerner. I explained that I had been to the north before—in fact, I went to university in Manchester. She let out a sound somewhere between derision and pity. "That's hardly north, is it, love?"

I look like the Michelin man. Except not as color coordinated. Darren sweeps an eye over my outfit. How come he's warm *and* manages to look sophisticated and rugged?

"I see that Mam kitted you out appropriately."

I don't dignify his sarcasm with a response. I'm not sure if he thinks he's being funny or if he's trying to be irritating.

But then I'm not sure if I *am* irritated.

Odd.

I can't remember when last I was so unsure about so many things. I want to tell Darren that I feel better for my marathon sleep. Better than I've felt for as long as I can remember. I want to tell him that I seem to have woken up with a new and startling sense of clarity and while I don't agree with his point of view, I do accept it. Grudgingly, I respect it. He's argued his case well. But I can't say this because if I do, how will I explain that I want to stay an extra night? How will I explain that, despite my expectations, I like it here? It's peaceful.

And terrifying. I am trying to be honest with myself, at least. I thought my battle was with Darren. But now I see that, if it was, I've lost.

I do like him.

He's sexy, witty and intelligent, which I've come across before. But more than that, he's also gentle, decent and straightforward, which is an entirely new experience for me. I do like him, very much, and by admitting as much I realize that I have a whole new war to wage. I fear my opponent is much tougher, more devious and ruthless than Darren could ever be. I'm at war with myself. I like him, but hate myself for doing so. Because isn't this what I've been studiously avoiding all my life? I know I should pack my bag immediately and get on the train back to London. I should take myself well away from this danger zone.

But I can't.

I know if I leave now, Darren will always be with me. I'd wonder if he were for real. I'd fantasize, despite myself, that his outlook on life—open, honest, optimistic—is a possibility. I'd be ruined.

If I stay, there is a reasonable chance that Darren will expose his true self, which surely can't be as amazing as I currently believe. All I can do is maintain the cool exterior, which I've nurtured for twenty-six years, and hope that by spending more time with Darren I begin to bore of him. Not my strongest strategy ever, but my preferred option by virtue of the fact that it's my only option.

We begin to walk along the shoreline. I expect and dread that we'll settle into an uncomfortable silence. Instead Darren chats happily. He's nauseatingly well informed about the local sites and history.

"Lewis Carroll is reputed to have written much of *Alice in Wonderland* while sitting on these sands looking out to sea."

"Really?" I don't turn to see where he's pointing.

"In the Roman times a signal station was likely to have been erected on this spot."

"Fascinating." I'm rather pleased with the tone I hit. It's an enthusiastic enough word choice but the manner I deliver it hints that I've had more fun scouring ovens.

"Let's head to Flowergate. We can pop into the Sutcliffe Gallery."

He drags the girls and me around a billion sepia pictures. After staring at four million, seven hundred and forty-five of them I begin to admire his tenacity. The shots are absorbing, but I'm doing my level best not to betray that I think so. Darren matches my feigned disinterest by feigning oblivion to it. This game-playing is exhausting, even for a pro like me. We move on, crossing the river. Darren points to a church in the distance.

"The original dates from 110 A.D. Can you see the graveyard? That's where Dracula is allegedly buried." I smile to humor him.

"And that's St. Hilda's Abbey, isn't it?" I ask.

Darren nearly keels over with shock. "Absolutely."

I'm gratified that he doesn't ask how I knew this but instead assumes that I'm one of those terribly impressive people who know all sorts of facts about a diverse range of places and topics. A person like Darren. He's so obviously delighted with me that I can't resist elaborating.

"Did you know that the original abbey housed both men and women, but was destroyed by the Danes?"

"In 867," he adds, nodding his head enthusiastically. It's so cold I can almost see ice in his hair but his smile shoots spears of warmth through the town. There's a direct hit in my knickers. I reflect on this and consider jumping into the river and swimming away, a long way away. Less dramatically, I resume my commentary. "Hilda was a relative of King Oswt's, wasn't she?"

"Correct." Darren is orgasmic. Knowledge *is* power. Luckily he doesn't ask where I gained such a detailed grasp of the history of his home town, Smallsville. He's so ridiculously pleased. A little part of me would hate to disappoint him. Truth is, Fi sent me a text message through my mobile with this and a number of other facts about Whitby. We always research our subjects thoroughly.

"Would you like a closer look at the abbey?" he asks. The abbey is on a cliff top. I could do with the workout. I nod and we set off. "What do you think of Whitby?"

I think it's cold and I think it's unfashionable. I never thought I'd be pleased to see a Woolworths' and greet it as though it was Harrods' food hall. But just as I'm about to say this I turn to Darren. He's looking out to the sea. It's shimmering turquoise and lustrous waves are breaking on the sand, which looks pink and peach by turn. I can't see any of the grayness that had been so prevalent earlier.

"It's overwhelming," I mutter, which is at once truthful and vague enough to satisfy.

Darren grins widely. "Isn't it? I knew you'd love it. It's such a riot of color and smell and sound. My senses feel electric."

His skin looks cold and transparent, which is perfect for hanging on such strong, jilting cheekbones. My senses feel electric, too, but I'm not sure that it has much to do with the smell of fishing nets and creosote. We begin to walk through the cobbled streets. The children surprise me by not whining about having to climb up a couple of hundred steps; in fact, they are keen to do so—they want to look at old gravestones. Darren doesn't seem to think this is at all odd, so I can only assume it's a northern thing. The walk takes quite some time, as I go to extreme lengths to avoid being anywhere near a seagull. I swear Whitby seagulls are baby elephants in fancy dress. I'm almost deafened by their constant, hungry squawking. They look fierce, and while it may be lucky to be used as a bird's public toilet, it's a pleasure I can do without. I buy ice creams for the children and me. Darren's determined to act his age and points out that it's freezing. Charlotte looks at him pity-ingly, as though he is a lost soul. I can smell fish and chips, or more specifically, I can smell vinegar seeping into newspaper and, as we climb higher, I can smell smoke from the chimneys. It's different.

We finally reach the church and while the girls run off to find Dracula's tomb I puff furiously on a cigarette, not caring if it's tak-ing me one step nearer to joining Drac.

"Have you heard from the studio?" asks Darren.

"Oh yes. Dozens of calls. They can't seem to muddle through without me."

"Really?"

"Really." I don't tell him that Fi has found a replacement for him. Because if I do tell him, he's bound to ask me why I'm still here.

"I'm sure they can't do without you, Cas. I mean such an intel-lectually challenging program needs your unique input."

I'm stung. I thought we were having a nice time, even among the tat and bric-a-brac. I'm trying—why can't he?

"Why do you hate me, Darren?" I ask directly.

He looks genuinely surprised. He must be taken back by my straightforward approach.

"I don't hate you. I like you. I just don't like the program."

Hmmm. He likes me.

Hmmm. Obviously not enough. Part of me wants to change the subject. Talk to him about the jet or herring industries. Indeed both those subjects suddenly appear riveting. But I can't. Darren has thrown down the gauntlet; in fact, he's spat at the family crest. I have to respond.

"But it's my program. I thought of the concept."

"And you are proud of that, are you?"

"I am. Very. TV6 was in deep trouble until I came up with this. People could have lost their jobs."

"Why couldn't you think of something instructive?"

"I think this is," I nod wryly. "It's a warning, if anyone is sensible enough to listen. Infidelity is out there. I think I'm helping civilization come to terms with itself."

Didn't we do this last night? Why bring it up again? I'm never going to agree with him. I know why I wanted him to see my point of view: it was to get him on the show. But why is he so urgent about my seeing *his* point of view? What can it possibly matter to him? What does he want from me?

"Your show doesn't help anyone. It *cheats* civilization." He's raising his voice. Which encourages me to remain irritatingly calm. I adore the upper hand.

"It captivates 8.9 million viewers. Actually 9.1 million last show. Di called to tell me."

"Oh, I admit that it holds attention, and consumes energy while ignoring the fundamentals of life." He's stamping on the pavement and I don't know if it's because he's cold or furious. He's waving his arms around and a woman, walking her dog, is looking at us.

"So?"

"Your program incessantly touches the audience but on a superficial level." I stare at him, uncomprehending. "Television doesn't require any acceptance of responsibility. Every one of your viewers who has hoped for an infidelity has committed a small betrayal of standards. But no one, except the poor sucker on the show, has to answer for his or her actions."

I touch my temples. I can see his argument but he's wrong.

"No, Darren. Television merely reflects and observes society. It should not be blamed for the degeneration. It might not be pretty, but I'm just telling it how it is. Why does it make you so angry?" I sigh.

"Why don't you admit it makes you furious?" he asks.

I shrug and lick my ice cream. "Do you want some?"

"Go on, then." We stop and he licks my ice cream. He has to

hold my hand steady to do so, because it's shaking. It must be the cold. He's right—I shouldn't be eating ice cream in January. His tongue is pink and slim.

"I don't buy your thing about collective responsibility, society, the greater good, blah blah. Bugger it. The more people I meet, the more disappointments I see."

"So who are you responsible for?"

"Myself. And I look out for my mother, Issie and Josh when I can."

We both fall silent. I stare at him. Looking directly into his eyes, which I rarely do, at least not when he's looking back at me. My stomach hiccups. It's stress.

"I won't be on your show." And he manages to sound genuinely upset by this. "That's not how I could help you." I shrug. To be frank, I'm not even sure I want Darren on the show any more—I'm almost certain I don't.

"Don't worry about it. I'm used to helping myself." I walk on briskly, not waiting to see if my rebuff hits as deeply as I hope it will. He doesn't need to know that I don't need him any more. It's much worse than that.

I just want him.

I call Bale and am relieved that he's in a meeting. The best I can do is leave him a message. I lie. I tell him that Darren is very near to agreeing to being on the show, that it's imperative that I get him to agree and that he can't call me because the battery on my mobile has run out. I am aware that the opposite is true—in all three cases. But I don't believe in hell.

When Darren and the girls arrive back home, about ten minutes after me, I am sweetness and light incarnate. I often pull this stunt with men. One minute moody, the next a delight. It makes them grateful. It's getting late, we've missed tea and more criminally we've made the girls miss tea. Mrs. Smith offers to make sandwiches but I can't eat. I'm churned up. Sarah takes the kids home for their baths. Mr. and Mrs. Smith, Shelly and Richard decide to go to the pub. They ask if I want to join them. I'm absolutely desperate for a drink. As soon as I agree to go, Darren grabs his coat and says he's coming too. He obviously hasn't done enough baiting for one day.

The pub is heaving. It's full of raw and rough-looking fishermen. Who, surprisingly, look quite sexy despite their wellies. They wear black skullcaps and oilskins, which are for real, rather than a fashion statement. I seduce the Smiths, offering to buy the drinks, and I even go so far as to join them in drinking the thick, treacly stout that's obviously their favorite tipple. The pub is filthy, tasteless, well worn and patently loved. Remarkably, I soon forget the sticky, ripped lino that curls to expose a far stickier wooden floor, I ignore the tattered cushions, ragged flock wallpaper and frayed rugs as I melt into alcoholic oblivion. By my second pint, try as I might, I can't find anything shabby. Instead I'm surrounded by laughter, warmth and goodwill. It swirls like cigarette smoke, sticking to my hair, clinging to my clothes and penetrating my essence. By my third pint Mr. Smith (senior) seems the wisest man I've ever known. His stories about Whitby are fascinating and his silences are profound. I forget my fears that the locals probably still indulge in cockfighting and even say so to Mr. Smith. I try to dilute my prejudice by admitting it's entirely unfounded.

"Prejudice is rarely anything else," he comments.

Shelly and Mrs. Smith seem actively jolly. We play several riotous games of dominoes and I win, which satiates my competitive streak for the evening. Richard is gregarious and well informed. He's heard from Darren that I have "extensive local knowledge." Much to my amusement he tumbles my source. "Someone from your studio told you about the abbey, did they?" I nod, nervous that he's blown my cover with Darren. He winks conspiratorially, taps his nose and adds, "Mam's the word." I'm so grateful I want to kiss him. And Darren?

Darren is unprecedented.

Darren is all of the above. He is sexier than the fishermen. His anecdotes are more wise, fascinating and profound than his father's. He's more fun than the Smith women, even at their most jolly. He's charmingly competitive. He is more discreet than Richard—I don't think anyone else notices him rest his hand on my knee. Like the happy atmosphere, he immerses me. He clings harder and longer than anything I've ever known.

Which horrifies me.

I'm drunk. But not too drunk, as I already hope the hangover comes with a sense of proportion.

At a quarter to nine I announce that I have to go back to pack. Darren says he'll walk with me and I'm grateful when Mrs. Smith says that she wants to go home too. In my slightly woozy state I know that if Darren wanted to touch more than my knee I'd definitely let him. When we arrive home Darren goes straight to the front room. Mrs. Smith stays in the kitchen to fold some clean washing into piles for ironing and I drink a reservoir of water.

"Had a nice day, pet?" she asks. I nod enthusiastically. "You can tell. You're a proper beauty when you smile. Really gorgeous." She leaves me alone in the kitchen, with the compliment for company. I feel brilliant. The word "gorgeous" rolls around my head.

Gooorgeous.

Gorggessss.

Gorgeous.

I receive a lot of compliments—some from men who want to screw me, others from the girls at TV6 who are too terrified of me not to compliment, and compliments from Mum, Issie and Josh. Mum's my mum and while Issie and Josh are probably genuine enough, those two say nice things about everyone. In my book, indiscriminate affability cancels out the worth. But Mrs. Smith's compliment is something really special. I get the feeling that she doesn't dish them out that often.

The back door swings open and Linda tumbles in after a fun-packed evening hanging around the bus shelter. She interrupts my thoughts.

"You look like the cat that's got the cream."

"I think I am." I smile back. "Cup of tea?" I've put the kettle on before she answers. Now she's grinning.

"You seem much more at home here after just forty-eight hours."

"I am. Maybe it is the sleep, or the sea air—"

"Or being around our Darren."

What's she implying? She's bloody cheeky for a teenager. No, thinking about it, she's absolutely normal for a teenager. I don't comment, but instead concentrate on displaying the chocolate digestives on a plate. She says, "He always has this effect on women."

Naturally.

"Always?" I venture.

Linda rolls her eyes. "Well, look at him." Fair point. "Women watch him in the street. Everyone fancies him, from Charlotte's friends, to mine, to Sarah's. Even Mum's friends, come to think of it." Someone has thumped me very hard. Suddenly I'm sober. "It's just the same with the women in London. I noticed when I visited him last summer hols. There was this constant stream of women dropping in on him. 'Do you fancy a drink, Darren?' 'Can you loosen this lid, Darren—oh, you are so strong!' 'Oh, a man who can cook—Darren you are very special.' "

I don't really like what Linda is telling me but her impressions are hilarious and I can't help but giggle. Besides, she wouldn't be telling me all this unless she was saying that I'm somehow different. Would she? Well, maybe she would. After all, she's only seventeen. Perhaps this is her unsubtle way of telling me that she (and he) have seen it all before.

"He is a good cook," I comment. "He made me cheese on toast last night and it was really special."

"Special!" Linda is derisive and she's within her rights, considering what I've just said. I catch her eye, which is clever of me, considering the speed at which she is rolling them.

"Not you as well! I thought you'd be impervious!"

"Me what?" As soon as the words are out I regret them. She's youthful; she's likely to tell me.

"You've fallen for him."

"I haven't."

"Really, you haven't fallen for him?" asks Linda.

"Really."

"What a shame, because I think he's fallen for you."

Hallelujah, hallelujah.

Linda picks up an apple and takes a hungry bite, shrugs and leaves me to my thoughts.

Where is the cheese box? The fresh herbs? The avocado? The fridge is heaving but there is nothing I can eat. I'm faced with a dazzling selection from Rowntree and Cadbury. But fish fingers, Alphabite potato wedges and Heinz sauce were not what I had in mind for a romantic dinner for two. Where is the adult food?

What am I saying? Romantic? I've never had romantic dinners before.

Strategic, yes, but not romantic.

Still, the end result is the same: sex. So it's simply a case of semantics.

I have to have sex with Darren. It's obvious—why didn't I think of it earlier? A surefire way to dispel any fanciful notions that I may be inadvertently harboring. Having sex with Darren would bring him down to the same level as everyone else I've ever had sex with. He's definitely not going on the show now, so there would be no concerns about a lack of professionalism if I slept with him.

Nor would there be any possibility of seeing him again, which erases the possibility of tiresome consequential scenes. And as he is as sexy as hell, well, why shouldn't I have a crack? I brush away my New Year's resolution in the same way that every other year I sneak an extra fag or drink.

Unaccountably, I'm nervous. I have expertly seduced the most dazzling and dull array of individuals. Darren must be like one of them. He *must* fit into one of my types and as soon as I identify the type, I can select the most appropriate strategy. I rule out anything obvious that I would try with my bimbo boys. I rule out anything dishonest that I would try with the less scrupulous dates I've bagged. I rule out anything that requires a fake identity—he knows me too well already. I look at my clothes. An ensemble of things I've borrowed from Shelly and Sarah, plus the one or two practical pieces that Issie insisted on stealing into my case. I look dreadful, so I rule out anything that is entirely dependent on my couture. I only have tonight, so I rule out anything that requires a long lead time. I had thought of cooking for him—such an act of selflessness, the candles and, if all else fails, the wine would have the desired effect. But having seen the contents of the fridge and also considering how notoriously difficult it is to cook in someone else's kitchen, I rule that out too. Yet I'm leaving tomorrow. I really do have to catch an early train. Bale will go ballistic if I delay any longer, unnecessarily so in my opinion. Fi can handle the film crews until I get there.

I look at my watch. It's 9:15 P.M.

It's now or never.

Never is not an option. I'll have to wing it.

I track Darren down in the front room; he's listening to Radio 4. "Let's go out. I assume there is a restaurant in Whitby that's still open after nine?" I challenge.

"Plenty. Get your coat."

CHAPTER
Eleven

DARREN USES THE TERM "RESTAURANT" much more generously than I would. You can, after all, buy food at a hot dog
stand, but I doubt that A. A. Gill would repeat purchase. The
"restaurant" has about half a dozen assorted tables, which have
between two and six variegated chairs scattered casually at each.
There are tablecloths but they are plastic, red and white checked.
There are flowers on each table but they too are plastic. There is
music but it's from a jukebox. However, the candles are real and
the food is good, although the choice is limited—spag. bol. or
nothing—so we have the spag. bol. Darren also orders a bottle of
house red. Neither of us bothers to ask if there is a wine list. There
are three other couples in the restaurant and one woman has
brought her dog. Loose tits and tummies surround me. This is not
the sort of place where I usually hang out. The only mercy is that
I'm so far from home that no one will recognize me. I am amazed
that Darren seems as comfortable here as he did in the Oxo tower.
I couldn't be uneasier. I'm terrified that the provincial drabness
will rub off on me. That I'll start to think wearing blue and green
together is acceptable or that a good night out is getting trollied in
a threadbare pub. Oh no, it's happening already. I have to make
my move quickly and get back to civilization before something
irrevocable happens to me.

The food and drink arrive. Darren is very quiet and my con-
founding lack of wit irritates me. I'm never stuck for words.

Why now, when I want to be dazzling? I know the end result I'm looking for. Surely getting him to sleep with me can't be that difficult can it? Right now it seems impossible. I sigh and gaze around the restaurant. I notice a couple of empty nesters asking the waiter to take their photo. I watch, amazed, as he doesn't show the disdain or pity that he must be filling his head. They grin and raise their glasses artificially. I'm just about to say something scathing when I notice that Darren is also looking at them and he's smiling.

Fondly.

"Isn't that marvelous?" He nods at the ugly couple. He doesn't seem to be aware of how dreadful they are, but instead starts going on about how great it is to see couples of that age happily married, still in love. I interrupt and point out that the couple are probably on a dirty weekend, and as Blackpool and Brighton were full, they've opted for Whitby. He smiles, ignores me and continues on about how he really believes in fidelity, friendship, familiarity.

"And fucking," I add. Let's cut to the chase.

"Lovemaking is part of it. Of course, that's important."

He means this junk and the strange thing is that, as he waxes lyrical, I *almost* begin to believe it, too. His optimism is infectious. It must be the wine. In the nick of time I recover.

"Christ, you're wet," I spit nastily. I'm not sure why I'm being nasty. Perhaps it's habit.

Darren refuses to take offense but smiles. "Maybe, but I prefer it to being a cynic."

"I'm not a cynic," I bite back. "I'm a—"

"Realist," he finishes for me. "I take it that you don't believe in everlasting love?"

"Everlasting love!" I snort my contempt. "There is no such thing. People use each other, wear each other out and then move on. You see it all the time. I bet you believe in the Loch Ness monster and Father Christmas, too," I snap. I look at Darren and his jaw is clenched. I'm not sure if he's angry or upset. Turns out he's both.

"Why can't you be civil? I'm doing you the favor here, remember. You invited yourself to my home. Has it been so awful for you, being here with my family and me?"

For a moment I'm floored. I sigh, sip my wine and answer honestly.

"No, actually it hasn't been awful at all. I've . . ." I hesitate and then take a deep breath, "Really had a great time. You have a lovely family."

Darren relaxes immediately and beams at me. "I hoped you had but I couldn't be sure. One minute you're laughing and the next you're—"

"What?"

"Well, snarling, for want of a better word."

I sigh again but accept his observation. "I do believe people fall in love, or at least lust, or something. We are a very weak species, generally. But they don't stay in love, again because they're too weak. Someone always gets hurt. And in my view it's better to avoid any messiness altogether."

"Aren't you being a little bit extreme?"

"I can't see a middle lane. Just a tiny bit in love doesn't seem to be an option."

"Now I do agree with you there." He pauses and then asks gently, "Do you remember the other night at the Oxo restaurant?"

Was that just three nights ago? It seems a lifetime.

"I asked you what *really* hurt you." I nod. "And then I realized it was none of my business and changed the subject." I nod again. "I wondered if you considered it my business yet? Because I'd really like to know what hurt you so badly that you shut down?" He drops his eyes, not looking at me as he asks this question. He's playing with the condiments.

I'm amazed he cares and I want to explain it to him. I wonder if I can.

"It's just that I'm not prepared to accept the flotsam and jetsam of humanity." He looks up quizzically. "The debris that passes for a relationship," I moan, weary with it all. "Look, it doesn't exist. This exciting love thing that you are obviously searching for, it doesn't exist. I know I've had sex with over fifty men and I've never made love."

I fall silent and wait for his reaction. He doesn't look shocked or horrified by my confession. Which—irrationally—irritates me. I really want him to be disgusted with me. It would certainly be easier if he walked away now. Or I did. But I'm not sure I can. He's waiting for a more thorough explanation.

"In my experience, and as I've mentioned it's wide and varied, people use each other and when they've finished using they leave." I pick up my knife and scrape the edge on the plastic tablecloth. I note the irony that a rather bad cover version of "Don't Leave Me This Way" is playing in the background.

"Who left?"

The way his voice breaks between the words "who" and "left" means it is absolutely impossible for me to resist.

"My father." Stupid angry tears well up from nowhere. I'm stunned. I've kept them at bay for twenty-six years. Why now? Darren sweeps the tear away with his thumb and for a nanosecond the palm of his hand is in contact with my chin. It blisters my skin and oddly soothes it in the same instance. I look at him and despite my years of experience, despite the fact that I've only known him for a few days and despite the fact that he is devastatingly gorgeous-looking—which should always be a warning sign—I want to trust this man. I think I do trust him. Which is dangerous. I have to get a grip.

"Look, I'm sorry. Can we forget that?" I push away my tears and his thumb. "It's been a long week and what with you pulling out of the show, I'm under a lot of pressure." He looks hurt. Which is exactly what I want. I want him to feel guilty. I look around the restaurant, desperate for a change of subject. Unless Darren has very strong views on flock wallpaper or plastic flower arrangements, I'm pretty stuck. The evening's gone AWOL I had thought that by pudding (it's packet trifle, so the term "pudding" is perhaps philanthropic) we would be flirting and talking exclusively in *doubles entendres*. Instead I'm drenched in big stuff, emotions, feelings of betrayal and, more extraordinarily, feelings of trust and possibility. The stuff I arduously avoid.

"You are lucky to have so many brothers and sisters," I comment. I admit this isn't exactly a change of subject—we are still on the personal; but it's his personal rather than mine. Which is a far safer zone. "All this hugging and kissing stuff you do to each other, I think I'm on an American chat show."

Darren smiles. "Aren't all families the same?" When I don't answer he stops smiling and simply adds, "Well it makes for interesting Christmases."

"Our house was always quiet. When he left he took—besides the regular income and the mock crocodile suitcases—the fire from the belly of our home. The rows stopped, for which I was grateful. My mother never cried or shouted again. But for that matter she never laughed or giggled either. She settled into an eerie calmness."

How had that happened? I'm on about me again. I look at my empty glass. Darren sees it as a hint and refills it. I don't argue.

"She cooked for me, washed and ironed my clothes, attended my parents' evenings at school, ensured ends met. She was perfectly adequate in every way. But I've often thought that the day my father left, I lost my mother too. It seemed she decided that loving was too risky and settled into the sanitized safety of simply caring for me. Even looking back, it seems unfair. I'd never leave her." I wish I'd shut up. I'm boring myself, never mind Darren. I mean it's hardly the most entertaining anecdote that I could have come up with, is it? Yet I can't stop myself.

"I'm not blaming her. I mean I understand where she's coming from. But occasionally it would have been nice if she could have read a fairy tale and closed the book without sniping that the prince would have a new woman by the end of the year."

Darren smiles sadly and I force a wry grin back. "Side by side, we worked our way through Christmases and birthdays, holidays in Devon, O-levels, A-levels and finally university. Mum ironing and singing her anthems, "Does Anybody Miss Me?" and "If You Go Away." My formative years. She is a fine mum and I know she always did her best for me. But sometimes I wish that my father had left behind brothers and sisters to fill the rooms and disguise the sound of the hissing iron and the clanking radiators."

We both wait silently as the waiter lowers two cups of coffee on to our table. I'm sure it's instant, it's served in the type of teaset that you collect from garages and with a plastic carton of UHT milk. Still, the waiter presents it as though he'd grown the beans himself and he was serving it in a seventeenth-century silver service. I would be annoyed that he's interrupted our conversation but I like people to be involved in their work.

Darren asks, "Do you look like your mum or dad?"

"I have two pictures of my father and, to my eternal disappointment, I am the image of that callous, deserting bastard. The pictures were taken in 1965 and 1973. The first is a wedding picture. I rescued the half my mother cut away."

Darren looks bemused. Of course, he comes from a family wrapped in bliss—how could he understand about wedding pictures being cut in half? I try to explain it for him. "Oh, don't worry, it wasn't a violent, passionate act. She was very calm about it. She wanted to keep the pictures of herself because she did look wonderful, so she carefully cut around her dress. I remember her using my round-ended scissors from a play weaving kit. She sat at the kitchen table for two days. She erased him from the wedding photos, the ones of my birth, all holiday snaps. Everything. It was a thorough, systematic extermination of all evidence that he ever existed. I stole the 1973 picture before she got to it." Darren doesn't interrupt. I check he's listening. He is. He's put down his coffee cup. Deliberately I pick mine up. "That was the year he left us. It's a picture of him helping to blow out the seven candles on my birthday cake."

How could he have left us, me—the very spit of him?

"Do you miss him?"

"Miss him? I don't even remember him."

We both fall silent again. I determinedly chew the mints. Just to show that I'm not bothered. It's difficult to swallow.

"For years after he left I tried to imagine what his life was like. When I was in a traffic jam I wondered if he was in it too, or another similar one. When I listened to the radio I wondered if he listened to the same channel. But I didn't know and I'll never know because I know so little about him."

"You could trace him," suggests Darren gently.

"I don't want to. He's made it clear where I fit in to his life— i.e. I don't. He never paid a penny in alimony or even sent a birth-day card. He's given me one thing in my life and I'm grateful for it. He's taught me about loss. He's saved me from ever having a bro-ken heart." I try to grin. "I've turned my heart to steel. In fact, even my closest friends question if I have one at all." I've always believed this.

"You have a heart to break, Cas, just like everyone else."

I'm indignant. There's no call to be insulting. "I do not," I assert defiantly.

"So what makes you think you are different? Your extraordinar-ily high consumption of sun-blush tomatoes? Because, besides that, you are pretty similar to everyone else."

"Am I?" I ask, outraged.

"A bit sexier maybe, a bit cleverer." He ambushes me with compliments. My outrage is melting and being replaced by pure delight. "You are just the same, Cas. You can fall in love just as easily."

Angry again, I retort, "No, I can't. I'm not good on intimacy. I don't like people. They are stupid and disappointing."

"Not everyone. You like me."

"You are so vain." And so right.

"You want to cop out of the human race, then? You can't just hide away, secure because you are not involved, not risking."

"I have. I am."

"Just because your father let your mother down doesn't mean you can't find love."

"If not him, who?" I laugh but my voice is unnaturally high.

"What?"

"If my father couldn't love me, which man can?" I'm going for closure.

"I'd like to have a go."

Bingo.

Fuck no.

It's unnecessary. I want to sleep with him. But he doesn't need to lie to me. He doesn't need to give me a cheesy line about love. I'm surprised. I thought he was above that. And it is obviously a cheesy line because he can't mean that he wants to have a relationship with me. I've spent the last three days telling him how little I believe in, or care for, such things. Not that this is the first time that I've been faced with this kind of declaration. Men are always telling me they love me. Always have done. But I know they don't mean it and sometimes they know they don't mean it, too. It's just a rather rudimentary ritual. It's more polite than just asking for a fuck. I rarely sleep with men who go for the love angle, unless I'm certain they don't mean it. If I suspect they do mean it, I forgo the sex and turn them into good friends—using their devotion for practical purposes whenever my lawn needs mowing or my garage needs clearing.

But Darren's different.

I don't think he would talk of love unless he was serious. But then, how can he be serious after all I've said? I do want to sleep with him because I fancy him like mad. But I can't possibly sleep with him if I think it means more than just sex to him. It will just get complicated. I don't want to hurt him. He's a nice guy. I must be absolutely transparent about how I feel about him.

If only I knew.

"I don't think you are the right man to try and love me, Darren," I grin brightly. It's a fake grin and fake brightness.

"Why is that?"

"Well, you're not my type."

"Why not?"

Why not! Why not? God, this guy is arrogant. "Well, you're a bit too serious and, erm, homely, for me." Darren looks at his empty cup. I feel like the bitch everyone says I am. I try to make amends. "I'm not saying I don't fancy you. I do fancy you. I'd be happy to fuck."

"Sex is not supposed to be separate from love." Darren stares at me horrified and yes, I think it is disgust I can see there. Well, that should make things simpler.

"Aghh, but I've had *great* uncomplicated sex." I try to cheer him.

"Yes, but have you ever made love? All that variety. The flings, the shags, the affairs, the nameless wonders—" He waves his hand, dismissing the men in my past, just the way I do. "You've never had love. It's just too easy to avoid."

"I don't need it," I say matter-of-factly.

"You think you are so brave, don't you, Cas?" I never indulge in these conversations. They lead nowhere. They lead to—"Well, you're not. Being brave is trusting. Being aloof is easy." I stifle the yawn. Go, Einstein. I reassure myself that it is only his pride that is hurt. "You use your parents and your career to avoid intimacy because you are scared."

"Did you go to college to come up with that?"

We glare at each other over the single bud vase with the plastic flower and the empty wine bottle that is doubling as a candle-holder. I know enough about men to realize that pursuing this scenario is going to waste my time. Darren's too intense. Someone would get hurt. Yes, he's a shag, undeniably fanciable, but it's not worth it. He has bunny boiler written all over him. He obviously cares for me and I simply can't allow myself to feel the same way. I admit it would be tempting to allow myself to believe that the intensity and the caring could last. But it simply doesn't. And what if I do feel the same? What if I do . . . care for him? Where would it lead? Nowhere, that's where. I've got to be brutal to be benevolent.

"You are obsessed with love. It's not your fault. It's popular culture. You're right, TV does have a lot to answer for. This ridiculous ideal, which doesn't exist, is touted in every song, poster and book. I'm sure if the Beatles had sung songs about world peace we'd be war free by now."

"They did."

"Oh, well not just the Beatles, then, but everyone." I try to joke but he remains deadly serious. He's not going to let either of us off the hook.

"Do you know what I think? Searching for love, the One, it's such a lot of wasted energy. It's embarrassing. I'm embarrassed for the human race. I think we should move on. I blame Shakespeare! Love, it's insane. Get the bill."

It's excruciating. Darren and I traveled home from the restaurant in silence. I went to bed immediately. This morning I had my breakfast with Linda; Darren was out walking the dog. It's pouring. I packed and he came home to drive me to the station. We've traveled the entire distance without using a double-syllabled word. It's a disaster. Being here is a disaster. Opening up is a disaster. Teasing Darren is a disaster. I take solace in the fact that soon I'll be on the train to King's Cross. I can go directly to the studio and make my peace with the increasingly irate Bale. I can finish the filming and manage the editing for this week's show and by Saturday night I won't even remember Darren's name. I am determined that he'll be consigned to history.

We arrive at Darlington station. The only sound is the swish of the overworked windscreen wipers. Darren gets out of the car with me. He goes to see when the train is expected and I wait on the platform. He comes back to the car, looking yet more miserable and pitiful than before.

"We've got nearly an hour to wait. I'm sorry, I should have checked the timetable before we set off."

"It's OK. I should have done that." We fall silent again. "You don't have to stay. I can wait in the café." The plan is that Darren is spending the rest of the week with his family. He isn't due back in London until Sunday night. I'm relieved—I couldn't stand having to do the entire journey with him in silence.

"I'd rather wait. To see you safely on the train."

"Make sure I do leave, hey?" I try to joke but I suddenly feel horribly lonely. Inexplicably, I realize I don't want to leave things like this. I don't want to get back on the train and go home to my flat. I don't want never to see Darren again. I've been kidding myself. This wasn't ever about whether Darren appeared on the show or not. His appearance would have made a strong show. His devastating good looks would force me into tuning into *The Generation Game*, so I can only imagine the meltdown effect he'd have on the rest of the British population, yet he's not, nor was he ever, essential to the show. We have replacements. I came to Whitby because I wanted to be with him. I don't understand why I did, but I did.

I still do.

Is he going to leave me alone here on the platform? If he does, I'll scream. He's staring at the ground. I follow his gaze and try to concentrate on what he's saying.

"As a child I used to think petrol puddles were rainbows that were a casualty of a nasty road accident." He smiles shyly, seeing how I'll relate to such an intimate confession. He's expecting something cutting that would prevent an outpouring of memories. After all, memories only lead to knowledge and intimacy. The danger of liking the person. But suddenly I face it. I want to know more about this man. I want to know everything. What was the name of the teacher he had his first crush on? There must have been one. Who are his friends? Why does he have that little scar above his eye? Does he like pesto? Does he hate mushy peas? What does he think about amusement arcades? What does he fear most? What's he like in bed? Who is he going to fall in love with next?

Is there still a chance it could be me?

What?

"Should we go for a coffee?"

I agree immediately.

Darren doesn't want to go to the station café but opts for a small "Italian" café run by Iranian refugees. Their Italian accents are worse than mine are but their cappuccinos are convincing. We sit on the sticky wooden benches and face each other over the tiny Formica table. So tiny that our heads are almost touching. But then this is OK, as the cappuccino machine is making so much noise that I'd have to lean close to hear him anyway.

"About last night—I want to apologize," I offer. I'm not sure what I want to apologize for but I know that I feel awful. I want to tell him that I'm sorry for my toing and froing. I'm sorry for my ice-maiden act. And most of all that I'm sorry that I haven't been able to trust him.

"No, I should apologize. I rushed things." And while the words are kind the tone is curt.

"It's just that we hardly know each other." This comes out sounding like another criticism and I want it to be an explanation for my caution.

"I wasn't proposing, Cas. I was just suggesting that we could try to get to know each other. I admit I was a bit hamfisted. But look, it doesn't matter. You made your feelings perfectly clear."

But I didn't, did I? I couldn't have because I can't. Make things clear. It's mud. I want him. I fancy him. I respect him. I like him. He intrigues me. I'm in trouble. It strikes me, as I sit in yet another one of our silences, that our relationship to date, such as it is, has been a series of rows and silences. Which proves my point that intimacy always leads to cruelty and aggro. I look at Darren and he looks dejected and delicious. I am unaware of anything other than my pulsing sex, aching breasts and throbbing lips, all of which could be relieved if he'd just kiss me. He's not going to and I can't be tortured like this any longer. I stand up and I swear the room is partying. I put my hand on the table to steady myself. It's hot in this tiny café.

"Look . . . goodbye . . . and . . . thanks for the coffee."

It's frantic and hurried and amazing. He touches my hand. He's not trying to restrain me. But he has. I'm rooted. His finger is resting gently on my wrist. I'm shackled. I'm ignited. I kiss him. He kisses back. Strong and dark. Engulfing. I've never kissed before. Or if I have, they were poor dress rehearsals. This is it. All the words that have fallen between us suddenly disappear, they are superfluous. We're left with naked silence. Stripped to desire. He tosses a few quid on the table and, not waiting for the change, we dash out of the café, into the rain. He points to an alleyway behind the station. I'm already heading that way; I have an in-built mechanism that helps me to locate dark streets and other possible places for fornication. The rain is still pelting down, hitting the pavement and vaulting up again. It falls through the afternoon darkness in nasty, spiky, drops, but I don't care. In fact, I'm grateful: the vicious elements mean that the streets are empty. I'm boiling over with anticipation. He takes a tight hold on my arm. We cross the road, not checking for traffic. Darren flings me up against the wall, barely pausing to check for privacy, I wrap my coat around him. His lips mesh into mine and we're kissing so hard I can't tell them apart. He scrabbles with his flies and then sinks into me. I stare into his eyes and he stares back, never losing me. Not for a second. It feels amazing. It feels important. It feels right.

He's climbing, he's filling, he's plugging. He completes me.

It's over in minutes.

I'm already scared that this will never be over.

CHAPTER

Twelve

SOMEONE IS HOLDING HIS or her finger on my door buzzer. One of the inconveniences of my loft apartment is that it has nothing as old-fashioned as a spyhole. It is impossible to know who is at the door without talking to them, by which time it is impossible to pretend not to be in, if that is the desired course of action.

I long for the visitor to be Issie. Possibly Josh, but ideally Issie. And yet I am terrified it is. What will I tell her? What can I say? How can I possibly begin to explain my behavior over the past two weeks?

Buuuuzzzzzzzzz.

This persistence demands my attention. If I ignore whoever, I'll spend the rest of the afternoon wondering who it was. I drag myself toward the intercom praying it's not Bale or Fi.

"It's me," says Issie. "Where the hell have you been? Open up instantly."

I'm relieved and press the release button. Within moments she is pushing open my door. She's really pissed off with me, so much so that she doesn't bother to kiss me. I'm aware that offense is the best form of defense so I demand, "Why didn't you use your key?"

"Lost it," she shrugs, immediately apologetic. I tut and start making noises about the security risk and the inconvenience of getting a replacement cut. Once she's appropriately subdued I ask, "Have you looked in your dressing-table drawer?"

"No."

"Well, I think it's in there. With the socks."

"Why would I keep keys with my socks?"

"Beats me, Issie, but you do."

This exchange takes place while we move toward the kitchen. It's four thirty on a Sunday afternoon. Which seems the perfect time to pour not just healthy but bionic G&Ts. I certainly need mine. My interlude with the key doesn't throw Issie completely.

"What's been going on, Cas? It's not so surprising that you disappear but normally it's work-related. I called the studio and they said you had laryngitis. I called here but there was no reply. You weren't hospitalized, were you?"

I take a proper look at Issie for the first time since she arrived, and I feel pretty dreadful. She is extremely drawn and nervous-looking. I realize I'm a worry to her. Then again so are lost puppies, the axeing of trees, and the absence of clean, running water in India. Considering the issues Issie involves herself with on an ongoing basis, my going AWOL for over a week is small fry. We look at one another and she pauses, immediately suspicious.

"You don't look ill. You look really well."

It's true, to be direct—I'm a goddess. My hair, black and shiny as a matter of course, is positively glistening. My smile, previously used only for effect, is now a permanent fixture. My skin has always had a pale and interesting hue, but now I'm sporting rose-red cheeks.

"Why didn't you call me, or Josh, or your mum? We were demented. What the hell is going on?"

She's going on and on and on. Question after question after question. Few of which I'm inclined to answer and those I am more willing to respond to are far too complicated. I'm relieved when she abruptly stops mid-conversation flow, but only momentarily, as I soon realize she is staring at the dirty crockery left over from this morning's breakfast. Normally anally tidy, I have not cleared up. This and the fact that the assorted debris discloses that the breakfast was saturated fat endorsed (as opposed to freshly squeezed orange juice and an ounce of Bran Flakes—my usual) astounds Issie.

"It's not just the eggshells that have been broken, is it?" Her tone is both suspecting and delighted. I shake my head and look at the slate tiles. I wonder if I can distract her by pointing to the grime under the fridge. I doubt it. "You've broken precedent, too, haven't you? You *never* feed men breakfast. Who's been privileged like this?"

"Darren." Simply. Unusually I haven't the energy or inclination to fudge. In fact, I want to talk about him.

"Darren?!" Uncomprehending. "The last time I spoke to you, you'd had a huge row. He was about to take you to the station. You were coming back to London *alone*. What happened?"

I thought I'd explained: Darren happened.

I tell Issie about the train ride to Darlington, the swimming baths, and the walks on the beach and the graveyard. I know I'm giggling, blushing and gushing (even in this state of near-hysteria I'm gratified to note she also thinks a walk through gravestones is odd). I tell her about the pub, the restaurant and finally the hissing cappuccino machine. I tell her that suddenly (while sitting over an itchy, orange Formica table) it occurred to me. Suddenly I knew, more clearly than I've never known anything in my life, that I wanted him. I wanted him beyond reason or rationale.

"Whoa there." Issie holds her skinny hands in front of her, trying to block the overload of incomprehensible information. She used to do this when we studied Russian language at night classes. Although I am trying to be clear, it's understandable that Issie feels she's neck high in the sludgy waters of an unknown territory. She naturally assumes that when I say I wanted him, I mean sexually. Exclusively sexually. A fair assumption in light of my history.

Inaccurate.

She lights one of my cigarettes, without asking.

"I thanked him for the coffee and *tried* to walk away but—"

"But?"

"He put his hand on mine and said, 'You're welcome. The plea-sure really was mine, Cas.'" I repeat this conversation in a stupid drawling voice, which is actually nothing like Darren's voice. It's just that I am aware that what I'm saying is serious stuff. I hope the ridiculous voice will serve to make the story funnier, less intense.

"Noooo." Issie latches on to the idiotic voice, hoping it's a lifeboat. She assumes I'd find this action inane. Any man, trying to get inside my knickers, should know never, ever to appear senti-mental once, never mind twice. I can't stand it.

Usually.

"And did he say your name like, Kez." She says my name as though she is a drunk David Niven impersonating Jimmy Tarbuck. Unaccountably, her mocking makes me ashamed. It's always felt fine to be harsh and heinous; now it seems puerile. Darren deserves better.

"Er, to be frank, no."

"But his hand was clammy." Issie, understandably discon-certed, is still holding out for the reassurance of one of my "scathing dismissal" stories, as supplied on countless occasions. Scathing dismissal stories make Issie feel better about the fact that she is horribly needy and couldn't be stinging to save her life. My cruelty to the opposite sex evens things up for her. It's no use. I'd like to help but I can't lie.

"Actually, it was cool and smooth."

Issie nearly spills her G&T on the floor as the shock makes her overestimate the size of my coffee table.

"Careful," I grumble, thinking about the Purves and Purves carpet.

"When you say you wanted him . . . ?"

I take a deep breath. I force forward. "I just couldn't leave him."

As best as I can, I explain it to Issie. I tell her that the pots are still dirty because I can't bear to wash him away. I even tell her that the sheets are rank for the same reason.

"Sheets? When did we get to sheets?" she squeals.

I could tell her about the first time. No sheets, just a dirty brick wall. Hurried and frenzied. My coat left damp and grubby, in need of a clean. My scarf sticky with dried love, because I used it to wipe his dick.

And I know that if I tell Issie this she'd think this is in character, it's what she expects of me. It's what I expect of me. But if I elucidate and add that while the act was undoubtedly basic and animalistic, it was also bashing against the surreal. We were wrapped in a pure light that made us *us*. Distinct and apart from anyone else, we floated in an individual time dimension that no one else knew about, or could ever visit. There was a secret, silent acceptance that hearts and flowers and all that they have come to symbolize were an option, even for me. I was *there*. I was involved.

He completed me.

Against an alley wall.

What would she make of that? Only one way to find out.

I tell her the stuff I'd vowed not to tell her. I can't do otherwise; it bursts out. I'm overpouring with Darren. Thoughts of Darren. Memories of Darren. Images of Darren. I'm not nervous exactly; it's something different to nervous. I'm excited, I'm exhilarated.

I'm terrified.

Issie listens to my garbled account of events to date; she says nothing but is wearing a ridiculous smirk on her face. The smirk broadens to a grin and then it widens an unfeasible fraction more. She's beaming as I tell her that I didn't get on a train back to London that Thursday morning, or Friday, or Saturday for that matter. Instead we booked into a tiny country house. As I repeat these facts the image of Darren licking me out, which has been more or less permanently burned on my mind, becomes 3D again.

We are in bed, limbs, sheets and senses entangled and confused. Yet as he asks, "Here, do you like it here?" I experience an unparalleled sense of clarity and certainty. I like it there, very much. I recall my fingers (which had never looked so slim and tapering) being swallowed into his thick, black hair. I'm lying on my back and looking down at my body and his head. It's nodding slightly as he moves his tongue a fraction to send me beyond consciousness. That bit was slow. But then that was our fourth time. Or was it our fifth?

Issie is quite traditionally dumbfounded.

"We stayed in bed for three days. In the end we were more or less evicted."

I smile to myself as I think of the exasperated chambermaid begging us to leave our room so that she could clean it.

"After that, after listening to each other's breathing, dreams, thoughts, we became . . . necessary to each other." I struggle, then come clean. "I couldn't let him go home alone."

I'd have lost part of myself.

"Instead I asked him back to my apartment."

Because if not, I'd have missed his singing in the bathroom. I'd have missed him tracing kisses from the end of my hair, to my scalp, past my ears, to my jaw line, then up—finally to my mouth. I'd have missed the sound of his pee hitting the loo.

"He left this morning. He had to go to the Cotswolds—a tree with measles."

Issie is quickly piecing together my story. She's counting days on her fingers. She looks confused. She must have put two and two together and, quite unusually for Issie, she's come up with four.

"He stayed here for a week?"

"Yes."

"But you never let men stay at your flat for more than twelve hours. That's your rule. What did you do for a week?"

"Well, besides the obvious, which took up a substantial amount of time, we went to the pub, I met his flatmate, Jock. We went for a curry, we watched vids."

"You dated."

"No." I think about it. "OK, well, yes, I suppose."

"What about work?"

"Work?" What an odd question.

"What did you tell Bale?"

"You know, I told him I had laryngitis." I'm irritated that she wants to talk about work.

"But Cas, when you had an emergency appendicitis you discharged yourself early because the hospital staff wouldn't let you use a mobile phone. Illness doesn't stop you working. Bale won't have believed your story about laryngitis. Why did you say laryngitis? You've never had it. Do you have any idea what it's like? How long it lasts? How contagious it is?"

Issie's panicking.

She moves toward my bookshelves and starts rooting around for a medical journal. She's obviously going to look up laryngitis. Which is sweet of her, but why is she so concerned? I can hardly bring myself to be bothered.

"You could lose your job. You are in deep do-do."

I try not to giggle at the expression and instead I think about Darren. I smile, widely, remembering how he hesitated by the door. We'd both been trying, for a week, to get back to work. We'd both been trying, for a week, to stay glued together. Issie notes my serenity and yells, "Aren't you worried?"

What can I say? If she doesn't get it, it proves to me what I have long suspected: Issie has never been in . . . Issie's never felt like this. It would be pointless to explain that he let me warm my (eternally) cold feet on his (eternally) hot shins, or bum, or bollocks. It would be futile to elaborate. The thing is, from that first kiss my head spun but my life stopped wobbling. I hadn't even known it was wobbling before. I know what his hair smells like. I know where he is ticklish. I've licked the inside of his nostril. I had sex until I was raw, but for the first time ever, it was entirely to do with love. My body does not feel like a gambling chit, a bargaining tool or a funfair ride. The world is Technicolor.

All of this from me! The confirmed steel heart. Poor Issie, how could she possibly understand? I consider myself the more perceptive, intuitive, sagacious of the two of us and I have no clue how this happened.

I make a move toward the kitchen to pour us both two more gigantic G&Ts. I carelessly slosh gin into the glasses and splash some tonic on top. Issie stares. She's incredulous.

"No ice?"

"It's in the freezer," I reply, heading back to the settee.

"And lemon?" I ignore her altogether. Normally I insist on measuring the drink carefully. Pouring the gin over three ice cubes and adding a slice of lemon and lime (my own speciality). I prepare G&Ts with the same care and attention that most people reserve for cooking a three-course gourmet dinner. Today I can't be fussed. To be honest, the preparation of G&T is not interesting. It's not Darren.

I pat the settee and Issie joins me. We both curl up in front of the open fire. It isn't real. It's a very good natural gas impersonation, which is cleaner and easier. Admittedly they don't give off quite the same aroma but the difference is minuscule and I'm prepared to sacrifice that small piece of authenticity for an easier life.

"Since he left this morning I've tried to distract myself by watching videos but every one I selected was about love and stuff." I throw my arms in the air, exasperated. "Four different videos, I tried. I put on a selection of various CDs and read the first page of a bunch of novels; but every way I turned I bashed up against poignancy."

Issie's smirking again. "It surprises me that you have romantic books and vids."

"That's the point, Issie. Before I met Darren they were just novels and films; now they are *romantic* novels and films. It's weird. The very fact that I find them romantic shows that—"

"That you're in love."

"Don't be so bloody stupid," I snap hastily. Issie doesn't meet my eye but concentrates on sipping her gin. "I'm not in love." She doesn't say anything. "I'm not," I insist. "Popular culture is so manipulative."

We are silent, watching the flames flicker. I'm thinking of Darren and me rolling around in front of it, behaving like a couple of proverbial soap stars. I don't care what Issie is thinking of.

"What are you afraid of, Cas?" Oh, she's thinking of me.

"I am in love." The words resonate around the room. Booming and thundering into our lives. Saying the words aloud is at once a relief, and also the most horrifyingly, scary moment of my life. "I am in love with him."

"Really! Reallyreallyreallyreally?!" Issie jumps up and this time the G&T does go flying. I scowl as I stand up to get a cloth from the kitchen. I quietly sop up the G&T.

"Yes," I sigh, overwhelmed for the umpteenth time today by my own emotion. We are both stunned and enjoy the confession. Issie is delirious. It's as though I've just told her I've won the lottery or that she'd won the lottery.

"How do you know? When did you know? Oh God, Cas, how amazing."

I smile, making the most of my moment.

"It was when we booked into the country hotel. Terrible place, floral carpets and cluttered reception, covered in flyers advertising darts matches and provincial craft shows. He had a bag with him."

Issie looks uncertain. I clarify.

"He'd packed condoms, toothbrush and clean boxers. So besides being mouthwateringly desirable, interesting, intelligent, moral and funny (all admirable qualities but not the ones that normally fly my kite) I realized he was presumptuous and cunning too."

"Jackpot," she smiles.

"Exactly," I confirm, and I can't help it—I actually clap my hands.

I luxuriate in the memories and Issie is bathing in possibility.

"Did you know we'd end up here?" I'd asked. He dribbled champagne (house, but who cares) into my mouth from his, silencing me momentarily.

"I didn't absolutely know." Mischievous.

"But you expected it?" Disgruntled.

He moved his lips from mine and attached them to my nipple, while he poured more champagne into my tummy button. He inched toward the alcohol lake, kissing and caressing my shoulder, my collarbone, my waist. He lapped up the champagne while I silently thanked my personal trainer—the two hundred sit-ups a day were worth it.

"I didn't expect it. I hoped for it. I told you, I'm an optimist," Darren grinned. His lips were wet with champagne and my cum.

Artful audacity is the icing on the cake. Suddenly Darren seemed dangerous. When had he got ahead of me in our sexual chess game? Had he won? Had I? Could we both?

It seems unlikely.

Cold, steely fear puts a hand around my throat, the grip tightens, squeezing the happiness out of me. My heart, which has been residing in the roof of my mouth plummets. What have I done? What *have* I done? This is the disaster I've spent twenty-six years trying to avoid. I am not prepared to throw caution to the wind after just two weeks.

It would be nonsense.

I won't do it.

I can't do it.

This is the worst thing that could have happened. Because now I believe in all the stuff on TV, radio, novels and cinema. It's true. You do know when you meet the One.

Your muse, your purpose, your explanation to life.

And suddenly life is shiny and glossy and worthwhile. But if the films and songs are right about falling in love, the chances are they can offer some insight into the outcome of entertaining such emotions.

Pain.

Lots of it.

Isn't my mother living proof?

Every second I was with Darren was exhilarating. Every second was heartbreaking. Constantly plagued with what could go wrong. When he said he loved me I was blissed out, ecstatic but petrified too. When Darren was with me I believed it. I believed it all, the happily ever after, the possibility that everlasting love is an option. But my confidence is ebbing away. It's unrealistic to expect Darren to stay with me every minute of every day but when he's not with me I'm too small to fight my own demons. It was OK in Whitby when we were constantly with each other—of course he couldn't be unfaithful or leave me. But now . . . where is he now? Maybe he's not in the Cotswolds. Maybe he's with another woman. The reality is that love never lasts; falling in love is asking to be hurt, deceived and betrayed. I feel naked. I look at Issie but she's oblivious to the cold chill in the air. I know she's thinking that if this happened to me, absolutely anything is possible.

But it's not.

"Of course, it can't go on," I state, making my mind up only in the seconds that the words form in my mouth.

"What?"

Turns out Issie's lottery ticket got thrown out with the garbage. Shame.

"It's impossible." My tone is more certain than my mind.

"But you've just said you love him," Issie is spluttering.

"I do," I snap. "At this moment I love him completely, utterly, desperately, clichédly. But if I carry on like this the next thing you'll know is that I'll be giving him a pet name and wanting his babies." I sound more harsh and resolute than I feel. I hope my voice convinces my heart.

"And what's so terrible about that?"

If I'm not mistaken she actually has tears in her eyes or perhaps her contacts are playing up. Poor Issie.

"Well, let's take it through to its logical conclusion, shall we? What if he doesn't feel the same? What if I care for him more than he cares for me?"

"But from what you said he sounds besotted."

"Well, men always are at first, aren't they?" Even Issie should know this. Especially Issie. "Then when the girl's hooked they stop calling. The power in every relationship sits with the person who cares least."

"That's where you go wrong, thinking that relationships are about power."

"*I* don't go wrong, Issie." I lay a heavy emphasis on the "I." "This would never have happened if I'd stayed in town. It's just that Whitby was, I don't know, beautiful, romantic." I continue to search for the correct word, "different."

"Cas, are you sure it's the scenery and not him that you are talking about?" I glare at her. "He sounds genuine," she pleads.

"OK, well, scenario number two. Assuming he feels the same way that I do—"

"He does, doesn't he? I know you think he does," squeals Issie.

I hardly dare suggest it. I think of him nibbling my fingers, brushing my hair, and looking at baby photos of me.

"Well, for the sake of this argument, let's say he does. Then what?"

"You could marry and live Happily Ever After."

As though it really were that simple. How naive! Issie obviously hasn't learned anything from her years of being my friend. I explain it slowly and clearly, as I'm beginning to suspect she's hard of hearing.

"There. Is. No. Such. Thing. Yes, we could marry but sooner or later (and it probably would be sooner, as these intense affairs are always the first to burn out) he'd let me down. Or I'd let him down. And that would be hell. If he can make me feel this good"—as though I was born the moment his dick delved into me—"imagine how foul he could make me feel if he left."

Issie hides her face in her hands. "Who are you trying to convince?"

"No one," Me. Me. I'm trying to convince myself, but at the same time I'd be more grateful than Issie could possibly know if she proved my argument is guff. But she can't because I'm right. I'm certain I'm right. I have to stop this going any further.

"Cas, you're thirty-three now, not seven. And just because your parents' relationship didn't work doesn't mean there can't be successful relationships."

I glare at her. Although Issie knows everything about my mother and father's divorce, we have an unwritten rule that we never discuss it. I am not the type to bleat on Oprah.

"Issie, one in three households are single-people households. Three in four couples who co-habit split up. Nearly one in two marriages end in divorce. Look at the facts." "The facts" have been bursting (uninvited) into my consciousness all afternoon.

"But think about Sharon and Ozzy Osbourne. They've been married forever and they are blissful."

"That's one example, Issie."

"There's the Queen and Prince Philip." I snort. She's desperate.

"There's Mr. and Mrs. Brown in the baker's on *Teddington Crescent*."

"They're fictional."

"There's my mum and dad."

"But your mum hates your dad."

"Not at all. She only pretends to. What about those couples on your show who didn't fall into temptation?"

"It's only a matter of time."

Issie raises her eyes skyward.

"Oh, Cas, you poor thing."

What can she mean? My mistake was allowing myself to become besotted by Darren. A mistake but not irrevocable. Not if I act swiftly and certainly now.

"Issie, can I come and stay with you for tonight?"

"Of course, if you want to. Why?"

"Because I know if I see him I'll weaken and I'm expecting him to pop by late tonight, when he gets back from the Cotswolds."

"Oh, see him, pleeeease."

"I can't, Issie. I'm not playing games here. This isn't a way to make him more interested. I have to sever all contact immediately. I can't allow this to continue. I can't make myself vulnerable."

I simply can't. Not won't. Can't.

I whizz around my bedroom and start throwing some clothes and cosmetics into a bag. I hardly pause to consider what I'm selecting, but I do stop to smell the sheets and to take him in one last time. He is why I was born a woman, but he can never, ever know because while I can only just bear walking away from him, I know I would be inconsolable if he ever left me.

This vulgar state of being "in love"—it's bound to be only temporary. The sooner I get back to my ordinary routine the better I'll feel.

It will only be a matter of time.

Very little time at that, probably.

Probably.

I pull the sheets off the bed and push them into the washing basket.

Issie realizes that she's not going to change my mind so instead settles for changing the subject. As I stuff a hairbrush and knickers in a bag she tells me that the sad loser guy from New Year has called. They've seen each other a few times. Issie's excited because they play Connect 4 together. I can't forgive him for letting his mother fix him up. Issie chatters on but I can't keep track. I'm sure it's delightful but I'm not sure I care. How has this terrible thing happened to me? How has this wonderful thing happened to me? How can it be both at once? I've seen enough to know that it is a messy, complex, filthy state of affairs at the best of times—i.e. when you want to be in love. This is by no means the best of times. I thought I was immune. I thought I was somehow better or different—certainly cleverer. Now I understand no one is immune.

As we put on our coats, Issie sighs, "You haven't been listening to a word I've been saying, have you?"

"I'm sorry, Issie. I've spent my entire evening forgetting about Darren," I smile sadly.

"Why are you doing this? Don't you think there's a possibility that you are snuffing out a genuine chance of happiness?" she coaxes.

"No. It's an exercise in damage limitation."

"I don't understand you, Cas."

"Really? How odd. I thought I'd made myself crystal clear." Except of course I'm lying. I don't understand me either. The bit I do understand, the fact that I *am* in love, only serves to confuse me further.

I lock the door behind me and Blue-tack an envelope to the door. It's addressed to Darren and the letter inside simply says:

Don't call.

CHAPTER
Thirteen

WORK IS AS FOUL as I thought it would be. Bale didn't swallow the laryngitis story because Fi, the bitch, showed him a photo of Darren.

"Laryngitis, my arse."

"No, actually it's a throat infection," I snipe back. It is a weak retort but I'm out of practice. I've been being nice to people for two weeks, for God's sake.

"I saw his picture, Jocasta. You were shagging. Getting your end away while the rest of us carried the can. It's shoddy. It's unacceptable. What do you have to say for yourself?"

Bale has selected his glass office for this public flaying. I know that however angry he is, he has to appear more so for the benefit of the rest of the team.

"Nigel, you are getting this out of proportion." I only ever call him Nigel when things are desperate. I consider leaning over his desk and creating an illusion of intimacy by touching his arm, but I can't bring myself to do it. "OK, so I trailed a candidate for the show and OK, it turned out to be a duff call because I couldn't persuade him to be on the show, but it was worth the gamble. If he'd appeared, it would have been the biggest show ever."

"Why?"

I knew that would get him.

"This guy objects to the show on moral grounds: social and individual. He's startlingly handsome and very articulate. If he'd agreed to be on the show there isn't a person in the country who would have wanted to oppose his decision. Not the lace industry, the manager of the John Lewis wedding gift service or that bishop." I toss the latest list of complaint letters to Bale. "The viewers would have united. He'd have taken away the last shadow of doubt about the show. People would have clambered to appear."

"But you couldn't persuade him?"

"No, I couldn't," I reply to my hands.

"You tried everything?" He holds on the word "everything" and we both know what he is asking. Did I sleep with Darren to get him to appear on the show? Yes and no. This answer is far too subtle for Bale to comprehend.

"Everything." My face is aflame.

Bale leans very close to me and I can see the blackheads nestling in the crease between his nose and cheek.

"Maybe you're losing your touch."

"What an arse!" I complain to Fi, as there is no one else around. Most of my team have decided that it's wiser to keep out of my way for a while. Fi is either braver or more stupid than the rest.

"I thought you'd need some company." She hands me a double espresso. I wince as I swallow it back. It's some time since I've drunk such strong coffee. It tastes like creosote.

"It's not as though anything went wrong while you were away," comments Fi.

She really is a bitch. I think it's time to remind her who the guru is.

"Yes. Well done, Fi. I saw that the ratings had stabilized at 9.1. Don't worry that you didn't get an increase with your shows. I thought they were very competently filmed, no matter what the punters thought," I smile at her and she hesitates, not knowing whether she should smile back or not.

"You're pleased, then?"

"You held the fort. Well done." The words say one thing, the tone another.

"Have I upset you?"

I sigh. I know I'm being a cow. Fi has produced two good shows. Without her there would have been no possibility of my taking off to Whitby, never mind staying for a week and then pulling the laryngitis stunt for another week. She's made a few minor cock-ups with the paperwork, she hasn't responded to any of the log-room calls and she hasn't helped Ricky or Di with any of the decisions they needed to make on scheduling or marketing. But, all in all, she's done a fine job. It's not her fault that I feel like crying, laughing, shouting, dancing and howling, while smashing and kissing everything in my eye's view. I'm turbulent. And misunderstood. Most notably, by myself.

"No, really, you have done a great job," I assure and this time I do it with a bit more enthusiasm. Her face breaks into a massive grin.

"I hoped you'd be pleased. Now tell me what really went on. I want details."

Fi pulls up a chair and we huddle around my PC. It is not my usual style to indulge in girly confidences but I haven't said Darren's name aloud for hours. If I don't say it soon I'll erupt. I tell her some of the things that I told Issie. I tell her about the train journey, his family, the swimming baths, the walks and the "restaurants." I've been talking for about twenty minutes solid and I've only just caught Fi's expression. She looks bewildered.

"What?"

"Cut the foreplay, get to the shagging."

I stare through her and think of the lovemaking. I can't tell her. For one thing, some of the language is potentially shocking, even for a Scand. And two, it's private. It's Darren's and mine. I can't turn him into a character in a short story. The phone rings and Fi reaches for it.

"Jocasta Perry's line, Fi Spencer speaking." I turn to my e-mail and let Fi deal with the call. I note that she's blushing. Then she giggles. Finally she says, "I'll just check." She covers the hand set and behaves like a pantomime dame.

"It's himmmmm," she mouths.

"Whoooo?" I mouth back; it appears it's contagious.

Fi flaps her arms up and down and rolls her eyes. In less enlightened eras she'd have been consigned to the ducking chair for less.

"Darren."

"I'm not here."

Fi looks perplexed. She makes excuses to Darren and then carefully copies down all his contact numbers. As she hangs up she passes me the note with the numbers on.

"So you did sleep with him." Her tone has changed considerably from before the call. I don't deny it; I just shrug. "And now you've lost all interest," she concludes. I wonder if this is what Darren has surmised. "Christ, Cas, you are such a love-them-and-leave-them merchant that I'm beginning to think that you were born a man and had a sex change. How can you resist him?"

I take the numbers from her and put them in the bin. "If he calls again, tell him I've left the company."

Because of the bishop's letter, Bale and I spend the entire day working side by side. The directors are metaphorically urinating all over the leather chairs in the executive suite. It's not that any of them are particularly godly—far from it. But one or two of them are hoping to be mentioned in the Queen's next honors list. Offending the Church is only one stop away from offending the government. Bale and I talk to the duty officers who work in the log room and fully analyze the complaints and compliments that the show has received since its conception. The duty officers are loyal and pragmatic and go some way to reassuring Bale that everything is cool. I suspect the loyalty is inspired by George, the duty office manager, who talks to my breasts.

"People are always more likely to complain than praise. The Great British public complain about everything." George shrugs; my breasts don't comment but let him continue. "This bishop thing, don't sweat it. It's always the mad ones who complain. I've had letters saying that we are biassed against smokers, that they don't like the color of the dress that the newscaster is wearing." I don't interrupt to say I have some sympathy—our newscasters are sartorially challenged. "During the Rugby World Cup we received complaints about the TV angles, that the Union Jack was upside down."

"Was it?"

"I don't know. They said Shirley Bassey was miming, which was definitely a lie. That the action was too much for epileptics and migraine sufferers. We are no longer a nation of shopkeepers but a nation of whiners."

I'm pleased—these examples discredit the people who complain, they seem petty and small-minded. I thank George for his time, with my special smile. It's wasted because as wide as it stretches it doesn't stretch to my breasts.

Bale and I also meet the scheduling and marketing departments. By midday we have a convincing response for the executive committee and, although we have the entire afternoon scheduled for debate, I know it won't be longer than an hour before the meeting breaks down and someone walks out. It's inevitable, with so many egos in the room. I'm delighted when my prediction comes true. The only director who really does object to my show is bullied and humiliated sufficiently for him to leave in disgust within an hour. We agree to take our response to *The Times*. I am packing away my electronic Filofax when Gary, the commercial director, taps my arm.

"Well done, girl." I smile. He nods enthusiastically and his mop of blond curly hair bounces up and down, putting me in mind of a cherub. It strikes me that I wouldn't have drawn this comparison before my foray into sentimentality. I'm disgusted with myself. I try to concentrate on what he's saying.

"Buoyant Term one. Going gangbusters. Twelve up. First stab, six up. The star performer in the quadrangle. Product categories are all up. Deal credit no deal debt. All thanks to ambitious penises. Well done, girl."

I haven't a clue what any of this means. The language is deliberately ambiguous. But Gary smiles at me and as I have only ever seen him smile when he talks about football, I figure that the commercial director is happy.

Next I plough through my mountain of e-mail. It's hard to concentrate, because although I've instructed Jaki to divert all my calls through to her, I still jump every time my line rings. Which it does about every four minutes. At the end of the day Jaki relays the messages she's taken. Despite my instructions Darren has rung twice.

I spend the early evening running through interview tapes in the editing suites. I need the best available material for next week's show. I'm not leaving it to the editor. I'm being conscientious plus to make up for going AWOL.

And to avoid thinking about Darren. It should be easier not to think of his gut-churning smile if I'm busy.

"You've quite a way with these stooges," comments Ed the editor.

"You think so, do you?" I don't take my eyes off the monitors.

"Yeah, you resist being patronizing, talking in short sentences and in single syllables. Quite a gift—the common touch."

"No one's ever accused me of that before," I comment drily.

"No one would guess how terrifying you are." Ed looks at me. Nervous, never sure how I'll take his jokes. I smile mildly and we both concentrate on the interview.

The monitor is showing the film I made the day before I met Darren. The case is one where some bloke left his wife for some girl. The girl is now unsure if she can keep him, even though they plan to marry in a month. She thinks he wants to go back to his wife. This, I suppose, disproves the theory that one wife is as good as the next. I'm interviewing the wife. She's a rare breed, a shy Scottish woman. Her abrasive vowels rasp, "If I were famous it wouldn't bother me so much—the stained carpet and chipped skirting board. I'd accept that he chose her."

"I might be able to give you both."

That's my voice on the monitor, offering her false hope. At the time I had thought that a bit of fame and glamour would make her happier. And there was a chance that he'd choose her. But rewatching the tape, just two weeks on, leaves me with an uncomfortable feeling in my stomach. Is it right to—? I stop the thought as it's forming, and for the zillionth time today, I curse Darren.

"They hate my accent," she's wailing.

"No, they hate your long legs and massive tits. That's their motivation. Objecting to your accent is a diversionary tactic," I assure.

"You are a true pro," says Ed. "Dishing out that sort of compliment is certain to get them onside. She'll get your man for you now."

"Actually, Ed, I just meant it," I say as I close the door behind me.

Unusually I decide to take a bus home. I don't want to be alone in a cab. I don't want to be alone with me. I don't want to be me. I've never felt so confused and miserable in my life. And yet I wouldn't have swapped it for the world. That's the worst of it.

I look at my watch and allow myself two minutes thinking about Darren. Twenty minutes later the bus arrives. There is a huge ad for aftershave painted on the side of the bus. The model has a look of Darren. Similar eyes but not as beautiful.

The bus is a mistake because the driver won't accept my £50 note and laughs when I explain that I don't carry loose change as it ruins the shape of your pockets. In the end some skinny guy behind me offers up the £1. It's embarrassing. I am about to glare at him for his impertinence but as I catch his eye I noticed that he also looks tired. Maybe he isn't paying my ride in hope of one in return. Perhaps he just wanted the queue to move along.

"Thanks," I mutter. He briefly nods, self-conscious about his own act of goodness. He's probably aware how very un-London he's being.

I go upstairs and sit at the front. I wish Darren were here with me—we could pretend to be driving the bus. As soon as I have this thought I hate myself. There. See. That's where this kind of shenanigans leads. Pathetic sentimentality! How do I know that Darren would pretend to be driving the bus? I'm acting like an arse.

Usually public transport is anonymous. That's why we are happy to pay inflated prices for an unfeasible short ride—it's part of the deal. No one will talk to you and if they can possibly help it, they will avoid looking at you too. Except for drunks who use public transport for the exact opposite reason. I rarely notice whom I'm traveling with, but today it's as if I am looking with new eyes. Nothing is anonymous; everyone seems to be acting significantly. The guy next to me, besides suffering from terrible BO, offends me on another front. He's wearing a headset, which he's singing along to. Naturally he's singing a song about everlasting love, which frankly is a load of crap. Not just his voice. I move seat and find myself sitting behind two teenage girls. They are reading Cosmo. They do the quiz to find their perfect men. If only it was so easy. As they read the questions aloud to one another I mentally answer them. I'm mostly Bs. By the end of the quiz the girls discover that their boyfriends are mummy's boys and misogynists retrospectively. I discover Darren cannot be improved upon.

When I get home I see that the answering machine light is flashing. I listen to the messages as I run a bath.

"Cas, it's me," chimes Issie. "Just ringing to see how things went with Bale today. Give me a call later if you want to. I'll be home from the gym at about ten."

I smile, knowing that she's slipped in the words "the gym" to impress me. Much to Josh's and my surprise Issie is following through on her New Year's resolution. She has a place in the London Marathon and is training hard for it. The second message is from Josh.

"Hey, Babe, how are you? How was the north? I'm going to the cinema tonight. Some sub-titled bollocks that Jane wants to see. I'm sure it will be very worthy and depressing. It's on at one of those arty cinemas that don't even sell Häagen-Dazs. I'll call you tomorrow."

Poor Jane sounds as though she's history. I am beginning to relax. The third message is from my mother, complaining that I didn't visit on Sunday. A spasm of guilt shoots through me. So all's well on the Western front—these are the messages that I often come into on a Monday evening. I am back on familiar territory. Darren has been a bizarre distraction but now I'm fine. I'm safe.

"Cas, it's me." His voice saws into my sanctuary and I'm delirious. I'm disgusted. "I guess you are still at work. If you are there, please pick up." The voice pauses. "I guess you're not there. I got your note." He makes a sad little sound which sounds strangled somewhere between a laugh and a sigh. "I knew you would do something like this. I knew you'd panic. But if you'll let me talk to you—" His voice breaks and he coughs. "Look, I had a great time the last two weeks. So did you." He sounds urgent now, a mix between anger and frustration—which I'm used to inciting, and tenderness—which I'm not. "If it's any consolation, I'm scared too." Then the tape runs out. I stand perfectly still and try to to understand what I'm feeling. My God, there we have it, I'm feeling already. Not thinking, like I was a couple of weeks ago. Suddenly I'm feeling!

He did sound genuine. What does he mean, he's "scared too?" As well as who?

I listen to the message again. And again. And again. In fact, I listen to it twelve times. By the twelfth time one thing is clear. I've lost it. I press the erase button and go to bed. Darren who?

Smith.

CHAPTER
Fourteen

BEING IN LOVE IS JUST AS PAINFUL as I always expected it to be. I wake up every morning and my first thought is of Darren. In fact, as my dreams are also littered with him, I'm beginning to find it difficult to distinguish between the two states. They smudge together. I'll be driving into work and I'll see him in every car and on every street. The excitement of spotting him is tremendous. The disappointment that it never is him is side-splitting. I walk into the TV6 building and always look around to see if he's in reception, which is a ridiculous thought, considering how much he loathes the studio and all it stands for. I listen to weather forecasts for Whitby, even though I know he's in London. How could I ever have thought that Whitby was Smallsville? Now it's everywhere I turn. TV6 is setting a new drama there; on the news yesterday there was a small piece about the myth of Dracula and there was a shot of the cemetery we visited. Issie's parents have just bought a caravan and Whitby was one of the first places they visited. Whitby is suddenly the center of the universe. Every time the phone rings I leap and while I always listen to his messages, several times, I haven't returned any calls.

Initially he called often and left complicated messages. Jaki begged me to return them.

"Call him, Cas. He doesn't believe you've left the firm."

"I've nothing to say to him."

"Well, at least tell him that! If not for your sake, for mine.

My workload has practically doubled since I started taking his calls."

"Then you weren't working hard enough in the first place," I replied, without looking up from my screen. "Contact reception and get me a new extension number and next time he calls tell him I'll inform the police if he keeps pestering me."

Darren has called around to my flat twice. Both times he conscientiously left a note detailing when he'd return, so I moved to Issie's for a while. He took the hint. The visits stopped. The calls stopped. Except for the occasional one, late at night, when he's obviously drunk—just a dulcet "It's me." He still sends me e-mails. He no longer sends long notes asking me to get in touch; now he simply sends links to websites that he thinks might interest me. Articles on Audrey Hepburn, surveys on TV viewing habits and yesterday an update on the latest divorce statistics released by the government. I wonder what he meant by that? It's hard to read significance into any of the articles he sends, as he doesn't introduce them or sign off with anything personal. Which I suppose is a blessing. Imagine if he wrote "best wishes" or "love" or "all my love"—I'd turn into Issie, analyzing the significance of each word, when there isn't any.

Facts about him erupt into my consciousness when I'm least expecting them. One moment I'm checking interview scripts, the next I'm thinking about his arguments on the collective responsibility of programming.

Which is bollocks.

But he did argue his case stylishly.

If only my thoughts of him stopped with recalling his arguments. I send myself to sleep each night remembering the way his lips felt hanging on my nipple and I wake up smiling. But only for the nanosecond it takes for my brain to explain to my heart that there will be no repeat performance.

Ever.

It seems that I know a million things about him because I'm always considering, remembering, recollecting. Yet there is so much that I don't know. I examine trees and wonder exactly what do tree surgeons do. We did talk about his work but I'd like a clearer picture. I'd like to be able to imagine every part of his day. I wonder what his flat is like and what car he drives. Then I remind myself that it is safer I don't know these things because the less I have to forget the better. And really it is only a matter of time before he's annihilated from my mind. I comfort myself with the thought that in the beginning, everything is fascinating. The way they part their hair, the way they blow their nose, their views on government policies toward third world debt, how they like their tuna steak. Every manifestation seems enticing, but if I were still with him these things would have already become tedious. It would be impossible to keep noticing these things if they were constantly before me. The commonplace is not rare and beautiful. Interesting. Precious. Like all my memories. It's better that I have the luscious intensity intact rather than sullied through everyday wear.

I'm aware that I sound like Issie. But it's under control.

I prescribe my usual antidote and work is hot. Full of despair, betrayal, rage, depression, sweaty palms and tight throats, but other people's, not mine. Weddings bring out the worst in people, which is ideal for my purposes. The British public don't disappoint me in their levels of paranoia or jealousy; contestants fall through the doors realizing what a perfect opportunity for revenge a wedding is. Who could ask for more? A huge stage packed with an audience of the stooges' nearest and dearest (plus 10.6 million viewers and rising) available to witness the humiliation. It's a fact that during preparations for a wedding small problems escalate. A decision about a buttonhole—carnation or lily—can be make or break; therefore the turmoil that the choice between Carol and Lily can wreak should not be underestimated.

My response to the bishop's letter ran in all the quality press. Which created just the correct amount of indignation. Calls were made for the government to intervene by issuing TV programs with certificates of classification, similar to the cinema. A sensible suggestion with which no one with any common sense could argue. Luckily the tabloids misrepresented the issue and reopened the old debate on freedom of the media and "big brother" censorship. The uproar is tremendous. Although the tabloids fail to articulate a sensible counter-argument to the idea of classification, there is enough contagious anger to keep the issue (and most importantly the show) in the headlines for weeks. I am delighted with the controversy. There are a number of distinct advantages, besides the incessant snowballing of the number of potential guests. I have been given the go-ahead to shoot *Sex with an Ex* episodes from now until July. Advertisers are more confident and are pledging big advertising budgets, which has allowed me the opportunity to extend the channel's program schedule. We've bought four massive films, which are set to secure huge audiences. We've put more money into the *Teddington Crescent* soap, securing better writers and sets that are not made of tissue paper. We've also introduced a number of entirely new programs—quiz shows, sitcoms and docusoaps. I am Midas.

The only disadvantages of *Sex with an Ex* being a runaway success is that Bale has become more "hands-on" in the management of the show. Like all good bosses, his main strength is identifying a winner, created by someone else, and stealing it. Bale has never had an opportunity to pull a fast one like this on me before—I'm normally too sharp, too many steps ahead of him. But this time I unintentionally handed him the opportunity on a plate. Bale describes my trip to Whitby as my "wild-goose-chase period." He frequently cites it as an act of misjudgment and irresponsibility. The implication is, of course, that if I've been so heinously stupid and irrational once, there is always the danger of my doing the same thing again; perhaps when even more than a tight schedule is at stake. My twelve-year exemplary CV counts for nothing. I would resent this treatment but I know the rules we play by in this industry—I made most of them up; so I simply have to take it on the chin.

At least publicly.

Privately I'm plotting ways to circulate pictures of Bale in woman's underwear, which I procured from his latest wounded jilt. She happily offered them up to me, as she has been giving Bale head for three weeks, on the back of his promise that "he'd see her right in the firm." In fact, he saw her right *out* of the firm with nothing more than a P45 for her effort. She'd taken the pictures during one of their more bizarre sessions. She gave them to me and I gave her a letter of recommendation based on some of her talents, other than those Bale sampled. I also suggested she concentrated on her shorthand, rather than hand jobs. But I expect the advice will have fallen on deaf ears. Once you find yourself on your back, on the back of a promise, you never get up. I'm not sure when, or if, I'll ever run the pictures on the Internet but I like knowing I have them.

Bale's insidious presence affects the entire show, largely because he doesn't understand it. The success of *Sex with an Ex* is its spontaneity. Now speculation has been annihilated.

We have telephone lines set up for those wishing to be on the show, which are manned by counselors. I rarely handle the interviews these days, but have a team of psychologists to do so. The channel gets involved with the stooges' wedding preparations from a very early stage in the engagement, often selecting the ring. We attend most dress fittings and censor the guest list. We bear the entire cost of any weddings that actually manage to limp to the altar but, worse than twenty parents, we exercise our right to advise on all aspects, from cake to consummation. We have teams that are specially selected for their sympathetic qualities or at least their ability to feign sympathy convincingly, and they become the friends of the stooges. We become indispensable to the ordinary people who wish to compete. Because it is about competition. Whom will he choose? Does she love me alone? Nothing is left to chance. It's now very rare that when the lights go down the contestant's confidence drains and they find themselves asking, "What am I doing here?" It's unlikely because they've been rehearsed, tutored, scripted, groomed to an inch of their lives. They know how to act if they are humiliated in front of millions (ideally a woman should cry and a man should be violent, but we sometimes turn this expectation on its head to create an extraordinary effect). They know how to act if their partner remains faithful (sweet relief mixed with assured confidence). They practice how to sit, walk, hold their hands, cry, punch and kick. I personally feel the show has lost its bite but Bale is so paranoid about the big bucks which are rolling on *Sex with an Ex* that he won't hear of returning to a more impromptu approach. I could argue my case but, unaccountably, I'm not as fired about the show as I have been in the past. I'm more concerned with getting some new shows off the ground.

I call a meeting to discuss some new ideas. I watch the team cluster through the glass partition. They no longer look like the anxious relatives of the sick, as they did last August. It's amazing what six months and over ten million viewers can do. They look happy and confident, proud and exhilarated. Stick that in your pipe and smoke it, Darren Smith.

"Hey, guys, how are you?"

"Hanging," replies Tom. I stare my rebuke. It's a lie. I've seen Tom's tackle and even the most generous description would not stretch to "hanging."

"Cool."

"Top."

"Smart," reply Mark, Jaki and Gray respectively. I hope they understand that I am responsible for their feeling of euphoria.

"Pleased to hear it. Now to business." I glare Ricky out of his chair at the top of the table and sit there taking command of the room. Each team member gives a brief update on their department. Gray reports the massive revenue increases in sponsorship and advertising. I was expecting this; the others gasp, happy and astonished. Di gives us more good news, announcing that the exec. committee has increased our team's marketing budget by 250 percent. Tom and Mark immediately start debating where we should go for lunch.

"Quo Vadis?"

"No, the Ivy."

"Grow up," instructs Fi. "There are more important things to discuss." She's learning.

"Like what?" spits Mark.

"Like what next?" I reply. "We have to stay hot." We bandy some ideas around.

"A follow-up to *Sex with an Ex*. You know, how are the couple doing? Did they make the right choice?" suggests Jaki.

"That's really obvious," snarls Fi.

"But cheap," Jaki defends, knowing it's me not Fi she has to impress.

"You're right, go for it," I instruct. "Write it up as a proposal. Make it sexy. Get some visuals."

"How about a series on serial killers?" suggests Tom. "Compare and contrast the Yorkshire Ripper, the Moors Murderers, that Dr. Death guy." I concentrate on concealing my disgust.

"Or something more broad, like tyrants and despots. Stalin, Hitler, Pinochet—we could have an audience participation deciding who was the most vicious," adds Mark.

"Too gruesome," comments Gray, and I'm relieved that someone has articulated my killjoy thoughts. "Let's stick to what we do well, humiliating and exposing the normal blokes."

"Yeah," says Ricky. "We could follow guys on their stag weekends. You know, get shots of them licking Guinness off prostitutes' breasts or being tied naked to a lamppost.

"Good idea," enthused Fi. "We could film the hens puking into their handbags singing 'Let Me Entertain You' while taking their bras off."

"No, no. I think we should go more up-market," comments Di.

I want to kiss her.

"Let's do some undercover work on politicians and fat cats. Let's film them standing on bar tops or licking Guinness off prostitutes' breasts."

I want to kick her.

"Or we could do a series of celeb profiles?" I suggest.

"Absolutely," enthuses Jaki. "Dig up all their dirty past, lots of photos they'd rather not see published."

"No," I shout, marginally more forcefully than I intended. "Something more"—I hesitate, nervous of how my suggestion will be received—"profitable."

"Well, skeletons in the cupboard are profitable. The advertisers are bound to see the appeal and put loads of money behind it," comments Fi.

"I mean emotionally profitable. Perhaps we could do a show about how celebs are getting along with their millennium promise or, if they didn't make one, perhaps we can get them to pledge something improving now."

"Maybe," mumbles Ricky. But he doesn't sound that enthusiastic. I look at the others but they are all steadfastly concentrating on the cobweb in the right-hand ceiling corner of the room. I'm embarrassed, but push on.

"OK, maybe that's not too keen, but I'm just trying to think of something more educational than the current mix."

"Absolutely."

"Quite right."

"Definitely agree," chorus the cobweb-gazing brigade.

"Do you?" I smile enthusiastically.

"Yeah, like a program on cross-dressing. Now that's educational."

"Or something on plastic surgery. Perhaps some horror stories of women desperate to keep their husbands and prepared to go to amazing surgical lengths to do so—all the better if the operations have gone wrong."

"Don't be so stereotypical," shouts Fi. "What about male plastic surgery stories? Penis extensions—now there's a tale to tell." The room erupts into sniggers. I don't join in. I'm relieved when someone suggests that we need to go to the pub for a "break from the intensity." I'm praying that the salt and Linneker versus cheese and onion debate will overwhelm, and that the original subject of the meeting is forgotten.

CHAPTER
Fifteen

I HAVE NEVER WORKED SO HARD in my life as I have these past few months. Or, more honestly, work has never been so hard. I fail to notice spring; the bit of me that appreciates green buds and blue skies was only ever a small constituent of my makeup, and has now been snuffed out completely as I surround myself with schedules, deadlines, target revenues, TVRs and ARPs. I'm not busy enough. I decide that my social life needs new impetus, so I attend every party, reception, premiere, dinner and event that I'm invited to. Recently I've broadened my life experiences to include visiting Le Cirque du Soleil, participating in a pony-trekking weekend in north Wales and an all-day aerobic session for charity, attending two hen nights (both with essential stripping policeman) and joining Issie's pottery class. For all this frivolity, I have no fun.

This indiscriminate acceptance of invitations has filled my hours, but there have been two annulling consequences. The first is that I've discovered that my previous opinion on mankind (considered by many to be harsh) was in fact generous. People are generally much more tedious than even I estimated. The women I meet are unilaterally obsessed with their waistlines and, as often as not, individually obsessed with some waster. The men I meet are as per my original evaluation. They are insincere commitment phobes or spineless and married. And while I personally am still resolutely avoiding commitment, I dislike this characteristic in others. In the past I was able to endure the trite lines and clammy hands at least until the morning after the night before. Now it's impossible for me to fake interest for as long as it takes most of them to fight their way to the front of the bar queue. Issie is thrilled that I am sticking to my New Year's resolution.

"Other than Darren you haven't had any casual sex this year." She blushes. "Well, including Darren you haven't had any *casual* sex."

I don't comment.

The second consequence of my indiscriminate acceptance of invites is that by making myself more available I have made myself less desirable. I worry that I am gaining the reputation of being one of those people who attends the opening of a marmalade jar. For this reason I have resolutely turned down all invitations for this weekend. I refused an offer to fly to New York to "shop till I drop." The guy who made the offer was being euphemistic. He actually wanted me to shop until my knickers dropped. I said no to a reception at the Tate Modern tonight and no to drinks with the team. I refused a dinner and fancy-dress party tomorrow, and a lunch on Sunday with friends. Issie is spending the weekend doing some intensive training with a group of people who are also running the London Marathon and Josh is taking Jane to the country. Not for a romantic weekend, but to bin her. He mistakenly thinks this is the gentleman-like thing to do. Issie and I tried to explain that, almost certainly, Jane would prefer to have her heart broken on her own territory, but Josh pointed out that he'd lose his deposit on the hotel room if he no-showed. As they are both out of town I'll spend the weekend without human contact.

I am hopeful, expectant. I'm looking forward to being alone with my face pack, fridge and remote control. I sit down with a highlighter pen, the television section of the *Observer* and a bottle of gin. I circle my TV viewing for the night. *Coronation Street*, a documentary on Brooklyn Beckham (that's our show), *Brookside*, *Friends*, and then I'll switch to cable for a movie. I catch sight of the date and automatically calculate that it's one month, three weeks, five days and eight hours since I last saw Darren.

Only quarter of an hour before Corrie starts.

Thirteen minutes.

Another nine minutes to go.

Still quite some time yet. I think I'll ring Mum.

"Hi, Mum."

"Oh, hello Jocasta, dear, how are you? I was just talking about you to Bob."

"Who?"

"Bob, you know—"

"Your neighbor."

"Exactly!"

"What were you saying?"

"Sorry?"

"What were you saying to Bob?" I'm beginning to regret the call.

"I was just saying I wonder how Jocasta is."

"Well, I'm fine."

"Pleased to hear it."

"And how are you?"

"Oh, I'm fine, except for the old problem." I have no idea what the "old problem" is, although doubtless she's told me on countless occasions; nor do I have any desire to find out. I move the conversation on.

"I called to ask if you fancy going shopping tomorrow. Unaccountably it's a Saturday and I haven't got a wedding to go to." I hadn't realized that I'd called to ask this, the fifteen minutes alone before my viewing started has obviously weighed in heavily. I wait for her gushing thanks that I've decided to offer up an entire Saturday, even though it's not her birthday or anywhere near Christmas. Instead she surprises me.

"I expect people are a little nervous about inviting you to their weddings, what with your show and everything. Well, dear, I'd love to go shopping with you, but Bob and I are going to a craft fair and it's been in the diary for some time. I can't let him down— I know he'd be most disappointed and I'm looking forward to it too."

I don't ask what kind of man enjoys a craft fair; nor do I commit myself when she adds hopefully, "How about next week?"

I put the phone down and turn the volume up.

While it's been a constructive weekend (I've filed my nails, both fingers and toes, I've tidied my cutlery drawer and I've descaled the kettle and the showerhead), by Sunday afternoon I'm beginning to wish I'd accepted the invite to lunch. I've read the Sunday papers, including the small ads for the removal of unwanted lines, fat and hair, as well as those for the addition to breasts and penises. I've watched a backlog of recorded programs and all the soap omnibuses. In fact, most of my entertainment and all my food has been generated from radioactive boxes. Although I have ample time on my hands, I can't be arsed to drag myself to Tesco's or even Cullen's. There really is no point in buying fresh herbs and vegetables, chopping and sautéing for one. Instead I search my cupboards for inspiration. I don't find it. I can't think of a recipe that happily combines peanut butter, Carr's water biscuits and All Bran. The contents of my fridge are neither useful nor ornamental. There's a molding jar of capers and another of anchovies (bought for a dinner party), Tabasco, Yakult and Red Bull. Of course, there's the foundation bottle of champagne, but even I don't like drinking Veuve Clicquot alone. Instead I defrost things unsavory. Cardboard food from cardboard boxes—singleton's food.

I can hear some kids playing in the nearby park. As far as I can tell the objective of the game is to see who can produce the most piercing scream. Very entertaining, if you're eight. I wonder what Charlotte and Lucy are up to? An airplane passes over head. In the mid-distance I can hear the intermittent hum of an articulated truck whizz from factory to storage warehouse. I'm depressed. I must be. The truck seems poignant. I look around for a vessel to use as an ashtray. All the ashtrays, saucers, teacups, plant pots that are in spitting distance of my sofa are full to overflowing with ash already.

While me-time is all very educative, the most overwhelming lesson appears to be that I'm pretty miserable company. Even the fact that Saturday's show was a corker, and the scheduling department have already rung me to tell me we've reached 10.4 million viewers, fails to cheer me. The worst of it is, I'm not entirely alone.

As I move around my home I see Darren sprawled out on his stomach reading the Sunday papers, or I find him squeezing oranges in my kitchen, or I bump into him coming out of the shower. Naked and powerful with a white towel around his hips and water drops dripping from his hair to the carpet. But the carpet is never wet because he's only in my head and he's never in my bed.

I remember Darren first coming into my flat.

"Nice pad. Did you buy it lock, stock and barrel from a style magazine?" He'd grinned and turned to kiss me. I flung my coat on to the back on my settee, not bothering to hang it in the cupboard. I kissed him back and didn't take offense.

"Funny. Issie thinks this place is impersonal, too. I think it's anything but. I bought an empty shell and built my apartment from scratch. What could be more personal?"

Darren wrapped his arms around me and held me tightly. I breathed him in. I was shaking with the newness of it all. It was new that I was talking this way. It was new that a man was in my home and I was sharing my life, even for a week.

I stare at the windowpane, concentrating on the raindrop race, which Darren taught me. The idea is you choose a raindrop and the other person chooses another raindrop, both roughly at the same height and ideally at the top of the window. The winner is the one whose drop reaches the bottom of the window first. I win. Naturally—I'm the only one playing. I can't think of anything to amuse, charm or hearten me. Not even the fact that Josh's girlfriend will be having an even more shit time than I am. This just proves my theory about the insanity of getting involved. I pray Josh will call me soon with a debrief—I need a distraction.

I decide to replace the catchy tune of my clunking radiators and purring fridge. I force myself out of my cozy window seat and examine my cassette and CD collection. Uninvited, the memory of Darren discovering my CD collection barges into my head.

"You put some music on while I pour some drinks," I'd instructed, moving toward the wine rack.

"Interesting music collection," he commented.

"Normally described as eclectic. It's a testimony to ex-shags."

"Ah, I see." And he probably did, because I believe that he understood me entirely, past and present. Which is my problem.

"The Smiths and the Cure represent your adolescent angst years."

"Correct. Actually I was an extremely buoyant adolescent but my lover was an anger ball so I faked an avid interest. Red or white?" I held up both bottles, trying to ignore my own last sentence. I realized that by faking an avid interest I'd set a pattern for a lifetime.

"Red. Something full-bodied, if you have it."

It impressed me that Darren managed to politely knock back the plonk in Whitby without showing any snobbery or distaste when he obviously knows what he likes when it comes to wine. Maybe it was a mistake to make such a fuss about drinking Blue Nun, especially when Mrs. Smith had bought it especially for me. Not that it matters. None of it matters.

It still gnaws.

"And I take it that Lloyd Cole, Tom Waits, Lou Reed, Pet Shop Boys and Scott Walker are attributable to your student years?"

"Spot on. Phil, Paul, Iain, Greg and, er, Mark respectively."

I poured the wine and handed it to him. As I reenact this scene I use a coffee mug, which is pretty inadequate.

"Your music tastes are certainly wide and varied. REM, Blur, Red Hot Chilli Peppers, Ruben Gonzalez." Darren sipped the wine and smiled at me. The smile then, as now, hit directly in my chest, exploded and hurled shrapnel to my throat, back of knees and knickers. I'd never felt so fine. I hurt all over.

"Not my taste in music but in men. Those CDs are credited to Nathon, Andy, Tom, Dave.

"The Judds!?" Raised eyebrow.

"I know—awful, isn't it? Peter. Take heart, his appalling musical taste was compensated by his expertise in the sack. At the time I'd even have forgiven white socks."

"I can't take heart. I'm jealous of every last one of them." He turned and kissed me ferociously, nearly causing me to spill my wine. He began to unbutton my shirt. His fingers teased my skin, first my collarbone. Then trailing past my breast, threading down to my stomach.

I absolutely force myself back to the present.

It's bleak. I thought I knew all there was to know about loss, but not having Darren in my life is so vile that I wonder how I get up in the mornings. I feel like Dorothy on rewind. Instead of hitting the yellow brick road and finding myself in Technicolored Oz, I've been shoved into a monotone existence. I don't enjoy parties, or bars, or clubs. I don't like being with people, I loath being alone. I don't zing, I don't sparkle. I don't slice with my tongue. Even work seems lackluster. I wonder how I ever thought this life was fulfilling, let alone exhilarating. Life now sags around me. I'm nauseous with loneliness. It engulfs me.

I wish I'd never met him.

I don't mean that. I hate myself for being so disloyal. I know that I would do it all again. I'd still get on that train. It was already too late the moment I collided into his eyes in the interview room. I'd thought I was so damn smart. So elite. So untouchable. Yet while it hurts that only his ghost—and not his irresistible self—is in my sitting-room, him in my toweling dressing gown, me in his jumper, both of us soaked in love and cum—I know I am still in control.

Oh, only just, I admit that.

I left *him*. He didn't leave me. He doesn't know how I feel. He doesn't know how vulnerable I am.

Only I know that.

The phone rings, breaking the sound of being alone. I pounce on it. It's Josh. I know this before I pick it up.

"How'd it go?" I'm ridiculously interested, as I'm desperate to break myself out of my own indulgent apathy.

"Awful," he groans.

"Mmm." I sound sympathetic because I am. "Did she take it very badly?"

"She cried." Most of Josh is upset but a tiny bit of him is triumphant.

"Mmm."

"It's worse doing the dumping than being the dumpee." I doubt he means this.

"I wouldn't know," I remind him.

"No, of course not. You've never been dumped."

"What is the point of sticking around long enough to get your heart broken?" I challenge, more cheerfully than honestly. Strangely I haven't been honest with Josh about my feelings for Darren. Josh assumes Darren was another brief and unimportant encounter. I can't tell him how I feel because saying it aloud makes it more real. I must bury my feelings for Darren. I must.

"What did you tell her?"

"Oh, you know, the usual stuff."

"It's just not right?"

"Yes," he agrees enthusiastically. Although I love Josh, I'm irritated by him. I sigh, thinking of all the women who've ever cried because of the words, "It's just not right." Why do men only discover this when they roll off the sticky Durex?

"I know what you're thinking, but I really didn't want to hurt her."

I relent. After all, I've known him since he played with Action Men and I played with Sindy dolls. Now it's the other way around, I can't simply abandon him. He starts to tell me about the ditching. It doesn't take long; he's a boy. If Issie were telling me about her dumping some bloke or other, we'd spend hours. We'd start with describing what both parties were wearing. We'd talk about the location selected for the scenario. It's very important to choose the correct ground. His place is good because then you get to choose when to leave and he doesn't have to stumble home in a veil of tears. Or somewhere neutral, like a bar or a party. Not his mum's. She simply won't see it from your point of view. And not—under any circumstances—your own place. He might decide not to leave, insisting that it's possible to make a go of it. It never is. Calling the police in is ugly. I know—I've done it. Now if this were Issie it would be a different story. Issie would tell me everything. She'd punctuate it with "and then he said," "and then I said," "and he looked as though . . ." However close we are, Josh has too many Y-chromosomes to do this. Instead he has to act all disinterested and hard. He blows it when he asks me if I'll go around.

"I'll be there in ten." Of course I'll go to him. I'd walk hot coals for him.

Josh likes to think he lives in Islington but in fact he lives in King's Cross. He lives in a ground-floor flat, which can most adequately and efficiently be described as "masculine." Until his thirtieth birthday, Josh steadfastly refused to pay as much as a cursory glance toward interior design, cleanliness or comfort. He lived in squalor—not that he seemed to notice. In fact, he often joked that filth and disorder were his best friends. I was never sure if he was referring to his domestic arrangements or me and Issie respectively. Josh only ever washed up if the corner shop had run out of paper plates and he changed his sheets less frequently than his women. His bathroom never benefited from Ajax, Jif or Domestos, all of which could be Greek islands as far as Josh was concerned. His items of furniture were my mother's cast-offs, the things she absolutely could not force into her home. This foulness was not poverty-induced, simply a male blind spot, as inexplicable as the fact that when men do become interested in their home (thirtieth birthday or marriage, whichever they meet first) they cover the squalidness in blue.

Blue walls and tiles, blue fabric, blue crockery, blue cutlery, blue loo roll, blue napkins and napkin rings (which have only ever been used once—the thirtieth birthday dinner party), blue settee, blue bed and bedding, blue dust pan and mop and finally a blue toothbrush. When Issie or I ever visited Josh while he was decorating we were always overly animated, fearing if we stood still for too long he'd paint us blue too.

As I walk into his flat, I'm thinking that if Josh introduced buttercup yellow in his hall or a deep red in his sitting-room it would be a vast improvement.

"Josh, why are the lights dimmed?" I ask and immediately turn them up. I start to laugh. "Oh, I see, to show off the candles. Are you indulging in a Druid-type self-loathing session?" I kiss him on the forehead and wave the bottle I've brought.

"It's a '94 Château La Croix de Mouchet. I was saving it for a special occasion but I'm not sure when that'll be so I thought I'd bring it around." I march directly to the kitchen to forage out some glasses.

I bump into the biggest floral arrangement ever.

"Who are the flowers for, or should I say from? God, Josh, this place looks more like a seduction scene than a dumping ground." I suddenly guess what's going on. "No, she didn't buy you these just before you ditched her, did she?" I'm shocked at the stupidity of some women. "And you accepted them." I'm less surprised by the callous nature of most men. "Bastard." I smile. He'll know I'm joking. Josh doesn't answer but takes the wine I'm offering and clinks my glass. I continue chattering, glad of the company, for what it is. Josh is not at his sparkly best.

"God, I've had the loneliest weekend," I confess.

"Really?"

"Don't look so pleased about it, Josh. You know you and Issie are indispensable to me. You don't need to prove your point by both going away at once. I started having the most maudlin thoughts. I even wished there was a wedding to go to. Now isn't that a hoot?"

Josh brightens. "Do you really?"

"What?"

"Wish there was a wedding to go to?"

"Well, since my choice this weekend was that or eat Coco Pops, by the hand directly from the box, yes, I'd prefer the wedding." I pat the settee next to me. "Come on, then, sit here. Tell me all about chucking Jane." I stare at Josh. "Hey, you look quite shaken. Are you regretting it?"

"No." He shakes his head definitively.

"So?" He pauses for the longest time. Something is definitely upsetting him. "Good God, Josh. You're not ill, are you?" I'm suddenly terrified.

"No. Not ill."

"So what's up?" I link my arm through his. He shuffles awkwardly, pulling his arm away.

"I don't know how to put this."

"Just say it, whatever it is," I encourage. Why the sudden hesitancy? Josh and I have always spoken freely to one another. What can he have to say that's so dreadful? Suddenly he lurches for my hand.

"OK, I'll just say it. Will you marry me, Cas?"

"Ha ha." I sip my wine.

"I'm serious," he insists.

I look at him. His eyes are shining earnestly.

He is.

Shit.

"Well, it's a bit of a surprise. I don't know what to say."

Probably anything but that. It's a bit lame. It's awful. Luckily Josh is too nervous to notice my inadequacies. He reaches behind a cushion and pulls out a Tiffany ring box. He magics a thick cream rose from somewhere or other.

"Bloody hell, Paul Daniels is proposing to me." I laugh but my laugh is hollow and echoey. It doesn't fill the silence. Josh notices the silence too.

"Bugger, forgot the music."

He jumps up and puts on his CD player. "Ground Control to Major Tom" blares out, which makes me laugh and Josh swear. I know he's spent the afternoon walking around the house with the strainer on his head, singing along.

"Fuck, not very appropriate." He swaps to Frank Sinatra singing "I've Got You Under my Skin." I'm grateful for this small diversion.

"You're serious, aren't you, Josh?" I ask his back.

"I am." He tells the wall. After fiddling with the bass and the volume for a while Josh comes back and sits next to me. He doesn't sit quite as closely as he usually does. He's not actually touching me, but he is close enough for me to notice that he's shaking and there's sweat on his upper lip.

"Did you buy the ring for me or Jane?" I ask.

"You, of course!" He sounds insulted.

"Just checking." I grin nervously. "I wondered if this was

impulse or you'd given it a lot of thought." His face implodes, I rush on. "Well, it's obvious that you've given it a lot of thought, but I wasn't sure if it was me you were thinking of." He looks even more appalled. I realize I'm an arse. "God, I'm sorry, Josh, that's a terrible thing to say. I'm nervous." I start to giggle. "I've never been nervous with you before, Josh."

"Well, I've never proposed to you before, Cas." Josh pauses. "Or anyone."

"So why?"

"We're good for each other. We are alike. We've known each other for ever. No other woman ever makes me laugh the way you do. Other women bore me."

I'm still buying time. "So you are ready for monogamy? I assume we'd play it conventionally?"

"Yes, I'm ready. I'm bored of attaching myself to the next thing that comes along and attracts attention. Other women seem sameish. You're different." He pauses and I know he's struggling. "I think it's always been you. I think that's why everyone else seemed inadequate. I think you are the reason I've bounced from one conquest to the next."

"Are you sure it's you who thinks that? It sounds suspiciously like my mother's theory. This proposal isn't the result of her finally grinding you down, is it?"

Josh smirks. He doesn't answer my question but continues, "And I figured that you don't have any other plans." His smirk relaxes into a wide grin. "I mean you don't let men hang around long enough for you to even learn their surnames."

Smith.

"It is true our getting married will delight your mum. Look, marriage is the logical next step—think government tax breaks."

"Very romantic." I laugh.

He turns suddenly serious. "I'll make you happy, Cas. We love each other, don't we?"

"It's just that this is so unexpected."

Josh laughs. "Actually, not at all. I've been waiting for years to tell you how I feel. I suppose, conventionally, I could have started by kissing you or asking you out for a drink."

"We're always going out for drinks together," I point out matter-of-factly.

"Exactly. I've been at a loss as to how I should let you know how I feel. I don't know if I'd ever have got the courage but recently you've changed. You seem more serious. I knew the time was right. What do you say, Cas? Can you imagine being my wife?"

Josh is my best friend. He's mymateJosh. And here he is, mymateJosh down on one knee, a rose in one hand and a diamond cluster in the other. He's right: marriage is a ceremony that is sanctified by logic, government tax breaks, law and thousands of years of repeat performance. Josh is kind, strong, wealthy, intellectually stellar, he worships me, he does not mind my tantrums or my unmade-up face and, if that wasn't enough, he's good-looking.

None of this would convince me to marry him. I look at Josh and suddenly Darren's face looms.

Josh is safe. I'd be safe. I'd never end up torn and bitter in the divorce courts. Because much as I care for Josh, I'm not overwhelmed by him. He'll never make my heart gallop, so he'll never be able to splinter it. A network of middle-class lifelines would constantly buoy us up. Dinners out with our mutual friends, who are interested and interesting. Evenings in, playing Trivial Pursuit, and charades at Christmas. Then later there'd be prep school for the kids and exotic holidays. I like all these things. These beacons of sanitized security seem like a possibility.

I've tried to fill my Darren-bereft days in an assortment of ways. None of which have been successful. But if I were with Josh, if I marry Josh—I let the concept roll around my head—I'd be safe. Marrying Josh will stop me doing anything really terrible, like getting drunk, and calling Darren, and telling him how I feel. Marrying Josh is the ultimate protection. It's complex. It's risky but it's my only chance.

"Yes."

"Yes what? Yes we love each other . . . or yes you'll marry me?"

"Yes and yes."

"Aghhhhhh. God, I'm the happiest man in the world. Oh my God. Should we ring Issie?" Josh does a funny little star jump and as he lands he wiggles his hips, claps his hands and punches the air. "No, no, best ring your mum first, or my parents—, what do you think?" Josh is dashing around his flat, fitfully searching for his mobile, although there is a perfectly good landline.

"Champagne? Do you want champagne?" He keeps turning to me and blowing kisses and punching the air again. I've never seen him so happy. I had no idea. I had no idea I could make him this happy. And I'm . . . I'm happy too. Calm happy.

"Well, isn't it traditional for you to kiss me? Kind of to seal the deal," I offer.

"Christ, yes. Sorry, Cas. I've been meaning to do this for twenty-six years."

I pretend I haven't noticed that he is now sweating profusely. I ignore the fact that he clumsily bangs my teeth and, for a moment, I'm behind the bike shed with Barry Carter. Soon we inch into it and soon I like his kissing. We're both too practiced for it to be anything other than technically brilliant.

I arrive early and seat myself facing the wall so that Issie can have the view of the restaurant. I take off my ring and put it under my napkin so that I can surprise her. Then I put it back on again— better to do the Taaaaddddddaaaa and hold my hand out as soon as she arrives. Maybe not. Back under the napkin. I'm nervous. I just wonder how Issie will take this. After all, Josh's her one and only real chance of marrying. I'm joking. I know this isn't the case, but it will irrevocably alter the dynamics. Well, does it have to?

No, it doesn't.

Yes, it does.

Issie will be delighted for us both.

Surely?

Certainly.

She's here. She kisses me, orders a Bloody Mary and cuts to the chase.

"What's your news?"

Deep breath, "I'm marrying Josh."

The restaurant stops. There isn't a clinking glass or thudding plate. At least I can't hear one. I watch Issie's face, waiting for her reaction.

"You're marrying Josh?" she whispers. She pauses and takes a sip of my water. Issie is obviously a little taken back.

But she's pleased.

Isn't she?

Well, she's not actively unhappy.

Is she?

"Yes, I've just said so, haven't I?" I smile broadly because engaged woman smile all the time and Issie knows that. I order some wine. She fiddles with her napkin. I look at the menu. She doesn't. I wonder which one of us will change the subject first. Issie and I have only ever been 100 percent truthful with one another. Except for the occasion when I failed to tell her Josh fancied her. But that was years ago and it worked out for the best. It would be so embarrassing now if they had slept together. Anyway the point is Issie has only ever been 100 percent truthful with me. I don't want her to skirt this if she has an issue.

But I'm not keen to confront her brutal integrity just yet.

But I hope to God she doesn't talk about the weather.

Stay with me, Issie.

"I've got to be honest with you, Cas. I'm shocked."

"Why?" I bluff. But I know why. Why is because I've never shown any romantic interest in Josh and I've always been actively opposed to marriage.

"Because you've never shown any romantic interest in Josh and you've always been actively opposed to marriage."

I glare at her. The waitress brings Issie her Bloody Mary (which is downed in one) and tells us what the specials are. I get her to repeat it twice. Issie says she'll have "That." I ask for "the same." Neither of us has any idea what we've ordered.

"Haven't you always said Josh would make a great husband?" I encourage.

"Yes," she admits.

"Haven't you always said I should marry? Allow closeness, trust, stop hiding from intimacy?"

"Yes," she admits.

"So what's the problem?"

"I didn't say I had a problem."

"But you so obviously do."

"I think you are being defensive. Do *you* think there's a problem?"

"No. I don't have a problem."

"Good."

"Yes, it's good."

The waitress comes back with the wine, water and bread. I'm delighted and greet her as though she is my long-lost sister. It becomes clear that she's not going to draw up a chair and join us. I watch her scuttle back to the kitchen, leaving me alone with Issie and her interrogation.

"What about Darren?"

"Darren?" The bread in my mouth won't be swallowed. I chew and chew but it simply won't go down. I drink some more water. "Darren who?" won't wash.

"Darren taught me a lot." I take a deep breath. "I owe him a great deal. He opened my eyes to the possibility of intimacy being an option for me."

"Don't speak to me as though I am one of your TV executives," she snaps. It's unlike Issie to be down on me. I think about what I've just said. It does sound like pretentious wank. But then I'm new to this game of speaking your heart. I'd always been content with speaking my mind, which is easy in comparison.

"Darren was important," I admit.

"You fell in love with him."

I can't tell Issie the truth. I can't tell her that marrying Josh is the ultimate armor. She loves Josh as much as she loves me and she wouldn't forgive me. I have no choice but to rewrite history.

"No, Issie, Darren was an infatuation." Firm. Denying Darren hurts.

"You *said* you were in love." Rigid.

"I was wrong." Reasonable.

"You said you're never wrong." Irritating.

"I was wrong about that too." I'm almost shouting. I take a deep breath and have a stab at regaining some self-control. "Darren told me things that no one else could tell me and he taught me to look at things differently but I didn't fall in love."

She stares at me with naked disbelief. "Oh, so you can't quote every single word he ever uttered to you? You didn't laugh with him? You don't talk about him constantly?"

Fair point.

"Darren was . . ." I'm struggling. ". . . exhilarating and amazing but he was a stranger. Women don't fall in love with men they've just met."

"Of course they do!"

"Why are we talking about Darren? It's Josh I feel secure with. Josh I've known forever."

"That doesn't sound like love to me, it sounds like the safe choice."

The waitress arrives with our food and we call an uneasy truce over the table. We sulkily eat our goat's cheese salad and glumly glug our wine. This isn't what I wanted. I wanted her to be happy for me.

"I admit Josh doesn't send my stomach into a somersault."

"The way Darren did."

I ignore her interruption. "But that's to be expected, I've known Josh forever."

What am I supposed to say?

Obviously Issie's disappointed that things are changing, but things can't stay the same. I wish they could have. Meeting Darren changed everything. I'm lonely in crowds now. But I'm a survivor and marrying Josh is my best survival tactic. While I'm sorry that it makes Issie uncomfortable, I am completely without option. I push on.

"Darren was about sexual attraction. I got carried away. I know I said some pretty crazy things at the time." I glance at Issie and try to work out if I'm convincing her. I can see by her face that she wants to believe me. Almost as much as I want to believe me. I press on. "Josh wants to marry me. I love Josh. He's like a brother to me." Issie tries to interrupt but I hold my hand up to stop her. "Maybe, at the moment, Josh loves me in a different way. But two people rarely love each other equally, in the same way, at the same time. We've years together, we'll even up." I pause for maximum impact and then I plead, "I'll be a good wife to him." I mean this. I plan to be perfect. I'll try to make it up to Josh for not being in love with him. I'll take fastidious care in putting his needs before mine. He can chose which side of the bed to sleep on. And I'll attend all his work functions. I'll even learn the rules of rugby. Josh will get a good deal.

Issie pauses and thinks about what I've said. We sit for an eternity.

Finally she mutters, "I can't believe you'd play games with Josh, so I have to believe that you are genuine about this, Cas." She stares at me for about two hundred years.

"I am." Her face relaxes into a broad, delighted and assured smile. I force a tight, relieved smile. I've often condemned her for being too trusting, saying she invites people to wipe their Manolo Blahniks on her soul. Now I'm grateful that she's so ingenuous.

We are through it. Everything is going to be brilliant from now on.

I show her my ring. She ooohs and ahhs, appropriately. She says that she definitely will not wear pink, lilac or frills. I reach into my bag and pull out the Amanda Wakeley Wedding Collection brochure. We both giggle shrilly and generally allow ourselves to get completely overexcited.

This is what girlfriends are born for.

CHAPTER
Sixteen

A WHOLE NEW WORLD OPENS UP in front of me. An entirely novel conversational track. An individual way to relate to my mother, Josh's mother, aunts, neighbors, women I meet at dinner parties, restaurants, art galleries, the gym—my Ph.D. in *Brides and Setting Up Home*. What had I talked about before I had the cluster on my finger? It surprises and delights me that wedding preparation is an admirable substitute for sex. Which is a good thing because Josh and I have decided not to rush having sex.

"Why?" Issie doesn't understand.

"Well, we're both finding it a bit harder than we imagined crossing over from friends to lovers."

"Isn't that a fairly major detail, since you are planning on getting married? Aren't married people supposed to be lovers?"

"Yes, and friends." I sound defensive. "We thought of getting through the initial embarrassment by just getting pissed and shagging each other. After all, we've both done it to other people often enough in the past. But now that seems so tacky and cheap. I realized that the reason I can't rush this is because I want it to be really special. A few more months without sex will be good for me."

"It might grow over, you know," teases Issie. I throw a cushion at her but we both shut up as Josh comes into the room with a tray of wine and Pringles.

"Why do I get the feeling you were talking about me?" He sits in-between us. Issie and I exchange glances.

"Just singing your praises," Issie says.

Little white lies are a way of life. Issie could hardly say, "Oh, actually we were just talking about yours and Cas's vow of celibacy."

Although in the past we did discuss every aspect of our lives. The nitty gritty, not just loose morals but, when traveling in India, loose feces too.

Tonight after Issie leaves I'll tell Josh what we were really talking about. It's a small shift in the dynamics, almost imperceptible and certainly not important.

Issie's brother is designing our wedding invites so Issie has come around tonight to help us decide on the wording. Which is the other tiny change—Issie rarely pops around just to hang out anymore. She only ever visits when she has a reason. Still, there are plenty of reasons—choosing dresses and flowers, repainting Josh's flat, returning a casserole dish. Her visits are just as frequent, so it's not really a problem.

"So, Issie? Have you decided are you going to be the bridesmaid or the best man?" asks Josh.

"I'm going to be the bridesmaid. I like the outfit better."

"You like me better," I screech playfully.

I notice she doesn't answer me but instead asks, "So where are you getting married?"

We answer simultaneously and differently.

"In London," I say.

"At home," says Josh.

"At home," I offer quickly.

"In London," he presses.

"We haven't worked out the details," I smile apologetically to Issie. Wisely, she doesn't comment.

"We do have a date," says Josh. I snuggle closer to him.

"Well, that's good," smiles Issie. "When?"

"June," I say.

"July," says Josh at the same time. We both laugh. "Look, don't mind. Do what you want. I'm just thrilled. It's going to he the best party ever." He leans in and kisses me. I wiggle away because I don't want to embarrass Issie.

Josh leaves for rugby practice and Issie and I set to on Project Wedding. I approach it exactly as I approach projects at work.

"OK, we need a list."

Issie jumps up and finds paper and pen. I grab a bunch of bridal magazines and I open the bottle of Chardonnay.

"So you are still working on when and where?" says Issie quietly as she carefully writes "Cas and Josh's wedding" at the top of the page. Her handwriting is round and childish and familiar.

"July and Esher, Josh's family home."

"Good progress," grins Issie. "Which church?"

"A church? I hadn't thought of a church."

"They usually feature."

"I was thinking of a civil ceremony. Maybe in a garden or a smart hotel?" I cross my legs underneath me.

Issie gently probes, "Have you discussed this with Josh? I mean he's quite godly."

"Considering he plays rugby," I add.

We both laugh. It's true Josh is a long way from being a bible basher but he does believe in God and goes to church at Easter, Christmas and at least two or three other times a year. I do recall him taking his godfather duties very seriously when he became godfather for the children of his head of chambers. I'd sort of put it down to brown nosing. But maybe not. I consider it.

"Of course he's godly, Issie. He went to a posh school which had obligatory Mass. Look, I'll discuss it with him."

"Well, if you are hoping for a July wedding you'd better discuss it pretty damn quickly. It's April now. I take it you mean this July?" She's doodling hearts and bells on the corner of the list.

"Yes, I mean this July."

We move on and begin to draw up a list of costs. I'm somewhat perturbed to discover that tradition has it that the bride's parents are supposed to pay for just about everything; the groom's parents get off with the odd bunch of flowers and the rings. I doubt very much that my mother has had a secret trust fund that magically matures as I meet Prince Charming. I think her budgeting for my wedding would truly have been a leap of faith; I'd hardly indicated that I was marrying material. Unless I want to give my guests' sausages on sticks and cheese and pineapple chunks, Josh and I will have to pay for the wedding. I hope that won't offend anyone. People have been acting rather strangely recently. Indeed, if I'd had a pound for every time anyone had said the words "traditional," "the done thing" and "expected," I'd be a millionaire. I'm surprised that these words have been showered on me with such frequency because I'd never heard them previously in my entire life.

"OK, so what else needs to be included in this project plan?" I ask.

"No one could ever accuse you of being overly romantic, could they, Cas?" grins Issie wryly.

"I just want to be well organized."

She shrugs and then reverts to the bridal magazine; I revert to the wine bottle.

"Well, for the service, civil or church, you need wedding rings and a form of service. You need to select music and readings. You'll have to consider cars, photographers and guest accommodation. There is a lot to think about. You'll need a guest list, and an acceptance list, lists of menus, lists of drink, gift lists. There are caterers to consider. You need to book a photographer and videographer. If I were you I'd decline my dad's kind offer to bring his cinecamera along. It's older than I am. What type of reception do you want?"

"There's only one type isn't there? The after-ceremony type."

Issie rolls her eyes. "Sit-down meal, buffet, melon balls and chicken or something a little less traditional, Asian, sushi, Italian,

Mexican? What about your silverware, napkins, menu design, flowers? Are you going to invite children? And if so, you should consider their menu and an entertainer. What about the favors, the balloons, the seating plan? Round tables or square? Who's going to sit in the seat that is traditionally saved for the father of the bride? Will you have speeches? Will you make one?" She finally draws to a halt.

"Oh, I see. Well, what do you think?" This is the question Issie has been waiting to be asked all her life.

"Well, if it were me, I'd want it to be sit-down and with a seating plan. I wouldn't try to mix oldies and youngies—because that only works in books, I'd allow the people with things in common to sit together. I'd want tuna carpaccio, followed by tempura fish with chilli salad and Parmesan polenta and then summer berries, which I'd have stacked in huge mounds as table centerpieces. I wouldn't have a traditional cake but I'd have a bitter chocolate profiterole mound instead."

I'm left stranded somewhere between horrified and admiring. When has Issie had time to think of all this? Then I remember she does this imaginary wedding thing instead of t'ai chi.

"Er, sounds good. Let's have that."

"You can't have that! That's what I'm having!"

I don't point out that Issie isn't even seeing anyone on a regular basis. It doesn't seem like a nice thing to do.

"Well erm . . ." I'm unsure what to say next. "I don't really mind and I'm pretty sure Josh is relaxed about it too. Let's ask my mum. She'll love getting involved. Planning my wedding will cheer up her drab little life."

"I'm not sure she thinks it's drab."

"Oh, come on, Issie, she must! Before she married she lived an exemplary life of purity and chastity—which can hardly be a barrel of laughs. Then she fell uncontrollably in love with her husband, he exited stage left and ever since she's put her life on hold by refusing to get over him."

"Is that how you see it?"

"Is there any other way?" I'm already dialing my mother's number, so I can't be sure, but I think I hear Issie say something about three sins I'm clear of. I watch as she moves her finger down the magazine page as she reads, which I find quaint and touching. The finger stops and hesitates.

"What about insurance?" Asks Issie.

"Insurance? What will I need insurance for?"

"Theft of pressies, damage to the dress, damage to the marquee."

"It's a wedding, not a rave."

"The loss of deposits due to the cancellation of the wedding."

We both pause.

"Well, let's get an estimate."

My mother picks up the mantle. She works steadily throughout the summer and does a marvelous job of knocking the day into shape. Full of zeal, she organizes everything from the church to the caterers, tactfully asking Josh's mum's opinion every step of the way. The wedding has a profound effect on everyone. Josh's mum has become more animated than I've ever seen her before, drinking less and smiling more. As I don't have a father to do the traditional patriarchal stuff, Josh's father happily adopts the role. He invites everyone he's ever met to the wedding, talks about the "forthcoming happy event" and, I swear, he's even taken to swaggering. This would be infuriating behavior except, a more happy consequence, he has decided that keeping a mistress is incongruous with his current self-image. For the time being at least, he has given up his philandering. Josh is delirious. Issie hasn't actually voiced any objections. Everyone is as happy as pigs in mud. I'm relieved to be freed up from the hassle, as I can now turn back to concentrating on my work. With vengeance.

I have returned to my routine of five trips to the gym a

week, cycling into the office by 8:30 A.M. and working through lunch. However, I don't often stay late now because Mum organizes imperative meetings with the dress maker/vicar/caterers/videographer/photographer/florist, etc., on a more or less continuous basis. But then I like to be busy. I exist in a huge waft of tissue paper and ribbons with a sprinkling of rose petals.

"Someone has parked their bike in my space. Deal with it," I bark at Jaki. "Ricky, do you have the runs for last night's shows? Di, Debs, have either of you seen the papers today? We are mentioned in the *Guardian* for our storyline in *Teddington Crescent* and in the *Sun* for the documentary on stars' babies and the *Star* for *Sex with an Ex*. Pretty good crop for one day, I'm sure you'll agree. Get a response out to all three editors by 10 A.M."

Jaki puts a double espresso on my desk.

"What did you watch on TV last night?" she asks.

"No time, I was at a tiara fitting." We take a moment to smirk at each other.

"Morning, darling," shouts Tom generally to no one in particular.

"Afternoon," we chorus as it's 8:45 A.M. Tom looks wounded—he's probably never been in the office so early before.

The status meeting runs exactly to plan. Gray tells me that we have received two complaints from the ITC about offensive language, but, or indeed therefore, the ratings achieved for most of our shows are as expected. The entire team negotiates with him over the predicted ratings for next season's schedule. As the advertising and sponsorship director, it is in his interest to put in "stretch predictions." The rest of the team see this as setting unfeasible targets. I settle the matter by diplomatically choosing a number mid-distance between the two extremes. Ricky updates me on scheduling. I'm only half listening because I notice Debs isn't listening at all but instead staring at her screensaver of George

Clooney. I'm irritated by her lack of commitment. I tune back in to Ricky.

". . . So net net what they are suggesting is to push back *Sex with an Ex*. I'll say OK, shall I?" If he hadn't closed his file quite so swiftly and tried to walk away faster than Road Runner, I mightn't have noticed.

"What did you say?"

Ricky sighs when he realizes he's stuck with my undivided attention. He has no choice other than to tell me the full tale.

Ironically, because of the success of *Sex with an Ex* TV6 is a bit flush with cash, which we've invested in box office hit movies, a move that I'd sanctioned. Now the Strategy and Scheduling Department are suggesting we take on the other commercial channels by showing the blockbuster films at a time which will necessitate that *Sex with an Ex* is pushed out of peak hour. Why didn't I see that coming?

"There's not much we can do," shrugs Ricky apologetically. "Their case is watertight. The *Sex with an Ex* viewership has stabilized; we can pull more viewers in with an Arnie Schwarnie film. There's more violence."

He's right. I sigh and nod.

"OK. Say we agree."

"What, just like that?" asks Fi, amazed. "Aren't you even going to try to think of a way to make *Sex with an Ex* bigger?"

"Look, Fi, you've got to learn which battles to fight. See the bigger picture. We are responsible for the channel, not individual shows."

"But the show was your idea."

"Fi, I have loads of ideas. Ten million viewers is an excellent achievement for a show of this nature. Far beyond anything we expected when we set out. Let's not get greedy. We'll pull in 12 million with the right films. And besides which, it's not as if they are suggesting we ditch *Sex with an Ex*—we're just moving it out of peak."

"Well, if it were my show I'd be fighting tooth and nail to keep it in peak." spits Fi, with far more passion than I'd ever seen her display before.

"It's not your show."

As part of my self-protection campaign against Bale sidelining me, I have started to increase my own public profile. In interviews with the national press I make it clear that my personal contribution to the channel is colossal. I also make the most of my less cerebral attributes. I figure that Bale will be keener to keep me sweet if I am a public sweetheart. I'm mid-interview with a journalist from one of the big women's glossies, when Jaki announces that my mother is in reception.

"I'm sorry, we're going to have to leave it there. I'm taking my mother out for lunch," I smile apologetically. The interview has been more demanding than I expected. The journalist and I are playing a very sophisticated game. I know he likes me but he's pretending not to; it's a matter of professional pride. I'm pretending that I'm still trying to win him over, although I know he's eating out of my hand.

He grimaces stiffly, trying to decide if I planned this interruption in the hope that he'll mention my lunch date with Mum in his article. If I have planned it, he won't mention it. If I haven't, he will. It would, after all, provide a human angle, which is notably lacking. In truth, it's a complete coincidence. Their paths wouldn't have crossed if Mum wasn't tyrannically anal about promptness and this journalist wasn't stereotypical in his tardiness.

"Just one or two more questions." I agree and smile a candy-coated smile. "You receive an enormous amount of complaint letters about the nature of your lead show *Sex with an Ex,* from parents, teachers, local governments. Even the Church of England has condemned you—"

"I'm agnostic," I smile my interruption.

He ignores it. "How do you feel about the charge that you are advocating adultery?"

"Quite simply, I'm not. The ratings are just as high if the couple stay together. I see TV as a nationally authorized culture. I don't force anyone to watch or to participate in the show." I parrot my answer, barely suppressing my yawn. It doesn't sound as convincing, to me, as it used to. I hope it convinces him. I think of a new bit to add. "The British public is far too intelligent to be dictated to. Will you write that up as a direct quote?" He nods shyly. I know he's annoyed with himself for being acquiescent.

"Finally, how do you feel about the label that you're 'the voice of your generation'?"

"I haven't heard that one before." I titter and twitter in a vain attempt to convince him that I'm harmless. "Truly? Off record?" I don't think I can maintain this syrupy exterior for another minute. It's such a strain. He nods.

"I'm not the voice of my generation because I'm far cleverer, far more compassionate and far crueler."

He mulls over what I've just said. I suspect he regrets agreeing to keep that off record. It's the best quote of the interview.

If only he knew what it meant.

I stand up, indicating that it's time for him to go. Jaki ushers the journalist out of the office and brings my mum in.

"I'm sorry, I'm running late." I blow her a kiss and my apology as I grab my jacket and handbag off the back of the chair.

"Jaki, I'm taking Mum to lunch and then we are going to choose her outfit for the wedding. I'll be out most of the afternoon."

This isn't a problem because I do such long hours I feel entitled to take an hour or two off. Other than my team, most TV6 employees don't arrive until 11:00 A.M., for many the real work doesn't begin until after sobering up from lunch. "Keep checking my e-mail as I'm expecting an important decision from the executive committee, regarding the budgets for next year. I'll keep my mobile on but don't call me unless it's an emergency. Don't put anyone through except for Darren."

"Darren?" repeats Jaki astounded. About two thousand watts charge through me.

"Did I say Darren? Oh, I meant Josh." I'm scarlet, so I delve into my handbag pretending to be looking for a tissue to blot my lipstick and I'm not even wearing lipstick.

"Why did you say Darren?" asks Jaki.

"Oh, it must have been that journalist. He was asking the same kind of questions that that Darren bloke asked about the show. You know, did I feel responsible for the nation's adultery? Do I feel guilty for being the catalyst to so much aggro."

My hands have suddenly got a life of their own. They are scratching my nose, moving my hair behind my ear, itching my leg. They won't stay steadily on my hips or by my sides. Jaki and Mum are both staring at me very closely. "They were a lot alike, the journalist and er, thingy, Darren. They were both unrealistic, misguided, moralistic pricks. Sorry, Mum." I'm apologizing for using the word "prick" before she demands that I do.

Sorry, Darren. Somewhere deep inside I feel treacherous.

"Who's Darren?" asks Mum.

"Nobody. Some guy who didn't appear on my show."

"Sex on legs," says Jaki matter-of-factly.

"Sorry dear?" My mum's pretending she doesn't understand.

"Very Jude Law, but kind of more dangerous, muckier," adds Jaki. My mother still looks bemused. "Very Rhett Butler," clarifies Jaki.

"Oh, I see."

My mother and I collapse gratefully into the chairs in the Selfridges restaurant. We are carrying heavy bags and light purses and therefore truly euphoric. It's quite an achievement. We've managed to buy Mum an outfit for the wedding, which we both like. *And* the said purchase has been completed without either of us resorting to sulking, glowering, blackmail or tears. We are on a roll, so despite already having lunch, we now order a traditional tea with scones and sandwiches. I won't touch the cakes or cream, of course. Fanatical about my food before, now I'm going to be a bride, I am rabid. Still, Mum's delighted and only worries about the extravagance for the briefest of times. She does what she always does nowadays, whenever we are together: she delves into her bag and produces the *How to Plan for Your Wedding* book.

"Have you spoken to your hairdresser?"

"Yes. I've made two bookings. One so she can practice putting my hair up and then one for the wedding day. But I'm playing with the idea of getting my hair cut."

"Oh, not your lovely hair." Mum looks as though I've just suggested sacrificing vestal virgins to pagan gods.

"I'm too old for such long hair. What do you think of a sharp bob or a Zoë Ball crop?"

Evidently not much because my mother simply ticks the box entitled "hairdresser" and moves the conversation on.

"Have you informed your bank and building society of your name change and ordered new business cards?"

"I don't think I'll change my name."

"Oh."

"Well, it's one less job," I defend, concentrating on sipping my Earl Gray. My mother speaks a million words with her silences. Finally she moves down the list.

"You have to choose the flowers."

I instantly know this isn't going to be as simple as picking out something fragrant and pretty.

"I was thinking hydrangeas and—"

"You can't have hydrangeas."

"Why?"

"They're unlucky. They represent boastfulness and exposure."

"Well, which are the lucky ones?"

"Roses are always good. They stand for love, innocence and thankfulness, depending on the color. Or something delicate like heliotropes, which represent devotion and faithfulness, with a bit of lemon blossom. They stand for fidelity in love."

"It's bollocks. What did you have?"

"Lemon blossom."

"There's my point."

My mum looks away. And I know I've hurt her. I can't quite say sorry.

"Oh, OK, heliotrope and lemon blossom it is."

She smiles, relieved, and I'm embarrassed at how easy it is to please her.

"Have you thought about your honeymoon?"

"I'm leaving it to Josh. Which probably isn't all that wise, but it is traditional. Will you have a discreet word with him, Mum? So that he doesn't book anything too active. Don't let him book a trekking holiday to the North Pole or a canoeing safari. Beach and bars will suit me fine." My mother makes a note.

"Has he chosen his ushers and best man?"

I stare at her with incredulity.

"It's not me that's asking, it's what the book says. Here, look: 'Check your husband has chosen his ushers.'" She points to the page.

"God, they assume we all marry simpletons, don't they? The implication is that he couldn't wipe his own nose unassisted." My mother and I treat the surrounding tables to looks of disdain and disbelief.

"So has he chosen his ushers?" she asks.

"No," I reply and we both giggle helplessly. I like this relaxed Mum. When the giggles subside, I say, "I am grateful, Mum. Thank you. I know it's a lot of work."

Mum glows and simpers. She carefully cuts her scone into halves and then quarters. There has been a mass of work and I don't know how I'd have coped without her. I hadn't expected to care about the fairy-tale day but as it approaches I really do want it to be perfect. I want a perfect bride with perfect hair, dress and makeup. Perfect Mum with all her friends attending and a hat that suits her. Perfect guests who are happy with the food and seating plan. And a perfect husband, which Josh is.

"We've had a lovely day, haven't we?" asks Mum.

"Yes," I agree.

She doesn't pause. "Issie mentioned a Darren to me. Pass the jam, dear." She's desperately trying to be disingenuous but she's had no practice. I, on the other hand, am a veteran. I reach into my bag and pull out, from acres of tissue paper, the shoes I've just bought for the wedding. They are covered in tiny beads, zillions of them. They are certainly the prettiest pair of shoes I've ever seen.

"What do you think, Mum?"

"They are beautiful. Wasn't Darren the one from the north? Didn't you go on holiday with him?"

Issie really is rent-a-mouth.

"It wasn't a holiday. It was work."

Mum falls back on the etiquette we have used for a thousand years. She refills my teacup and cuts me a slice of cake. She does this with the precision of a geisha girl. I try to be patient until the little ceremony comes to an end. It is only now that I realize she always uses this ritual to buy time. She has something important to say and she is carefully considering how best to phrase it.

"Josh is a lovely boy."

I smile, this is fine. We both know this.

"He's been like a son to me in some ways, over the years, and certainly like a brother to you. I'm sure he loves you very much."

"Er, Mum, this is hardly headline news. We are engaged to be married next month. Isn't this the usual state of affairs?"

Mum reaches across the table and puts her hand on top of mine. "Do you love Josh?"

"Mum!" I'm shocked. When my father informed my mother about his affair, she could not believe it. Quite literally. I watched, from the doorway of the kitchen, as she ran to him and hung her arms around his neck. She smiled sweetly, hopefully, up at him and asked if he could possibly love the other woman as much, no more, than his wife and daughter. She had expected him to see sense and tell her, "No, of course not." That way we could all sweep the whole silly business under the carpet. Unfortunately, my father was unaware of the script. He'd replied that, yes, regrettably, that was the case. My mother reeled from the shock. It was at that moment that she began to construct the elaborate safety net that would protect her from any such horrors and indignities again. The most notable components of the net are that she doesn't readily show affection (I can count on one hand the number of times she's deliberately touched me). She never talks about love. And she never asks questions to which she doesn't know the answer. It bothers me that in a single afternoon, sitting in the Selfridges restaurant, my mother has broken all three of her own rules.

I figure it's a bit late in the day for my mum to take up the role of adviser. Just because I've let her choose the flowers and menu doesn't mean I want her opinion on every part of my life. She's my mother and therefore understands nothing and knows less. She's always let me pretty much make my own mistakes and learn my own lessons. Why start interfering now? Anyway, I am suddenly *piqued* with myself. Marrying Josh isn't a mistake. It is the right thing to do. He's kind and decent and easy-going and everyone likes him and he's got great career prospects and he's a good cook.

And he's not Darren.

I glare at Mum but she won't be intimidated into shutting up. Instead she says, "I'd hate to think that all I'd taught you was sacrifice."

• • •

I put Mum in a taxi, which very nearly spoils the day because she thinks a taxi is frivolous and sees it as yet another example of my decadence and "odd ways." I simply think it will save her hat box from being crushed on the tube. We all but have a stand-up fight, but we are reunited when the cab driver is rude to us and tells us to get "bloody in, or bloody out, the bleedin', bloody cab." I take another cab and rush back to the studio in time to sit in on the interviews of a couple of possible candidates for next week's show. The interviews finish at 7:45 P.M. and when I return to my desk I find the department empty, except for Fi.

"You're here late," I comment.

She doesn't reply directly but grunts and glowers. I remember my mild, but public, rebuke earlier this morning and calculate that she's probably still sulking with me. I try to restore departmental harmony by telling her about the interviews.

"There was this archetypal Essex girl . . ."

It may be that she wasn't from Essex at all, but from Edinburgh or Exeter or anywhere in-between. But it's shorthand that Fi will appreciate. The girl had been describing her ex-lover. His CV read like the admission book to the Priory. A compulsive womanizer and gambler, whose idea of a day's work was a sticky-fingered sweep around the local shopping center; a louse in every way but redeemed in her eyes because he was "a real salt."

I stared at the girl, non-comprehending. "An Essex term, I presume?"

"Salt. Salt of the earth. The real thing. A fucker," she elaborated.

"Quite," I smiled. Knowing she'd make great TV and the warm-up act would be able to wallow in innumerable Essex jokes.

"Hey, Fi, what does an Essex girl say after her eleventh orgasm?" Fi shrugs. "Just how many are there in a football team?"

It's an old gag, but Fi appreciates my effort and finally allows herself to smirk. I know I've won her around when she says, "I'm just packing up. Fancy a drink? We could go to the Brave Lion."

I'm about to decline, as is my habit, and explain that I have thirty plus e-mails to clear, when I suddenly think of my mother's fretful face in Selfridges.

If only I could leave it there.

I know that if I stay in the office on my own she'll haunt me, so I shut down my PC and grab my bag.

"Are you all right?"

"I'm fine."

I'm not. But what can I say? How am I going to explain it to Fi, of all people? We clink glasses and sip our G&Ts.

I wonder what she meant? Sacrifice?

Fi is using her fag to orchestrate the tune playing on the juke-box. It's playing "Always Something There to Remind Me," which seems poignant. Fuck, I'll be reading horoscopes next. I wish pubs would stick to ambient music. Sentimental lyrics and alcohol are a lethal combination. I charge toward thoughts of work, and away from ones of my mum, or Josh or the wedding.

"So tell me, Fi, if *Sex with an Ex* were your show, what would you be doing to 'make it bigger'?"

Fi looks shamefaced. "Err, sorry about this morning. I got wound up. I was being ridiculous. As you said, I should choose my battles."

"Apology unnecessary," I grin. "It's good you are so passionate about your work." Or at least I think it is. "Tell me, what do you think of the show at the moment?" I ask this to give the impression that I value her opinion. It's a motivational thing I learned on a course. Fi sucks the lemon slice from her drink.

"Honestly?"

Suddenly I *do* value her opinion.

"Yeah, honestly."

I'm indignant that she's implying that I like to hear anything other than honesty. Then I remember that I often accept half-truths, exaggeration, insincere compliments and uncalled-for criticism, knowing that they are blatant lies. It's the oil that eases the wheels I call my life. Exaggeration—of anything from quoting the sales figures to qualifications on a CV—is routine. Insincere compliments and uncalled-for criticisms are always the result of someone else having an agenda. Usually the three Ps: promotion (securing theirs, ruining the chances of mine), pay raises (earning theirs, negotiating mine), promiscuity (all of the above).

Half-truths.

This is more uncomfortable.

This is horrendous.

I drain my G&T. Issie and I are dealing exclusively in half-truths at the moment. I find it totally impossible to be frank with her or, for that matter, my mother or Josh. To be frank with them I'd have to be honest with myself and although I have briefly considered this, I've rejected it as the lunacy it so obviously is.

"Want another drink?" Fi is up and halfway to the bar before I nod my response.

The full truth is I have not forgotten Darren. I had expected that by now his name, if mentioned, would call a blank. That momentarily I'd struggle to place him and on placing him I'd be indifferent, cool, unconcerned.

I think of him more or less continuously and a fleeting thought sends me into a flurry of, of, of . . . Happiness.

Pure unadulterated happiness. I'm happy he's on this planet somewhere. Even if that where isn't anywhere near me. All this and I'm marrying someone else in four weeks. I force myself to return to Fi. What were we talking about? Oh yeah, honesty.

She puts the drinks on the table.

"Yes. Honestly, what do you think of the show at the moment?"

"Well, it's fine." I raise an eyebrow. "Very good," Fi corrects. I raise the other eyebrow. This doesn't create such a fetching effect but at least my expression corresponds with my thoughts. Fi sighs. "It's lost its bite. There are no surprises." She's right.

"Any ideas?"

"A few." I wonder if she's going to share them. She must have invited me for a drink just for this opportunity. The opportunity to say, "Actually I've sketched out a couple of ideas and a business case," and then to reach for her satchel. I pause. She doesn't do this. I'm surprisingly relieved. Frankly a ten-hour day is enough for anyone.

"Another thing." Fi hesitates and examines her nails. I notice that, somewhat out of character, her nails are bitten, stubby runts of nails. I wonder what's making her nervous. Or has she always bitten her nails? I can't remember.

"Go on, what other thing? Actually don't, I'll get the drinks and then you can tell me." Odd that our glasses are already empty. I engage in that necessary hand-to-hand combat with other pushy, overaggressive and well-dressed Londoners. Luckily I'm served immediately. It takes a rare barman to ignore me (and a rare bar-woman to serve me). I squeeze my way back to Fi. I feel as though I've just spent six weeks in army training. Sensibly I've bought us both two G&Ts; two doubles, actually. Well, it saves having to tackle the assault course for at least another fifteen minutes.

"Go on. The other thing?"

"You."

"Me?"

"You. You've changed."

"I'm wearing eye shadow—maybe that's it. I read that eye shadow was in again," I defend.

Fi stares. She can't decide if I'm being deliberately obtuse or uncharacteristically thick. The truth is, I'm nervous. I neck both my drinks as though they are water. Fi pushes her spare one in my direction.

"Maybe it's the engagement but—" she's steeling herself. Deciding whether to be brutally straight or not. She ploughs on. All I can do is admire her stupidity. "You just don't seem as interested."

"I'm very busy," I snap with indignation.

"Of course." Assuring.

"I can't be expected to do everything." Defensive.

"Certainly not." Insincere.

"You're managing." Petulant.

"Absolutely." Condescending.

"I'm not as interested." Truthful.

Truthful. Fuck. That's unprecedented. I swill back another huge glug of gin.

"Oh shit, Fi, what can I say?"

Fi tilts her head, silently nods and I want to say something. I want to confide in her. I mean, I really like her. OK, it's quite a sudden intimacy, I have been resisting becoming matey. It could be something to do with the several gins that I've necked in as many minutes, but I want to talk to someone. Anyone. And Fi is the one in front of me. Two actually. There are suddenly two Fis in front of me. And a whole pile of glasses. I shake my head gently from side to side.

"Maybe because now you are getting married you are slightly less cynical and the program is no longer as appealing?" offers Fi.

Maybe.

She could be right. I want this to be the answer.

"Or maybe it's simply that you are really busy with other things. I mean before you got engaged absolutely everything came *after* work—your friends, your family. Maybe you are simply reprioritizing because you are busier now."

Yes, the endless lists. I'm suddenly chilled as a flash of panic hits me. Have I given the list of hymn choices to the organist?

What does she mean—"everything came after" my work?

Fi's saying something else. I try to listen. The room is carousing. I touch my head but it still thinks it's a spinning top.

"When did you get engaged? March, wasn't it?" She doesn't wait for my confirmation. She drags heavily on her cigarette. "Yet I'd say that your disinterest stems back further than that." I freeze. "Back to January. Did you make a New Year resolution not to work as hard?"

I glare at her. Both Fi and I know that she's pieced it together. She isn't absolutely spelling it out and this could be for one of a number of reasons. Either she's not drunk enough, or she still has vague enough recollections that I whip hide rather efficiently and I'm her boss, or she hasn't a lot of cash with her and she can't afford to offend me as she needs me to buy her drinks. I pause and consider what her reticence can be attributed to. Fi takes advantage of the pause by going to the bar and buying some more drinks. So she has plenty of cash, then.

As she sits down I blurt, "It's Darren."

"Darren who?"

"Darren Smith." I resist adding "of course." How can she not know who Darren is? How come his name isn't embroidered on her consciousness? I feel gelded.

"Smith? I always think that's such a pointless surname. It doesn't throw any light on the matter of identification."

I scowl at Fi. Smith is a strong name. Where would England have been without black smiths and gold smiths and plain smiths? A slightly embarrassing recollection tickles my conscience. I vaguely remember thinking Smith (and Darren) were stupid names. Over the last few months this has changed somewhat; I've been associating Smith (and Darren) and, more specifically, Darren Smith with strength, goodness and downright horniness, rather than pseudo names for adulterous couples embarking on a dirty weekend. I hunt out the more familiar part of my nature, my ability to be Machiavellian.

"Darren. You know, that stubborn git that I tried, and failed, to get on the show," I prompt Fi. I'm trying to give the impression that he was a no mark in my grand scheme. This is stupid. Talking about Darren is stupid. Why am I doing this? It's dangerous. Fi hadn't associated my peculiar and sudden squeamishness with Darren and I should be relieved. I shouldn't be pursuing the topic. Because *no matter what* I am marrying Josh next month. Josh who isn't a risk and isn't a bad option. It's stupid to bring up another man's name in conversation.

I can't stop myself.

Saying his name aloud is a relief.

And anyway I'm only talking about him. Perhaps talking about him will help me clarify the situation. It does need clarifying because—I'm certain this is just the drink—but suddenly I can't remember why I didn't return his calls.

"The beauty? The horn?" asks Fi.

"Hmmm. Was he? Yes, I suppose, in a very obvious way he could be described as attractive. I'm more referring to his arguments on collective responsibility, taste, decency and erosion of public standards."

I force myself to look at Fi. She's staring right back at me. It's obvious that she doesn't believe me. That's because she wasn't born yesterday. I suddenly sober up and know I have to change the subject. My mind is whitewashed. Blank. Vacant. Clean.

"I slept with him."

"I know that." Fi waves my confession away with a beer mat. It strikes me that when other women confess this type of thing the reaction is usually a little more stunning. Fi goes on to explain why she's not that astounded. "But you sleep with everyone."

"Actually I don't. Not anymore. I haven't slept with anyone since Darren."

"Not even—"

"Not even Josh."

Fi looks as though she's just received news that there is intelli-gent life on Mars. More, that they are male. I take a deep breath.

"We tried but—well, it was awkward, and so we thought it's probably just the pressure." She doesn't seem to be following me. "Josh says it doesn't matter."

But patently it does. Josh must be wondering how, since I've slept with half the male race in London, I can't have sex with him—my fiancé. It is a good question. He's lovely. I've slept with men I barely knew, never mind liked. Why the sudden capricious nature? Sex has never been in my head, firmly staying where it should be, in bed. Except for the mind fuck games which I played, but that was entertainment. I don't do sentimentality or lamenting lost love.

At least I didn't.

I got on. So there was never any issue about, "I like him but I just don't fancy him." Now I have problems with every aspect. His smell. Not that he smells terrible—the reverse is true. Josh always smells beautifully coiffured and doused in aftershave. But I want to smell *him*. His fingers, his armpits, his feet, his sperm.

But then I don't.

"Well, you know, it was bound to be difficult because we've known each other so long, in such a different context." I look at Fi again. From her face it's clear that my explanation is mud. "And so we thought we'd wait until after the . . . you know—"

"Wedding?" prompts Fi. I'm grateful.

"Yeah, the wedding."

"But the real reason is because you've still got the hots for Darren."

"I'm not saying that."

"Oh, I thought you were."

Another cab. This time to Josh's. I find him in front of his PlayStation. Without taking his eyes off the TV, he tells me that there's beer in the fridge.

"This is an unexpected pleasure," he yells through to the kitchen. "What's on your mind? If it's the ushers, don't worry, your mother's already called me. And she mentioned the honeymoon, too. I've canceled the bungy jumping from Sydney harbor."

I bring my beer back into the living room and don't waste any time trying to work out if he's kidding or not.

"No, nothing to do with wedding arrangements, I just—look, put away the PlayStation. I've a couple of other dials for you to play with."

I sort of dive on to him, quickly fastening my mouth on to his before he can comment on my terrible seduction line. I hastily unbutton his shirt and push it back off his shoulders. I frantically kiss his chest and neck while tearing at his buckle.

"What's the rush?" he asks as he tries to turn my hasty pecks into lingering kisses.

"It's time now," I insist. "We've waited too long."

It's encouragement enough. After all, he is male. He jumps up and walks to the bedroom. I follow him. We undress ourselves quickly. He folds and hangs up his clothes. We get into bed and have sex.

He wants to please me, that's obvious. He strokes my head and thighs and caresses my breasts. I bury my head into his neck and squeeze my eyes shut. It's pointless. Darren is tattooed on to the inside of my lids.

It's fine, absolutely fine. I even have brief waves of orgasm, although I don't quite achieve a full climax, but then, I rarely do.

I lie on my back and stare at the ceiling. Josh props himself up on one arm and lies facing me. I pull the duvet up to my armpits. He strokes my hair.

"I'm sorry that was all a bit quick."

"No, no, it was—fine. Great." I'm desperate for a cigarette.

"Really, you, er, enjoyed yourself?" He wants to believe it. "I mean, did you, er—"

"Yes, really, I came. Well, just about."

Relieved, he reaches for his cigarettes. "Well, that's good, then."

"Yes."

He hands me a lit fag and I edge up the headboard so that I can smoke it. I'm gripping on to the duvet like a Victorian virgin. We smoke in silence and then we stub out in silence.

"Do you think we are doing the right thing, Josh?"

"What—a big wedding, rather than something small and intimate? Absolutely. It's going to be a great party and we've both got loads of people we have to invite—my family, your colleagues—and a few we actually want to invite. A big wedding is definitely right for us."

I hold my breath. As I let it go, unscheduled words tumble out. "No, I mean by getting married at all." Double jeopardy. Gin-induced soul-searching, the worst kind.

"Well, even if we simply lived together you'd still have to have sex with me," jokes Josh. I turn to him and see he's terrified. He coughs. "Was it that bad?"

"No," I smile, messing his hair and planting a big kiss on his cheek. "You are every bit as good as you've always said."

We laugh, me and mymate Josh. I feel more relaxed with Josh than I have done since the engagement. Obviously it was the sex thing that was stressing me out. It's better to have got that over with. I feel I can talk to him again. I push on.

" I just worry that neither of us know how to do this. Neither of us have ever sustained a relationship for any length of time—"

"That's because we were with the wrong people. We are meant for each other."

Of course.

"But my parents are divorced and yours just stay together to spite one another. Hardly ideal role models." Why am I trying to reach for the self-destruct button? Marrying Josh is what I want to do. Why am I putting doubts in his mind?

"Loads of people manage."

"Loads of people mess it up too," I counterargue grimly. But then I remind myself: those who don't make it through are the ones who marry for the wrong reasons, for lust, for passion, because they are irrationally in love. Josh and I are quite different. We are marrying because we are alike. We are compatible. We are comfortable.

Fine.

Josh puts his hand under the duvet. He rests it on my thigh. He moves his thumb in circles. It feels like he is dragging my skin in the wrong direction.

"Again?" he asks.

Again? I hadn't thought about again. But of course there's an again. And again and again.

"I'm a bit tired actually."

"No worries. We've got all the time in the world." Josh turns away from me and is asleep in seconds. His breathing is deep and relaxed.

A lifetime of doing it again.

My feet are ice blocks.

CHAPTER
Seventeen

B ALE HAS COME UP WITH his most ridiculous, irritating and inconvenient idea yet.

"A party?" I'm incredulous.

"Yes, Jocasta, you know the sort of thing—music, drink, merriment."

"But what for?"

"For the troops, of course. To thank them for all their hard work during the difficult times, to celebrate these delightful ones."

Bale, nearer the bile of human meanness than the milk of human kindness, has never been within miles of being altruistic. I can't credit it now. I wonder which young PA he has his eye on. I assume that there must be someone he wants the opportunity to befuddle. Even so, it's a lot of expense to run to just to get someone drunk.

"Come off it, Bale. What's really going on?"

He comes clean. "It's a tax break. I have to spend a certain amount on staff training and recreation."

"I see." I consider it. A party isn't a bad idea. If it takes place after I get back from my honeymoon I'll be tanned. I begin to mentally run through my wardrobe, considering what I should wear to cause the biggest sensation.

"All right, I'll look at organizing something in August."

"Too late. All the invoices need to be through by the end of July. The party must take place this month."

"In that case, no can do." I can use this phrase with Bale—he still thinks "ciao" is an acceptable greeting. "Someone else will have to organize it. I'm getting married on the twenty-first." I point out the obvious to him. "Less than three weeks' time."

"We'll do it before the wedding." Bale reaches for his *Playboy* desk calendar. He concentrates on the numbers in among the cleavages and tight butts. "Today is the second. Let's have the party a week on Friday—that's the thirteenth. You're not superstitious, are you? No, you're not the type. That gives you another week before your wedding to clear the invoices." Bale stares at me: "You always throw such good parties."

I want to tell him that this isn't in my job description. I want to tell him that I have a number of other projects that need completing before I go on holiday. I want to tell him to go and screw himself. But there's something in his eyes that tells me this isn't up for debate. I know I'm being tested. Am I efficient and committed enough to pull off a huge corporate event the week before I get married? Or am I demob happy?

The bastard.

"No problem," I smile and skip out of his office.

"Bugger!" I yell, once I'm safely behind my screensaver.

"What's up?" asks Fi as she passes my desk.

"The usual. Bale," I groan. "He's piling up my workload just to see if I fuck up. I could really do without it."

"What's he asked you to do?"

"Arrange a party."

"A party? Great," enthuses Fi, miscalculating the reaction I want by about as much as is humanly possible. She sees my thunderous face and adjusts her jubilant one accordingly. "Not great."

"No, not great," I snap. "Besides all the final touches for my wedding, I have to close the books on this quarter's budgets, write a presentation to the executive committee, oversee the production of *The Murder Trilogy* drama, secure the contract on the coverage of the Tour de France, get the final episode of this series of *Sex with an Ex* in the bag and approve the casting of the Scott family in *Teddington Crescent!*"

By the time I finish my list there's more than a passing resemblance between my face and Barbara Cartland's wardrobe.

"OK. OK, I get the picture. Calm down, pink's not your color," says Fi. She puts her hand on my shoulder. "I have some capacity at the moment. I'll help."

"You will?"

"Sure." She sounds nonchalant and not at all like the life-saver she undoubtedly is, I want to kiss her. I settle for something more conventional.

"Thank you."

"No problem."

Fi and I make a great team. She takes charge of arranging the party: decides the theme, arranges caterers and alcohol. She finalizes the guest list, which extends beyond staff, to include the press, minor celebs and competition winners; she sends all the invites. Fi works around the clock for two weeks. I am really impressed by her commitment and friendship. Whenever I see her, she's awash with project plans, inventories, rosters and registers. She is nearly continual on the phone trying to drum up guests, PR interest, entertainers and glassware or she is sending e-mails, faxes and couriers to cajole, influence or sweet-talk whoever into doing whatever.

This leaves me free to tackle all my other tasks. It's imperative I leave work in shipshape condition. I really don't want to have to be making long-distance calls throughout my honeymoon. I work like a madwoman. Long hours and high levels of concentration cause my head to ache, eyes sting and temples bulge. By the time it gets around to the thirteenth I have emptied my in tray and signed off all the projects that are imperative. The only thing left to do, in the week between the party and the wedding, is close the books on this quarter's budgets. Then after the honeymoon I can come back to—

Well, to whatever is in my in tray.

"All done!" I send my last e-mail of the day with a flourish of satisfaction.

"Oh good. I was worried that Cinders wasn't coming to the ball," says Fi. She's scrabbling under her desk trying to retrieve a kitten-heel shoe. We are both high on the spirit of having achieved what was demanded of us. Despite the unreasonable nature of the demands.

"What, and miss your party? Not for the world."

She's dressed in a white sequined Moschino number. Very ice maiden meets LA débutante. I couldn't have chosen better myself. She's obviously taken great care and spent her dowry.

"Are you getting changed?" she nags.

"I haven't thought about it." Fi pulls a face. "OK, OK, I'll look through my filing cabinet. There's bound to be something to wear in there." I know she's worked hard and wants everyone to appreciate her effort by making an effort.

Fi has plumped for a theme of black and white. She said this was largely to do with the invitations being sent out so late in the day; the guests are mostly media luvvies, and a dress code stipulating one or the other of these colors won't cause any problems. Despite the brief, I emerge from the loos, fifteen minutes later, with freshly applied lipstick and a scarlet Johanna Hehir dress. It's clingy, flowery and feminine. I believe in the importance of an entrance.

I follow the noise of laughter and clinking glasses and the heady perfume of fat waxy lilies up to the roof terrace where we are holding the jamboree. The lifts part and my first impression is top. Waiters, dressed in Paul Smith, carry trays of champagne. There are dozens of lanterns and fairy lights everywhere and while it's still too light and warm for them to be anything more than decorative, they are certainly that. There are sculptures of huge chess pieces scattered about. I'm not sure what their original purpose was intended to be but they are being used as giant ashtrays and bar stools. There are luxurious, white, faux-fur rugs hanging on the walls. The food looks exquisite; it also follows the theme of black and white—piles of scrumptious-looking caviar followed by attractive miniature summer puddings, made entirely with black-berries and served with heavy dollops of double cream. Fi has done the correct thing by serving small amounts of delicious-looking food. It barely matters what it tastes like, as most of the guests would rather polish the shoes of the entire British army than consume unanticipated calories. Still, the media luvvies look the part; as my mother would prosaically say, "They scrub up well." The room is awash with every label in the alphabet, from Armani to Versace.

The effect is magical.

I help myself to a glass of champagne and look for someone useful to talk to. Fi prevents this by hurtling toward me.

"OhmygodOhmygod," she screams.

"What? Have I lipstick on my teeth?" I ask, rubbing my teeth with my finger. As I do so I notice there's soap stuck in my engagement ring; I take it off and start to gouge it out with my fingernail. Something is certainly upsetting Fi. She looks as though she is hyperventilating.

"I am so sorry. I can't think how it happened. We used mail merge. His name must have been on the wrong list," she gabbles.

"Whose name?" I ask. But Fi can't answer because she's staring at something behind me. She looks like a rabbit terrified and trapped in the headlights of an oncoming truck. I turn.

I'm the rabbit.

"Darren? Darren?" I can hardly believe it is him. For months I've been trying to convince myself that seeing Darren again would be the worst thing that could possibly happen to me, but now I'm actually facing him, I have to admit it feels like the best. The crowds around us dwindle and there's just the two of us. Which is a nightmare because my tongue is cleaving to the roof of my mouth and I can't think of anything at all suitable to say. I slip my ring in my pocket.

He's breathtaking. He's everything I've been imagining and remembering for the last six months, but more.

I'm expecting an onslaught of anger and recriminations and try to head them off by putting us on a polite and formal note immediately.

"Are you here for the party?" Then I shoot myself. Or at least that would be a suitable penalty for such a banal conversation starter but I don't have a gun handy.

"I suppose I am," he says, half grinning and wincing at the same time. My La Perla knickers hiccup.

"Good, good. I'm so pleased." I like this sentence more. It is at once honest and straightforward. Honesty and the ability to be straightforward are things I know Darren admires. "I didn't expect to see you here," I rush to clarify. "Not that I invited you." That sounds awful. "I mean. I didn't send out the invites." He looks confused. "Well, it's not your sort of thing, is it?" My voice finally falters and then draws to a halt. I suspect we are both relieved.

We stand awkwardly watching other people enjoy themselves, until eventually Darren asks, "Will Trixxie be coming along?"

I'm crushed. He's here for Trixxie. Not me.

Not that he could be here for me. Not after I've ignored him for six months.

Nor should I want him to be. I'm engaged to Josh and I don't do casual sex any more. I try to tell myself that my jealousy is a lazy hangover from my other life.

"I don't know. I don't think even Fi knows who she's invited, judging by the look of confusion on her face when she saw you. If

Trixxie is coming she'll be late," I add sulkily. He's grinning. No sign of disappointment that Trixxie may not appear. Maybe he just thought of her because I was behaving like an incompetent. I add, "It's quite a select gathering."

"I'm touched."

In case he thinks I am, I clarify, "And your name got on the list by mistake. A fault with mail-merging the wrong list."

"Ha," he guffaws. He actually throws his head back and laughs out loud. As ever, I'm not sure if he's laughing at me or with me. But I don't care. I just like hearing his laughter. It cheers me. It is definitely the most exhilarating sound I've ever heard.

"You don't change, do you?" he asks.

In fact, I do. I have. And if I tell him I'm engaged that would prove it.

My mouth is welded together.

I wait for him to walk away but he doesn't. Instead he asks, "What did you think about that article on Ian Schrager's latest hotel?"

"Sorry?"

"Or the one on the Balinese spas?" He is referring to the web pages he's e-mailed to me. The one on the spas was the last one he sent, nine weeks ago. "It's just you never said." Darren stares at me and his stare could shatter granite. Every one of his e-mails had been selected with peculiar care. They always referred back to some conversation we'd had in the halcyon period. The two weeks when we behaved as a couple. The two weeks when we were a couple.

I cough up my voice. "I—I often visit the Starsky and Hutch site." The side of his mouth twitches a fraction. "And the one about historical Oscars. In fact all the articles were interesting."

Darren nods. It's a tight, tense nod. Hardly perceptible. I need a drink. I daren't move toward a champagne tray, in case Darren takes the opportunity to leave, so instead I flag down a waiter and insist he fetches us a couple of glasses.

Darren accepts the glass but he doesn't look comfortable.

"What should we toast to?" he asks.

I consider suggesting that we could toast to my engagement. But I don't.

"To, er, you. You look well. Let's toast to you," I suggest.

"No. That would be far too unchivalrous. How about to *you*? You're always well, aren't you?" I don't quite know how to answer that. He doesn't sound 100 percent genuine. I shake my head warily. "Proposing we toast to us seems a bit off key," he snipes.

"Suppose so," I mutter reluctantly.

"I've got it. Here's to *Sex with an Ex.*"

I catch his eye. "Er, *Sex with an Ex,*" I mutter, because really, here's to it. But can Darren mean that? He can't be toasting the program. He loathes the program. So does he mean a genuine ex? Me? Is he flirting? I clink my glass. I hope he's flirting.

I can't believe my luck. I keep expecting him to make his excuses and go and talk to someone else but he doesn't leave my side. Instead he attentively fills my glass, fetches me caviar, walks the room with me, allows me to introduce him to innumerable colleagues. He stands outside with me when I feel overwhelmed by the heaving throng and then he dances with me when I feel so happy that all I want to do is fling my body in random, jerky movements to the thumping bass. He stays right by me, carefully watching my every action, listening to my conversations with other people, and he seems to be happy to do this. We both behave as though we've seen each other every day for the last six months. Darren doesn't publicly rebuke me for my terse note and sudden disappearance; he doesn't refer to a single aspect of my despicable and undoubtedly confusing behavior. I don't know what to make of this. Am I so insignificant to him that he can't even summon up the curiosity to ask me why I behaved so strangely? But if that is the case, why spend the evening with me? If I were more trusting, the only conclusion I could draw is that he wants answers but he won't embarrass me in front of my colleagues by demanding them. He's too polite. He cares too much.

Believing that he cares at all sends me into a state of near hysteria.

Throughout the evening he is a delight. He charms and amuses everyone. He chats to Debs, Di and Jaki, who are enraptured with his good looks and general affability. Trixxie stands speechless, with her jaw hanging open as she listens to his theories on why women find Robson Green irresistible.

"She's literally mesmerized by you," I tease him.

"No, it's drugs," he grins modestly.

I watch as Darren works his sorcery on the celebs who normally make it a rule not to be impressed, or even civil, to anyone other than their next paycheck. He grips the "gentlemen" of the press by quoting their own articles back to them and having an informed opinion on the broadest range of subjects—anything from the ins and outs of India's election systems to the GDP per capita in Japan. He even impresses Bale, who, desperate to meet Darren, follows him around the room and contrives to collide in the urinals. In our two weeks together I'd painted a bleak, but accurate, picture of Bale which must now be coloring Darren's judgment. Whilst happy to talk to everyone from the bar staff to the chairman, Darren steadfastly avoids Bale and won't treat him to more than a casual wave across the room. And while everyone is captivated by Darren, I am bewitched. He is just as funny and interesting and polite and sincere as I remembered.

He is more sexy.

I feel as though I am swimming in champagne. Bubbles of euphoria zip through my body where blood and lungs and my nerve system used to be. I feel giddy and light-headed and light-hearted too.

Fuck—what if someone tells him about the engagement before I can?

I saw my way through the crowd of women who are congregating around him. It's slow progress and so I eventually whisper to one of them that Robbie Williams has just arrived. Fickle, they rapidly disperse, leaving Darren to me again. He looks relieved.

"Enjoying yourself?"

"Yeah, it's great meeting your friends." There's a "but" in his voice and I'm glad.

"Fancy going somewhere less frantic?"

He agrees immediately.

We leave the party and start to stroll aimlessly along the river. We take a similar route to the one we took in January, past the National Theatre, the Royal Festival Hall, the Hayward Gallery, the Queen Elizabeth Hall. We walk on to Westminster Bridge and stop to look at the London Eye.

"Impressive, isn't it?" comments Darren.

"Very," I agree.

"This is what I love about London. The space, the crowds, the progress, the history. The morphing culture."

So he starts to tell me about what he does with his time in London and how he ended up here in the first place, why he left Whitby and also how much he misses and loves it. I ask him about his family and he gives me their news. Sarah's expecting another baby and Richard and Shelly had a lovely wedding day. He shows me a photo of Charlotte receiving her certificate for swimming twenty-five meters. The image of her tiny, wet and shivering body, erect with pride, makes me smile. I ask dozens of questions but he can't give me enough information. I hadn't known I could miss anyone so much.

"They often ask about you," he says.

"Do they really?" I'm aglow.

"Yeah, they have a pet name for you."

"What?" I ask tentatively, not sure that I want to know.

"Naomi Campbell," he grins.

I start to laugh. "I'm going to pretend that is because of my fetish for shoes and modelesque looks rather than my stunning ability to throw a hissy fit."

Darren laughs nervously, too frank to confirm or deny my suppositions. His nervousness makes me laugh louder. I'm laughing at myself and it's OK because I'm part of the Smith family jokes. He tells me how his sick trees are. And makes me laugh again with descriptions of his new flatmate. We talk and walk for hours. We leave the river at Charing Cross and start to head to St. James's Park; we pass Buckingham Palace and march on to Hyde Park.

I can't remember exactly when he took hold of my hand. I think it was when we crossed the Mall. I have never held any man's hand in public. It's so territorial, so tacky. Their hands are always clammy and it's difficult to walk in a straight line with someone hanging on to you.

Don't let go.

I'm firing on all cylinders. It's been a particularly warm evening, so there are still hundreds of people on the streets. Including the terrorists of the speed walker—tourists, roller bladers and pensioners. But tonight their stop-start-stop styles, dangerous speeds or dithering steps don't annoy me. They seem like part of the tapestry. As do the *Big Issue* sellers, the gangs of Euro-trash teenagers, the groups of friends finishing their picnics, the traffic wardens, the dog walkers, the mounted police riding up Birdcage Walk and the other happy couples.

Other happy couples.

Other happy *couples*.

"My feet are aching." I finally submit. "Let's go and get a drink somewhere."

"OK. Where?"

"Dunno. It's late and this is not my end of town."

And I want to take a hotel room.

It's just like that. Because besides all the hand holding, and the conversation, and the laughing, and the fact that I was desperately proud of him at the party, there's something else. There's my breasts, which have taken on a life of their own: nipples upturned and out-turned, aching, desperate for him to clutch and ply and grasp and tongue. And there are my exploding knickers. Creamy with desire. Dizzy with craving.

We hail a cab within seconds, which is fluky and seems to me to be a sign that this is meant to be. Unashamed, I instruct the cabby to take us to a hotel.

"Which one?"

"Any," I reply, irritated by the interruption, for by now he is interrupting. He's interrupting Darren's long, filthy looks of undisguised want.

The cab pulls up outside some hotel. We pay in a daze, wildly overtipping. We muddle through the inconvenience of having to check in and decide which paper we want in the morning. And just as I think we are about to stumble in to bed in a stupor, Darren stops in the foyer.

"We have to talk."

"We've done nothing but talk all night," I say while tugging at his jacket sleeve, impatiently trying to drag him toward the lifts.

"Talk about us." The only topic we've avoided.

"But you're a boy," I joke.

Darren won't be deterred and leads me to the hotel bar. I reason that a drink is a good idea. I haven't had one since I left the party, which will have been near nine o' clock. It's nearly twelve now; I'm in serious danger of sobering up. In the past I've often found myself in London hotel bars. I know the form. There will be a waiter who shuffles in a manner that is ostensibly discreet. Eyes averted, addressing us as "sir" and "madam" rather than anything that hints at our real identity. The waiter will ensure that we've located the loos, knowing that the purchase of condoms will be necessary and as likely as not somewhere to throw up the night's excesses. He will take away the dirty ashtray and leave a clean one; he'll leave a small bowl of cashew nuts and a cocktail menu. He'll expect us to get heinously drunk in an attempt to shed responsibility and any visions of consequences and he'll expect us to leave a massive tip before we stumble to our bedroom. Darren breaks precedent by ordering a lemonade. His boyish choice makes me giggle until he says, "And you, Cas? I suggest we keep a clear head."

I want a double vodka and a fuzzy head but I order a mineral water. We don't say anything in the time it takes the waiter to go to the bar, fix our drinks and return with them. When the drinks do arrive neither of us suggests a toast. The silence clings to my brain and congregates in my nose and throat, suffocating me.

"Why?" The question, disgustingly direct, shocks me. Darren is naively expecting an equally open response. He wants truth to shape all his dealings. Whilst when I stumble across it (which is rare) I view it as an obstacle. The late hour and the raw expectancy in his voice defeat me.

"Is that an all-encompassing 'why'? Why didn't I call? Why didn't I return any of your messages? Why did I dodge you when you came to see me?"

"No, Cas, I know the answers to those questions." He does? How? "I know why you ran. I know you are terrified of commitment and I reasoned that I couldn't do anything about that except wait. I hoped time would show you that I'm serious about you. If I hadn't known at least that much about you, how do you think I could have brought myself to speak to you this evening? Don't you think I was blistering with anger and"—he pauses—"pain? But I reasoned that while you hurt me you didn't do it to be cruel, although you were; you did it because you didn't know how else to behave. You hurt because you are always hurting. That's why I didn't rail at you this evening. Believe me, I wanted to."

He pauses and I look at him. His eyes are a mass of confusion and wisdom, certainty and terror. I feel so ashamed. If he had ranted at me I could have walked away. I could have sidled back to the sanctuary of aloofness, feeling justified that he didn't understand me and never would. But he does understand me.

"I never stopped thinking about you, Cas. I never stopped wanting you. What I'm asking you now is why won't you *allow* yourself to trust *me*."

So he's worked it out. I'm impressed—it shows dedication. But then I know he's the dedicated type. I wonder how to answer his question. After all, he's never let me down, hurt me or disappointed me. In fact, he consistently exceeds my expectations. He has attributes and characteristics that I thought had died out with Merlin and Arthur's round table. And even then were myths.

I can't think of a logical reason why I wouldn't trust him.

I can't think of a convincing lie. So I do the next best thing. I tell the truth, a part of the truth, something like the truth.

"I do trust you."

Darren's face, previously tight and anxious, melts into the broadest grin. He takes my chin in his hand, tilts my head and kisses me. The kiss is strong, absorbing and complete. Darren is satisfied with my answer; he thinks that his six months' wait on the sidelines has brought me to my senses. And so we move toward the lifts, to the bedrooms. I trust him but he shouldn't trust me. I am engaged to Josh. And while I know now, for certain, that I made that promise for the wrong reasons, I did promise. Poor Josh. Poor Darren. And if I could bring myself to like myself more, I'd feel sorry for me too. I know I should pull away from Darren, stop him kissing me, stop kissing him back and tell him about Josh instead. But I can't. I'm a coward. Whilst Darren has been the epitome of reasonableness thus far he won't understand that my fear of loving him drove me into an engagement with another man. I hardly understand it. And I want him so ferociously that I don't know how I'd continue to live if he stopped kissing me now. So while Darren's kissing me, and illuminating my skin with his strokes, and warming my consciousness with the words he's uttering, I am making another promise. This time to myself.

This will be the last time.

One last fling before I return to Josh. I may trust Darren but I don't trust love. And while Darren has arrived in my life with a certificate of authenticity, he's not carrying a lifetime warranty. Josh does. I plan to enjoy every moment of tonight and I'll make memories that will fortify and edify me for the rest of my life.

That's what I plan.

We fall on to the bed and he forcefully and repeatedly kisses me. My legs entwine around his, our hands race to rediscover every curve, crevice, ravine and fissure of each other's bodies. We shed our sticky clothes in a matter of seconds as our skin burns and bleeds into one another's. He kisses, strokes, licks every inch of my body. Exploring the obvious parts—my shoulders, my tits, my thighs, discovering the discreet parts, my toes, the crook of my elbow, the space between my fingers. I consume him. Tasting his sweat and smelling his sex. I concentrate on the feel of him, which bits of his body are rough, which are smooth. I become familiar with the texture of his hair, all his different hair. His thick, glossy locks, the downy fuzz growing in between his buttocks, the hairs on his chest that thicken and become more coarse around his groin and the bristles that grow on his chin, right now, while I'm with him. I listen to his heart and his breathing. Both becoming quicker and less controlled. I smell him. I taste him.

I see him.

The second before he enters me, he grabs my head in both his hands and he looks at me. He stares.

He knows me. Me with his pubes stuck to my cheek, him with

my sex on his lips. I tighten my muscles in my thighs and groin in an effort to cling on to him. To keep him exactly where he is now. In me. With me. I wonder how I walked away from this. I wonder how I'll walk away a second time.

It's faster and faster and tighter and harder. I can feel my body responding and the response is rising. It's coming from my toes, circling up through my legs. But it's started in my fingers too, which seem to be lost in his hair and then running up and down his back. My arms ache with the exquisite brilliance of it. My head spins with the same shocking ecstasy. The intense feelings of luxury creep up my back and through my heart, meeting in my stomach. The meeting fulfilled in acute spasms of rapture. I jerk with sex. I jolt with sex. And when he screams out that he loves me I brim over with a feeling of gladness.

Suddenly everything is crystal. This is the last piece of the jigsaw, the glass of freezing water on a blisteringly stifling day, the hot, creamy chocolate after an afternoon on the piste, the sunshine on a wet pavement after a summer storm, the thing the songs go on and on and on about. He's it.

Exhausted and sweating, we fall on to each other.

I watch him execute the logistics of falling to sleep: peeing, putting a glass of water on the bedside table, adjusting the air conditioning, discarding the duvet and selecting a sheet instead, and I'm fascinated. I watch him turn on to his side and see that as his breathing calms, his shoulders rise and fall steadily. I tuck tightly into him. My breasts on his back. His bum nestling in my pubes. My legs folded into his, finishing with my toes in the arch of his ankle. And it starts to fade. The throbbing anger, cynicism and mistrust that I've carried around for twenty-six years starts to fade. As does the terrible feeling of loss and grief that I've been soused in since January. I am simply full of love and hope and possibility. The revelation that we are imbued with something more interesting than physical gratification is velvety. The recognition that I,

too, have a need for and ability to give respect, friendship, love and
passion sings around my head. This man is my destiny. This man
is my life. Fuck it, I'll risk it. So he doesn't come with a warranty—
so what? I'll risk it. And I'm so lucky to be able to.

"Cas, you awake?" Darren's whisper interrupts my thoughts.

"Yes," I whisper back, although I'm unsure who we're being
careful not to disturb.

"I was just wondering."

"What?"

"Will you marry me?"

"Yes."

I know. It's slightly unconventional that I am technically
engaged to two men.

CHAPTER
Eighteen

HERE I AM IN THE MIDDLE of realizing a dream, a dream I didn't even realize I had, and it's good. Really good. Wow. That shit about better to travel hopefully than arrive. Losers. Better to arrive spectacularly and I have.

I have! I'm drunk on euphoria (and only a little bit of fear). I want to bottle the experience and keep it on my dressing table. I know he is *it*. The One. The only one. I'm not sure how I'll maintain this constant high. But I believe it will all take care of itself.

We stay in the hotel all morning, excitedly talking about when and where we'll get married. Darren is thrilled when I admit that there's nothing I'd like more than to marry in St. Hilda's Abbey, Whitby.

"You mean the church near the abbey. The actual abbey is decayed. It doesn't have a roof."

"No. I mean the abbey. I want to be outside in the open."

"We can look into it. I'm not sure of the rules. I suppose once ground is consecrated, it's always consecrated, long after the roof has fallen in." He pauses and kisses a mole on my back. "I didn't think you believed in God. What are you doing? Keeping a foot in each camp?"

"No, it's not that. It just feels right. The abbey is so beautiful. I felt calm there."

We both confess to a hankering for a winter wedding.

"Although it will be freezing, so you have to consider erect nipples if we are getting married outdoors. They can ruin a photograph," I comment.

"Can they?" From his tone it's obvious that he doesn't think so.

I can see me in a long fur dress and him in navy velvet. I can see it all so clearly. We talk about children, how many and their names! Then we agree that we had better get up and start telling people. I freeze. Telling people that I'm marrying Darren necessarily means telling them I'm not marrying Josh. I'm terrified and horrified. I can only imagine the pain and disappointment I'm going to cause. I turn to Darren and consider confessing everything to him. I'm sure he'll guide me, and advise me on how best to handle this awful situation. But the words don't fall out of my mouth. Instead we agree to negotiate a late checkout. I try to thrust Josh to the back of my mind. We order champagne and drink it in our room. Later we order lunch, "our meal" (because we already have "our" things)—cheese on toast which I can't eat. So instead we celebrate with more loving. At four o'clock the chambermaid and the manager hover, then hammer outside our door, insisting that the room has to be cleaned, as it is booked by someone else for tonight. Reluctantly we drag ourselves out of bed and into our clothes.

We say goodbye to one another in the hotel lobby, but then can't quite separate, so Darren walks me to the tube even though he is catching a bus. We say goodbye again at the ticket barrier but then decide to buy a ticket for him, just so that we can say a final goodbye on the platform. We wouldn't have parted at all but I have arrangements to meet my mum and Issie at my flat to do a final fitting of the wedding dress. The wedding to Josh, that is.

"I expect his reluctance to let you out of his sight was because he isn't sure when, or indeed if, he's ever going to see you again," snaps Issie.

"Of course he knows he'll see me again. He trusts me. *I* trust me. We're going to see each other every day for the rest of our lives." I giggle and do a small on-the-spot jig. I'm just so full of energy! My mother and Issie stare at me from their seats on the settee. Their faces sort of spoil the moment.

"Aren't you pleased for me?"

They exchange looks.

"Aren't you going to congratulate me on my engagement?"

Issie tuts, "Which one, Little Miss Changie-Mindy?" I notice my mother put her hand on top of Issie's in a futile attempt to calm her.

"It does seem a little sudden," comments my mum. Trying to walk the tightrope between tact and instruction.

"It's not sudden, I've felt like this for a long time. I've just found the courage to admit it. I haven't changed my mind, just my heart. I am still sure that infidelity, shallowness and cruelty are out there. I just no longer believe it is my only option."

"You know, you're right. Infidelity, shallowness and cruelty are out there," shouts Issie. "And do you know something else? They are right here too. *You* epitomize them. What about Josh?"

Of course I haven't forgotten him. I admit that I've worked hard in the last twenty-four hours not to think of him, but he's been with me all the time. He's the shadow on my intense euphoria. Which is heartbreaking, because I do believe that all he ever wanted to do was make me happy.

"I can't marry Josh," I state sadly.

"Well, I realized that you weren't planning on becoming a bigamist," screams Issie. Her mouth is wide open and her face is the same color as her tonsils.

I kneel in front of them, hoping, rather than expecting, they'll understand. Issie flings herself back against the settee; my mother moves a fraction closer to me. Although it's hardly a herald of angels, I take this as a sign of encouragement. I try to explain. "I didn't believe in love—I couldn't understand why anyone would.

When people talked about love it was like reading reports about war in a far away country—it just didn't seem real. And then I . . . well . . . I guess . . . I . . ." Issie and my mother are staring at me, which is a bit off putting. "Well . . . fell in love."

"Visited the war zone, so to speak?" says my mother. She sounds unsure.

I plough on regardless. "But it was really scary, so I . . . well . . . I . . ." Bugger—when did I start stuttering? "Ran away." Issie tuts like a budgie. "But once I knew the war zone was real, really real, I found it impossible to ignore. Marrying Josh would be a halfway measure, like sending food parcels."

"You want to be a foot soldier rather than part of the Red Cross," says my mum. She still doesn't sound confident. Hearing her repeat it back to me like that, I realize how bizarre my analogy is. So I try something more conventional.

"I am so sorry that I'm going to hurt Josh. But don't you see? It would be much worse marrying him when I don't feel about him the way he does about me."

"Yes, I see that," says Issie. "That was my point all the way along."

"Darren makes jokes funnier if he laughs at them and he makes the room more homey when he enters it. He makes water cleaner, nights blacker and stars brighter if he notices them. I hadn't wanted to admit that love existed, that I'd made such a monumentous, disastrous misjudgment. But I have to, because I love him. Even when I'm asleep." At this point it seems a genuine possibility that foreign tongues have possessed me.

"I, I, fucking I. That's all we ever hear from you, Cas. What about thinking about someone else for a change?"

I stumble backward, nearly overwhelmed by the power of Issie's words. She rarely swears and never says fuck.

"First you hurt Darren by just walking away from him, then you pick him back up when you feel like it—"

"It isn't like that, it's—"

She waves her hands in front of her, cutting through my objections. Imagine Issie's little, skinny hands being so powerful and effective.

"You are so selfish." She's on her feet now and pacing around the room. "OK, so you believe in love now—let's have a party!" She stamps her foot and with anyone else I'd have been tempted to laugh, but since this fury is coming from Issie and directed toward me, all I can do is listen.

"No, on second thoughts, let's not. Let's examine your ridiculous behavior instead." I think I prefer the first option, but then I don't think this is a genuine choice situation. I listen to Issie as she begins to list my crimes against humanity. The way she explains it, it appears that I have more in common with Imelda Marcos than a love of shoes. ". . . The horrible way you've treated your countless lovers. The stupid destructiveness of *Sex with an Ex* and finally your selfish, fucking, engagement to Josh." With each accusation Issie raises her voice a decibel. I fully expect the people in the flat above to bang on the floor and ask us to keep the noise down.

My insides are raw. I want to tell her that I wasn't awful to all my lovers and anyway most of them didn't really expect anything too laudable. I want to tell her that the show saved jobs. I want to tell her that I love her *and* Josh and never meant to hurt either of them. But all these arguments seem hollow and pointless. She's heard them before. She was never that impressed. Anyway she's gone.

The door bangs behind her.

I turn to my mother. "Do you think she was disappointed because she's not going to be bridesmaid next week?"

"Don't joke about it, Jocasta," replies my mother sternly. "You always rush to hide pain in jokes and it comes across badly." Subdued, I follow her through to the kitchen. She opens the fridge and pulls out a bottle of Veuve Clicquot.

"We can always depend on you to have champagne in the fridge," she comments. "I've always thought that is so stylish of you."

"Have you?" I'm so stunned I'm momentarily diverted from pondering Issie's outburst. I'd always assumed that Mum thought champagne was decadent. The only bottles my mum keeps in the fridge are brown sauce and tomato ketchup. My initial surprise is superseded by the fact that my mother expertly opens the champers and pours it into the glasses without spilling a drop. I don't think I've ever seen my mum open champagne in my life.

"Do you think Issie's right?" I want to know where I stand, but I'm not sure how much more straight talking I can take.

"Yes," replies my mum, without taking her eyes off the drink she's pouring.

"Oh." We both silently watch the bubbles fizz and then settle, and I wonder if I'm going to have any friends left, if I get through this at all.

"What are we celebrating?" I ask apprehensively.

"It's not quite as simple as that, is it? I mean we could raise a glass to your new engagement but that would seem rather insensitive toward Josh. Poor boy."

I stare at my shoes. "If only I could turn the clock back."

"You can't. Ever," states Mum. And as if to prove her point I notice that the only sound in the kitchen is the clock ticking.

Then in a kinder voice she adds, "But do you know something? I'm proud of you."

"Proud of me?" I can't believe it.

"Yes. You've recovered. You aren't letting your father ruin your life."

"Like he did yours, you mean," I mutter glumly. I really don't want to be reminded of my father right now. All too clearly, I remember the innumerable occasions that my mother moaned and grumbled about him. I received the subliminal message loud and clear: men are bastards.

Not all of them. I remind myself.

Expecting an onslaught of bitter regret and fury from my mother, I cling to the thought as though it were a shield. Not all of them.

"He didn't ruin mine, darling. I have a lovely life. Bob and I are very comfortable with one another."

"Bob?" I'm amazed. Surely her life is dished. Why else would it be so quiet? Except of course if she likes it that way.

"Yes, Bob." She smiles and doesn't elaborate. Thank God. I've had enough monumental shocks and surprises in the past twenty-four hours to last me a lifetime. I've discovered I'm capable of loving. I've learned Darren loves me and revealed that I love him too. I've got engaged. Again. I've heard Issie say fuck, I've seen my mother open a bottle of champagne. I could not stand knowing that she has a sex life.

"I'm proud of you for falling irrationally and uncontrollably in love. I didn't know if you'd ever have the grit to do it. I thought your father and I had denied you that on top of everything else." She pauses and then adds, "Well done, Cas!" I think she's going to slap me on the back but she hugs me. It's a small, tight hug—not exactly the huge grasping to the huge bosom that you see in movies, but then my mother hasn't got a huge bosom.

It's the best hug I've ever received.

We pull apart and grin at one another. I think I've just come first in the egg and spoon race. I must have because my mother is every bit the proud parent.

"Issie," I groan.

"Don't worry too much about Issie, she'll come around eventually. She's too kind not to want to see it from your point of view," smiles Mum. Then she adds, in a tone I'm much more used to hearing from her, "Not that you should dismiss what she said—it was spot on. You have a lot of bridges to mend, and maybe some of them will never be repaired."

I can't bear to think about that.

"Now come and tell me some more about Darren. When will I get to meet him? Don't forget to bring that bottle of champers." She takes my hand and leads me to the sitting room.

Mum sits on the settee and I sit next to her. We while away the early evening with chatter about Darren and, more shockingly, Bob. I tell her the big things that make Darren wonderful and some of the small things too.

"He raises his eyebrow and it is sooo sexy. And he kind of ruffles his hair in a boyish way."

"Bob does that too. Not that he has much hair. Which does, I suppose, encumber the effect." We laugh. "Maybe you and Darren would like to have tea with Bob and me on Sunday."

I think of a compromise. "Or we could all go to a restaurant."

She sees it as that and meets me. "Yes, that's a good idea. We can get dressed up. Make it a bit special."

At some point I ease down the settee and find myself half slumped, half draped across Mum. My head is on her lap and she's playing with my hair. She runs her fingers over my scalp. I have Darren. I have Mum. I am as safe and as loved as a child.

Buuuuzzzzzzzz.

"Wonder who that can be," I mutter, annoyed that my bonding time with my mother is being so rudely unglued.

Buuuuzzzzzzzz.

"Are you expecting anyone?" asks Mum.

"No." I drag myself toward the intercom but before I open the door it opens from the outside and Issie falls through it. She's fumbling with her keys and mobile and handbag, which she drops, scattering tissues, money and makeup everywhere. I'm thrilled to see her.

"Put the TV on," screams Issie. She's tense and still angry, which incites her to forcefully yell, *"Now.* TV6." Yesterday this sudden boldness would have been unusual; now the unexpected is all that seems available. I do as she says.

I hear a familiar theme tune.

"Sex with an Ex? But the series is over."

Issie shushes me.

"Hello. Thank you very much and welcome," says Katie Hunt as she bounds on to the stage. Her tits are trembling and, to make the job of the close-up camera easier, her shirt is unbuttoned one more button than necessary. "Well, ladies and gentlemen, have I got a treat for you!" She winks cheekily, the way I taught her to.

Issie hands me a gin and tonic, which I take unquestioningly. I see that she's poured Mum a sherry.

"Tonight we are featuring our very own 'voice of our generation,' only days before her wedding. We are going to see if she's ready to say 'from this day forward,' or is it a case of 'from this lay forward.' " The audience erupts into loud oohs and phwas. "Our celeb was given the opportunity to appear on the show but has declined, so instead we'll meet her fiancé, Joshua Dixon. A big hand, ladies and gentlemen."

"Josh!"

The gin and tonic slips out of my hand on to the floor. The glass smashes and the liquid spills in all directions. None of us moves to mop it up.

"Josh—you don't mind if I call you Josh, do you?" Katie purrs. Josh shakes his head, always one to be taken in by a pretty face. *"Can you tell us a little bit about yourself and your relationship with your fiancée, Jocasta Perry. Tell us why you are here tonight."*

"Cas and I have known each other since we were children."

Ohhhhh, chorus the audience, no doubt incited by the stage manager holding up a big sign reading "how sweet." We have other ones reading "shame" and "condemn." The signs were Bale's idea.

"*I love Cas. I've always loved her, right through school, university, and when we both got jobs.*" As Josh is saying this, photos of Josh and me appear on screen. One when we are about eight and he is pushing my swing. I'm grinning, a gappy, toothless grin, and kicking my legs high. You can see my knickers. Josh looks intense and as though he's working hard to push me higher. In fact he was trying to push me off the swing so he could have a turn. Of course he was. He was a brother to me.

"I've always loved that photo," says Mum. I scowl at her.

There's another one of us at university, getting our degree certificates. Josh is adjusting my gown. Then several others, where we are doing our own thing. Josh in his chambers, me at various parties or functions. The thing they have in common is that I'm always surrounded by men and holding a glass of champagne; Josh is always alone.

"Why haven't they shown any of you working?" asks Mum. "Or any of Josh partying? He's such a cheerful young man and he seems a loner in these."

"Exactly. That's what they want to imply." I rake my hands through my hair. I know exactly where this is going and I'm quite powerless to stop it. Issie pats me on the knee. We don't take our eyes off the screen.

"*Cas seems quite a party girl,*" pursues Katie.

"*Well, she is,*" confirms Josh, and in case he's misinterpreted, he adds, "*But I like that in her.*"

"*When did you get engaged?*"

"March, this year."

"*So you've waited for Cas for twenty-six years. You staying at home, while she's been having a high old time. I hope she's worth the wait.*" Katie turns toward the camera and grimaces.

We don't get to hear what Josh replies. Even if he was honest enough to admit that he didn't exactly hang around in the wings for twenty-six years—more like bought shares in Durex, the audi-

ence don't get to find out because the camera cuts to some affi-
davits from my friends and colleagues. We see them say, *"Up for
it," "Game on," "Wild," "Fun," "Skilled"* (laugh), *if you know what I
mean."* The audience has no idea what question was asked or how
the interviewee was led into a certain response. They could have
been talking about my attitude to work. They could have been
talking about someone else. I know this because at TV6 we aren't
always that consistent in our approach to interviewing for *Sex with
an Ex* and we edit for maximum entertainment—rather than
authenticity. In the past I've advocated this. Now I'm regretting it.

Katie gets Josh to talk about how he proposed to me. The audience lap up the cream rose, dimmed lights, huge diamonds. He
omits to mention the fact that the weeping of the freshly ditched
Jane was still echoing around the flat. Nor does he mention his
New Year's resolution or the tax breaks.

Fair enough. I wouldn't either if I were him.

Josh talks about all the preparations, cost and care for our "big,
traditional wedding." He doesn't say that my mum has done all the
work. They cut to lots of footage of Josh talking to caterers, florists
and the guys who erect the marquee. I can only assume this
footage was filmed especially because, to my certain knowledge,
Josh has not visited any of these people to actually plan for the
wedding. My mother confirms this when she comments, "But
that's not the florist we are using." She looks at me and corrects
herself, "Were using. That's not the florist we were using. Why do
you think Josh is talking to them?"

She's far too innocent for me to be able to explain.

"Josh, it's clear to see that Jocasta is a bit of a flirt."

The words cut. A neat incision.

*"But why did you contact the studio? Is there a particular ex that
you feel might threaten your relationship?"* Katie Hunt tilts her head
to one side and smiles sympathetically. I've seen her practice that
in the mirror in the loos.

"There's this one guy. Darren Smith."

The incision rips to a wider gash.

They play a film of the TV6 party. Even in this stupefied state I have to credit the editor. It's a fine piece of work. Because the cameras were concealed and I obviously haven't signed a release form allowing TV6 to film me, they have had to use a black stripe to obscure my eyes. But since they have just shown numerous stills of me, the strip doesn't conceal my identity. I just look sinister, a bit like a masked madame at a brothel. The film starts with a shot of me slipping my engagement ring into my pocket. This is repeated four times and then it shows me greeting (a masked) Darren. Cut to me beaming like a Cheshire cat. It shows Darren being attentive toward me, bringing me caviar and champagne. They speed that bit up and, because of my animated hand gestures and his vigilance, it looks as though I am bossing and directing him on an endless stream of jobs. Fetch this, bring that, go there and come here. Cut to Darren and me dancing together. We were actually dancing to an innocuous cover version of "Let's Twist Again" but TV6 have dubbed in the husky, throbbing voice of Rod Stewart singing "Da Ya Think I'm Sexy." The camera angles are such that I look as though I'm gyrating my groin almost in Darren's face. Cut to me trying to get through the crowd of women hanging 'round Darren. Again this is speeded up, and by shaking the camera, the effect achieved is one of violence. It looks as though I'm shoving away the competition. There's a bit where we were chatting exuberantly, my hair cloaking our faces, it looks as though we were snogging, at it like hammer and tongs. We had openly left the party together. But by editing two different bits of footage, one of Darren going to the loo and another of me going out of the room for a moment to take a call on my mobile, it looks as though we deliberately left separately and then met furtively outside the building. If this were a film about anyone other than Darren and me, I'd be thrilled.

Darren.

I watch Darren and me walk along the river. I was right—we did start holding hands by the Mall. I see us get in a cab and arrive at a hotel. The masks hide the look of longing and apprehension in Darren's eyes and blank out the moment where the caution rinsed from mine.

It all makes sense now. That's why we were able to get a cab so easily—a plant. The cabby *knew* which hotel to take us to. The one with hidden cameras in the lobby, bar and corridors. That's why breakfast arrived even though we hadn't ordered it. TV6 needed an affidavit from the bellboy that we were in bed together. That's why the manager couldn't let us stay at the hotel for another night. Too right they needed to clean the room out—more like they needed to collect evidence.

I'm right. The film finishes with a number of shots of the debris of our love. A camera pans around the bedroom we left. Empty bottles of champagne, discarded sachets of bubble bath, crumpled sheets on the bed and used condom packets in the bin. The last two shots cause the audience to titter. There is no voiceover. No accusations are actually articulated because if they were I could sue the hides of TV6 but the implication is clear. The masked woman, identifiable as Jocasta Perry, has betrayed Josh, the smiley, affable chap on the stage. I feel betrayed. Exposed. Dirty.

Katie Hunt is exhilarated. Her obvious excitement is bordering on sexual arousal. She tries to contain it as she turns to Josh.

"So how does that film make you feel, Josh?"

There are no winners.

Poor Josh. Despite having watched every episode of *Sex with an Ex* it is clear to me—his former best friend—that he had no perception of the humiliation, upset and pain he was about to bring upon himself by opening this Pandora's box. The same could be said of me but doubly so.

How had I ever thought this showing of bloodied sheets was entertainment? How could I have ever thought that it was OK to reduce love to petty gossip and to aggrandize betrayal to something glamorous rather than grubby?

Josh looks worn and defeated. He tries, but fails, to summon his charming smile. The audience sigh collectively. He looks as though he's going to cry. Oh my God, he is crying. It's excruciating.

"*As I mentioned, Jocasta Perry was invited on to the show but refused to appear.*"

"That's an outright lie. I'll get my lawyers on to that," I snap, but I know the situation is beyond help or hope. TV6 have made a calculated gamble. Even if I sue for invasion of privacy, as this show has been much more obtrusive than any other, they have a hit.

"*We do, however, have a recorded interview with her.*"

They show footage of me in a meeting, presenting on *Sex with an Ex.* I am not wearing a mask because I made this film for TV, to publicize the show. I gaze brazenly at the camera. I am in fact talking about the show when I comment, "*Sex with an Ex* is unbeatable. Risky, dirty, cheeky and above all fun." But I know that the millions of viewers watching think I am talking about Darren.

"*And let's leave the final word with Darren Smith,*" beams Katie.

Close-up of Darren leaving the station after having seen me on to the tube. Even the black stripe over his eyes doesn't make him look comical—he looks more like a modern-day Lone Ranger. He leaps up the steps three at a time. He reaches the top of the steps and leaps in to the air, punching it. Cut to me, winking and saying, "Cheeky and above all fun," air punch, "above all fun," air punch.

Issie and my mother stay silent as the credits roll. I switch off the TV.

"What did that last bit mean?" asks my mother.

"Do you, do you—" Issie's struggling. "Do you think Darren was in on it?"

I pelt her with a silencing glance and she looks at her shoes. I finally find my voice.

"How could they do that to me? I hate the studio. I hate the media."

"Er, you invented it. It's your baby," points out Issie with uncalled-for reasonableness.

"This isn't a baby. Babies are cute. This is Frankenstein's monster's more vicious big brother." As I say this I know she's thinking this serves me right. I also know she's correct.

My eyes flick with tiredness, my head aches. I'm suddenly freezing. I go to my bedroom and unearth a jumper and some socks. Back in the sitting room my mother and Issie are sitting still, like statues, where I left them. I pull my jumper tighter around me. The chill seems to be coming from the inside.

"So do you think Darren set you up?" persists Issie.

"No." I'm horrified that this thought has entered her head.

"You're certain."

"I'm positive. Issie, I trust him."

"It's just that he did seem to forgive you rather too easily. He might be a saint, but it seems more likely that he was part of the plot and wanted revenge."

"You're wrong." He couldn't have faked it. I know it was absolutely real. Everything from the party, to the walk along the river, to the hotel. He's my fiancé, for God's sake.

Hmmm.

But even considering that, I trust him. I keep hold of *my* pictures, him singing into the bathroom mirror, my hands toweling dry his soapy back after our bath, him shining his shoes with the little polishing kit they leave in hotel rooms. I don't allow the film to replace them. I know what I know.

The telephone starts to ring. Foolishly my mother answers it.

It's a reporter from the *Mirror*. I take the handset from her and hang up. It immediately rings again. I disconnect the phone at the wall. Issie looks out of the window. She's right to expect to see the pack.

I start to think of the people who must have been involved in this set-up. Bale certainly must have given the go-ahead. But Bale has not betrayed me. Betrayal requires an atom of self-awareness. With Bale this kind of behavior is closer to animal instinct. Unpleasant as I've always found him, I can certainly believe that he'd stitch me up in this way for ratings. He'd sell his mother to the white slave trade if he thought it would make good television. But he's not bright enough to have come up with the idea. That must have been Fi. I don't want to jump to conclusions, but Fi knew how I felt about Darren. She was unusually keen to help me arrange the party. I bet she suggested the party to Bale in the first place. Of course—why else would she have enough time to help me out? Bale makes sure all his staff are on overdrive all the time. She sent out the invitations and she never makes mistakes, mail merge or otherwise. How could Fi do that to me? I thought we were friends.

But were we?

Was I ever a real friend to her? When she joined the station she had tried to be agreeable but I made it clear our relationship was strictly business. I recognized the fact that she was fiercely intelligent and ambitious. I was threatened. So instead of developing her potential, working her into the team, recognizing her achievements, I tried to contain her talents. All I've taught her is ruthlessness, selfishness and egotism.

Still, she seems to have learned those lessons pretty well.

And it's not just Fi. Debs and Di must have been working on the publicity for this. Jaki must have cooperated too, because the press have my telephone number and address—personal details that only Jaki has. Katie Hunt was having a great time exposing me as a bitch and I gave her her first big break! What could I have possibly have done to offend her? Maybe she just thought I was fair game. Tom and Mark may have held a grudge because I slept with them and then dumped them. Gray because I didn't. Ricky's trickier. What have I done to hurt him? Failed to comment on how fetching he looked in his new Diesel shirt. I think of the time that he needed me to negotiate a schedule change with the homophobe executive. I'd agreed to go to lunch and then stayed with Darren. I didn't even remember to cancel the date. The executive never forgave Ricky and has made his life hell in a thousand small ways since. Obviously Ricky felt I'd let him down. And Jack the cameraman? Ed the editor? Mike on sound? How we've laughed about that—"The mike Mike," we roar. Jen on special effects? We've shared KitKats! And then, when it came to the crunch, they all betrayed me. These are depressing thoughts but the worst of it is I know that I deserve it. It doesn't surprise me that I failed to inspire any loyalty anywhere with anyone. Because it has been my mantle: no trust, no honesty, no fucking possibility. I'm being treated badly because I treat people badly.

My mother and Issie stare at me cautiously, waiting to see the result of mixing the mortal cocktail of resentment and humiliation. They are expecting me to swear that I'll never ever trust anyone again. Cautious before, impenetrable now. It wouldn't surprise them if I insisted on leaving the country, where my impenetrable aloofness would be further enhanced by the fact that I'd be struggling with a phrase book. They are waiting for the fury and the vows that I will never, ever confide, trust, respect or love again.

Instead I say, "I'd better call Darren."

CHAPTER
Nineteen

"J OSH."

Silence.

"Josh, it's me, Cas." I guess that this is more information than necessary, in the light of our history.

"Well, hello, little lady." He sounds suspiciously joyous, which I know can't be the case.

"Josh, are you drunk?"

"Yes, and you'll still be beautiful in the morning." He sounds wounded, regretful and disgraced.

"Oh Josh, I'm so sorry." The inadequate words fall down the telephone line.

"Which bit are you sorry about, Cas? The twenty-six-year friendship? Agreeing to marry me? Committing infidelity in front of 12.4 million viewers, or the color of the bridesmaids' dresses?"

I smile. I love him for being kind enough to joke with me, even though I am pretty sure I can hear his heart splintering at the other end of the phone.

Twelve point four million. A record for the program and TV6. It's now unlikely that *Sex with an Ex* will be ousted into another time slot to accommodate blockbuster films. Fi's done her job. The irony is that I helped her to bring about my fall. If I hadn't been so determined to boost my own public image, by insisting on appearing in every tabloid, magazine and chat show, my marriage would never have been so interesting to the general masses. If I hadn't created resentment in the journalists by manipulating them, maybe, just maybe, they wouldn't be so keen to put the Russell & Bromley in now.

The press have jumped on the exposure story, inciting yet greater interest as each day passes. A number of the chat shows have run opinion pieces, asking their viewers to ring in and vote for who I should marry, Josh or Darren. The qualities also ran the story, turning it into a modern-day morality tale. And indeed all my ghosts have visited me: past, present and future. Josh is far too cute for anyone to want to consider his part in this, so the blame has been well and truly, and entirely, left at my door. The moral condemnation overlooks the fact that 12.4 million silently vindicated my infidelity by being entertained by it.

I understand.

The more vehement the condemnation of me is, the more entire their absolution. Clean hands. I don't blame them. I haven't exactly advocated collective responsibility in the past. Besides which, it *is* my fault—even I know that.

The florist who had been booked to provide flowers for the wedding is suing me. He claims that as *Sex with an Ex* filmed a substitute florist, he was denied the publicity, which was rightly his. I don't think this will stand up in court, but a number of other suppliers have jumped on the bandwagon: the caterers, the cartoonist and the manager of the reception venue are demanding that they be paid in full. Even the vicar is looking for a public apology and, more secularly, compensation for the bellringers. But then I guess the fact that the number of weddings has declined by 35 percent since the first episode of *Sex with an Ex* is reason enough for the church to feel aggrieved.

Past guests of *Sex with an Ex* have emerged in droves. Reselling their stories with a new spin, i.e. how I incited the infidelities (which is not true—there are enough careless people in the world without me having to do that). Other guests say the channel gave them money to commit infidelity (untrue); others say that I offered sex for them to cooperate (lie). Nothing is so bad that it cannot be said of me.

Every one of my exes who could come forward, without jeopardizing his own relationship, has done so. Exactly how I give fellatio is now a matter of common knowledge. As is where I get my hair cut, how many fillings I have, how much I paid for my apartment, my bra size. I have been laid open, unmasked.

"I take it the wedding's off, is it, Cas?" Josh asks.

I think I hear hope in his voice. Which is worse than all the above. I know his heart rate and breathing have quickened. I know his mouth is parched and his stomach somersaulting.

"Cas, I'm sorry about the show. I should never have agreed to do it. I didn't know they were going to stitch you up that badly. I didn't approach the studio, they approached me. They didn't stick to the rehearsed questions. I didn't—"

"I know," I sigh, cutting him off. He needn't explain. I'd assumed the best of him, blaming him for little more than naïvety. It is a pity that Josh didn't have enough confidence and trust in our relationship, and therefore put us both through this. But he was right not to trust me, so the pity and shame is mine. "It's not your fault, Josh. I'm sorry they used you—"

"Can't we just put it behind us?" Hopeful.

"No. We both know I can't marry you." Firm. "I am sorry they used you to get at me but I'm more sorry that I used you." I take a deep breath. "I love you, Josh, but I'm not in love with you. I agreed to marry you for the wrong reasons." For the first time I understand what the expression "cruel to be kind" really means; I'm not using it as an excuse to dump someone who's outgrown his use, become tedious or I've simply stopped fancying. Dare I add the next bit? "And I don't think you are really *in love* with me." I hear him take a sharp intake of breath. It sounds as though I've punctured his lung. I've certainly punctured his dreams.

"What the fuck do you know, Cas?" he snaps drunkenly.

"Not much," I admit. I pause. There isn't a gentle way. "But a bit more than when I agreed to marry you. I am so very sorry, Josh."

"But it's so humiliating. The invites have gone out." He's pleading with me, nearly begging, but instead of the cold delight that I used to derive from impassioned accounts of unrequited love, I hurt for him.

"Please, Josh, don't say any more." If I wasn't so swollen with sadness I'd be amused that he hopes that anyone who's received an invitation will still consider it valid. All Britain knows I'm not going to be wafting down the aisle in a cloud of silk and lace this Saturday.

"You don't believe that thing about the One, so aren't I as good as the next one? Better than none?"

"Josh, you're wonderful. You'll make someone a fabulous husband," I say truthfully.

"But not you." There's no need for me to comment. "And are you planning to keep the champagne on ice for your wedding to Darren?" he asks sarcastically. "Your adulterous friend." I try to be patient and remember he is within his constitutional right to be bitter and livid. I don't say that sleeping with Darren wasn't infidelity. Sleeping with Josh was.

"You know we can't ever see each other again?" he threatens.

This is complex. A fat tear splashes on to my telephone directory. Crying is now significantly more natural than breathing.

"If that's what you want," I say, knowing this is not what I want but I have to respect his wishes now.

"You realize what I'm saying. There will be no one to fix your washing machine, or check the oil and water in your car. No one to send out for pizza in the middle of the afternoon because you and Issie are too engrossed in your movie to move your arses." He's trying to sound angry, but I can still hear the tears in his voice.

"I'll miss you. I love you. I'm sorry," I squeak and I put the phone down.

I know I can get in a plumber, take the car to the garage and order my own pizza. I can do it alone, but I'll miss him. I'll miss his stupid jokes and his stories about court. I'll miss his hugs and his cooking. I'll miss our shared history. I'll miss his friendship.

Darren.

His face cuts in to my consciousness, explodes and sends tiny particles of emotion hurtling into my heart, knocking me sideways. It doesn't feel secure, it feels risky, but it feels safe too. I don't feel certain, but I am sure. It's right and it is fractious. I can't marry one man knowing I am in love with another.

The odd thing is, I've lost Darren.

Quite literally.

I have spent the last four days trying to track Darren down but he's vanished. His mobile is switched off. And when I went to his house his flatmate told me he hadn't seen him since the night before the TV6 party. I went to his laboratory and office to ask for him. No one had seen him for a few days. It was suggested that he might have been consigned to an away job. But if anyone knew where that might be, they weren't going to tell me—public enemy number one—no matter how much I cajoled, threatened or pleaded. Issie sees his disappearance as an admission of his involvement in the set-up; Mum's reserving judgment but as the days have slipped by, and there's been no contact, her face has become increasingly fraught.

I know he wasn't in with Bale and Fi. I don't know why he's disappeared but I know he didn't betray me.

So, after all my years of skepticism, mistrust, selfish hedonism, I find I have landed here, exactly where I was scrupulously avoiding.

In love.

But alone.

I guess that's evidence that there is a God, or at least my fifty-three cast-off lovers would think so.

I return to the office on Thursday. It's a difficult journey into work as journalists are constantly trailing me. One of them is more tenacious (or junior) than all the others and has been camped outside my door since Saturday. He's obviously unsuited to sleeping rough and now looks as bad as I feel. Seeing his chilled and crumpled state this morning, I take pity on him and pass a few pleasantries and offer him a cup of tea. He looks at me suspiciously but is too cold to turn down the tea. It may be July but it's a British July.

"You shouldn't believe everything you read, you know. I'm not Cruella De Vil." He takes the tea. "Are you planning on trailing me all day?" He nods. "Well, I'm driving to work. I might as well give you a lift." He doesn't know whether to accept my offer. Naturally he's trying to discern what my ulterior motive could be. There isn't one. I'm too worn out to formulate a come-back strategy. I'm not even sure that I want to.

I arrive at the office by 8:15 A.M., and although I haven't managed to go to the gym I enter with my kit bag over my shoulder to give the impression that not only is it business as normal, but I am healthy and sane. I'm wearing a charcoal-gray Armani suit—emotional armor—and dark glasses to hide the bags under my eyes, induced from lack of sleep and endless crying. But then I do work in media and as long as the glasses are designer no one thinks twice about my wearing them inside.

I walk through the glass, open-plan offices, cursing (not for the first time) the architect. Had he considered my public humiliation when he put together his design? I nod to a few faces and ignore the sniggering and whispering. I walk the marathon to my desk, sit down and put on my PC. I ring Jaki's extension number.

"Jaki, can you bring me a double espresso, please," I ask, as I do every morning.

"You're back!" She doesn't trouble to hide her disbelief.

"I am. I had summer flu. But I'm back now."

"Er, glad to hear you're better," she stutters.

"Thank you, Jaki. Can you bring me my diary? Oh, and can you make room in it so that I can see Bale today."

"Well, actually your diary is clear."

I get it, but pretend not to.

" Fine, then I'll have time for some invoicing and it shouldn't be difficult for you to get me an appointment with Bale." I hang up.

Bale agrees to see me at 11:00 A.M. In the meantime the entire staff studiously avoid me. My leper-like state is due to the widely held belief that luck is catching—both good and bad. When I was fast-tracking my way through promotions I'd been an extremely popular girl. Trixxie is the only exception. She does pop by my desk to say hi. But then I suspect that in her drug-induced state she has no idea what happened on last week's show.

I choose to wait until five past eleven before I walk into Bale's office. Fi is sitting there already.

"Bale, you've put on weight," I smile. Pleasantries over, I close his office door. He reminds me of a walrus, his pink fleshiness indefinitely merging nose into lip, lip into chin, chin into neck into chest and suddenly we arrive at his feet. I try to think of his good points. I can't. He doesn't even close his mouth when he chews his food. I turn to Fi. She, on the other hand, looks magnificent. Triumphant, glowing. I think of Lady Macbeth. She's wearing an Alberta Ferretti suit, which, as I've never seen it before, I can only assume was bought from her ratings-achieved bonus.

"Nice suit, Fi," I comment. "I didn't realize that they took blood money at Harvey Nics. Thought it was just charge cards."

"Oh, come off it, Cas. You know the game." She looks sensational and I know for certain that my team will now be worshipping at the temple of Fiona. They can't see through her. Because they are dazzled. She's dazzling.

"Have a seat, Cas," offers Bale. I note it's the low one. They'll tower inches above me if I sit in it.

"I prefer to stand."

"Oh, not stopping?" asks Bale. They start to snigger.

"Did you catch the show on Saturday?" asks Fi. Which sends them into raptures.

"Have you seen the runs? Aren't you going to congratulate us on the ratings? You always said a show with Darren Smith would break all records," pursues Bale.

"Ratings? Ratings? Is that all you think about?" I snap. Despite my vows to remain cool and calm throughout.

"Yes, Cas." He thumps the desk and suddenly turns serious. "Ratings are all *I* think about. And up until recently, when you fell in lurve, that's all *you* thought about."

Slapped face. Even this repulsive cliché knew more about me than I did. I don't think there's any point in my trying to explain that the cost of ratings rocketing is hearts plummeting.

"You let us down, Cas. Running up north after that hippie gypsy. Coming back with loads of mumbo-jumbo ideas on emotionally profitable programs. You're a disappointment."

"Just because Darren isn't a materialistic, hedonistic Fascist that does not make him a hippie gypsy," I yell back. I think about it for a moment and then add, "And anyway what's wrong with hippie gypsies?"

Bale and Fi roar with laughter. Her boobs and his belly bounce up and down as their laughter ricochets around their bodies. I stay still.

"I expect this type of thing from you, Bale, but you, Fi—you've surprised me. How could you do this to me?" Fi stares back, insolent and unashamed. "You knew that Josh and Darren would both be hurt and that I'd become public property."

"Yeah, I heard that Dazza did a runner," sneers Bale, "Bad luck, Cas."

"Still, look on the bright side," comments Fi. "There's been so much publicity about your abilities in the sack that, besides Darren, absolutely every man in the country wants to shag you."

"And the bright side is?"

"Oh, come on, Cas. You've never been one to turn down a shag."

"No," I sigh and rub my forehead. "Not in the past." I'm sick of the small talk. "Well, as jolly as it is passing pleasantries with the pair of you, I think it's time I got to the point. I'm resigning."

"Accepted. I was going to fire you, for your recurring absences without doctor's certificates, but then we'd have to negotiate severance pay. It's so much cleaner this way. Although not as financially advantagous to you," he taunts.

I don't care about the money. I turn to Fi.

"I've got to hand it to you, Fi. I thought you were going to have to fuck Bale to gain his favor. Instead all you had to do is fuck me. Good choice—I'm far prettier."

I let the door slam behind me.

I walk out of the office, past my desk. I don't even bother to empty my cupboards. I walk to the lift, through the reception and keep walking out of the door.

And I surprise myself, because as the door swings behind me, I feel better than I've felt for a long time.

So I get my hair cut. All off.

"My God, your hair!" squeals my mother when I pop around to see her and Bob on Thursday night.

"Don't worry, it's not an act of self loathing or penitence. I just wanted . . . I don't know . . . a change."

My mother looks as though she's about to cry and so I'm grateful when Bob says, "It's very fetching, Cas." Bob's OK, quite a decent bloke, once you look past the brown cords.

"Thanks." I force a smile across the fish fingers and beans. I see him gently nudge my mother.

"Well, I expect it's a good idea to herald a new beginning," she stutters heroically. "You might shake the press for a day or two."

My head's much lighter—I estimate that my hair weighed pounds—but my heart is still heavy. After supper I turn down the offer to stay the night and hurry to catch the tube.

I spend the next day on the telephone. I recall Darren's mobile, flat, lab and office. No joy. I make a list of National Parks and call each one of them to see if he's working with any. He's not. I then start on London's parks and when I still don't unearth him I try twenty or thirty others up and down the country. There are plenty of sick trees but Darren's not ministering to any of them. I walk the streets hoping to spot him. It's futile. I then gather my courage and call the Smiths in Whitby.

His father answers the phone.

"Hello, Mr. Smith. You probably don't remember me." I had the impression that my stay at the Smith household passed Mr. Smith by. I was merely an interlude between *Countdown* and the chat shows. "It's Cas Perry. I'm a friend of Darren's. A sort of friend." Somewhere between archenemy and fiancée.

"Hello, pet, of course I remember you. When you came on the telly, I said, 'Wasn't she the one who was up here, chasing our Darren?' And Mother said I was right."

I'm a bit stuck for what to say next. The fact that Mr. Smith referred to my "chasing" Darren is bad enough but my worst fear is confirmed: Darren's family saw the show.

"I've seen your picture in the paper, too."

Marvelous.

"Well, I was just ringing—it's a bit awkward really. You see, I need to talk to Darren and I can't find him."

"Aye."

"Well, erm, I was wondering if you'd know where he is."

"Aye."

"And whether you'd tell me." I cross my fingers. In fact, they've been crossed for days now, which makes it very difficult to hold a cup of hot coffee and almost impossible to tie my trainers.

"Well that's something else. I'm not sure I can do that. I'll have to ask Mother. *Mother*," he bellows.

I have a vision of Mrs. Smith running along the corridor in a waft of baking smells and fury. I am terrified and want to put the phone down. But if I do I'll never find Darren. Mr. Smith has put his hand over the handset but even so I can still distinguish distinctive wrathful mutterings: "No better than she ought to be, the cheek of her, I'll give her what for." I am paralyzed with fear and now can't put the phone down, even if I wanted to.

"Yes?" she barks. "Who is this?"

"It's Cas Perry." Meek.

"Who?" Insincere.

"Cas Perry, Darren's friend." Tentative.

"Hardly!" Outraged.

"Mrs. Smith, I can imagine how angry you are—"

"Oh, you can, can you?" She sniffs. "I doubt it."

"But I really do need to talk to Darren," I persist.

Silence. I can hear the cogs of her mind whirl around.

"I won't help you."

The phone goes dead and I'm left with the cold, continuous tone that tells me no one wants to speak to me.

I wonder if he is there? Perhaps he was in the yard kicking a ball around with Richard. Oblivious to the telephone wires that I am trying to crawl through to reach him. Or perhaps he did know I was on the phone and just didn't care.

Saturday is red hot. The sun is pouring in though my windows. Insensitively cheerful. I consider that this is the fine weather I hoped I'd wake up to on my wedding day; now the sun's mocking me. I pull down the blinds. I look around my flat and try to think of something to do to while away the next fifty-odd years. Throughout the last few days I have tidied, ordered, arranged and rearranged every aspect of my life. My cereal packets are arranged in descending size order, my knickers are arranged in color and date purchased order, my cosmetic bottles are separated into sections—face, body and hands, and then subdivided by brand, and my CDs are alphabetically categorized. Everywhere I look is tidy, neat and trim. It's ironic that I know exactly where to locate the list of who I sent Christmas cards to in 1995, but I've no clue as to where to find my fiancé.

Besides the physical tidying up, I've had time to do a bit of mental cleaning out, too. I've written a list of the things that have gone wrong. Or more specifically, and much more humbling, the things I've done wrong. I approached my list methodically, subdividing my crimes into categories: "Darren," "Mum," "friends," "work," "lovers," and an all-encompassing "general." The same themes recur in each section. I've selfishly pursued my own peace of mind, ruthlessly trampling on the feelings of others. Worse, I've justified my behavior by sulkily holding a grudge against my parents for having the audacity to make their own decisions and live their own lives. I think of Fi's question, asked in some grotty pub after we'd both become careless with alcohol. "Couldn't you have just, I don't know, muddled along like the rest of us?" Yes, in retrospect I suppose I could have. Should have. After all, I was given enough chances. Why didn't I see that my mother was teaching me about love, not restraint? She loved me so much that she put me before anyone else for years. Why did I have to resent that and see it as a pressure? I had amazing friends, and how did I repay them? By bossing one and using, then humiliating, the other. Issie's and my friendship is held together by a very slight thread right now. I know that the only way I can possibly hope to keep her as a friend is to learn to deal honestly and fairly. Josh, my dearest friend, is lost forever. I can't see how either of us can ever recover from this. Too much hurt pride on his side. Too much shame on mine. I used my power at work childishly, thoughtlessly. I was so heady on the success of ever-increasing ratings and advertising billings that I was blinkered to the destruction the program was wreaking. I now force myself to consider every aspect: from the woman weeping in my reception on Christmas Eve to the silk farm that had to close down after their exports decreased so significantly. I wonder how many lives I altered the course of with *Sex with an Ex?* Was it fair to involve myself, and the general public, in people's loving and living? Would those people have muddled up the aisle if it hadn't been for my intervention? And if they had, would it necessarily have ended in disaster, as I'd always maintained? Perhaps it was unfair putting such emotional pressure on individuals just before their weddings. Perhaps it hadn't been a flat playing field. I realize now that *Sex with an Ex* was not much more than an elaborate way to try to prove that my father was the rule rather than the exception.

I had boasted about dealing in desolation, but I hadn't a clue what desolation was.

I feel sick. I stand up and walk into the kitchen, trying to put some distance between me and the ugly list.

I pour myself some Evian and hold the cold glass to my forehead. It soothes the aching momentarily, but I'm aware that my actions are similar to those of an air hostess asking "Chicken or beef" seconds before the plane crashes.

I pick up the pen. My ex-lovers. I'm resolute that the majority knew where they stood with me. Hearts and flowers were not part of our dialogues. These men were mostly the ones with wives or girlfriends. The ones who wanted a quick-no-questions-asked bonk, and I supplied it. But had the wives and girlfriends been in on the deal? Unlikely. Now, I wonder how many times I caused a heart to sink as those women found my telephone number scribbled on a scrap of paper. And what if some of the men, especially the single ones, were surprised that I never called back, and a little hurt, perhaps insecure? Is it possible that Issie is right and men have feelings too? I think of Darren, I think of Josh. Of course it's possible that they have feelings.

My neat list has become a random mind map, with arrows and circles like Venn diagrams connecting one action to another. Looking at the amount of ink I've spilt this morning, it's not surprising that Darren has walked away from me. I don't deserve him.

I am so sorry. And this isn't simply because the press are trailing me, the show exposed me, the country and most specifically Darren hate me. I'm sorry because I got it wrong.

I don't deserve Darren, but he does deserve an explanation. I have to find him.

The phone rings and I fall on it.

"It'smeIssie," says Issie quickly, establishing that it's her rather than Darren. She knows I really only want to hear from him. "I didn't know whether to ring."

"I'm glad you did." I am. I am indescribably grateful that Issie was only able to sustain her state of acute pissed-off-with-me-ness for about two hours and has allowed her fury at me to fade somewhat. I guess that's the only good thing that came out of the show. Issie couldn't possibly turn her back on me in my hour of need; the fact that the rest of Britain loathes and despises me serves to increase Issie's commitment to our friendship.

"Has he called?"

"No."

"You still think he's going to?

"Yes."

"Why?"

I realize that I'm in serious trouble. If Issie, the last of the great romantics, has no faith in this ending in a tulle and organza number then I must have more chance of winning the lottery, on a roll over week, than ever getting an opportunity to talk to Darren.

"I've told you Issie, I trust him. He proposed to me. Darren wouldn't do that just for TV."

"And I've told you, he might do it for revenge. After all, you did sleep with him for two weeks, all the time giving the impression that you were pretty committed, then you vamoosed. There's not a man on earth who would take kindly to that type of behavior. His pride was kicked into touch. Don't you think that it's possible he's getting his own back?"

"I know he had nothing to do with the program, Issie." I'm trying not to become irate with her, but my personality transplant hasn't been so entire that I can stay patient in the face of a constant barrage of criticism of Darren. "Look, Issie, why don't you ask Josh if he thinks Darren was involved in stitching me up. *He* must know." I place a heavy emphasis on "he"; if I can distract Issie with Josh's crimes for a while, maybe she'll get off Darren's case.

"Would you like me to do that for you?" she asks enthusiastically.

"Do it for you, Issie, so that you believe in Darren. I don't need anyone else's word."

We sink in to a huffy silence. I know I can outsulk Issie. I haven't even counted to three before she offers her olive branch.

"OK, supposing you are right and Darren wasn't knowingly involved in your unrestricted and unmitigated humiliation, why do you think he's done a disappearing act?"

"It's obvious, Issie. He thinks *I* set *him* up."

"Oh."

Issie is far too straightforward to pretend not to see why he'd make this assumption. She doesn't even blame him.

"I should have told him about the engagement!" I berate myself.

"So what are you going to do from here?"

"Good question. I need to talk to him but I've looked every-where. Work, home, pubs. I've even walked the streets but it's futile. London's a big city; England's a big country."

"Well, actually, it's quite small in geographical terms—"

"It's colossal when you are hunting someone who doesn't want to be found."

"And of course he may not be in England, he may be abroad. He could be anywhere."

I wonder if the position of Job's comforter is currently available in some other time dimension, because Issie has all the qualifica-tions.

I sigh. She's right. I suddenly feel so small and the world so big.

"Issie, there's call waiting bleeping. Do you mind if I ring off?" We both know I'm hoping it will be Darren. We both know it won't be.

"Fine. I'll call you tonight," says Issie.

"Hello," says a tiny voice on the line. I try not to drown in the disappointment that it is a female voice as I struggle to place it.

"Linda?"

"Yes. Hello, Cas." Linda sounds nervous and young. Even younger than her seventeen years.

"Linda, I'm so happy to hear from you."

"Oh. Are you? I don't know if I should be talking to you."

"Yes. Yes, you should," I urge. "Linda, I know things must look terrible from your point of view. I have done some very bad things, but you have to know I didn't set Darren up on that program." I'm speaking very quickly because I guess I have only a finite amount of time to convince her. She sounds on the edge of putting the phone down.

"I know," says the tiny voice.

"You do?" I'm so relieved I can't say any more. To have some-one believe in me is an overwhelming relief.

"I said to Mam that you loved our Darren. But Mam said I

only believed that because I'm seventeen. No one else believes that you do."

"But *you* are right, Linda. You *are* right. I do love Darren," I repeat hysterically. It matters to me that she believes me.

"Mam said I mustn't call you."

"I see."

"It's just that Darren called last night and he mentioned that he might go to the Natural History Museum today and I thought you might—"

"Linda, Linda, I could kiss you," I yell down the phone. Of course, his favorite building. That's where he goes to do his thinking. Suddenly my mind is splattered with a vision of Darren's childhood bedroom. Aladdin's cave meets Treasure Island meets Batman's cave. With the zillions of books, the cardboard models, the Meccano eco-system and the painted Milky Way. "Thank you, Linda. Thank you so much. I promise you you've done the right thing. I love you Linda!" I drop the telephone, grab my keys and fly out of the flat.

CHAPTER

Twenty

IRUN TO THE TUBE, my feet thudding on the pavement, my blood thundering to my heart, my heart pounding. I run all the way to Tower Hill station. I pass the happy crowds drinking pints in the street; they leer and jeer at me as I'm sweaty and not wearing a sports bra. I keep running. Although I usually run eight miles in the gym every day, I haven't been since "the show." Not that I've been afraid of the inevitable pointing fingers (they like notoriety better than celebrity at our gym—the receptionist nearly orgasms every time she spots Jeffrey Archer using the treadmill); it's just I've had no motivation. Every moment has been consumed with finding Darren. So now I'm panting heavily. Then again, the shortness of breath isn't just to do with the rapidly decreasing levels of fitness. It's also excitement. Hope. Possibility. A long shot. But a shot.

At the tube station I realize that I left the house in such a hurry that I didn't pick up my purse. When did I become so disorganized?

"Please can you let me have a ticket?" I smile sweetly; it really is my most dazzling.

"Where to?"

"To South Kensington."

"£1.80."

"I have no money." The smile is frozen and stuck to my face. The ticket officer snorts. "We're not operating a charity."

"Pleeeease. It's an emergency. I have to get to South Ken." I have abandoned my tone of pleasant authority and I'm begging. He's impervious.

"Mind along. There are other customers. Ones with money."

I stay still.

"Pleeeeease." I think I might cry. Tears that I've managed to hold back for years are now constantly threatening and erupting. The officer doesn't even look at me.

"No money, no ticket. Bugger off."

That's the proverbial straw. Huge, ugly overwhelming sobs storm out of me. I'm not sure where they come from—certainly not just my mouth, but my nose too and perhaps my ears.

"I've got to get there. He's there. He's there," I sob, which is ridiculous on many counts. For a start, the Underground officer doesn't know who I am or "he" is, and anyway, he cares less. Secondly, I don't *know* if I'll find Darren there. There's snot on my arm and days-old mascara on my cheeks. I'm blind with tears, boogies, regret, frustration, pain and loss. I slump to the floor. It's too much. I can't act any more. Years of acting as though I don't care, then I care, and now I've hurtled past caring, straight, slap bang into despair. It's too much. Life without Darren is not enough.

"I'll pay her fare." I hear the lazy, warm drawl of an American accent. "She sounds kinda desperate." I daren't believe someone is being kind to me. The recent, constant volley of abuse has left me bereft of hope. I can only assume this guy has just arrived in England or that he doesn't read any newspapers. My Good Samaritan kneels down next to me and the crushed cans and cigarette stubs. This isn't easy for him, because he's obviously a man who enjoys a good breakfast, and lunch and dinner too by the look of it.

"Hey, ain't you that girl on the TV?" he whispers as he hands me the ticket.

"It wasn't how it looked," I defend through my tears.

"Nothing ever is." He staggers to his feet and offers me his hand. I let him pull me up.

"You're not a journalist, are you?" I ask nervously. He shakes his head and then melts back into the throng of people busy sight-seeing.

I consider it. I look up and see a security camera. It is just possible that this is another set-up. That guy could be a plant.

Get a grip. Only Linda knows I'm coming here. She would never be part of a set-up.

But I could have been followed. I'm still breathing shallowly and quickly. The guy looked honest. Unlikely though it seems, I think he was just doing a good thing. I don't waste any more time thinking about it. I push my ticket through the machine and dash to the platform.

The sand and gray building creates a swell in my heart and I allow myself to hope, because, maybe, just maybe, he's in there, the Natural History Museum. I realize I have the money problem to face again. At the desk I lie and say I've had my bag stolen. The staff are far too polite to laugh outright at my claims.

"Have you reported the theft, miss?" asks the huge, South London bird.

"No," I admit. "I am planning to."

"What, after you've visited the *Tyrannosaurus rex?*"

"Yes."

"Naturally."

I'm very short on patience, a life trait exasperated by recent events, but somehow I hold it together long enough to persuade the staff at the museum to let me ring Issie. She gives them a credit card number and they give me a ticket.

I burst through the turnstiles and then run directly to the galleries. I charge up and down the three flights of stairs, constantly looking to my left and right. I can't see him. I rush through the huge corridors, popping my head into all the exhibitions and restaurants as I pass by. I see innumerable creepy crawlies with their wings fettered; I see fossils, stuffed eagles and tigers. A taxidermist's dream. But no Darren. I check the exhibitions on crystals, mammals and dinosaurs. I see every animal, vegetable and mineral in every state of growth, maturity and decay, except for Darren. I do this all twice. After an hour and a half of frenetic and futile searching I find myself back in the main lobby. Other than attracting numerous odd looks and lots of unwanted attention, my wild goose chase hasn't achieved anything.

Of course it hasn't.

I sit under skeletons of dinosaurs, surrounded by Gothic arches and earnest foreign voices reading to each other from the guidebooks. It's pretty spooky. I've searched the entire building; he's not here. It was ridiculously far-fetched to hope he would be. Why didn't I ask Linda some more searching questions? Like what time had he planned to visit? Was it a definite plan? I'd been so delighted to get even a sniff of a lead that I hadn't followed it properly. I can't call Linda back. She'll get into trouble if her mother knows she's been in touch with me. I feel dumb and hopeless. The gargoyles obviously knew this all along because they look as though they are laughing at me.

I need to get some perspective.

I go to the cloakrooms. As usual there is a massive queue of women with bladders the size of peanuts. I stand listlessly, too exhausted to fidget impatiently or terrify anyone into peeing more rapidly. I catch sight of myself in a mirror and I'm shocked. I look like a down and out. My new crop requires minimum attention, a quick comb through, some gloss and then a ruffle to erase the effects of the combing. However, I haven't thought to carry out this simple operation, so my hair is tangled and snarled at the back of my head. Nor have I thought to change my clothes, apply any

makeup or eat since the show. Normally slim, I know I look ema-
ciated. Up until now, I've been with Wallis Simpson, but now I
see—a woman can be too thin. I've smoked to abate hunger, to
distract and comfort myself. The smell of stale fags lingers in my
hair and clothes. My skin is gray and my eyes have sunk to the
back of my head. I am a human ashtray. I splash cold water on my
face and then decide to revisit the dinosaur collection; at least they
look rougher than I do.

For three hours I slowly amble around the galleries and while I
admit that fishes, amphibians and reptiles are interesting in their
own way, they can't compete with Darren for mind share. Whilst I
learn that dinosaurs lived between 230 million and 65 million
years ago, I can't imagine it. I've been without Darren for a week
and it seems like an eternity. I also learn that they lived on land
and could not fly but walked on straight legs tucked beneath their
body. I consider writing to the consistency editor in charge of film
at the studio, because I'm sure I've seen blockbusters with flying
dinosaurs, but I don't have the energy. I visit the human biology
gallery and watch a film on reproduction and the growth of babies,
which makes me feel squeamish. Not just because of the blood but
because it's proof, if I needed it, that love and life—and living that
life—are special and miraculous. I sigh and check my watch. Four
thirty. I'm hungry. I decide to visit the Life Galleries one more
time and then, reluctantly, I'll call it a day. Go home, have some
pasta.

The Life Galleries are really spectacular. A series of exhibits
demonstrating that each individual animal, plant and person is
just one component in a complex system. There are some cool
special-effects holograms of the atmosphere, hydrosphere and
lithosphere. There's a reproduction of a bit of the rainforest, with
sound effects of pouring rain and screeching birds. There's a bit
about oceans and coastlines. The sound effects change to crashing
waves and seagulls.

Whitby.

Him.

It could be my imagination but I think I can smell the sea.

Less romantically there is a stuffed rattlesnake and a decomposing rabbit.

I walk through howling gales and head toward the funky bell music, which puts me in mind of the stuff that's played in Camden market or in flotation tanks. I head along a dark corridor toward a series of mirrors that are arranged to reflect and refract light to create the impression that you are standing outside the earth and you are watching the hydrosphere. Water recycles endlessly, in all its many guises, water, steam, ice. I don't quite understand it. But the scale and silver holograms are awesome.

Darren.

Suddenly there are hundreds of him. I can see Darren. He's right next to me. He's left, next to me. I reach to touch him but my hand plummets through space. I *can* see him. He's in front of me, and he's behind me too. I look up, he's above me. Then he's gone.

My breath surges out of my body, creating a vacuum. I can't breathe. It gushes back in again, nearly knocking me over.

He was here. It was him. I try to work out where he must have been standing, and which were mere shadows and visions of him created by the mirrors. I can't calculate it. But he can only have gone one of two ways: back through the rainforest to the Waterhouse Way corridor or forward toward the Visions of Earth exhibitions.

Creepy crawlies or lost in space?

I pelt toward the Visions of Earth exhibitions. A series of six statues, representing different aspects of life on earth, are dominated by a dramatic sculpture of earth, which revolves between two giant walls. The walls depict the solar system and the night sky. I collide with a party of overseas schoolkids, universally noisy, happy and overexcited. They're all dressed in blue and merge into one homogenous mass of rucksacks, acne and pony tails.

He's in front of the party.

He's ascending the giant escalator that takes you up through the solar system.

I have no time to consider English tradition. I shove and barge and push my way through the queues of schoolchildren. They object noisily.

"There's a queue, you know, madam."

They try and elbow me back, but their attempts are pathetic in the face of my love and panic-induced strength.

"Excuse me. You are going the wrong way."

But I'm not. I'm finally going in the right direction. I fasten my eyes on Darren's head and don't drop the link. He isn't aware of me and I don't call out. The schoolchildren dividing us may prove to be too much of an obstacle if he decides to run. The escalator rises through sheets of beaten copper, which represent the core of the earth, and we are accompanied by Indie music, which represents the poor taste of the curator. I pass the stars Ursa Major, Draco and Ophiuchus at an achingly slow speed. I want to stamp my feet and although I've squeezed past a number of other gallery visitors, by intimidating them with my sense of urgency, I'm stumped now I've reached a woman with a double buggy. Short of climbing over her, I'm stuck.

At the top of the escalators I turn right and follow Darren though volcano eruptions and earthquakes.

"Darren," I scream. "Darren!"

But my voice, usually powerful, doesn't cut through the natural disasters or the fourth-form chatter.

"Darren."

He turns.

For a moment he doesn't recognize me because of the haircut and the unfashionable grunge look.

"Cas?" As the word edges from his brain to his vocal chords I see his face flicker in surprise, disbelief, pleasure and then settle in irritation.

"This is a coincidence." Darren puts his rucksack on the floor and folds his arms across his chest. My brain computes that he's saying don't come near. My stomach is oblivious; it becomes gymnastic as I see the muscles in his arms flex.

"Not really. I've been looking for you." I don't mention Linda's tip-off. I don't want to get her into trouble. "I've been here for hours," I stutter. He looks surprised. I push uphill. "I tried everywhere I could think of in the last week." I scratch my nose and pause. I'm looking for a credible place to start our conversation. He looks around too. I wonder what he's looking for.

"So where are the cameras?"

Ah, I see.

"There are no cameras—well, none that I know of," I add nervously. He makes a sound, a mix between a snort of contempt and disbelief, which forces me to assert, "I had nothing to do with the show."

"Really?" It's just one word but I don't think a half-hour soliloquy could have communicated his disgust and sarcasm quite so clearly.

"I know it looks bad—"

"Bad," he yells, attracting a number of curious stares from the wild children. "Bad isn't how I'd describe it. I'd describe it as vile, corrupt, damning. You've made an arse of me, Cas, you've—" He's shouting and stuttering. "You've fucking hurt me. I can't believe you, *even you,* would sink so low. You slept with me for TV entertainment. You accepted my proposal for TV entertainment. What sort of animal are you? I can't believe it!" He's spraying angry spittle and his face is contorted with pain.

He's magnificent.

"Well, don't believe it, because it's not true. I didn't know that

we were being filmed." I try to grab hold of his arm. He violently
jerks away from me as though I'm unsanitary.

"You were engaged to Josh!" he fumes.

"Yes," I confirm simply, dropping my arms to my side again.

"You were engaged and you didn't think to mention it?"

He's still shouting and we are now collecting a small crowd of
onlookers. I don't think he's noticed. The teacher tries, but fails, to
move the children along. She's right—this may be a PG certificates' viewing, bad language and violence threaten.

"Well, yes, I thought of it. But—"

"And you accepted my proposal?"

"Yes. But I didn't lie to you. I was going to tell you—" It
sounds faulty, even to me.

"When? Before or after you married Josh?"

He's really furious. He is spitting, not blood, but pain and tension. His face is splintered into trillions of anxious particles and I
can't look at him and see the whole face. I can only see a hurt
mouth, angry nostril or a ferocious eyebrow. Desperate eyes.

"I wasn't going to marry Josh. Not after I'd met you again. I
didn't have anything to do with the show." I'm trying to sound reasonable and in control. It's a tough act. "I love you. Just you. I'm in
love with you and I have been since we were in Whitby."

It's a relief saying the big words.

"So why were you engaged to Josh?" Darren asks the floor this
question. For the moment the anger has subsided and lapsed into
a sadness. I like it even less. Deep breath. I know this is my last
chance. And chance is probably far too generous a description. I
choose each word carefully.

"I was scared I'd end up like my mother. Or at least how I
thought my mother was. Falling in love was too risky. I knew that
I'd be safe with Josh. He loved me more than I could ever love
him, so he'd never be able to hurt me."

"Didn't you think how unfair that was on him?"

"Not really," I sigh. There's no option, other than to be honest. But the truth is so unflattering. I can't imagine my looking more unsightly.

"Jesus, Cas, do you know what you've just said?" Darren suddenly looks up and his gaze punches me. "Josh is one of the few people I thought you truly loved. I had been heartened by your relationship with him because I thought it as indelible proof that you were capable of loving and the hard-bitch act was just that, an act. But you've just admitted you didn't even *think* about him. He was just another piece in your game."

"It was what he wanted."

"I doubt he wanted a wife who didn't love him."

"It wasn't like that. I don't think I knew how to love then." I try to wave the thought away.

"I heard you, Cas. I saw the program. You said sex with me, and I quote, was 'risky, dirty, cheeky and above all fun.' I didn't hear you tell the world you loved me. Why not?" He doesn't let me answer but gives in to his anger again. "Because you don't. You've made all this up because Josh has dumped you, and the studio has dumped you, and all Britain hates you. I'm nothing more to you than your only option."

"You're wrong."

"How many kick backs am I supposed to take, Cas? What's an acceptable number? First I'm 'too serious and homely.' Then you fuck my brains out. Then you disappear. Then you're back and then you fuck my heart out and this time we get engaged and then that turns out to be for the tittilation and edification of your audience. You ignored my calls, threatened to call the police."

Put like this it sounds bad.

"You act like a psycho. How do I know that this latest declaration isn't just another publicity stunt? How can I trust you?"

"I just know you have it in you, Darren. Some people have and you are one of them."

I concentrate on the slight cleft in his chin, and on the exact color of his eyes. I note the way he moves his hands and the precise shape of his wristbone. I consume it all because there is a real possibility that I'll never see any of it again. If he walks away I'll live in a permanent eclipse. I look at the group of schoolchildren, who are all but splitting with laughter and jeering. "Can we go somewhere more private to discuss this?" I hiss through clenched teeth.

"What's the bloody point, Cas? Our relationship is public property. Posh and Beckham have more privacy."

I get the feeling I'm being tested, but I'm unsure of the nature of the exam. I certainly haven't prepared. I navigate through with as much sincerity as I can. I am conscious that behind me there is a reconstruction of an earthquake. Every fifteen seconds the world shudders and cracks up. I wonder if Darren also thinks this is ironic.

"I was very scared, Darren. Loving you so much left me petrified. Ecology is your thing, isn't it? Piecing things together for the whole picture? Come on, Darren, think about it. Think about where I was coming from. I'd never seen any good come out of loving. My father didn't love either my mother or me enough to stay. He left her, us, brokenhearted. My mother did her best but it wasn't just the money that was limited after he disappeared. She reined in her affection, or at least her displays of it. She was awash with caution and distrust. I wasn't taught to love. I was taught to be wary."

"Wary, Cas, not wicked!"

I ignore his interruption. "I know it's not an excuse, only an explanation. Before I hit puberty, I was certain sex and love were incompatible. And then the endless stream of lovers seemed to confirm my theory. There was man after man who was prepared to betray me or use me to betray someone else. I didn't want to be a victim. I wouldn't allow myself to love. I didn't even think I was capable of it."

There's lead stuck in the pit of my stomach, but at least I have Darren's attention and that of every member of year four *l'école de* Sprogsville. Where is this going? How can I tell him that loving him seemed like the worst thing that could have happened to me, but at the same time the best? That I miscalculated lots of things when I was young. Now I see that to have a figure like Barbie's I'd have to have an eighteen-inch waist, a forty-inch leg and a head the size of a beach ball. Spaghetti hoops are not the world's most exquisite culinary delight and Donny Osmond isn't sexy.

Being made happy by love is an option.

I notice that the neck of my T-shirt is wet. I touch my face and discover that I am sobbing. Fat, globular tears are falling at such a rate that I'm soaked.

"I'm sorry it took me so long to get here but I've learned I am capable of loving. I did not set you up. I know how you feel about the program. And for what it's worth, I see now that you were right. You have to believe me, Darren." I wonder if there is any point in telling him that I've left TV6. I doubt it. He'll probably believe the papers and think I was sacked. My face is aflame. My heart literally aches, a filthy agony. I try to read his thoughts. I know he'll be trying to understand, but will he be able to? And even if he does, will he care? He leans back against a glass display case. The fact that he needs propping up can't be good for me.

Can it?

He rubs his eyes with the balls of his fists.

"Believe me," I plead.

He shakes his head. Very quietly, almost inaudibly, he whispers, "I don't think I can. I'm sorry." And he looks it. He looks devastated. Wounded. "I wish I could." He bends down and picks up his rucksack and starts to walk out of my life.

For a week I have vacillated between regret, fear and desperation. I've howled and cried privately. I've fought to appear collected and not too indulgent in public. I've been dogged and exposed. Discussed and dismissed at a micro and macro level. The experience has left me weak. The small amount of residual energy I had left was consumed while reasoning with Darren.

Wham.

Suddenly I'm whacked with an emotion that is straggling between passion and ire. Anger refuels my body and the resurgence explodes in torrents of undefined fury. Not the premenstrual monster that inhibits my body for three days every twenty-eight. Not the spitting anger that I used to feel when the ratings weren't robust or a production assistant had made some duff decision. Not the intense irritation I feel when Issie throws herself at some worthless oink. Or the scornful vexation that I've felt when Josh mistreated some bimb. My anger is much more . . . painful than that. The storm of irritation and hurt began to climb the Richter scale. Swelling up through my stomach, into my chest and heart, exploding—a veritable whirlwind—in my head.

"IS THAT IT THEN, DARREN?" I scream. "That was your crack at being in love?"

He turns back to face me. "Well, I think it was pretty crap actually!"

Being unreasonable is all I'm capable of again. I'm so bloody desperate. I don't know how to stop this inevitable, needless disaster.

"You've been loved and adored all your life. Swaddled. Protected. Encouraged to believe the best in people and here you are falling at the first serious hurdle. I thought you were better than that. You are better than that. Don't you dare walk away from me." I stamp my right foot. "Don't you dare stop trusting me." Then my left. "You said you loved me. Easy fucking words." He's right in front of me. I spray some spittle into his face.

"OK, so I came to it a bit late in the day but I do believe in love and I do think that out of the billions of people in this world you're the one I should be with." I jab my finger at him accusingly and I want to stamp again and flay my arms. There's so much anger inside me and it doesn't know how to get out.

"I've stopped being terrified by the 'what ifs.' And I know you're not my father. And I know that I shouldn't judge everyone by his iniquitous standards." The hairs on the back of my neck stand viciously erect. Tears poke mercilessly at my eyes. "And I'm sorry that I've hurt so many people in the past before I came to this understanding. I am so sorry. But trust me now. I did not do this for the bloody, fucking, crapping, pissing ratings."

I think that even if I'd gone to a posh school, I'd have been struggling to come up with more appropriate vocabulary, under the circumstances. I give in and stamp my feet, harder and harder and harder and faster and faster and faster. The tears explode from my eyes and fall harder and harder and harder and faster and faster and faster. Eventually I am worn out.

Exhausted.

Defeated.

I stop stamping and try to find some equilibrium. My breathing is fast and desperate, my feet are throbbing with the violence of my stamping and my head is sore with shaking. I cannot look at Darren or the schoolkids. It is so intensely embarrassing. Over the last few days I've lost everything: both my fiancés—one my love, the other my best friend, my job, my privacy and now my reason. I've been cheated, deceived and humiliated. I've felt despair and loneliness and regret.

I take stock.

All that and I still believe in love.

Which means that just when I thought I'd lost track of the game, I've won.

I have Mum.

I have Issie.

I have learned a lot.

I force myself to look up at Darren. My heart cartwheels. I rub the back of my hand across my face, cleaning up the excess of smudged mascara and tears. I pick up my museum map from the floor, where I'd thrown it.

"Do you know something, Darren? The irony is, I never stopped believing in you. I never thought you'd betrayed me. Not for a minute."

We are both breathing deeply. Staring at one another. Our faces are a potent cocktail of anger and forgiveness, love and lust, trust and fear, potential and endings. Hope.

It's all been so intense, right from the beginning. Euphoric, desolate, euphoric again, desolate plus. What now?

Minutes go by. Neither of us says anything. Neither of us moves.

"Do you know the Camarasaurus weighs twenty-five tons?" asks Darren.

"Yes," I say carefully, and then add, "It's a plant eater, so I suggest the grapefruit diet." It's a weak joke but Darren's face hints at a smile. He takes my arm and starts to lead me through the galleries. His fingers singe.

"So you've seen the dinosaur exhibition?"

"Yes." I'm shaking.

"Have you seen the blue whale?"

"Yes."

"So you've seen enough of the Natural History Museum for one day?" I feel as though I'm behind a number of veils but as he asks each question a veil drops and instead of feeling exposed, I feel more confident. I can see more clearly.

"Yes."

"Do you think you'd like to go for a beer?"

This time I nod. I'm incapable of finding my voice. We leave the museum and go out into the London sun. We stop on the steps of the museum and squint at the brightness and crowds. Darren turns to me.

"Do you still believe in me, Cas?" he asks. His voice is patchy with emotion but it is still velvety and I recognize possibility and opportunity glimmering there.

"Yes."

"Will you give me another chance?"

"Yes. I will. A huge, fat, full YES."

I'm home.

Up Close and Personal with the Author

CAS IS INITIALLY QUITE DIFFICULT TO LIKE. WHAT MADE YOU WANT TO WRITE ABOUT SOMEONE WHO IS SO MANIPULATIVE?

It is very easy to write a character that is everyone's best friend and is entirely sugar and spice and all things nice. The "conflict" in the novel would then have to be that she came up against an adversary who was completely bad. In the real world people are much more complex than that. Good people do bad things. Mean people are often motivated by explanations that are not immediately obvious. For example Cas appears to be a super-bitch but she does care for her friends and family, she is simply vulnerable. It's a much greater test of my skill as an author if I can get the reader to like someone who doesn't deserve any admiration.

DID CAS DESERVE SOMEONE AS DELICIOUS AS DARREN?

Probably not, initially. But Cas does undergo a transformation. Darren literally brings out the best in her. Besides, true love is about loving someone even when they don't deserve that love. Darren also learns things from Cas. In the end she has more faith in him than he does in her and her faith has never been nurtured the way his has. Hers is the greater leap. I love Cas' spirit just as much as Darren's morals.

DARREN IS SO GORGEOUS. IT'S VERY EASY TO FALL IN LOVE WITH HIM. DO YOU THINK THERE ARE REALLY MEN LIKE HIM OUT THERE?

We can live in hope.

WOULD YOU THINK OF WRITING A SEQUEL TO *GAME OVER* TO REVEAL WHAT HAPPENS TO JOSH AND ISSIE AND WHETHER DARREN AND CAS ACTUALLY MAKE IT?

I doubt I'll write a sequel. Once I've finished a novel I like my characters to live in the imagination of my readers. However, I am a fan of happy endings so it is my belief that Issie does find true love. Perhaps, she'll meet a Doctor. Josh will probably marry a model with a heart of gold and have a bunch of kids. Cas and Darren stay in love and grow old together but I'm not sure they'd actually get married.

WHERE DOES THE INSPIRATION FOR YOUR CHARACTERS COME FROM?

Life sparks my imagination but I never write biographies of individuals nor do I try to reproduce people I know; my friends are saved that indignity. My characters are an amalgamation of a number of people I've met, watched or heard about, plus a great big dose of "but what if . . . ? ". The question "but what if . . . ?" is the one that kindles my imagination.

DID YOU HAVE TO DO LOTS OF RESEARCH TO WRITE THIS NOVEL?

Yes. I was lucky enough to have a number of friends and contacts who work at a UK terrestrial channel, ITV, which is one of the biggest in the UK. They kindly answered all my questions and introduced me to producers of real shows, so that I had a clear idea of the mechanics of a TV channel. They even allowed me to work alongside of them for several weeks so that I had a thorough understanding of the vibe of TV production.

In addition I sat in the audience of a number of live and recorded shows so that I could get a handle on audiences' reactions. I also became a regular visitor of the Natural History Museum.

WHAT DO YOU THINK OF REALITY TV SHOWS? DO YOU WATCH AND ENJOY THEM?

I watch them occasionally and something rather terrible about me enjoys them, but I'm not particularly proud of that fact. I think Reality TV is lazy TV. Producers no longer have to do much to produce a show. No time is given to clever scriptwriting, making beautiful costumes or training and hiring good actors. All that is required is a few ordinary people who are desperate for a bit of fame and don't mind being exploited.

IS THERE A SIGNIFICANT EX IN YOUR LIFE?

Not now because I have been married and divorced and so I guess my ex-husband is the most significant ex I have but I don't have any "what if" fantasies about him as I know exactly what being with him was like. I guess it would be amusing to know what my ex's were up to now and a rather vain part of me would be interested to know what they think of me.

DO YOU THINK SEX WITH AN EX COULD REALLY BE MADE INTO A TV PROGRAM?

Sadly, yes. I came up with this concept in 1999. My editor worried that the show was too far-fetched. Since then we have seen an explosion of Reality TV programs hit our screens and the concept of Sex With an Ex is rather tame compared to those shows, where people are prepared to marry on stage or live in a house for weeks with complete strangers, allowing the nation to watch them take a shower. I wonder if there are any limits left.

Then don't miss these other great books!